The Art of Dying

The Art of Dying

DOUGLAS LINDSAY

DI Westphall Book 3

MULHOLLAND
BOOKS
HODDER

First published in Great Britain in 2019 by Mulholland Books
An imprint of Hodder & Stoughton
An Hachette UK company

4

A CIP catalogue record for this title is available from the British Library

Paperback ISBN 978 1 473 69699 0
eBook ISBN 978 1 473 69698 3

Typeset in Plantin Light by Hewer Text UK Ltd, Edinburgh
Printed and bound in Great Britain by Clays Ltd, Elcograf S.p.A.

Hodder & Stoughton policy is to use papers that are natural, renewable
and recyclable products and made from wood grown in sustainable
forests. The logging and manufacturing processes are expected to
conform to the environmental regulations of the country of origin.

Hodder & Stoughton Ltd
Carmelite House
50 Victoria Embankment
London EC4Y 0DZ

www.hodder.co.uk

For Kathryn

I

In no particular order.

March 2006: As the senior SIS officer in the area, I interrogated a suspect in a small village outside Kabul. Two British aid workers were being held captive, location unknown. The suspect smiled when he told me they were already dead. The interrogation went too far. There was blood on my boots. I felt his Adam's apple pop.

January 2009: Zétény Kovács. Forty-three. Hungarian, working for the Russians. I threw him out a fifteenth-storey window in Paris. A classic of the kill-or-be-killed genre. I wasn't particularly invested in him dying, but he gave me no option.

Kiev, summer 2003: An affair with a Ukrainian journalist. Alina. She thought I worked for AP. She loved me. When I'd got what I needed from her, I left. Returned to London, didn't say goodbye. Maybe Alina got over it. I never heard of her again.

Stockholm, October 2007: A hit job. Not a killing, just the run-of-the-mill destruction of a political life. Someone in London didn't like the rise of an opposition MP. I wasn't told the reasons, though I worked them out along the way. Seemed trivial, but I had a job to do. Money, sex, intoxication, the trifecta of political downfall. She had issues with none of them, so I had to create them. Took less than a month. Lost her job. Might also have lost her marriage and her children, but I didn't hang around to find out.

December 2009: A fire-fight on the Rwanda–DRC border. I, and four others, fired Heckler & Koch MP5s into the jungle at unseen figures, for twenty-three and a half minutes. At some point the return fire ended. We went on our way. We didn't count the dead.

Those instances come to mind.

There have been others.

I was doing my job. It wore me down to the point where I gave it up, transferring over to the police service. They didn't haunt me, though. The victims. I didn't think about mothers grieving sons, broken lives or broken hearts.

And then a year ago a woman killed herself in front of me, a woman who'd spent the previous two nights in my bed. I stood and watched her, and all I cared about was the information I'd got from her before she died.

Sometime later she returned. Walked into my head in the middle of the night. Didn't say hello, just took her position in the line-up of guilt. I hadn't known that particular alliance of the lost and the damned had even existed. All those years, doing my job, or doing things that perhaps weren't necessary but which came with the job all the same. No guilt. That's what I thought.

Turned out they were waiting for me. Like highwaymen. Midnight robbers. Lurking in the shadows, come to take away my nights.

2

Five forty-five, early Saturday evening. I step out of the car and look up at the dark, cloudy sky. A second to adjust to being at work, to the damp air, to the evening. Recapturing the moment of the murder from fifty minutes earlier.

'Boss,' says Detective Sergeant Sutherland, as he walks up beside me.

'Iain.'

A quiet street down past the hospital in Dingwall, that bustles every time County are playing at home. The road leads down to the river as it opens out onto the firth, houses irregularly spaced along the way.

There are still some cars parked at uneven intervals, fifteen police officers already at the scene, a few more on their way from Inverness, a ragtag gaggle of spectators pushed back about thirty yards on all sides beneath orange streetlights. There are three TV cameras and two ambulances.

There are voices all around, conversations, shouting. There's one reporter calling out repeatedly, the same question over and over – *Have you made an arrest?* – her voice clear through the damp autumnal evening.

A few yards from where I'm standing, a teenage boy sits on the road, leaning back against the door of a police car. There is a bandage across his nose. He's staring at the sheet-covered corpse ten yards in front of him, his expression faraway, his mouth slightly open. A paramedic stands not far from him, looking down, a watchful eye. The other paramedic sits in the rear of the ambulance, her legs dangling over the side. They're waiting to be called to remove the victim's body.

Further back there's a guy standing with a blanket over his shoulders, holding a bandage against his cheek. I doubt he needs to hold it, as it looks like it's been taped to his face, but he's clutching the remembrance of the attack, as another paramedic stands beside him, her eye level a good six inches lower than his, looking up at him, speaking slowly.

'What have we got?' I ask.

Sutherland, who's been on shift since seven this morning, indicates the body without turning towards it.

'Thomas Peterson, aged fifty-one. He was at the game this afternoon with his son, Roddy,' says Sutherland, and he nods vaguely in the direction of the boy.

Just as bad as it looks. A boy staring across the road at his dead father. What's the official line on whether he should be allowed to just sit there? These moments, the last half hour, the death, everything about this scene, will be burned into his memory.

'The dad got into a fight when he had his kid with him?' I ask.

'He was attacked.'

'Unprovoked?'

'Far as we can tell. A guy in a hood ran up to him, swung a punch, then laid in. His kid made one attempt to protect his dad, and got batted. The fellow there in the blanket says he weighed in, and got banjoed for his trouble.'

'We don't know why he attacked Peterson in the first place?'

'The boy thought it might've been related to an incident earlier in the ground.'

'Go on.'

'Hibs have got the lad Sanga, you know him?'

Think about it for a moment, but I don't really follow it closely enough. There was a time when I thought my interest in football had waned as work and life got in the way, but really it's the awfulness of it all that did for me. The cheating and the time wasting, the clutched face, the preposterous fall, the haircuts and the tattoos, mobbing the referee, and more time spent on the training ground working on the goal celebration than on controlling a twenty-yard pass.

'He's French,' says Sutherland. 'Well, Senegalese, eligible to play for France . . .'

'Is that relevant?'

'Only in that he's black.'

'OK. Go on.'

'First time Sanga touches the ball, some guy behind them in the crowd makes a monkey noise. Just the one guy. Peterson gets to his feet, turns round, says something like, "Seriously? A monkey noise? What are you trying to do to this club?" Then he sits down, someone starts clapping, and then boom, hundreds of people are applauding the guy.'

'An everyday hero making a stand against racism.'

'Yep.'

'Any more monkey noises?'

'Nope.'

'Any further incidents during the game?'

'Nope.'

'So, do we suppose the guy who made the monkey noise bore a grudge?'

'There's no direct evidence, but so far it's all we've got.'

'You get a description of the assailant?'

'Still in the process, but we've got the boy, and blanket guy over there, although he already sounds a bit sketchy. We should be able to put something together.'

I look back to the boy sitting against the police car door.

'How's the kid?'

'Didn't want to leave.'

'You've looked at the victim?'

'Yep. Bloody. It wasn't a single punch, though some way short of an out-and-out pummelling.'

'OK, we should get the body moved.'

Sutherland turns towards the paramedic sitting on the back of the ambulance and makes a wheels-up gesture. The paramedic nods, looks over at her partner and the two of them get to work.

'You've been in to speak to the club yet?'

'Waiting for you,' says Sutherland.

'And the mother?'

'Should be here shortly.'

'Right. You get along to the ground. Speak to security. Have a look at CCTV. If Peterson and his kid were sitting in a section with season ticket holders, get as many names as you can. We should be able to get them from online sales too. We'll get a description from the boy and the blanket guy, see what we can match up. This won't look good for the club, so hopefully they'll be helpful. If it was the monkey man who did this, it shouldn't take too long to pin him down.'

'Boss,' says Sutherland, and he turns away.

He stops for a second, looks at the boy sitting on the ground, lifts his head to the air, smelling the evening, searching for rain, then walks quickly through the small crowd.

Led by Sutherland's movement, I do the same, tilting my head to the evening sky. Rain on the way. Then I walk over to the boy and stand next to him for a few moments, waiting to see if he's going to look up. He doesn't so much as glance at my shoes. He's watching the body being removed, face still that peculiar mix of shock and awe.

'Roddy.'

There's an entirely predictable pause of a few seconds, then he says, 'What?' without looking up.

'Can I get you anything? A drink? Or is there someone you'd like to call while you wait for your mum?'

A moment, then he turns his hand to show me the phone I'd already noticed.

'You don't want a drink?'

'I'm good.'

Give him another couple of seconds, while we both gauge how this is going to go. Sometimes you have to tiptoe, and sometimes you just have to step boldly forward.

'Did you and your dad come here every week? Were you season ticket holders?'

Patience. Can't look away from him, as he's as liable to answer with a silent gesture as he is with a sullen word.

'He wasn't my dad,' he says after a while, his voice low. 'And no.'

'He wasn't your dad?'

'Dad's in America.'

I automatically glance round at Sutherland, who's speaking to one of the officers on the perimeter.

'Mr Peterson was your stepdad?'

'Yes,' he says, then a strange, small noise escapes the back of his throat, somewhere between a rueful laugh and the sound of a sob catching.

'You live with Mr Peterson?'

'Yes.'

'Were he and your mum married?'

'Yes.'

His answers are carrying a lot of weight for a monosyllable.

'You didn't get along?'

At last he slowly turns his head and looks up. He studies me for a few moments, taking the time to decide whether or not he considers me worthwhile talking to, obviously determines that I've passed some strict teenage engagement test and says, 'He was an asshole,' although his tone is neither as harsh nor glib as the words suggest.

'How often did you come here?'

'Third time. He was an asshole the first two times as well.'

'Was he an asshole all the time, or just when he took you to the football?'

As the words cross my mouth, I can see the look on the face of some bureaucrat sitting in an office being shocked that that was how I just referred to the murder victim.

'Twenty-four seven,' he replies, and his eyes drop, as though he feels guilty for speaking so ill of his newly deceased stepfather.

'Tell me about the attack.'

'Some guy just came up behind him, lamped him on the head.'

'With a bat, a . . .'

'No, punched him. Didn't knock him out, or down even, just knocked him off balance, then he grabbed him, punched him another couple of times. Started hosing blood straight away. Jesus.' He pauses, winces at the thought of it.

'How'd you get that?' I ask, indicating the bandage on his face.

'Thought I should help him. The guy lashes out at me, tells me to fucking mind my own business. I mean . . . suppose I could've waded back in, couldn't I?'

'We wouldn't be talking now.'

Another quick look up, then he lowers his eyes.

'What kind of accent did the attacker have?'

'Around here, I suppose. Nothing specific. Bit of a ned.'

'You think he'd been at the match?'

'Probably.'

'You think he was the guy who made the monkey noise?'

'I don't know what that guy looked like. Wasn't like I looked round to see any of them.'

'Did your stepdad indicate if he'd realised who'd made the noise? If he'd engaged anyone in particular when he turned round?'

'Didn't speak to him.'

'At all?'

'Pretty much.'

I turn away for a moment, look around the scene. Give the boy some space.

Perhaps we just have a typical relationship between child and step-parent. The resentment at the break-up of the parents' marriage, the need to take it out on someone, the step-parent being the easiest available target.

It sounds old and worn, but then there are so many broken marriages, so many step-parents, that every conceivable outcome has been seen and done before, a thousandfold. Nothing new in the human world.

'Had he called out racism before? Were there any incidents at either of the previous two games you'd been to?'

A half-glance, then his eyes drop. A slight change in his demeanour. The front he's been bravely putting on to cover his distress slips. There's a little more of an answer to be given to this.

'Your face just did a thing,' I say, when the inevitable silence ensues. 'What was the face, Roddy? You have to help me out here.'

Bad wording. No one has to do anything, least of all this kid, whose stepdad just got murdered in front of him. The step from seeing death in *Call of Duty* to the real thing is giant, and it's going to affect anyone, even the coolest teenage kid on the block.

His head moves from side to side, a slow-motion refusal to answer.

'Tell me, Roddy,' I say, trying to get back on track.

'It's nothing.'

'I asked if your stepdad had said anything at a previous game, and there was something there.'

Another pause, and then the words, 'What's it matter?' are bequeathed reluctantly to the dank dark of early evening.

'We need to find the man who did this as quickly as possible. We don't want it to happen to anyone else.'

'What are you saying?' he asks, his words harshly spoken to the ground. 'If I don't help you, the next guy's blood'll be on my hands?'

'I didn't say that.'

'Like Tom's blood is on my hands? Is that it?'

'How could his blood possibly be on your hands, Roddy?'

'Jesus,' he says, cursing out the word.

'Roddy?'

'Fuck's sake.' Ready to talk now, grudging words leaked from between tight lips. 'The last game, I don't know, a month ago, we were here. Some guy behind us called that wee Rangers winger a black bastard. Tom was full of himself afterwards, full of outrage. I said to him, well you should've said something then, shouldn't you? If you're so full of outrage, *say something*.'

His head drops a little further. A small, hopeless hand gesture.

'Now he's dead.'

The body is in the back of the ambulance. Shortly it will be gone. The boy hasn't been paying it any attention since I started asking questions.

'The guy over there,' I say, 'the one with the blanket.'

He looks up at me for a while, and then turns towards the blanket guy. Gives him a few seconds' consideration, and then turns back.

'That guy was an asshole as well.'

'You know him?'

'Never seen him before in my life.'

'So, how'd you know he's—'

'Tom's dead and all he wanted to talk about was himself. My part in not even remotely preventing the murder. He'll be in the pub in half an hour pretending to be a hero.'

Smart kid.

'Don't take it for granted that the guy behind you in the crowd making the noise was the guy who did this,' I say. 'It could be entirely random.'

His gaze shifts to the side. He watches something over my shoulder; his eyes widen slightly, just for a moment, and then narrow again.

'Your mum?' I ask, without turning.

'Yeah,' he says, 'Mum. Here to make everything better.'

3

'I fought in the war.'

Robert Kane says the words with total confidence, but that confidence slowly drips away beneath my look from across the desk. *I fought in the war.*

He's still pressing the bandage against his face. He did not bleed, at all, though the single blow he received did result in some bruising. The paramedic reported there'd been no point in applying a bandage, and he hadn't been intending to, but then the victim had taken a selfie, posted it on Instagram, and a couple of his friends had replied telling him to get a bandage on it.

They'd argued, briefly, then the medic had shrugged and given him his *stupid bandage*.

'Which war?'

'Afghanistan.'

'Whereabouts?'

'Out of Bastion.'

'Really?'

'Sure.'

'How much fighting did you do?'

He doesn't answer.

'Which unit were you with?'

'51st Highland.'

'Territorials then.'

'If you want to call them that.'

'How long d'you do at Bastion?'

Pause, then he says, 'A fortnight.' Another pause beneath my withering gaze, then he adds, 'It was intense.'

'Did you discharge your weapon at all in that time?'

Nothing.

I give him another few seconds, but there's little else to be said on the matter. He spouted his line, some people might be impressed by it, and unfortunately for him, I'm not one of them.

'Tell me about the incident.'

'Of course. What d'you want to know, Officer?'

That tone.

'You didn't leave the game until after the final whistle?'

'Stayed right to the end, always do. It's only ninety-some minutes, what's the point of missing any of it?'

'Which section of the ground were you in?'

'Far end, West Stand. Went for a slash after the game, had a chat with Tony, but he was going off back up to town, I was heading for my car.'

'Where were you parked?'

'Ferry Road. I'm just heading out, then I see this guy punching the other guy.'

'Many people around?'

He stops his fairly quick flow of answers, looks away from me, narrows his eyes on a spot on the wall behind me. Placing himself once more at the scene. A moment, then he says, 'Not sure.'

'Why?'

'I was in the zone.'

I hold his gaze for a moment, and I can see the confidence drain from him in the same way that it did after he said he'd fought in the war.

'Which zone?'

'I write copy for a marketing agency in Edinburgh. Slater & Cummins. Got a pitch to prepare for Monday, was just running some ideas through my head. I was in my mind palace.'

'That's not what a mind palace is.'

'We've got a project on a new range of flavoured waters. *Water Just Got Interesting*,' he says, making a banner gesture.

'That's all you've got? *Water just got interesting?*'

Cheap shot, but he deserves it.

'It's punchy,' he protests, weakly.

I hate people.

'So what was it that distracted you from your water project?'

'I heard the kid shouting,' he says. 'His voice is quite high still, right? Heard that, looked over, and the kid was reeling backwards. The guy had just hit him.'

'You saw that, or you're assuming he'd hit him?'

'It looked like he'd hit him.'

'What was Mr Peterson doing at that point?'

'He was on his knees. The attacker, the guy, whoever he was, swung another punch at him, and he fell back. Man, blood just flew off him, you know, as he toppled backwards, face pointing upwards, and whoosh! So much, so much blood. I have never seen anything like that in my life.'

'And you fought in the war . . .'

'Is there another officer I can speak to?' he asks, although I think he's trying to be funny.

'Was Mr Peterson struck again before you intervened?'

'He was, but just the once. You know, at first, you have to take a moment, you really do, to establish what's going on.

'So the killer leans over the poor bastard, and gives him another bruiser to the face. More blood. And then I'm like, it's time for Bastion Bobby to make an appearance. So I got stuck in.'

I find it easy enough to ignore the facetious absurdity of *Bastion Bobby*.

'What happened?'

'He sees me coming, he straightens himself up and then it's just me and him, *mano a mano*.'

I let that particular piece of preposterousness hang in the air for a while, before indicating with a sceptical hand for him to continue.

'We duked it out for a few blows, then he caught me with a lucky punch,' and he indicates the bandage on his face, 'then when I'm out the way, he turns back to the dude, lands another couple of whoppers on him and legs it.'

If you're in the mood, there's a certain amount of sport to be had with the fool and his stories, but not today. Feels like I haven't been in the mood for a long while.

'The boy said you never landed a punch, the guy hit you once, you went down and stayed there.'

He doesn't answer, although as is so often the case, the answer is in the silence.

'Can you show me your injury, please, Mr Kane?'

'Got the bandage,' he says, indicating the bandage.

I play out the way the next two minutes could unfold, and contemplate just reaching over there and ripping the bandage off. Then I remember I can look at his Instagram account, and decide to step away from the confrontation. Within minutes of getting out of here, the guy is going to be speaking to the media, so I ought not to give him an *I'm-the-victim-but-the-police-treated-me-like-I-was-a-serial-killer* story.

I get quickly to my feet and he looks surprised.

'Constable Cole will be in shortly to take your written statement.'

'Wait, what? Can't I go? I've got to drive back to Edinburgh.'

'You can shortly, Mr Kane, but we'll need a statement, thank you. She won't be long.'

'Who won't be?'

'Constable Cole.'

'A woman?'

I save my most contemptuous look for last, then walk out the small room, leaving the door open behind me.

There are five of us watching a large TV screen. Sutherland and I, the boy and his mother, and PC Fisher, who we've made liaison between the family and the investigating officers.

Sutherland presses rewind, we watch the reverse whirl of black and white, then he stops the film and plays it again. It's a clear view of the section of the West Stand in which Roddy and his stepdad were sitting, around twenty rows in view. There's no sound.

The crowd is subdued, not densely packed, the action on the park obviously slow. A figure in a dark coat, four rows behind Roddy, cups his hands to his mouth, then lowers them, smiling. A moment, and then Peterson gets to his feet and turns. It's impossible to see from the angle how much he speaks, or if he looks directly at the man he's addressing. A few seconds, then he sits back down. A moment, and then someone a few seats along from him starts applauding. Shortly, about half of the people in view are applauding. No one within three seats of the perpetrator joins them.

It's the third time we've watched it. No one's spoken. This time, as the applause dies away, Sutherland stops the footage, looks at Roddy, and then indicates the man in the dark coat on the screen.

'Does this look like the man who attacked your dad, Roddy?' he asks.

Sutherland gives me a quick glance. Our eyes make contact for the most fleeting second, but it's a look that asks if he should have said stepdad rather than dad, and how could either of us possibly know which the mother would prefer? The minefield, the fine lines, of family politics.

'No,' says Roddy, quite sure of himself.

I look at the face on the screen. Just a face. Any old man. Impossible to tell from here what he could be capable of. We know, at least, that he's comfortable with overt racism.

'You're sure?' asks Sutherland.

'Yeah.'

'And the men on either side of him,' I ask. 'What about them?'

The boy takes his time. I also look, to see if there's anyone who meets the description he's given of his stepdad's assailant. Glance round at him, and he's still got his eyes on the screen. He's wanting to help, at least, which is positive.

'No,' he says, looking at me as he speaks.

'OK,' I say. 'Broaden it out, take another look. Is there anyone in the entire shot who resembles the attacker? And remember, they might have taken off a coat or a hat before they came to attack your dad. The hood will be down. They might not have been dressed as you see here.'

Another look at the screen, then he turns back, looking blank. He's got nothing.

I turn to Sondra Peterson, who's still studying the screen.

'D'you recognise anyone here, Mrs Peterson?'

She looks at me curiously, then her brow wrinkles and she says, 'Why would I?'

'You're studying it very closely.'

'I could be looking at the man who killed my husband.'

'Yes.'

Her eyes narrow a little more, but the look on her face is one of curiosity, like she doesn't fully understand why we're having this conversation. She's a bereaved widow, so why am I even speaking to her?

There's a flicker of a twitch in her right eyelid, which I noticed as soon as we met outside the football stadium. Nerves, guilt, worry, fear, grief, stress, fatigue, caffeine, the early symptoms of Parkinson's . . . Who knows?

You see everything with a bereaved spouse, and you can't go making assumptions. Peterson's wife's air of detachment could just be her way of holding it together, trying not to let herself go in front of her son, or in front of the police.

'D'you mind if we have a word with you on your own, Mrs Peterson?' I ask. 'The constable will sit with Roddy until we're done. It shouldn't take long.'

'Yes, of course,' says Peterson, and she squeezes her son's hand.

I glance at the other two officers, Sutherland turns off the screen, Fisher nods, and we head from the room.

'D'you know of any reason why someone would want your husband dead?'

Sutherland and I sitting across the desk from the widow. Away from her son, it seems now that some of the reserve has gone, the guard has dropped a little. She doesn't have to show the brave face for us that she did for him.

'What d'you mean?'

'Just like it sounds.'

'He was killed at the football,' says Peterson. 'Roddy watched it happen. Why should it be for any reason other than the one you mentioned ... the thing you pointed out already? The man and the noise.'

'Roddy didn't see his killer in the rows behind them.'

'Maybe it was someone else. Maybe it was some other reason.'

'That's what I'm asking.'

'No,' she says, sounding confused, 'that's not what I meant. Maybe it was some other reason at the football.'

'Roddy couldn't think of anything else of significance.'

'He's fourteen,' she says, brow furrowed.

'He quite understands what's going on around him,' I say. 'He was very aware of the significance of his stepdad standing up and telling someone off in front of people. And yet, he's also quite sure that that person wasn't the one who later attacked him. So, it could be, and here we have to consider every eventuality ... it could be that someone wanted to kill your husband, and then chose to do it just after a game of football so that it'd look like an act of soccer violence.'

'But how would they know about the monkey noise? The incident, the monkey noise incident?'

'They didn't have to. It could be a pre-planned attack, intended to look entirely random, intended to look like it was an attack committed by a drunk fan. We're sitting here concentrating on this small moment during the game, when it might've been completely unrelated.'

'Wouldn't they have hit someone else as well if that'd been the case?'

'Why?'

'If he was pretending to be drunk, randomly hitting people, wouldn't he have hit a few people to cover for the fact that he had one intended victim. I mean, that's what they do on crime shows, isn't it?'

'He hit your son and he hit the other gentleman who tried to intervene,' I say, although I know that's not what she means.

'But he was attacking Thomas.'

'Yes.'

'Well?'

'There is no *well* here, Mrs Peterson. We have no idea why your husband was attacked, so we, the police, need to establish who he was and why someone might have wanted to kill him. At the moment, we have nothing. We thought we might have, even if such a brutal attack would have been unusual for an act of petty vengeance, but it just vanished when your son looked at the footage and couldn't identify anyone. As a consequence, literally everything is back on the table. Everything.'

'Aren't you going to speak to other people at the ground? Weren't there any other witnesses?'

'Yes, there were, and we have a team of officers still interviewing at the scene. Sergeant Sutherland has already talked to the club, and we have further discussions with them scheduled for tomorrow. What did your husband do for a living?'

'What does that have to do with it?'

'Maybe nothing,' I say, reeling my tone in a little. The woman has lost her husband. We need to have this conversation, but I can give her space while we do it.

'He's the CEO of George Bailey's,' she says.

'The funeral directors in Inverness?'

'Yes, the funeral directors. Funny, eh? I know who to call.'

'How long had he done that?'

'He started the company seven years ago.'

'They say they're everywhere now. In every town and village, all over the country.'

'Yes. They're big. Very successful.'

'Who'll take over the running of the business now?' I ask, and there's an almost physical wince of pain on her face at this brutal introduction of reality into a conversation that she might well have been conducting as some sort of peripheral mental exercise. Going through the motions until she got to be back with her son. Although we cannot yet know these people, she will be feeling the pain of this a lot more than Roddy.

Whatever my superpower is in this game, it's not compassion. A career forged working on the margins, going rogue, interviewing people with a gun at their head, or a boot at their throat. Nine years now in the Highland police has not been nearly long enough to remove the rough edges.

'Are you all right to continue?' I ask, forcing the courtesy. Sutherland, who has witnessed this before, expressionless.

'Yes,' she says. 'It's fine. And I'm not sure, is the answer to your question. There'll be time to worry about that later.'

'Can you tell us about your first husband?' I ask, trying to get away from the clumsiness of the previous question. A somewhat scattergun approach while we establish what areas we need to draw on from her husband's life, but better that than asking her to consider the future. The future can wait.

'He's in Boston,' she says, although she doesn't sound at all interested in the question. 'North of Boston. He's a bum.'

'He doesn't work?'

'He's on a fishing boat.'

'He's a bum on a fishing boat?'

'All right, he's not a bum, not in the . . . I'm not saying he doesn't work. I get it, it's hard work on a fishing boat. He seems to enjoy it.'

'How'd he come to be north of Boston?'

'Huh. You know the movie *Perfect Storm*? Brandon, that was my husband, he was the only man on the planet who saw that and thought, *I want to do that. I want to go there.* I mean, if he'd been a fisherman already, maybe. But he was an accountant.' She embraces us both again with a look that says the situation was inexplicable. 'Seriously. The man was an accountant, earning, I don't know, sixty, seventy thousand a year. So, the summer after we've seen the movie, we go on holiday to New England. I went along with that, you know, whatever, it was a holiday. Nice enough place. We get home, then he says, first day back, *I love it, I'm moving there, and I'm going to get a job on the fishing boats. Start at the bottom, work my way up. Do whatever it takes to get a visa, Green Card, whatever.*

'I say, well *we're* not going, Sunshine, me and Roddy, we're not going, thinking, that'll put his gas at a peep. But, you know what . . .? He knew we wouldn't. He was leaving us, that's what he was doing. Running away. Mid-life crisis or whatever, I don't know. Shedding the wife and kid, see you later, alligator.'

'When was this?'

'Four years ago. If it hadn't been that, it'd have been something else, wouldn't it? There's always something with these people. Men.'

'When was the last time you saw him?'

'The day he walked out the house.'

'And Roddy?'

'He went over in the summer for two weeks. Went out on the fishing boat once, spent the day throwing up. Otherwise, spent most of the time on his phone.'

'How did Brandon feel when you re-married?'

'You'll have to ask him.'

'Is Brandon re-married?'

'Not so that he's told me, but I expect he'd have told Roddy, and Roddy would have said.'

I finally break the gaze and end the quick-fire questions. I get the feeling this isn't about Brandon. There are plenty of occasions when it's reasonable to bring the ex-husband into it, but usually not when he's fled the country to get away from his wife in the first place. Nevertheless, it's obviously much too early to discount him. The happy life of the fisherman could be the miserable life of someone who walked out, has no money, hates his job, doesn't want to admit he screwed up and is jealous of his ex-wife's rich second husband.

'You can tell us how to get in touch with Brandon?' I ask.

There's something in my tone that alerts her to the fact the interview is drawing to an end.

'Of course.'

'Thank you, Mrs Peterson, I think that'll be all for the moment. And I'm sorry for your loss.'

A pause, but she doesn't fill it.

'We'll do everything we can to find your husband's killer. If there's anything you'd like from us or anything you want to ask, you can get in touch with Constable Fisher and she'll see what she can do. Or, if you think of anything that might be relevant to our investigation, then you can give the sergeant or me a call.'

Her lips part for a moment, then she decides not to speak. The interview is done, the box has been ticked, and we move on through the preliminary conventions of the police procedural.

4

Thomas Peterson's body is lying on the long table, uncovered, naked and pale. The blood has been cleaned from his face. The damage done to the skull is evident. The nose has been crushed, and there are wounds that have clearly not been caused by human fists or feet alone.

The part of the conversation where I note these wounds and ask the question is unnecessary, and Dr Hamilton gets straight to the point.

'I'd guess a knuckleduster of some sort. Not just your classic, but something with a bit more of an edge to it. Spiked. Maybe not clinical enough to kill with one jab, but certainly something to increase the damage.'

Hamilton arrived from Glasgow as the stopgap police pathologist in Inverness after we'd brought the brief and unpleasant tenure of Dr Wade to an end, and the stopgap has now become a full-time transfer. There's a grim brutality about Hamilton. Around my age, probably, with the traditional world-weary look of the man whose trade revolves around the dead.

'How many blows? Was there one in particular that killed him?'

Sutherland is turned away, looking at his phone.

'Around eight or nine,' says Hamilton. 'Haven't identified a killer blow as yet. Perhaps there won't be one. A cumulative effect, as is often the case.'

'Any sign that he'd been in a previous fight?'

'None.'

'Toxins in his blood?'

'Had a heavy night last night, I'd say, but nothing since. No drugs, just whisky.'

'Anything you can add to the story of him leaving a game of football and being attacked?'

'No.'

'Like this?' asks Sutherland, and he holds forward his phone, showing a picture of a knuckleduster, a small spike on each knuckle.

'Exactly that,' says Hamilton.

Sutherland turns the phone towards me so I get a better look. A standard weapon of brutality. I look back and forth between the photo of the implement and Peterson's battered face to confirm the match for myself, then nod at Sutherland.

'He had sex this morning. I managed to get some DNA. We'll get that to you in due course.'

'He didn't have a shower after sex?'

'Wiped himself down with a L'Oréal Paris, Age Perfect cleansing wipe.'

'That's pretty specific.'

'Sorry about the detail,' says Hamilton, sardonically, 'I know you'd prefer if I'd told you he'd wiped himself down with a cloth, or maybe a loofah, or it might have been, I don't know, a *thing*.'

Can't help smiling. He reminds me of Dr Sanderson, and somehow the thought of Sanderson's death from cancer doesn't make me feel sad any more.

'How d'you find the DNA?'

'A pubic hair.'

'What colour is it?'

'Dark brown.'

Sutherland and I share a glance, having the conversation quickly through another silent look. Mrs Peterson is a near-perfect blonde, but then her colour likely comes from a visit to the hairdresser.

'And . . . can we take the hair?'

'Sure,' says Hamilton, his tone implying, as ever, that he doubts the police will do much of a job of taking care of the evidence.

'There was no other DNA to be had?' asks Sutherland. 'Sounds like it might have been a cursory clean he did there.'

Hamilton gives him a long, contemptuous look, then tuts loudly. 'The notion of the cursory clean itself comes primarily from the presence of the pubic hair,' he says sharply, 'but if, for example, that hair came from his underwear and not the sexual contact, then that notion no longer has primacy. Nevertheless, I will continue to do my job, and will let you know if anything else presents itself. In the meantime, may I suggest you do the same?'

'One more thing,' I say.

'Of course,' says Hamilton, with an amusing, forced patience.

This time I bring a picture up on my phone, and hold it towards Hamilton. Robert Kane, Bastion Bobby as he's known to no one but himself, and the picture he Instagrammed of his wound.

'This bloke was punched by Peterson's killer at the same time—' I begin.

'Yes,' says Hamilton, cutting me off, 'and as you can see, he was not punched with the same implement that was used on Mr Peterson. The blows with the enhanced knuckleduster were delivered with his right hand. This,' he adds, with a gesture that manages to dismiss Kane's injury as utterly insignificant, 'was clearly a softer punch from the killer's left.'

For a moment he looks like he's going to further toss Kane's injuries on the scrapheap of derision, and then he can't even be bothered to do that.

'Yes,' he says. 'I take it we're done now?'

'Thanks, Roger.'

And with that, Hamilton holds an open-palmed hand towards the door.

In the car, on the way back to the office, just off the Kessock Bridge. The rain has arrived, heavy, persistent. Almost ten p.m. An evening ruined, if either of us had had anything planned for it. I have no idea about Sutherland. For myself, I'm ready to go home, stick on two slices of toast and cut up some cheese, and have a couple of glasses of wine, and damn the mundane solitariness of it all. Before that, however, back to the station for a quick wrap-up with the team.

'Isn't it amazing,' says Sutherland, breaking the silence, 'how often people have had sex just before they get murdered? It's like the chances of getting murdered increase dramatically the minute you've slept with someone.'

There's humour in the words, but not in his tone. His thought processes are the same as usual, but there's no conviction in the levity.

'That'd certainly explain why I'm still alive,' I reply, tone not dissimilar. Think of apologising for giving too much information, but decide not to bother.

'And the damn rain,' says Sutherland. 'Someone's been murdered, and there are two certainties. A, they just had sex, and B, it starts raining.'

'On the other hand,' I say, slowing down as I come up behind a BMW that's idling through the evening, 'we're in the Highlands, and in the Highlands it doesn't just rain when someone's been murdered. It also, for example, rains when someone hasn't been murdered.'

'And the sex?'

'Someone has to be having sex,' I say glibly, and the guy in front slows a little more. We can see the light of his phone.

He's texting while he's driving. I nod to Sutherland to give him a short, sharp burst of the police siren.

Five of us in Room 2. At some point in the last couple of years, Mary started calling us the Murder Squad, although fortunately murder is still a rare occurrence around here. Sutherland and I, Constables Cole, Fisher and Kinghorn.

Room 2 as bleak as ever. Never the right temperature, windowless and unadorned by decoration. Warm and stuffy in winter when the heating is on throughout the station, cold in summer, when the heating is turned off and natural light does not penetrate. A whiteboard, where crime is recorded in intimate detail, little else on the walls. A table, seven chairs around it. In the corner, the *Ficus benjamina*, which Constable Cole nurses through the endless days of sunlight deprivation. Over time the plant has acquired its own status at the station. The ficus, guardian of Room 2, where evil is dissected.

'We'll make it as quick as possible,' I say. 'We can still try to retrieve a little of the evening.'

Two of them look at the clock, which is behind me on the wall, over my right shoulder, and I can see what they're thinking. There's very little of the evening left to retrieve.

'You can catch *Match of the Day* on iPlayer, Alice,' and she nods and drops her eyes. 'Fish, where are we?'

Constable Fisher glances at her notes, a pen in her left hand, which she quickly runs across the page of tightly packed, handwritten text.

'We've spoken to seventeen people who were in the vicinity of the attack,' she says. 'As usual, with that number of witnesses, we have an explosion of contradictions, but it boils down to this: the attacker was wearing a hoodie, and it must've been pulled tight around his face as it didn't come off during the assault. It all happened quickly, there was only one attempted intervention beside his son, that of Mr

Kane ... I don't think anyone was particularly impressed with him, but then, no one else was really in a position to criticise, and so, remarkably, they didn't.'

'In which direction did he flee after the game?'

'Down towards the river, then up the path, legged it across the railway line. And he could run. Sounds young and fit at least.'

'How are the descriptions of his face coming along? Are we going to get a decent e-fit out of it?'

Fisher looks at Cole, who's already nodding.

'It's coming together, I feel, sir. There's a certain consistency to the descriptions, the usual couple of outliers notwithstanding. We're going to get Roddy back in tomorrow morning and we'll firm something up.'

'OK, thanks, Alice. Anything from inside the ground?'

'Nothing yet,' says Fisher, 'still waiting on the list of names from the club, but they said we'd have them by morning.'

'Any intelligence on where the attacker came from? Anyone see him in the ground, walking out of the ground, any interaction before he attacked Peterson?'

'Doesn't look like it, sir,' she says. 'Came out of nowhere, though we can't say for definite either way whether he was at the match. We'll need to get into the club's CCTV.'

'Sure. Elvis, anything?'

'Think I got all the nutjobs, sir,' says Kinghorn. 'Everyone had a different story to tell, though none of them, interestingly, suggested the attack was subsequent to anything else. I wonder if we're looking at a pre-planned attack.'

'A hit,' I say.

'Yes, sir.'

'Yep, it's possible. Let's not go there just yet, but tomorrow we'll need to start getting into the weeds of the victim's life. Who he worked with, family etcetera. I think we can probably all go home now, though.'

I look around the room; there are nods of agreement. Instinctively Kinghorn yawns.

'Back in tomorrow, I'm afraid,' I say. 'We'll see if we can flex the schedules, and make up a day or two off later in the week.'

And so they rise, and the next chapter in the steady start of any murder investigation is complete. The constables leave the room, Sutherland in their wake, then he stops at the door and looks back.

'You're not coming, sir?' he asks.

'I'm on it, Sergeant. Go home, do whatever it is you'd normally do at . . . eleven p.m. on a Saturday evening . . .'

'Sir,' he says, an acknowledgement in the single word that he won't be doing anything, then he turns away, leaving the door open.

I look at the whiteboard. There is a photograph of the victim at the scene, bloody and beaten, and another of him lying on the mortuary table, face cleaned up, showing the bruising and open cuts, the collapse of his nose.

A death at the football, a straightforward act of violence, plenty of witnesses and a quick identification. That's how it could play out, an uncomplicated, linear process, to a swift conclusion.

Room 2, this suffocating space, which holds the remembrance of so much criminal malignancy, says otherwise. Of course we sit in here sometimes and discuss the mundane, the cases that are tossed out, the petty crimes and the divvying up of humdrum police duties.

Sometimes, however, it knows. We do not sit here for nothing. We will not sit here briefly.

'By the pricking of my thumbs . . .' I say quietly to the room.

Crap. I push the chair back and stand quickly, determined to rid myself of the fug that is descending. I look at the ficus, our dear green plant.

'Yes, I know,' I say, 'talking myself into it again. No reason we can't get this wrapped up tomorrow.'

I walk out the room, turning off the light as I go, the breath of movement causing the leaves of the ficus to move like seaweed in a low tide.

5

The beach is long, bleak, cold. I stand and stare into the distance. Low dunes to the left, topped by long grass bent horizontal, a flat calm, grey sea to the right. The cloud is low, the light dull. It's almost as if the scene is in black and white, the sand so washed of colour it looks grey.

Through the murk, out to sea, a light blinks intermittently. I watch it for a few moments. Maybe longer, I'm not really sure. It blinks four times. It stops. A short while later it blinks again.

Somewhere it feels like there's a fiddle playing, although I'm not sure I can hear it. I can feel it, that's all. What does that remind me of?

It is being played somewhere, but not here. Not on this beach, not behind the dunes, not out to sea. As though someone has added it to the soundtrack. An overlay to the scene, inserted into the mix at a later date. Perhaps that's why I can only feel it, rather than hear it.

After a while, I need to turn and walk forward. The beach is desolate, haunted yet by forlorn ghosts. For a while it seems there is no one else here, the view uninterrupted for mile upon mile into the misty, grey distance, yet eventually they come, and once they start they do not stop.

Here they wait for me, my midnight robbers, strangely sitting at desks, spaced intermittently along the sand, so that I never know when the next one will appear.

Tonight, Elizabeth comes first. Elizabeth usually comes first. Elizabeth, who killed herself in front of me a year ago, and who has since led the charge into my subconscious. She sits behind the desk, her eyes never leaving mine, and drives a knife into her stomach. Over and over, the movement repeated, in and out, blood gurgling up each time, spilling from her lips.

And on I walk, past the desk and the gurgling blood. Her eyes don't leave me, though when I look back she's gone. She's never there when I look back, tonight's scene playing out like every other.

Maybe she wasn't there in the first place. I like to tell myself that.

Just as I begin to think that there never was anyone sitting at a desk, there's another one. A man, on his own, bleeding from his left eye. His right eye, desolate, bitter, is on mine. He is a Taliban fighter. I do not know his name.

He disappears. I walk on.

An African man I do not know, his chest soaked in blood. Then Kovács, who fell from the window of the Paris hotel. They come and they go, never smiling, always dead.

There is another one, another desk. Or a table. More of a table than a desk, and at it there is a man eating dinner. He is sitting with his back to the sand dunes, facing the sea.

I stop.

I do not know this man. The people at the desks come and go. Elizabeth, the strange catalyst, remains the same. But this man, eating dinner, is new. I do not know him. I did not kill him. I do not think I wronged him.

He's blind. He's looking at his plate, but he can't see it. Yet, he understands things. He knows what's going on. He can see without seeing.

He, however, is not where I am. I recognise that. He's not sitting on this beach. He's eating dinner. He's in a restaurant. He knows there are seventeen others in the room. Fourteen diners, two waiting staff and a nurse. A male nurse. He knows the nurse well.

Across the water the light blinks. Bumped by an unseen ghost I shiver, look around hurriedly – there's nothing – and then turn back. Expecting the blind man to be gone, I'm taken by surprise that he's still there.

He doesn't look at me. The blind man, he doesn't look. On occasion I have seen people here, on this bloody beach, that I did not know, yet they had their place. I had hurt them, indirectly. I had ruined their life, indirectly. The widow, the mother, the son.

But not this blind man. That is not why he's here.

It makes no sense. I see dead people. On this beach, this walk of shame, I also see those I have hurt. I don't see people who are alive, sitting in dining rooms, allowing me to think what they're thinking, feel what they're feeling, know what they're seeing, even though they're blind. Perhaps he's a ghost already. That's where the blindness comes from. It's not that he can't see them, it's that they can't see him, sitting alone at a table.

If he's dead, then it might explain the other thing he can feel. That thing that's been coming for a while, and maybe is already there. The slow invasion, the creeping sorrow that lurks just beyond the boundaries of his understanding.

The words *a creeping sorrow* are in my head, and I don't know if they come from the blind man, or whether they are my own interpretation. I don't really understand it at all, which is perhaps not unusual. Eventually stories straighten themselves out, things become clear.

Finally I'm able to walk on. Up ahead there is a woman sitting at a desk. She looks forlorn. It is Alina from Kiev, who I loved and left. There is a hypodermic needle in her arm, leaking blood.

Sunday morning church service. 11.37 a.m. So wet and dark and grey outside, it's as though the sun has yet to rise. So wet and dark and grey outside, the church feels under siege, as if the darkness were caused by a host of demons.

The congregation is meagre, even by its usual low standard. Fewer than forty. Now that the children have gone off to Sunday school, their young parents alongside them, I can see only one other person younger than me in attendance. The familiar sea of grey hair of any church congregation.

I could have gone into work, yet I came here beforehand. Second time this month. Fifteenth time this year. The number ticks steadily upwards each time I attend, yet to lose track.

What am I looking for? I've arrested enough people who have used religion for their own gain that I think nothing of anyone else's belief. You can't trust faith, and I don't have any myself. Yet, here I am, sitting alone in a pew, completely detached from my surroundings. Maybe it's just a good time to think, that's all. Yes, when you live alone, every minute at home is time to think. But there's something about a church, whether there's a service on or not. It's built to make you think, even if you're not thinking about what the people who commissioned the building intended.

I realised it several years ago. One day in Washington DC. A tough visit, flitting between Langley and the Pentagon, the Americans riding roughshod. Funny how the current administration in the White House makes us all look back at the incompetent fools of the Bush years as the good guys, the glory days.

I had a couple of hours out in the afternoon, and went to the National Cathedral at the intersection of Massachusetts and Wisconsin to sit in silence. There were too many visitors for the silence to be complete, and then at five thirty the cathedral was given over to Evensong. Yet the sounds going on around made no difference. I could feel my head clearing as I sat there, the fog of war evaporating.

I need this more often, I thought at the time, and then didn't go anywhere near a church for years. This past year, however, the unseen haunting of Elizabeth Rhodes, the sight of her thrusting that knife into her belly, the sound of the blood, the gurgle, has me seeking something, even if I don't know what it is. It has brought guilt, and I should talk to someone, but I don't want to. I don't want absolution, I don't want to lay myself bare to anyone. And no one can tell, and no one's asking, so I don't have to make excuses for myself. So this is just for me. I'm going to church. This is me doing *something*. My head will be fine.

This morning I woke early, went for a walk through the deserted Sunday morning town, down along the Peffery to where the Conon meets the Firth. There were a couple of dog walkers. I sat in silence looking at the water, but couldn't shake the strange feeling of the middle of the night. The beach, the blind man who shouldn't have been there.

Walked back through the town as it slowly came to life, had smoked salmon, scrambled eggs, toast and coffee for breakfast while listening to Radio 3, and now I'm here. Thinking. Just not thinking about yesterday's murder, and what'll need doing when I get to the station.

'And when He had taken a cup and given thanks, He gave it to them, saying, "Drink from it, all of you; for this is My blood of the covenant, which is poured out for many for forgiveness of sins".'

Reverend Marcus pauses, and I have one of those brief moments of tuning in. *My blood of the covenant.* She's in her late thirties, younger than everyone else now sitting before her, but there's a gravity about her. For a moment it seems that she's staring straight at me, and then her eyes move to the side and continue on over the congregation.

'And how many of us have clung to that moment in the life of Christ? How many have stared into the darkness of our own failings and our own deeds, and thought, Christ died for me, died so that my sins may be forgiven?'

Another long pause. She has a beguiling voice, layered with tone. The words are almost unimportant. And yet, those words there, those particular words, felt like they were directed right at me. She can read every damned, guilt-ridden thought in my head.

I switch off again, forcing the words from my mind, allowing the minister's voice to wash over me with indistinct phrasing and warm, perfect sound. Look to the stained-glass window on my right. An angel in rich red and blue, Latin script down either side. The colour of the sky outside, such as I can make out, is heavy, dark grey. Naturally foreboding. As though, when the service is over, I'll leave the church and Sutherland will be there, waiting to inform me of the next murder. The follow-up murder to the one that's supposed to be an isolated incident outside a football ground. Or else I won't even get to wait until the end of the service, and my phone will shortly start vibrating, and I'll have to excuse myself and make my way out the back of the church.

There's a general, low rustle of movement around the nave, and I look up. Marcus has finished her sermon and announced the hymn to follow. How long have I been zoned out? It seemed like a quick sermon, yet it's almost ten to twelve.

I lift the hymn book, *I, the Lord of sea and sky*, and rise with the rest of the congregation.

I never sing.

No matter how few the number, there's never a quick evacuation from a church. The only way to exit the building in a timely manner is to get up and out before the rest of the congregation. I never choose to push my way dramatically to the front, instead sitting while the others inch slowly back down the aisle.

Behind the pulpit there is a large stained-glass window, the familiar jumble of dark, nineteenth-century colours. The image shows the martyrdom of Saint Sebastian, face serene, tied to a tree, and shot full of arrows. Blood drips from his wounds. A quick glance at the window would tell you little beyond the brutal death. Close study shows the incredible detail, the talent of the artists who created the window. And in the muddle of colour, it's all there. The angry mob, the arrows flying, blood on Sebastian's hands, the angels looking down, waiting to welcome him to eternity.

It wouldn't have been what was intended, but perhaps it's a fine metaphor for the demise of the church in Scotland.

What do they all think, these people? These passing few, the last generation to regularly and automatically attend church? Do they really believe in God, or is it just what they've always done on a Sunday morning? A certainty about their lives, a rock by which to anchor their week, a community of outward decency, a faith they need not question?

My generation and younger have always questioned. Besides, we have other things to do. Sundays are just Saturdays with marginally fewer shops open. And yet, here I am, sitting alone in the middle of a church pew, the organist still playing, a steady, unspectacular 'Jesu', the place emptying around me, wrestling with something. Just not faith, that's all. Haunted by a man in a dream who sees everything without being able to see anything at all.

The organ stops, the silence itself as sudden and abrupt as the sharp strike of a gavel. I look away from the window, realising that my eyes have barely moved from the face of Sebastian for the last few minutes, and look down the length of the church as the organist collects her music, rises slowly and walks down the few steps and through the side door. She does not look my way.

'The art of dying.'

I turn at the voice next to me. I didn't jump. It was as if I knew there was someone sitting there, right next to me, but had yet to officially acknowledge it to myself.

The Reverend Marcus is staring up at the window. I watch her for a moment, and then follow her gaze when she doesn't look at me.

'Unusual in a Church of Scotland building,' she says. 'Such a depiction of martyrdom of a saint, particularly Sebastian. The work of one of my long-ago predecessors, the Reverend Charles Blake. He insisted, apparently, against the wishes of his superiors. He must have been a man of singular panache to have carried it off.'

Here I sit in silence, staring at the window, nothing to say about the Reverend Blake.

'I sit in here from time to time, doing just what you're doing now,' she continues. 'Getting lost in his sacrifice. That someone could give of themselves like that.'

Saint Sebastian does not look back out at the congregation. His eyes are directed upwards at the angels as they await his ascension. Meanwhile, the Reverend Marcus's words hang in the air like those angels above Sebastian's death.

'Do you really believe that?'

She turns away from the window.

'How d'you mean?'

'Do you really believe the story of Saint Sebastian?'

A moment, then she smiles.

'Some suggest that he recovered from this, and was later clubbed to death after warning the Emperor Diocletian of his sins. But I don't think that's what you meant.'

I don't answer. I don't know the story of Saint Sebastian.

'I think perhaps you're questioning the romanticised view of his martyrdom, rather than the fact of it,' she says. 'If he did indeed die beneath a hail of arrows, would he have worn such an air of tranquility? Probably not. But I don't think the churchgoers of the nineteenth century would have been happy with a brutal representation of the true horror of death by the mob. Nor, for that matter, would today's congregation.'

'What's left of them,' automatically escapes my lips, then I hold up a repentant hand, mumbling an apology.

'That's all right,' she says, 'I can't argue.'

A beat. The church is completely silent.

'You're sitting here thinking about Mr Peterson, perhaps,' she says.

Another beat while I contemplate where this discussion can go, then I say, 'You read the news.'

'Yes. It's horrible. I was going to mention it this morning . . . I should have done, but then I saw you . . . I'm not sure why that stayed my hand. I just thought, maybe I'm stepping into a police investigation, maybe you wouldn't want me saying anything at all, not even the kind of achingly bland platitudes you'd expect from the pulpit. And, of course, Mr Peterson did not live in Dingwall, and was not generally known, as far as I'm aware, by the parishioners.'

I can't help smiling grimly at the honesty of the words *achingly bland platitudes*, and although I don't look at her I get the sense she's smiling too.

'You haven't managed to catch anyone.' I don't answer, and she nods. 'He could be an awkward man, but . . . well, if all awkward men were to be killed, there probably wouldn't be too many of you left.'

For the first time we look at each other. The gentle teasing, that look in her eye. If we were sitting in a bar at two in the morning, I'd have an idea where this was going. A recently emptied church, enveloped by the quiet of the graveyard, as though all the sound has been drawn out by those who departed, seems a different proposition.

It's not just the teasing and the look in the eye. Of course it's not. People tease all the time, it doesn't mean there's anything *two o'clock in the morning in a bar* about it.

'I wasn't thinking,' I say, ignoring the sudden arrival of subtext, 'you must have known Thomas Peterson.'

A beat while she adjusts to the change in direction, then she says, 'Yes. I'm afraid,' and she pauses, and indicates the pews, empty now, but not that much more populated during the service, 'our congregation is dying off at a somewhat alarming rate. And winter is coming,' she adds with a grim smile, 'when funerals arrive at a rate of two or three a week.'

'You'll be out of a job,' I say mundanely.

'No, I don't think so. The number of churches may be dwindling, but not as quickly, sadly, as the number of people who want to minister.'

Finally I break the look, glance over my shoulder at the open door at the back of the nave. There, at last, is sight of someone, an elder of the church, sorting pew Bibles into even stacks. Just from the quick glance I get the sense of the woman's OCD.

'We need to learn a bit more about Mr Peterson,' I say, the words sounding strangely prosaic. Why shouldn't I have this conversation with the minister? 'Would you be able to have a chat? Shouldn't take long.'

'You know what day it is, right?' she says, smiling.

Sky blue shirt, white dog collar, hair an attractive blonde bob with a perfectly cut, untidy fringe.

'You have places to be?'

'I'm afraid so,' she says. 'I need to go and join my flock in the church halls for the regulation tea and biscuits. Then . . . I won't bore you, but my Sunday afternoons are mapped out several weeks in advance, and then we have the evening service, when even fewer will appear in God's name. Perhaps we could find each other this evening, if you're still working.'

Damn. Another one of those moments. A perfectly acceptable, reasonable suggestion to navigate a scheduling difficulty, yet it feels weirdly like she's asking me on a date. Or, that I've asked her on a date and she's trying to accommodate me.

The triviality of the thought, the idea that I can't have a conversation with an attractive woman without me deciding there must be an underlying context, a chemistry, a *something* waiting to happen, induces a familiar feeling of self-loathing. The chemistry is turned off; I focus on the job.

'Sure,' I say, 'I'll give you a call. I'll see how the day goes, it might be we don't need you.'

She laughs, a curiosity on her face, having recognised the switch in my demeanour.

'Nice not to be needed,' she says, getting to her feet. 'Now, I should get along, the pensioners will be wondering what happened to me. And given that Mrs Bletchley saw us chatting, I dare say there'll be a fair amount of gossiping. They've been trying to marry me off to one of their sons, or grandsons, since I got here.'

I follow her out the pew, my renewed melancholy preventing me sharing in her amusement.

'Either that, or they all think I'm gay.'

She stops, as she walks up the aisle, and we look at each other for a moment. She's smiling.

'Some also say I talk too much. I take it you won't be joining us for refreshments in the hall?'

'I'd love to,' I say, drily. 'Next time.'

Another smile, and she turns and leads the way out the church.

Behind us I can feel Saint Sebastian, those eyes now turned towards us, following our path from the nave.

6

'Sergeant,' I say, walking into the open-plan. Sutherland is at his desk. The office is quiet, of course, but still a few desks are occupied. Fisher's here, as are Ross and Andrews. A quick glance into Quinn's office confirms that the Chief Inspector isn't present. 'Thanks for coming in,' I add.

'It's fine,' he says.

'What's the coffee situation?'

'Would you like me to get it?'

'I'm on it. D'you want one?'

Sutherland glances at the cup sitting beside him and says, 'Sure, thanks.'

Wander over to the coffee machine, which has space for two cups to run at the same time, and set them going. Two coffees with milk. Stand for a moment listening to the machine, watching the milk pour, and then hear the quiet of the office. A lazy Sunday.

'Anything new overnight?' I ask, and Sutherland lifts his head. His desk is about ten yards away. Some days it isn't really worth trying to have a conversation across the office because the place is bustling so much.

'Rammy inside, then continuing outside, the Drummond. Around ten people involved. That's your major incident for the evening.'

'Oil guys?'

'Oil guys and locals. A pub argument turned into a free-for-all. Like in an old western, but without the inherent

45

romance of John Wayne slugging some bum in the face over a beautiful woman.'

'Anything as a result?'

'Five injured, two overnight in hospital, one serious, but not life-threatening.'

'Is there a report?'

Sutherland indicates Fisher, who, tuned into the conversation, says, 'It'll be in your inbox in five, sir.'

'Thanks, Fish.'

'Say we banned alcohol,' says Sutherland. 'D'you think we'd have more time on our hands, once all the alcohol-associated crime and domestic violence had been taken off our slate, or d'you think we'd have less time 'cause we'd spend our lives hunting down illegal stills, illegal imports, gangs, smuggling, and all the associated crap? Same with the medical services. Would all the spare capacity it'd bring be used up treating people drinking meths, shoe polish and poisonous moonshine?'

'I have a plan for when I'm in charge,' I say, bringing the coffees to the desk and passing one over to Sutherland, as I avoid directly answering the question as though I'm a government minister on *Newsnight*. 'Super-high minimum pricing on retail sales, but reasonable pricing in pubs and restaurants. And I mean, mega-high, none of the wishy-washy fifty pence a unit. I'd say like thirty-five quid for a bottle of wine, seven or eight for a can of beer. But much cheaper in bars.'

'People would be upset,' says Sutherland.

'Not the people getting beaten up by their drunk partners. Not the people having to wait in A&E because of the Drummond lot.'

'There's a flaw,' says Sutherland. 'Those guys were drinking in a bar.'

'How many of them had filled up on cheap booze before they got there?'

'Decent,' says Sutherland, acknowledging the point. 'It'd put Oddbins out of business.'

'Pubs would thrive. Oddbins can change their business model. The plan cuts out pre-drinking, and more or less forces people to drink in public. Obviously it wouldn't eliminate alcohol abuse, but there'd be less, there'd be less crime, fewer injuries, less of a strain on the NHS. Everyone's a winner.'

'Tesco won't go for it.'

'They can sell more vegetables,' I say glibly.

'We'd spend our life chasing down illegal stills.'

'I'm not sure. We're not *banning* alcohol after all. You want a pint, so what do you do? Take the time to make your own? Risk drinking something in a plain bottle made by Big Alisdair at the bottom of his garden? Or nip down the pub?'

'Hmm,' says Sutherland, still not convinced. 'Anyway, it'd be a disaster for home dinner parties.'

I'd already started scrolling through my inbox, and now I look across at him. Can't help smiling.

'You're right, it's a total no-goer. The dinner party vote in Scotland's pretty substantial. Why, only six years ago I was at a dinner party.'

Sutherland smiles humourlessly, and then he turns back to his computer. The introductory conversation for the day over, time to get down to business, going through the motions of the start of every working day. The quick check of e-mails, deleting the dross, making notes, the two-line holding reply for anything urgent.

Early Sunday afternoon, and there are far fewer e-mails than there are on a weekday, there's nothing of particular importance, and I'm able to quickly close the inbox.

'Right, good to go. Where are we with Thomas Peterson?'

'Still waiting for County to give us the names of the ticket holders in Peterson's vicinity yesterday.'

'Can we hurry them up on that?'

'I'm on it. Alice is working with Tech to get the e-fit of the attacker. Roddy's been back in this morning, and we've also brought in three witnesses, including Action Hero Man, for their input.'

'Thought he was going back to Edinburgh?'

'Stayed the night at the Tulloch. We asked him to, he was happy to hang around the scene of his pugilistic triumph.'

A deadpan look across the desks.

'He used the words pugilistic triumph, didn't he?'

'Yep.'

'When will we have the picture?' I ask, deciding that'll do it for Bastion Bobby.

'An hour or two.'

'Good. We should aim to get it out this afternoon. Get it in the papers in the morning. Did you see them today, I haven't looked.'

'Much as you'd expect.'

'K. What else?'

'We have . . .' and he looks at his notes, quickly flicking through them, 'we have CCTV from outside the ground, the club did send that over. The view was blocked by a bus.'

'Really? You think the perpetrator picked his spot to make sure he wouldn't be caught on camera?'

'I do,' says Sutherland. 'There's no particular way to know for sure, but if it's true then that points far more to some kind of hit. Picking the spot outside the ground where the opposition team bus is parked between you and the only camera takes some planning.'

'We inch closer to this being specifically about Mr Peterson, rather than some random act of violence.'

'Yes. So . . .' and his eyes once more scan his notes, before they lift, and he looks over my right shoulder. 'Incoming,' he says, the word barely across his lips before the bark comes from behind.

'Gentlemen. My office.'

Chief Inspector Quinn breezes briskly past behind me, Sutherland and I share a glance, and then we get to our feet and follow the boss. Into the room, close the door behind us. We stand, while he sits down, then he tosses the *Herald* onto the desk, back page up, turned round so we can read the headline.

County Face Long Ban After Match Death Horror.

He lets us read it for several seconds, although I don't think he's intending that we read the small print, then he leaves the newspaper in place and leans forward on the desk.

'I know you're going to hate this, Inspector, but there are always local politics. It may not be your game to play them, but it's certainly mine. And football's football, wherever you go.'

Football's football, wherever you go ... I'm not sure which argument that phrase is supposed to win, but it doesn't really matter. Politics is always the heavy burden of the suits at the top of any organisation, usually taken on willingly nevertheless. The grunts on the ground just need to get the job done, while the suits always have to think about the bigger picture; what other people are thinking, whose toes are going to be getting stepped on.

At least, that's what they all want to believe, because by playing the game, they're making themselves part of it, increasing their own feeling of importance. By this means, the corrupt millionaires and the councilmen and the politicians stay out of jail and stay in control, in a giant, self-perpetuating merry-go-round, no matter how detached ninety per cent of these people think they are from it.

'There's not much that matters in this town any more, Inspector, but there's still County. And when this kind of thing starts appearing in the national papers, when this starts happening, then the shit starts flying. People start talking. And people are already talking, people are already saying things. People are assuming things. Me too, for a moment. And then half an hour ago I get a call from the ground, and they tell me that the victim's son couldn't identify anyone who was at the game, something for which you two were present. The young boy basically shot a hole in the theory that the victim was killed by a fan who bore a grudge. So, in fact, his murder quite likely had nothing whatsoever to do with County, nothing whatsoever to do with what happened at the football. And here I am, searching this report, and I've searched the Internet, yet I cannot see any mention of a statement from the police confirming this *fact*.'

He pauses, keeping his eyes on me.

'Did I miss something?' he adds, when I don't immediately jump in.

'The football club may be ready to declare their fans blameless, but we're hardly in that position yet, sir. We need to—'

'Well, yes, they are, and you know why? Because they *are* blameless. What else are you suggesting, Inspector? That some fellow from the crowd took offence at Mr Peterson, but he didn't want to get his hands dirty, so he calls some thug on his mobile and fixes up the hit. Twenty minutes after the game's finished, Peterson's dead, and our suspect is halfway down the A9 on the way back to his stately mansion near Kingussie?'

As time goes by, mine and Quinn's relationship slowly deteriorates. As he edges closer to retirement, the inevitable encroachment of the passing years, the inescapable end, he becomes more and more resentful, looking to lash out at any suitable target. Too pusillanimous to lash upwards, and too professional to lash out at the junior staff, he picks the person he assumes will not be affected. The easy mark, the victimless crime.

The only victim, in fact, is our relationship, and neither of us cares.

'We've only just begun this investigation, sir,' I say. 'We have to consider it a possibility, but it's still too early to say that Peterson was killed for some reason in his life outside of football. In fact, the most likely explanation at the moment is that some drunk thug, just having left the game, who didn't happen to be sitting anywhere near him, took to him out of simple badness, nothing else. If that's the case, then there's no way County will be getting a pass. Sir.'

He'll know I'm right, even if he won't outright admit it. Acknowledging the politics of the moment is fine, but issuing a premature statement purely to defuse the situation has far too much potential to backfire.

'I want you to get on to the club right now,' he says. 'You need to reassure them that everything's being done to get this matter wrapped up as quickly as possible. And if it turns out the club aren't liable in this in any way, then you need to tell them it'll be getting made clear to the media very soon.'

What else am I going to do? He's more or less just said, *I need you to do your job and do it well*, which is what I'd been intending to do in the first place.

'When Inverness calls here first thing tomorrow, I want to have something to tell them.'

It's rare for the men at the top to have a sense of perspective. Fortunately, the person at the top in Inverness is a woman, and she's far more attuned to the real world than Chief Inspector Quinn.

He opens his mouth, about to add something, but instead kind of half sighs, and nods in the direction of the open-plan. And out we go, leaving the door open behind us.

'Can you imagine what he'd've been like if they'd been playing the Rangers,' says Sutherland in a low voice.

'He would've been an explosion in an asshole factory,' I say, and Sutherland laughs darkly.

PC Cole, who's obviously been waiting for us to emerge, rises from her desk and approaches.

'Afternoon, sir,' she says, and hands me the mugshot of the suspect in the Peterson beating.

Sutherland stands at my shoulder looking at the picture. E-fits become ever more lifelike with each passing year, but they're still e-fits all the same.

'Thanks, Alice,' I say. 'What do we think?'

'I like it, sir,' says Cole. 'Roddy gave it his best shot. We fed in the views of the others, then when we had a more complete picture, we showed it to Roddy again and his face automatically brightened in recognition. It was like, pa-ding! You know how you see that sometimes?'

We all look at the picture.

'This is our guy,' she adds.

'Thank you,' I say, 'I'll take heart from your positivity.'

'You've run it through facial recognition?' asks Sutherland.

'Nothing, sir,' says Cole, directing her answer to me, even though it wasn't me who asked the question. 'Shall we go public?'

'Please. Standard procedures.'

'Yes, sir. Anything else?'

'We're good, thanks. Iain and I are going to speak to the club now. I'll let you know what comes up.'

'Sir,' she says. She glances at Sutherland, a quick, almost disparaging look, and then turns away.

I watch her go, and then look at Sutherland. He watches Cole walk across the open-plan. Suddenly he looks drained.

7

We take the car back down to the club. Might have walked under other circumstances, but the rain's tipping down, it's Sunday mid-afternoon, and we just want to get on with it. I'd not intended coming here until we'd heard something positive from them, Monday morning at the latest, but here we are, forcing the discussion with the club because the boss has ordered it. Politics.

'What's with you and Constable Cole?' I ask, halfway through the three-minute drive. No traffic, nowhere in Dingwall is far from anywhere else.

The rain is squally, the wind picking up, wipers on full.

Sutherland stares straight ahead, mid-bite of an old dough-nut he grabbed from his desk drawer.

'There's nothing with me and Constable Cole,' he replies.

'I could swear there's something with you and Constable Cole.'

I'm not smiling. I'm still annoyed by my conversation with Quinn, wanting to tell him where he can take his subservience to local politics, and looking to talk about something else. The palpable feeling of irritation in the car isn't helping.

There's obviously something between Sutherland and Cole, though I have no idea what. As I ask the question, I'm aware there's an outside chance I'm a part of it. Despite asking, I don't wish to know about that.

Sutherland gives me a sideways glance.

'I think your spider sense might be a little off on this one, sir.'

The briefest of conversations, the journey is done, and we are both saved from the awkwardness I unnecessarily started.

The e-fit of the suspect is on the desk of the head of County security, Moira Reynolds. She's studied it for nearly a minute, while we sit and watch her in silence.

Reynolds has blinked twice.

I recognise what she's doing, and I'm impressed. She's running the picture through a database in her head. An eidetic memory. She studies footage every week, she knows who to look out for.

Reynolds lifts her head, at the same time pushing the picture away. The movement is only a couple of centimetres, but it's a symbolic act. She's done.

'No,' she says. 'He's not one of our regulars.'

'But he could've been at the game?'

'Of course,' says Reynolds, with the stilted indifference of a continental European. 'I haven't seen all the footage from yesterday. I'll have finished by tomorrow morning. I'll give you a call.'

We've been here before, of course, talking to security, but Moira Reynolds is new. From the few minutes we've been with her, I'd say she'd have been able to pick up a security job somewhere a hell of a lot bigger than the local football ground in Dingwall. She must be here for love or the scenery, one or the other. No one with the level of skill and competence she's currently displaying would come here for career advancement.

'You have facial recognition software?' asks Sutherland.

This woman *is* the facial recognition software.

'Yes. Not entirely reliable, but I'll get it started on the picture.'

'And what about the people sitting behind Peterson, have you been able to identify any of them?' he asks.

'We can tell who paid for all of the tickets, the season ticket holders and the one-off ticket sales, except one to the far left of Peterson's line of vision, which was a match day cash payment. Of course, there's no guarantee that the person sitting in the seat is the same person as the one who bought the ticket. We'll compare with previous games, see how many are regulars. That should start to firm up the names.'

'And the Monkey Man?' asks Sutherland.

'The Monkey Man,' says Reynolds with a smile. 'You're a Wilburys fan?'

Sutherland looks curious, then glances over at me.

'Yes, Iain, you're a Wilburys fan.'

Sutherland shrugs and smiles awkwardly at Reynolds.

'Well, the Monkey Man is Mr Grey Davies,' she says. 'Been a season ticket holder with us for ten years. We've already sent a letter to warn him that if there's another viola-tion of any description, he'll be barred for life. We also note in the letter that we cannot rule out the possibility of police action, the result of which may well be that he's suspended for life anyway.'

She holds my gaze. The club has done what it has to do. Over to the police.

'We'll take his details. And those of the ones around him, if you're happy to give us those,' I say.

'Of course. We want this cleared up as quickly as you do. We can do without the kind of headline we got in the *Herald* this morning.'

'Can you check footage of that section of the stand from the rest of the game, please? So that we can see if—'

'Anyone left the game especially early, right,' says Reynolds, interrupting. 'Already done it. And no, there wasn't. Plenty of people on phones, however, so someone could have called in a hit job, if that's what you're thinking. Seems extreme, but it would hardly be the weirdest thing any of us had ever seen.'

'What about Mr Davies?' asks Sutherland.

'He used his phone. Five times. Barely off it, in fact. That moment when he made the noise was a rare exception.'

'And his first name is really Grey? Or that's a nickname?'

'That's the name on the season ticket.'

'That's not giving your kid much to live up to,' says Sutherland.

Reynolds stares blankly across the desk.

'You used to be a cop?' I ask. Something about her, but that's not it. Not a cop.

We have what we need for the moment, and my question is the way of wrapping things up. I expect to not really get an answer, but I can see her relax a little, then she says, 'GCHQ.'

'That makes sense. You were there recently?'

'At some point in the past, Inspector,' she replies, with a meagre hint of amusement. 'But I don't believe that it really pertains to your investigation.'

'Right, thank you,' I say. 'I'll be in touch again in the morning. We'll try to get this wrapped up quickly, and if we can be certain that the suspect wasn't at the game, we'll get that disseminated to the press.'

'You don't have to give me the sop, Inspector,' she says. 'I'm just doing my job. If this one is on us, we need to address it and look at our procedures. If it's not, then it'll do us no harm to look at our procedures again anyway. The PR people have their issues, I have mine.'

'We'll leave you to it,' I say, getting to my feet. 'If you need to contact me this afternoon or tonight, you've got my number.'

'Either way, it'll be first thing in the morning. No need for more people than necessary to be working on a Sunday,

Inspector. Mr Peterson isn't on the verge of becoming any less dead.'

I smile, Sutherland nods a goodbye, and then we turn away. By the time we've reached the door, Reynolds is already looking back at her computer screen. Door closed, and we walk along the short corridor.

'She's good,' says Sutherland.

'Yes.'

'So, what was with you and her, anyway?' asks Sutherland.

I glance at him curiously.

'There was nothing.'

'Hmm,' he says. 'I could have sworn there was something with you and her.'

A moment, then the penny drops. I don't look at him, but let him see me roll my eyes. He laughs lightly at my back.

Grey Davies is in his late forties, and has something peculiarly attractive about him. He's slim, with a thin, angular face, cheap, round spectacles, a small goatee and greying hair shaved short at the sides, coiffed into a small ridge on top. He's wearing a faded purple Dylan T-shirt, an unbuttoned, pale Harris Tweed waistcoat and beige shorts. He should look ridiculous – it's as though he's trying to prove he's nothing like his forename – yet somehow he pulls it all off.

A woman in her twenties answered the door, introducing herself, even before I'd spoken, as Candy. *Hi, I'm Candy*. The door to a lodge by the shores of Loch Garve in the Highlands being answered by a woman who looked like she'd stepped straight from a seventies LA porn movie, as the dark of a late-November early evening crept over the land, certainly slotted into the all-human-life-is-here theory of police work. Candy was wearing a long, cotton shirt, top three buttons undone, and nothing else. We didn't speak much. She directed me through the house, along a hallway that was a riot of art. Every inch on one side covered with contemporary oil paintings, shapes and blurred images in bright colours. On the other, a series of explicit etchings of a man and a woman making love.

Candy offered tea, coffee or something stronger. I refused all three. Through the kitchen, out the back, and Candy stood at the door pointing in the direction of the small wooden building at the bottom of the garden, on the shores of the loch, the lights from within bright in the night.

'That's his studio,' she said.

'Thanks, Candy,' I said. 'The etchings in the hallway. Those are of you and Mr Davies?'

Candy smiled and bit her bottom lip. 'What d'you think?'

Not really having anywhere to go with that conversation, even though it was me who'd made the mistake of starting it, I smiled and turned down the garden path. Knocked on the studio door. Davies invited me in with a wave, without even turning to look to see who was there, and now I've been standing for three or four minutes in silence, watching him paint.

It's captivating, despite, rather than because, of the subject of the painting. To his left there is a much smaller easel with a pencil sketch, all he seems to be using as a guide. As with much of the art inside, this is a self-portrait. The artist and his love, fighting a dragon. Both he and Candy are naked. The dragon is rearing up above them, wings spread wide, fire breathing over their heads, as Davies prepares to throw a scimitar into its belly, like he's throwing a javelin. His erection almost matches the javelin in size. Candy is in mid-dive, outstretched, back arched, breasts gloriously, and somewhat gravity-defyingly, pointed upwards, as she thrusts a knife into the dragon's heart. It's not entirely clear why the dragon doesn't just aim its fire at its assailants and roast them both.

'What's it supposed to be?' I ask, finally breaking the silence.

Davies holds his brush over the canvas for a second – he's in the middle of painting Candy's left thigh – and then he withdraws the brush, turns to look at me. When he sees that I'm joking, he smiles caustically, sets the brush down, rubs his hands on an old rag by the side of the easel, and then leans to the nearby desk, lifts and drains a cold cup of coffee.

'You'll be the police officer,' he says.

'Detective Inspector Westphall,' I reply, briefly holding out my ID.

He looks at it quizzically.

'Detective Inspector? You lot got nothing else to do? I got the letter from the County already. Hand delivered, *on a Sunday*. So, I made a stupid noise, I admit it. I'd been drinking. I'm going to write to the club to apologise, I'm going to . . .' and he waves his hand, round and round a couple of times. 'I'll apologise to anyone in the entire ground I offended, I'll apologise to the wee black guy, whatever his name is. I mean, is that not enough?'

I let him talk, although I realised pretty much as he started speaking that he has no idea why I'm here.

'You saw the papers this morning?'

'I read the reports on the game,' he says. 'Didn't think my intervention had that much of an impact. It would've been shite anyway.'

'There was a murder.'

Davies pauses at the shift in tack, thinks about it, and then nods. Totally unconcerned, it seems. He's a decent actor, or, of course, genuinely unconcerned.

'Last thing the club needs. And, look, I get it, me bringing my drunk, casual racism into the ground doesn't help anyone either. But like I said, I've apologised, and they really don't have to threaten to ban me for life, for God's sake.'

'I'm not here to talk about your drunk, casual racism, regardless of how much deserved opprobrium you receive as a result. There was a man three rows in front of you who stood up and told you off.'

Davies looks back at the painting. The top left quarter of the canvas is still clear. The etching suggests that it will be filled with a castle from the fantastical mind of Ludwig II.

'Made me feel stupid,' he says, chastened, 'but I suppose he had a point. I learned my lesson right there. Didn't need the letter from the club. Expect he was onto them, complaining. I mean,' and he turns round, 'point or no, the guy's a pious bastard. Just showing off. *Look at me, look at how righteous I am.* Virtue-signalling asshole.'

'His name was Thomas Peterson. He was the man who was murdered after the game.'

Davies holds my eye for a moment, and then, his face unchanging, he looks away, this time past the canvas, out over the loch, beautifully framed in dark grey in the huge picture window.

I watch him for a while, and then follow his silent gaze. The water is high, which is no surprise given the time of year, the constant falling rain. There's a wind blowing down from the hills beyond, making it look as though the loch is sweeping towards us in the dark.

'That's why you're here,' he says finally. 'You're asking if I killed him. Wait, no. You're here to accuse me of killing him.'

He turns now, his eyes expressionless, his mouth twisted in a downturn of resentment.

'You'll be loving this, I expect. Surprised you've not come with twenty hefty goons to huckle us off in an unmarked van.'

'Sure,' I say, 'because that's the kind of thing that happens. Look, a man who publicly embarrassed you was killed, that's all. No one's saying you did it, but we, the police, need to establish that it wasn't you, then we can move on. What did you do after the game?'

He lowers his eyes, seems to accept that he has to face the line of questioning, and says, 'I sat in the car park for fifteen minutes. I was on the phone.'

'Thought you said you were drunk?'

'I'd sobered up by the end,' he says, without missing a beat. Voice dead.

'You were on the phone throughout the game. Who were you speaking to?'

Another long pause, then he says, 'You'll have looked at my phone records already. *You* tell *me* who I was talking to.'

'We saw the CCTV of you on the phone. We haven't checked the records yet. But we will. Who were you talking to?'

'Candy,' he says.

'Why?'

'Really? She's my girlfriend. Why wouldn't I talk to her?'

'You live with Candy, then you go to watch a game of football, something you do every weekend. Seems odd that you would talk to her throughout. How long have you and Candy been together?'

'What does that have to do with it?'

'I'm trying to find an excuse for you,' I say. 'If you're in a new relationship, then maybe you're still at the stage where you can't get enough of each other. Maybe you're still madly in love. But then, would you have gone to the game in the first place, or wouldn't she have come with you?'

'Three and a half years.'

'It's not that, then.'

'Maybe we're having a crisis,' he says, finally looking up. 'People discuss things when they're having a crisis.'

'Were you having a crisis?'

He doesn't answer.

'The people you sit beside at the game. Friends of yours?'

'No.'

'What d'you talk to them about?'

'We're British. We don't talk.'

'You're not commuters on the six forty-one to Paddington. There's footage.'

'So, we talk a bit. They're just guys I know from the ground.'

'Did you speak about Mr Peterson's public rebuke?'

'No,' he says. 'It was embarrassing. No one was talking about it.'

'Did you, or anyone else, make any threat against Mr Peterson, directly to him or in private conversation?'

He smirks, looks away dismissively. Sometime in the past a police officer must have bottled that reaction, and been cursed by it. We see it so often. *How inane of the police to ask such a question!*

'Did you, or anyone else, make any threat against Mr Peterson, directly to him or in private conversation?' I repeat. Same words, same tone.

'No,' says Davies this time. 'I didn't, and didn't see anyone else doing it.'

You rarely get anything on a first visit. It's about establishing a basic framework, a starting point from which you can progress to looking for inconsistencies.

I turn away and look around the room. There's nothing similar to what he's currently working on. The rest of the art has been painted in various styles, but it all features the same subject matter. Candy. Even when he has included himself in the painting, the focus is on Candy.

Candy dancing; Candy sleeping; Candy staring forlornly out the window; Candy running through a meadow; Candy blasting a punk with a .44 Magnum; Candy smiling; Candy masturbating; Candy biting into a tomato, the juice exploding from her teeth.

In all the paintings, Candy is naked.

Despite the singular nature of the subject matter, it's tough not to be impressed with Davies's work. He has caught Candy so perfectly, so intimately, some of the paintings could be mistaken for photographs.

I turn back to him, realise he's been watching me the whole time.

'I'll let you know when we've completed our investigation into what happened at the ground, then you can come into the station.'

'Why?'

'At the very least you'll be getting cautioned for racially aggravated harassment under the 1998 Crime and—'

'Jesus . . .'

'—Disorder Act, and we'll see where we are with the murder investigation.'

'Brilliant,' he says. 'Now, are you just going to stand there, or are you going to fuck off and let us get back to work?'

And for today, at least, that will do it for Mr Grey Davies.

8

Sitting at a kitchen table, around and around the interview circle. Back at the first call of the day, talking to the Reverend Marcus. She has a glass of wine and I, playing it straight to the end of the working day, have a cup of tea.

'Thomas did *that*?'

'His son thought he'd goaded him into it.'

When I arrived, she asked if she could put some music on. For some reason, I imagined songs of praise or Gregorian chant, the kind of one-dimensional thought that depresses the hell out of me. She put on Sinatra, and currently 'The Best Is Yet To Come' plays softly in the background.

'That must have taken some goading,' she says.

'It's out of character?'

'He was a businessman. The only reason I can imagine for him doing something like that would be if he thought it'd get his name in the papers. He'd look like an anti-racist champion, and people would be falling over themselves to hand him the dead bodies of their parents.'

She sighs heavily.

'Not very Christian of me, sorry. I've seen Thomas at work, and he could be awkward. I'm not sure why he ended up in the line of work that he did, but presumably he just saw it as a worthwhile business opportunity. People will always need burying and cremating. People will always die.'

'When was the last time you saw him?'

'He'd taken over the undertaking business in Ross-shire, of course, so his companies arranged ninety per cent of the funerals conducted through our church. Having said that, he was the boss, and only occasionally got his hands dirty. I did see him a few weeks ago, though. Fforbes Robertson's funeral. That was huge. Absurdly so. Church service, the burial, the wake, all conducted with a solemn pomposity.'

She takes a drink of wine, masking a smile at the ways of families and the ceremonies in which they indulge. I can picture the Reverend Marcus conducting a renewal of marriage vows with a sceptical heart.

'He seemed worse,' she says, after taking the wine, and I realise that a certain amount of time has passed when I didn't say anything. Have to think about it, but I was staring at the glass of wine, the movement from the table to her lips and back to the table.

'How'd you mean?'

'He was edgy, but . . . Sometimes you can tell. Sometimes people are having a bad day, and they take it out on those around them. But there was a look about Thomas. Something was eating him, I'd've said.'

'Any ideas?'

Another smile.

'I didn't ask. Yes, compassion's my job, but not with him. He was a man who neither inspired it nor accepted it.' A beat, and then she lifts the glass and indicates me. 'You, on the other hand . . .'

I don't say anything, for a second hiding behind the mug of tea, like we see so many of our interviewees doing.

'You have a haunted air, Inspector Westphall. And there you are, a non-believer, sitting in church, lost in the martyrdom of Saint Sebastian.'

I continue to hide. Suddenly we're talking about me. I just

need to grab the conversation and get it back onto the death of Thomas Peterson, but I feel blindsided.

'We've never spoken about Elizabeth Rhodes,' she says. 'That must have been traumatic for you.'

We've never spoken about anything, the Reverend Marcus and I, bar small talk at the church door. I don't pedantically make the point.

'I know you're an officer, and you must see things all the time, but nevertheless, for someone to do that to themselves in front of you . . . Did you ever get counselling?'

She leans forward, so that the short distance between us across the table is reduced even further. It does not feel like much of a divide. The moment creates itself. Her concern, Sinatra, the wine. The wine, even though I'm not drinking it.

'No,' I say.

She looks troubled. 'Of course not. Why would you? You can, if you like, talk to me. One of the many reasons I'm here. And you can do that without having to admit to yourself that you need help.'

I don't respond.

'And I promise not to bring Jesus into it,' she adds, with a smile.

That finally has me smiling too, and although it hadn't been her intention, it does also break the spell that had briefly been cast. That thing that's there, the elephant at the table, it can wait.

'Thank you,' I say. 'I'll . . . Sorry, we should get on. Is there anything else you can tell me about Mr Peterson?'

She smiles at my clumsiness, holds my gaze for a moment, nods an acceptance of needing to move the conversation on.

'I'm not sure that I can.'

'Was there ever anything about money?'

'We always deal directly with the families, so no money exchanged hands between George Bailey's and the church.'

'Would you have any idea why someone would want to kill him?'

She splutters, with me asking the question as the wine touches her lips, then she coughs, light laughter emerging at the other side.

'Really? Is that a question you ask everyone?'

'Yes,' I say, not joining in her amusement.

I realise I need to complete the questioning and get out. I'm being drawn in, and I don't want to be drawn in by the Reverend Marcus. Not now. Not tonight. Not with my head in a funk, haunted by strange nightmares, in the middle of a murder investigation. Getting drawn in by Elizabeth Rhodes didn't work out so well for anyone.

'If they knew Mr Peterson, then definitely,' I continue. 'You never know where the answer's going to come from.'

'Well, I guess not,' she says.

'So . . .?'

'So, no, I don't think so, Inspector. When do you get off work?'

I drop my eyes to the wine glass. That's what she's asking. *It's nearly nine p.m. on a Sunday evening. Are you really going back to the station now, and if not, then why not finish the interview, have a glass of wine and relax? We don't need to talk about a woman who stabbed herself to death in front of you, we don't need to talk about the shadow that hangs over you.*

'I'll leave you my card, and if you think of anything, you can give me a call,' I say.

She puts the glass to her mouth, her lips smiling behind it.

'Or if you hear anything while arranging the service for Mr Peterson.'

'I'm not sure that that's what'll happen,' she says. 'He didn't live in my parish.'

'Of course.'

'Have a glass of wine.'

'I need to get back to the office.'

Now, I can't let go of her eyes. She captures me. I'd wondered when I made the decision to come here. I questioned whether I needed to. In fact, I knew that I didn't.

'And yet, you're here,' she says, continuing my thought. 'We're not that familiar, Inspector. There will be other ministers who knew Thomas better than I. There are many people to whom you could speak on a Sunday evening who knew Thomas better than I. And yet . . .'

We hold that gaze across the table. The sound of her voice, the teasing words, beautifully wrapping themselves around my head. I take another drink of tea, another regulation defence manoeuvre, and then push my chair back.

'Thank you for your time, Leia. Like I said, if you think of anything else,' and I fish a card from my back pocket and place it on the table.

The minister leans forward, elbows on the table, her chin resting on the backs of her clasped hands.

'Maybe I'll think of something later this evening,' she says, and I can't help smiling forlornly in reply as I turn away.

I fall asleep in the armchair by the window in my front room, the glass of wine I didn't take with the Reverend Marcus on the table by my right hand.

The transition from bleak and cold Easter Ross to the endless bleak and cold beach, the far distance out to sea lost in a lazy haar, always seems such an effortless journey. Somewhere there is the rumour of a fiddle playing.

The evocative, brackish smell of the sea. Transported in an instant to my night-time haunt, populated with the familiar cast of characters. Here the silence, a tangible player in the nightmare, here a woman leaning forward on a desk, her head in her hands, audibly weeping, sobs coming from her chest. I do not know this woman, but I know she weeps for her dead son.

I know I will see the blind man.

Here the sand, and here the dunes, and here the silent surf. Here is Elizabeth Rhodes, the suicide victim, whose death was not my fault, but whose death I witnessed, and whose death I affected not to care about. I thought she was always first. Always the introductory message. The lead-in, the heart of it, the reason we're all here. Then I remember that I've already seen her this night, and here she is, come again. She has not tortured me enough. Over and over, a knife in the guts for my attention.

She holds my gaze. I walk on.

A man sits at a stall, blood gurgling from his lips. Shot in the stomach. He's been here before. I must have killed him in the rainforest in DRC. Yes, that's it. That's why he looks at me like that. *But really, you were shooting at me, my dead, Congolese friend.*

I don't say that. I killed him. Zero sum game. No sympathy given, no understanding, just hatred.

Here we are. The blind man. Before him on the table there is a game of chess. I stop. The blind man does not look up. He's staring at the game. He knows where all the pieces are. It's not obvious whom he's playing. Perhaps he's playing me. Perhaps I make a move every time I'm here.

I don't remember playing chess before. Not against the blind man. Not in a long time. That week in Bratislava, waiting for Jürgen to show. Jürgen never showed. Maya and I played a lot of chess while we waited. It wasn't all we did.

I wonder if Maya will ever be on the beach, although I doubt it. I never hurt Maya. Maya was about boredom. Maya was about *something* to do. And for Maya, I was about boredom and something to do.

Maybe I was just lying to myself. Making an excuse to avoid any chance of guilt. Maybe Maya will be at the next desk.

I look to my left.

There is no next desk.

I turn back to the chess set. A piece has been moved. Bishop to queen's rook seven. I look at the blind man, but he does not look back. He sits in exactly the same position, awaiting my move.

9

Monday morning, back in the dire confines of Room 2, although this morning I've left the door open, in an attempt to allow some light into the room. Sutherland brought coffee, unbidden, which is very welcome. Kinghorn, Cole and Fisher also in attendance.

The rot of depression still sits in the middle of my stomach. An insidious juggernaut of melancholy that will not be appeased by the leaving open of doors, or the green leaves of the ficus.

'OK, let's get going,' I say, compelling the words from my mouth. 'Fish?'

PC Fisher gives her notebook a cursory glance.

'I've spoken to fourteen people who were sitting in the same section as Thomas Peterson on Saturday. None of them knew his full name, only one of them called him Grey. A couple of them thought his name was Davie.'

'Anyone overhear his phone conversation?'

Fisher smiles.

'One guy said he was talking, well, *shite* he said, to a woman. Says he tried, and failed, to zone him out. The guy on his left,' and she indicates the picture on the board, the black and white still photograph of the crowd, 'Angus, said he heard every word. Davies was talking to someone called Candy about shoes.'

'He made five phone calls during the course of the game,' I say.

'Every one of them was about shoes.'

People.

'I've got the request out for his phone records, and once we've got that, we'll be able to confirm whether all the calls were made to the same number.'

'K, so no one else had anything suspicious to report?'

'Literally nothing, and the only consistency was that several made the same gag about wanting the ref arrested.'

'Right,' I say, already mentally moving on to the next thing. 'Anything else?'

Fisher answers with an open-handed gesture, and I turn to Kinghorn.

'Elvis?'

'I got in touch with Mrs Peterson's ex-husband, Brandon Mahler,' says Kinghorn, and then he follows my gaze to the clock. 'I e-mailed. Thought I might be able to speak to him this afternoon, but turns out he gets up early to go out on the boats. Like, three thirty in the morning early.'

'He knew already?'

'The son had called him. Mahler didn't have much to say, just concerned about his kid, naturally.'

'OK,' I say, 'I don't think we need to do too much more on this. Maybe just a little more on his background to make—'

'Already done it,' says Kinghorn. 'I spoke to his brother in Edinburgh, he confirmed the story of the marriage break-up. Called his brother an asshole, but at least he was straight with everyone. He misses his kid, but he gets him every year and seems happy enough with that.'

Kinghorn pauses to run his finger down his notes, which, unlike those of Fisher, are written on an iPad.

'I've gone through his social media pages, Facebook and Instagram in his case, and the guy's clean. It's all sport, fishing and cat fails. I'll call his local police station in Massachusetts, but didn't want to do it too early. If they got a call in the middle of the night, they might think it's urgent. Maybe they're an educated bunch, but they don't understand the time difference. Not really.'

I'm not going to comment on one of my people being condescending about Americans. Sometimes, these dark days, it's hard to be anything else.

'Yeah,' says Cole, 'I went out with this American guy once who thought Britain was, like, literally just off the coast of New York. They really have no idea.'

'Didn't he notice the length of the flight to get here?' asks Sutherland.

Something in his tone. I glance at him, but then look away. Somehow, just for a moment, it's painful to look at him, his torment with Cole laid bare.

'I was in Chicago,' says Cole, dismissively.

'Elvis?' I say quickly.

Whatever it is with Sutherland and Cole, we don't need it in here.

'I'll call them this afternoon,' says Kinghorn.

'Sure. That aside, we're more or less ready to close this one?'

'I'll speak to the police first, but I'd say, if they have nothing – and I don't think they will – then I should move on.'

'OK, cool,' I say, and I turn to Sutherland, who's still looking slightly troubled. 'Iain, where have you got to? You've been looking at George Bailey's?'

'Yep,' he says, and with a snap of the fingers he's back. 'I called Mrs Peterson, and—'

'How's she doing?'

'I'd say she's medicated this morning, or hadn't woken up completely from whatever meds she took last night.'

'We do what it takes.'

'Yes, sir. So, I got a bit more background on the company, though she seemed reluctant to discuss it. She may have a point, but I did impress upon her our need to check.'

'Was the business on solid ground?'

'We didn't really get into that. It was established seven years ago, and right from the off they had a business model of quick expansion, which they did by buying over small going concerns, moving into a market and taking over.'

'Where'd the money come from?'

'She claimed not to know, but I did get the name of his business partner.'

'Not George Bailey?'

'There's no George Bailey. He took the name from *It's a Wonderful Life.*'

'Nice move,' I say. 'Was that whimsical or cynical?'

'She didn't say.'

'Who was George Bailey?' asks the ever-practical Fisher.

'Jimmy Stewart's character in that movie. He wasn't an undertaker, but he was the nicest, most helpful guy in cinema history. Who's the partner?'

Sutherland glances down, then says, 'I'm meeting Natalia Kadyrova in half an hour at the BBC in Inverness. Want to come?'

A beat.

Tick-tock goes the clock.

'What just happened in that sentence?'

'Why does she have a Russian name, and why are we meeting at the BBC?'

'Yes.'

'Well, her accent isn't as pronounced as a generic Hollywood bad guy, but her English isn't great. As for the BBC, we'll need to ask.'

I hold his gaze for another few moments, then glance around the room at the others. None of them say anything, as they await my assessment of this piece of news.

'I really hope this isn't going to be about Russians,' I say.

'Don't you read the news?' says Sutherland. 'Everything's about Russians.'

'Jesus,' I say, under my breath. 'I'd rather it was about God.'

'Peterson was also an elder at his local church in Conon Bridge,' says Cole, and I turn to her with a rueful smile.

'Thanks, Alice. What else have you got?'

She pushes forward the e-fit she created yesterday evening, and which has been sitting in front of her the entire time. It's the same image she had last night, so it's sitting there more as a focal point, a means of taking the emphasis away from herself.

'We've had a lot of returns already. A nil from County, as it happens. They're pretty definite the guy wasn't in the ground.'

'And how about the local pubs?'

'I went out to them all last night, and there's nothing so far. I was aiming to go back round this morning.'

'Yes, please.'

'We'll also get the photo up in shop windows, and so on, and we'll get Inverness to give it a push too. If it's unrelated to the match, and so far everything's pointing to that, then there's a chance he came from outside.'

'Yep, there is.'

'A couple of the calls we've had have been from Highland, and we've got a few others to check out.'

'OK, good. And you've looked into Peterson's wider family?'

'Yes, sir. So his parents, as we know, are both deceased. He has a sister in Muir of Ord. Husband, three kids. I've spoken to her on the phone, briefly.' She pauses, then says, 'Yeah, I don't know how to pronounce that,' and pushes her notebook round for me to see. 'We managed to have the conversation without me asking, or her introducing herself.'

Euphrosyne James is handwritten in Cole's familiar scrawl.

'James,' I say, drily. 'It's fairly common, thought you'd've heard it before.'

She looks at me deadpan, but amused nonetheless. Not quite confident enough to be able to treat that line like she would if it'd been delivered by one of her peers.

'Yoo-fros-nay,' says Sutherland, and Cole slings him the kind of vicious look that would've stopped an annihilating army of Visigoths on their way to Rome.

'Ancient Greek,' I say, to try to reclaim the room. 'One of the three graces, daughter of Zeus.'

'Not much to live up to, then,' says Cole, turning back to me, her tone noticeably softening in the brief course of the sentence.

'Other family?'

'No other siblings. There are a few aunts and uncles, some cousins. Would you like me to get—'

'Put a list together, thanks, Alice. I'll go out and speak to Euphrosyne first of all, regardless.'

'Sure. There is one surviving grandparent. Lives in a home overlooking the sea, near Dornoch. Unable to communicate, though. Not sure of the problem. Severe dementia maybe. The sister visits once a week, Peterson would go once every couple of months, but had been going more regularly recently.'

'OK, thanks. How about friends? That could be of more immediate concern.'

'Seems like he might have been one of those guys. You know, a lot of acquaintances, but friends . . . not so much. He was an elder at the church in Conon, as I said, and a member up at Strathpeffer Golf Club, so there are associations and quite a bit of involvement there.'

I'm nodding as Cole speaks. We got some of that from Mrs Peterson on Saturday evening. Business ownership, football fan, elder in the Church of Scotland, golf club membership.

You can find this man in every suburb and town and village in Scotland. The only surprise is that he supported the local team, and not Rangers or Celtic.

'OK, we need to speak to the church and golf club people, they can at least give us some more on what kind of man we're dealing with.'

I take a moment, look at the whiteboard with its various notes and photographs, then turn back and look around the table.

'Anything else?'

Nothing, bar a couple of head shakes.

'K. So far we have Russians, the undertaking business, County, the church, the golf club and a phone call to the American police. If anyone wants to find a link to Satanism, moon landing conspiracy, child abuse or a nineteen-seventies DJ, our crime bingo card'll almost be complete.'

They smile – even the lugubrious Cole – I get to my feet, and the meeting breaks up.

10

'You sure you don't want coffee?'

Kadyrova works in a tiny, second-floor office at the small building on the corner of Mayfield and Culduthel that houses the BBC offices in Inverness. A five-minute walk from the castle, close to the city centre, but already in a residential area.

We are in what Sutherland once described to me as our classic interview formation. Sutherland is sitting across the desk from the interviewee, while I'm standing at the window, looking out on a wet, grey day, across the road at the bare trees, no view through to the river that is only a hundred yards away.

Kadyrova looks like the kind of person who wants men to look at her, so I'll stand here for a while, staring at the road. The office is warm; Kadyrova is wearing a white blouse, top two buttons undone. Her hair is dyed blonde, perfectly to the roots, her eyebrows a pale brown.

'You need not worry, it won't be laced with polonium,' she says, her voice soft, with only the faintest trace of an accent.

That line has me glancing round.

'Russian humour,' I say.

'One must make the jokes out of this nonsense, or else noise gets too much.'

'No thanks,' I say, 'to the coffee.'

'Yeah,' says Sutherland, 'I'm good, thanks.'

'Very well. You need to talk about Thomas?'

'You'd already heard about him when the sergeant called?' I ask.

'Yes, of course.'

'How did you hear?'

'I listen to news. Do you listen to news, Inspector? The news is always good, even when it's bad.'

'Can you explain the situation here?' I ask, having turned away, asking the question while looking out of the window, the pane a blur of rainwater.

'Yes, of course,' says Kadyrova again. 'I come from wealthy family. Papa sent me to UK to set up portfolio of interests. We invest money in various enterprises. This includes Bailey's. He also allowed me to pursue own interests, and this is what I do here. I run small television production company. We make one-hour episodes of television drama.'

I turn back, catch her eye, then look around the office. There's a desk, which has a phone, a tray containing one slim brown folder, a small lamp and a MacBook, a drinks cabinet and another long piece of wooden furniture that serves no recognisable purpose. A few green plants are dotted around the room, and there are several paintings on the walls. Moscow in the winter. St Petersburg in the winter. An icon. Stalingrad. *Stalingrad?* There's also a calendar, with a picture of St Basil's in the snow, notes scribbled on various days.

'Anything we might have seen?' I ask, managing to look away from the scene of WWII horror, the Soviet flag flying over the scores of German dead.

'No,' replies Kadyrova, no hint of humour or disappointment. 'We have projects in pipeline.'

'And the BBC?'

'We rent office. There may be others who do same. It gives us access, puts us at heart of production community in Scotland.'

'In Inverness?'

'Everyone must be somewhere.'

'Some of your pipeline projects are with the BBC?'

'Yes, of course.'

'Tell us about your relationship with Mr Peterson,' I ask.

Kadyrova smiles, leans forward on her elbows, her hands clasped together on the desk.

'By relationship I take it you mean business, but, of course, we had sex in beginning. It was natural.'

'Did his wife know?' asks Sutherland.

'She wasn't wife when we started, and then he got married, and . . .' and she dismisses the idea of sleeping with a married man with a wave of an indifferent hand, then continues, 'we had sex a few more times, but I don't want to break up marriage. Also, I tired of lovemaking. Not so good.'

'When was the last time you slept with him?' asks Sutherland.

'Nineteen months ago.'

'Very specific.'

'March 8th, last year. It was Wednesday. Raining. He cried when I said it was over.'

That'll be the brutal honesty of the non-native English speaker again. Almost laughed at that line, but that would probably have been inappropriate.

'So,' I say, deciding it's time to move on from the sex, although it will likely need returning to at some point, 'you weren't in on George Bailey's from the beginning?'

'That is correct. Thomas expanded business slowly for few years, then when he needed injection of capital, he looked for investors. He found us.'

'How much *have* you invested in the business?' asks Sutherland.

'All details available at Company House.'

He gives her another moment, but it's obvious she's not going to add anything further.

'And have you seen any return on the investment?' he asks.

Kadyrova answers with a thick and heavy silence. She has closed down, and there won't be much more forthcoming.

'It's early days yet, I take it, regardless of how well the business was doing on the surface,' I say.

'All details available at Company House,' she repeats.

'You said.'

'Then we have no need for further questions.'

'Can you think of anyone who might have wanted to kill Mr Peterson?' asks Sutherland.

'Perhaps owner of one of companies he bought was upset,' she says.

'Can you think of any in particular?'

'Of course. I give you list of suspects. Would you like me to find out where they were between hours of five and seven on Saturday evening?'

Can't help but smile at the lovely, dry delivery. She's good, I'll give her that. Of course, she probably had five years at the FSB before she was sent out into the field.

'Is there any other information you have that could be of help to us?' asks Sutherland.

'I think not,' says Kadyrova, barely taking the time before answering. 'If I think of anything, I let you know.'

Summarily dismissed. She's had enough, and that's all we're getting. And the all, hasn't been very much.

'We'll likely need to speak to you again,' says Sutherland.

'I can be called back to Moscow at any moment,' says Kadyrova, her voice flat.

'I bet you can,' I mutter, and then nod at Sutherland, say goodbye to Kadyrova with a slight movement of the head, and then walk quickly from the office, out into the short, dull corridor and down the stairs.

II

Still in Inverness, though Sutherland and I have split up. The sergeant has gone to speak to the bank, and I've come to talk to an officer in the Highland Financial Criminal Unit.

Police Scotland are encouraging us all to use video links more and more, and it'll take over one day. But for the moment they're still stuck with my generation, the one that has grown up used to dealing with people face to face, and the generation that's also suspicious of the technology. And it's not as though they have a dedicated team of computer geniuses in Alloa working on the tech. We bought off-the-shelf video streaming software from an American company named VideoSquare. Maybe it's the ex-spy in me, but I don't trust it for a second, regardless of management's protestations about its security credentials. There's nothing truly secure in the online world. Nothing. Hasn't been since it started.

I'm in a small office on the third floor, on the other side of the desk from Inspector Dundee, who's keeping me waiting while she quickly whips through a series of papers that I placed before her a couple of minutes ago.

I don't mind the wait. Vaguely staring past the top of her head, out of the window, to the bland office front across the road. I can see a man sitting at his desk, his head in his hands. The way his palms are pressed against his eyes makes it look like he's crying. He is crying. The office is open-plan, but there aren't many other people around, and none of them are paying him any attention. And so he weeps in isolation.

Time is lost, as it so often is. Dundee stares at the papers, I look at the crying office worker. He lifts his head to look at his computer screen. Runs his hand through his hair. He's not so close that I can see him well, yet I get the sense of him like he's sitting directly opposite me. Or perhaps it's just that he and I are currently occupying the same emotional space. He looks like I feel.

He wipes his eyes with both hands, then sits back. Still staring at the screen. Rereading the thing that has brought him to tears. Now his hands lie impotently on the desk.

A woman walks by, sees his face, stops to talk. He can't speak. He tries, but can't get the words out. His face crumples and he points at the screen. She watches him helplessly for a moment, and then reluctantly looks at the screen, as if she's not sure she should. A moment, her hand goes to her mouth. She reads on, at the same time her other hand automatically finds the man's shoulder.

Inspector Dundee opens a drawer, takes out a small lunchbox.

'Sorry,' she says, 'd'you mind?'

A beat.

I have to readjust to where I am, what I'm doing here. I'd been consumed, for what was probably no more than half a minute, by the drama across the street. The man and his tears, the sorrow that draws in others.

I look at the lunchbox.

'No, go ahead.'

'Tied to the desk all day,' says Dundee, by way of obvious explanation.

She opens the box, lifts the fork that's been placed inside, wipes the handle with a tissue, takes a mouthful of food, seems to stop for a moment to savour it, then smiles.

'Couscous and roast veg, feta cheese. Can't beat it.'

Still got that gut feeling of pain inherited from a stranger, or which has been sitting here half my life waiting to emerge.

I need to get rid of it. Straighten my shoulders, breathe, pull on another skin.

'Inspector,' I say, 'thanks for seeing me . . .'

'You can call me Croc,' says Dundee.

'Really?'

'I was five when that movie came out,' she says, 'been Croc ever since. Could've been worse. My sister's called Eileen.'

'Come on,' I say, playing the game.

'Exactly. Every day of her life she gets that about ten times. Cursed.'

'What have you got for me?' I ask, trying to stay on track, having forcibly put myself there.

Dundee, accepting the change of direction, taps the paperwork as she takes another mouthful of couscous.

'What we have here, I would call a legal clusterfuck,' she says. 'I mean, you know the score, Inspector. I've had an initial glance, and there's all sorts of paperwork still to check, but so far I haven't found anything that we could even consider prosecuting. It's all above board.' She holds a finger aloft. 'But it's a clusterfuck all right. Business law, we know, is extraordinarily complex. It's like government wrote all the rules they needed on a single bit of paper, they sent it out to the private sector for comment, business replied with eight hundred thousand contradictory suggestions, and the government incorporated every single one of them into law. Or, more succinctly, it's like someone ate the law and shat out loopholes.'

'That doesn't mean, however, that even if George Bailey's was getting run by the loophole book, all at least legally above board, that someone, somewhere, isn't going to have been getting screwed,' I say.

'Bang on,' says Dundee. 'There are so many layers here, though I've yet to see enough to know how many, but it's very easy for someone who knows what they're doing to pull the wool over the eyes of someone who just thinks they know. Plus, you've got the other thing here, where clearly this business was being built to be part of a portfolio.'

'How'd you mean?'

'People who fund businesses like this, they're not bothered about long-term investment and profit, they're not bothered about staffing or peoples' lives, end product, anything. They're interested in short-term results, cutting costs, improving the viability of the company, and then selling it on. Return on their investment, thank you very much, and who can we plunder next?'

'They were massively in debt,' I say.

'Doesn't matter,' replies Dundee, taking in a mouthful of food. 'Everyone's in debt. Debt isn't a bad look. And, of course, it's possible that not everyone involved in the company knew about all the debt. Could be someone found out about it . . .'

She smiles at the implication. 'You'll need to speak to the bank,' she says, recognising as soon as she says it that the words are unnecessary. 'They might give you a better idea of who knew what and when, they'll have more signatures on documents.'

'OK, thanks, Inspector.'

A pause while I think about whether there's anything else I should be asking at this stage. Still early days, and though I feel underprepared, this is why I'm here. Sucking in as much information as I can.

I want to look past Dundee's head, across the street, but I stop myself.

'I think we're good,' I say. 'If I can ask you to spend another few minutes on it, get it clear in your head where we are, then you can take a look at anything else we send over within the context of what you already know.'

'Certainly.'

'You have the time?'

Dundee smiles. 'Of course not.'

I return the smile, and get to my feet.

'We never do,' I say.

I stand for a moment, sharing a look across the desk. Feels like there's something waiting to be said, though I'm not sure what. There are words in the air and one of us needs to grab them and speak them before this scene can move on to the next. Yet it's not the same as when I was leaving Marcus's house last night. This, thankfully, isn't that.

'Sorry,' says Dundee, smiling again, as though this peculiar silence has been her fault. 'I spend my life looking at paperwork, you're just about the first person I've spoken to all day. It's hard getting used to it, sometimes.'

'That's all right,' I say, feeling strange for accepting an apology that didn't need to be given.

'I woke to a peculiar dream this morning,' she says.

Odd. I could have said the same thing myself. For a second I wonder if it's going to be the same strange dream, yet I know that's not it.

I find myself sitting back down.

'I was in Motherwell,' Dundee continues. 'In the dream. I was in Motherwell. It's where I'm from, and I was younger. Maybe twenty. I'd been somewhere, not sure where, and I was contemplating driving home, then I decided to walk. And I was walking across playing fields that used to be down at the bottom of our road . . .'

'Houses now,' I say. Everywhere that once was is now a housing estate.

'Yes, houses. And I looked away to my left and there was my car, with me driving it. It was a red Mini, you know the Cooper, with the white lines on the bonnet and a Union Jack on the roof?'

'Did you have that Mini?'

'No, though I used to want one. But that was the me who'd decided to drive home. And then beyond that, walking a different route, and to my right, on other paths, were another two of me. So there were four versions of me, taking different routes home, all wearing the same clothes.'

'Dreams,' I say. 'They'll mess with the laws of space-time.'

'Hmm,' says Dundee. She's a fast talker, but as she retells her dream, her voice slows, mellowing, growing more contemplative. 'I don't know what to think of it. Clearly it was about decision-making, but was it saying that every time you make a choice, some part of you goes off in that other direction? That some other you, living another life, follows that path?'

'Given the number of decisions that everyone makes every day, that would be an awful lot of parallel lives. Each person would have billions.'

'Yes,' says Dundee.

'I've wondered about that before,' I say. Still haunted by the man across the street, still stopping myself from looking over. Will he still be crying? Will he have drawn others into the black hole of his grief? 'The breaking of the self into two. The schizophrenic literally becoming two people.'

Stop myself. There's nowhere to go with that, and it feels odd and uncomfortable to be talking about it out loud. Anyway, I'm a listener. A receiver of others' sad tales.

'What were you wearing?' I ask, not really knowing where the question comes from.

'Jeans, torn at the knee. Just the one knee, though,' says Dundee.

'Those were jeans you had when you were twenty, or were they like the Mini Cooper?'

'I never had jeans like that,' she answers.

Then she stands up and walks round the side of the desk, so that I can see what's she's wearing. A pair of faded jeans, torn at the left knee.

'Strange thing is,' she says, 'I tripped over on the way into work this morning. Tore my jeans. That's kinda weird, isn't it?'

I look at her knee. Through the hole I can see she's wearing one of those large plasters that come with every packet available at the chemist or the supermarket. There's a spot of blood in the centre where it's started to seep through.

'How did you fall?'

Dundee looks down at her knee.

'I don't know,' she says. 'It just kinda happened . . . Maybe there were other versions of me it didn't happen to.'

Dundee lifts her head, and holds my gaze for a moment. Then together we look around the small office, almost as if we might be able to see some sign of another Inspector Croc Dundee, one who didn't fall over on her way into work. And then, at last, together we find ourselves looking out of the window, back across the road, into an open-plan office.

We see a man, standing at the window, looking out, staring onto the street below. His eyes are red, his stare is vacant. He is alone.

12

I drive back to Dingwall, the few miles along the eight-three-five, feeling the colour of the weather outside. Hoagy Carmichael is playing. 'Winter Moon', the 1956 recording, slow and melancholic, wrapping you up in sorrow with the sense of it rather than the words. The clouds creeping down from Wyvis are now so low you can barely see the tops of the trees on the hills around Strathpeffer.

'Winter Moon' used to mean something, back in my foolish, romantic period when I first met Olivia. That night in Grindelwald, dancing on the terrace of the horrible hotel. A cheap room, and a poor meal, rescued by an acceptable Pinot Grigio. And then late in the evening the song had come on, I led Olivia out onto the terrace. We hadn't realised how beautiful the mountains looked at night from out there. I held Olivia close, our cheeks pressed against each other, and I breathed in the smell of her hair. And that night, when we lay in bed, making love into the early morning, the tune played throughout in my head. Warm and slow and beautiful, anything but melancholic.

A couple of years passed. We became tired and angry. An ugly, bitter relationship, fuelled by resentment. Yet, when the time came for me to give up London and move to the Highlands, I asked her to come with me. She said no and hated me for going. Then, in one of the many arguments that preceded my departure, when she was in the process of throwing everything we'd had under the bus, she said she'd hated Hoagy all along and was delighted that she'd never have to listen to him again.

To be fair to Olivia, everything we had belonged under a bus.

I've liked Hoagy even more ever since.

Sitting in a new café in Dingwall. The Coffee House. Not a chain, as far as I know, but it might be one of those chain cafés designed to look independent. Since neither Sutherland nor I have a hipster beard or a MacBook open in front of us, and we both just ordered a coffee with milk rather than a mint kombucha or a decaffeinated chai espresso latteccino, we stand out like the mundane police officers we are.

Even the simple coffee with milk request was turned into an event. Did we want Columbian, Costa Rican, Tanzanian or Ethiopian? Hint of spice, blackberries or strawberries? Or all three? We both just wanted a cup of coffee, and thus we were made fleetingly to feel like troglodytes.

Take my first sip of Costa Rican roast, having just given Sutherland the outline of my conversation with Inspector Dundee, such as it was. I skipped the part about her ripped jeans.

Not picking up the promised brown sugar aroma, or the undercurrents of apricots in the flavour.

Sutherland has been nodding as I talked, and when I take my coffee, indicating that I've wrapped it up, he says, 'Yeah, I've spoken to Croc before. Interesting woman. She helped on the Piebald case.'

'Of course.'

'Nice smile,' he says, matter-of-factly, a disinterested compliment. Sutherland has other women on his mind.

'Anyway, she says she'll get back to us in due course, though, you know, she's snowed under same as the rest of us. How about the bank?' I ask.

Sutherland takes a large gulp of coffee, then sets the mug down. The coffee order was so protracted that he ended up not ordering any food, presumably out of fear of having to distinguish between two hundred and eighty-seven different types of pastry, and he glances over his shoulder to the counter.

'You can eat later, Sergeant,' I say.

'Yes,' he says, turning back. 'So, she said it was clear George Bailey's were buying up, taking over the market, with the intention of selling on. Consolidation of the marketplace might have been a decent move anyway, but the investors, the people who were pulling the strings, didn't care. It was all about portfolio building and short-term profit.'

'Do we know who they are?'

'Aside from Peterson, there were three main players. Our Russian friend, Kadyrova, and two guys from the anonymously named Equity Capital. They're in London, so we either jump on a plane, or get the Met to speak to them . . .'

I give him a bit of a raised eyebrow, and he nods an unnecessary apology.

'It's fine,' I say. 'You can jump on the plane if it comes to it. They're not Russian, I take it?'

Sutherland lifts a page on the notebook that is resting by his left hand.

'Alan Westbrook and Davinder Singh.'

'We'll assume not Russian, then, although, of course, they could be working for anyone.'

I look around the rest of the café, for a moment yanking my mind away from the investigation, from the confusion of companies and names that any financial case boils down to. The place is half-full, and the sergeant and I are the oldest people here. Which means, of course, that I'm the oldest person in the room, by some stretch. The stark contrast in demographic between a church and a beatnik coffee joint.

Beatnik? *All right, Granddad . . .*

'These three,' I say, turning back to Sutherland, 'without getting into the specifics of money and transactions and why they do what they do, these are the three with the power? They controlled the business?'

'Yes,' says Sutherland, 'that's how it worked. Peterson was the founder, but in building the company he looked for outside investment. He gets the money from various sources, but in doing so, he ultimately cedes control of the enterprise. Now, it could be he signed up for it, not realising the extent to which he'd lose control. We might never know. Perhaps he was fully aware of what he was doing. The more we learn, the more it sounds like he was all about the money—'

'Yes.'

'—and he definitely wasn't the real-life George Bailey of the mortician business. But we don't know to what extent he controlled the flow of cash or, perhaps even more importantly, information.'

'The trouble with the business side,' I say, 'is that it's likely to be so convoluted, we could get tied up in knots for months. Whatever the reason for the murder, ultimately someone delivered the fatal blow. We need to find that person. We need to make sure we don't forget about fingerprints and identification, the fact that a man was killed in the street, right in front of his stepson.'

'I was thinking the same thing, in there, in the bank. That world, the financial world, is so rife with corruption, so open to it, and you know, most of it's *legal*. I mean, they can say it's not corrupt, because a law was passed, or there was a loophole, or there's whatever. But God, these people . . . There's so much stuff that should be corruption, which *would* be corruption in a civically run social democracy, but is entirely legal because some government minister brought it in six months before he swanned off to become a director at HSBC or GlaxoSmithKline, or Parker, Dick-Booth and Stephenson.'

I laugh. Even when you're feeling empty, sometimes the laughter still appears.

'Getting a little wound up there, Sergeant,' I say, and he smiles bleakly. 'Know a lot of Dick-Booths?'

'Oh, I think we've both come across plenty of them in our time.'

'I've had my fill for the moment. Time to get back to some regular, plain interviewing. Looking in someone's eye and trying to work out if they're lying.'

'Who are you going to start with?'

'Peterson's sister, Euphrosyne,' I say. 'I'll nip back to the station, touch base, then head over there. You want to come?'

'Why d'you suppose she'll be lying?'

'People see us coming, they lie. It's just how it is.'

He drains his coffee, as he indicates his agreement. And there we are, that's what the job does to you. Going to meet the sister of a murder victim, and our automatic assumption is that she'll lie to us about something.

We stop just inside the door. The office bustles, a busy Monday afternoon. Quick walk to the desk, check my inbox, contemplating speaking to Quinn, although I'd rather not, then head back out.

'Sir,' says Fisher, appearing beside me. She looks concerned. Something to say.

'Fish.'

'Inspector!'

Fish and I hold each other's gaze for a moment, Sutherland beside us, and then we all turn in the direction of Quinn's office.

'Anything I need to know?' I ask.

'We had the Russian consulate in Edinburgh on the phone a few minutes ago,' says Fisher.

'Seriously?'

'They had a call from a Russian citizen claiming to have been harassed by the police.'

I look into the Chief's office, then turn and direct the look at Sutherland. He has the same look on his face.

'You shouldn't have been so brutal, sir,' he says.

'If I'd know she was going to complain, I bloody well would've been.'

'Maybe next time,' he says, then he adds, 'I should get on,' and walks to his desk.

'Thanks, Fish,' I say, and walk into Quinn's office, closing the door behind me. There's a chair lined up opposite the desk, but I don't sit down. Not that Quinn is offering.

'You know how much I hate politics, Inspector,' he says. 'You know, right?'

'You wanted us to find a motive for the murder of Thomas Peterson that had nothing to do with football, which, I should say, we were already looking for,' I begin, hating that I'm having to justify myself. Just let us do our jobs, for God's sake. 'It made sense to talk to Peterson's closest business partner, which is what we did. We did not have confirmation that she was Russian until we spoke to her, and we did not, in any way, harass her.'

His arms are folded, as he boldly plays the part of the one in control of the conversation. OIC Actions and Consequences.

'And what did she have to say for herself?' he asks, which is the first sign that he's not going to berate me for it in the way his body language implies.

'She came over from Moscow with money to spend. George Bailey's seemed like a worthwhile investment. If we want to know the details of the company's finances, we can look it up.'

He smiles.

'A typical reaction,' he says. 'Have you looked them up?'

'On the agenda for this afternoon.'

'What d'you think we'll find?'

'Good question,' I say, relaxing a little, as it's apparent that Quinn is more on our side than I'd presumed. So, yes, he really is in charge of the conversation. 'Quite possibly there'll be financial difficulty. There was debt, but we don't know yet how much difficulty that was causing. Success on the surface so often masks turmoil. Where you have debt and turmoil . . .'

'People get murdered.'

'Exactly. But it could be fine, of course, and his murder is completely unrelated. Or it could be bad, yet his murder unrelated anyway.' I make the international gesture of infinite possibility, and add, 'Could have been the football, could have been any number of things.'

'Basically, too early to jump to any conclusion,' says Quinn. 'Yes, sir.'

'Which d'you think would be worse?' he asks. 'Having to deal with the Scottish Football League, or the Russians?'

I'm not entirely sure if he's being serious, but when I don't immediately answer, he looks at me questioningly.

'Oh, I don't know, sir,' I say glibly. 'On the one hand the Russians attacked Georgia, annexed Crimea, invaded Ukraine, infiltrated the Republican party, armed the Taliban, bombed hospitals in Aleppo, supported an attempted coup in Montenegro, malignly influenced elections all across Europe and helped the North Koreans with a nuclear weapon intercontinental delivery system, threatening to engulf the entire planet in nuclear holocaust. The Scottish Football League . . .? I'm not sure really . . .'

Quinn laughs.

'You're right. They did force Rangers into League Two, though.'

He smiles to include me in the joke, then frowns when I don't react.

'We don't want to mess with the Russians, but just because it'll be tough, isn't a reason for not doing it,' he says.

'Yes, sir,' is all I say, but I don't trust anyone in authority to make the right choice when it comes to messing with the Russians. When choosing between taking their money and doing the right thing, a lot of poor decisions have been made in the last twenty years.

'So, what's next?' he asks.

'I've spoken to the man who made the monkey noise at the game. Not really looking like he's involved, but we won't let it go just yet. I'll get Detective Sergeant Sutherland and the team to get onto George Bailey's company records, and any other associates who had an active interest in the business. We also need to speak to more members of Peterson's family, including his wife's ex-husband.'

'He's the chap in ...' and he looks around his desk, 'Massachusetts?'

'Yes, sir.'

'You're not going to need to travel to Massachusetts, are you? That might stretch the budget.'

He looks at me seriously, but I can tell that there's some attempt at wit behind it. Never at his most comfortable when trying to be human in front of his staff, at least he hasn't immediately jumped into the snake pit of taking the easiest possible route.

'Only if I can take *Queen Mary 2*, sir,' I say lightly.

He laughs stiffly, at the same time waving a hand towards the door.

'Thanks, Ben. You should get on. I'll speak to Inverness about the Russians, see if we can keep them at bay a little longer.'

I nod, can't quite bring myself to smile, then turn and leave the office.

Back at my desk, Sutherland asks, 'All well?'

'For the moment. I doubt we'll have too long in the clear, though. Someone will make a phone call, and then ...' and I finish the sentence with a thumb across the throat.

13

Late afternoon, darkness closing in. We're standing on the doorstep, bell rung, looking back over our shoulders at what we can see of Wyvis from outside the large detached house near Muir of Ord. The sky has cleared a little, the clouds are racing. For the moment the sprawling, flat summit of the mountain that dominates Easter Ross is clear, but it will likely be swallowed up in clouds and darkness by the time we leave. One of those days when the weather changes with the passing of minutes.

'I'm kind of expecting to be greeted by a Greek goddess,' says Sutherland.

Sutherland is not himself. The words remain the same, but there's something missing in the tone. Perhaps it's my own current detachment from real life, getting through the investigation one foot in front of the other, that prevents me delving too deeply into what troubles him. Ultimately though, it seems like it might be an affair of the heart, and as long as it doesn't affect his work, then it's none of my damn business.

'And how will that look?'

'You know, tall, long blonde hair, massive breasts, low-cut top.'

'A toga?'

'Yeah,' he says, drily. 'I'm expecting a toga.'

Sutherland's phone rings, and he turns away to answer as the door opens.

I hold forward my ID.

'DI Westphall,' I say, 'and Detective Sergeant Sutherland.'

Euphrosyne James is a couple of inches taller than me, has long, rich blonde hair, and the kind of chest that Sutherland was facetiously imagining. Dressed in a high-neck wool jumper and jeans, she's missing the toga, but has the imagined beauty of a Greek goddess. The parents may have taken a punt with the name when she was born, but it came off.

'Constable Cole called to say you'd be coming. Come in.'

She glances past me to Sutherland, who's standing still, listening, staring in silence at the field of sheep across the road.

A car drives past, slowing as it approaches the long bend. There's the angry, high bark of a crow from a nearby tree.

'The sergeant has to take a call, he can come in when he's done.'

I don't wonder what it's about. I'll hear soon enough. Perhaps it's related to whatever relationship troubles I imagine he's experiencing, though I really don't think he would take time out for that now.

'That's OK. I'll close the door over without locking it.'

I follow her into the house, through a hallway that has none of the abandon of a usual family home. No mess, neither discarded coats nor boots. There's an umbrella stand, a coat stand, a large mirror. A large painting of a sea battle, a wide, central flight of stairs, two doors off to either side, a further one at the end of the hall. She leads me into a sitting room.

It's like walking into a stately home long since given over to the National Trust and, like the hallway, barely looks inhabited.

Perhaps this is just where they receive visitors, such as the police, or young men with ten thousand a year wanting to marry one of their daughters.

There are two green leather double settees, and a maroon leather armchair. There's a hearth, which has a small but mature fire burning, lending an old-fashioned, smoky warmth to the room. The pictures on the wall are maps, battle scenes or portraits. There's also another large mirror above the mantelshelf. There are books on shelves on two of the walls, a freestanding globe and a writing desk against the window.

'Do take a seat,' says Euphrosyne James. 'Can I get you some tea?'

'No thanks. Just had coffee.'

'Very well,' says James, and we sit opposite each other on the double settees. 'We don't need to wait for the sergeant?'

'No, we're good,' I say. 'I'm authorised to speak without him.'

She smiles, but the smile says she's humouring me, without finding the line either amusing, or even appropriate.

'You want to ask about Thomas?'

'Yes. I'm . . . I'm sorry for your loss.'

There's a slight movement of her head, one that says either there's no need for the formality, or that she doesn't care that much at all. Or, quite possibly, that she recognises the investigating officer's words are not heartfelt. The automatic commiseration, delivered as instructed in page fifty-seven of a nineteenth-century police manual.

'Do you have any idea yet who killed him?'

'We're really just starting out on the investigation, putting a picture together.'

'It was two days ago,' she says.

For a moment I'm unsure if she's being serious, then I become aware of the loud ticking, and I glance over at the grandfather clock in the corner opposite the globe. Hadn't noticed the clock, the biggest single item in the room, when I entered.

'It's not television,' I say, turning back.

'These things take time in the real world,' she says, agreeing to let us off the hook.

'Sometimes we do know straight off the bat,' I say, 'but this is not one of those times.'

'Of course.'

'Can you tell me the last time you spoke to Thomas?'

My voice is softer than normal, dialling back the tone, perhaps aware I've been caught out in my fake condolence and need to pretend that I care.

'It's been a while,' she says. 'We were never particularly close, and after he married that terrible woman, we've had less and less to do with one another. I'd no intention of getting into some absurd bitch-fight with a sister-in-law I hadn't gone looking for.'

'There were never family get-togethers?'

'Occasionally we had lunch, but they were dreadful affairs.'

'When was the last time?'

'Ugh,' she replies, waving the question away. 'I don't want to think about it.'

I hold her gaze for a moment, trying to work out if that's avoidance, or disdain for the subject. Will probably turn out to be the latter, but safer to assume the former for the time being.

'Maybe you could think about it long enough to remember,' I say.

She smiles, continuing the air of someone doing the police a favour.

'It's been a few months, I believe. Maybe some time in the summer, I don't recall the exact date. You know how summer holidays are when you have children.'

She looks at me, searching for my agreement.

'And you've got a grandmother in a home near Dornoch?' I say, moving the conversation along.

'You've been doing your research. Yes, she's been there a few years now.'

'You got her admitted to the home?'

'Oh no, she did it herself, with Thomas's help. You can ask her, although you won't get a reply.'

'She doesn't speak?'

'Not any more. She'd had a miserable life. Grandpa, while being lovely with us, especially when we were children, was a dreadful man. Dreadful. Treated her terribly. We wondered if she would blossom when he died, but instead, after years of slowly shutting down, she just switched off completely. She arranged with Thomas to go into the home, and then she shocked us all by buying that terrible painting. Terrible. Goodness knows what she was thinking.'

'What painting?'

'Brueghel's *Massacre of the Innocents*. I mean . . . it does what it says on the tin. Babies being slaughtered. Ghastly. She just sits and looks at it all day long. I really don't understand.'

Brueghel's *Massacre of the Innocents*. I try to picture it. I look through Euphrosyne James until she politely coughs.

'Inspector?'

'Did she ever lose a child?' I ask.

'Not a baby, not an infant,' says James. 'Mummy died, of course, but even so . . . seriously?'

'When was that?'

A moment, while she looks surprised at the question, then she says, 'Covering all the bases? Well, I suppose you must. Mummy killed herself. She and Daddy divorced when I was twelve. He went off to live in New York. Enjoyed the bachelor life for a long time, then he married a woman two months younger than me. He died of a heart attack later that year. Meanwhile, Mummy stayed at home and brought up us kids. When we'd left home . . .' A moment, a deep breath. 'She slashed her wrists in the bath. Terribly mundane, I know.'

I don't comment. Another sad story. They are everywhere, after all.

'Anyway,' she continues, 'I really don't know why Grandma would look at that painting all day. Simply awful.'

'I presume it's a copy?'

'God, no. Cost her two-point-four million at auction in Sotheby's. Can you believe it?'

That does sound rather incredible and I don't need to ask the question. It obviously demands further explanation, which she begins with the wave of a hand as preamble.

'When Grandpa died it turned out he had millions in the bank. Millions. He'd never said. So, she bought the painting, and arranged, with Thomas's help, to move into the home. You understand, we're not talking about Brueghel the Elder's *Massacre of the Innocents*?'

I express my lack of art history knowledge with open palms.

'The father painted one version of it, which currently hangs in Windsor Castle. His son made a copy of the painting, and then returned to the theme many times. There are anywhere between seven and fourteen different versions. That's why it only cost two-point-four million.'

Perfect, I think. Let's bring the art world into the game, as if the labyrinthine machinations of big business aren't enough to plunge the investigation into the mire.

'And how did you feel, you and Thomas, about her spending the money that way? You'll split the value of the painting when she's gone, I presume?'

She holds my gaze for a moment, her lips pursing.

'We come to it at last,' she says, finally. 'The accusation.'

I hold the look. There's no accusation, just a natural question for the would-be inheritors of a couple of million pounds, on learning that their money was spent on art. One sees it often enough, when money is left to a new wife, or a friend or a cat home, or split unfairly. The anger, the torment, the court case. Hard to see where this fits into the narrative of Thomas Peterson getting murdered, but murdered he was, and here, staring us in the face, is another complication.

'Well, as you can see, I don't have to worry about the money. Thomas wasn't happy about it, of course, but then he was rarely happy about anything. He seemed to be doing all right, but he still objected. And no, we are not getting to take home half a painting of slaughtered children each. She's bequeathed it to the Kelvingrove in Glasgow.'

From all quarters they come, pieces to be fitted into the puzzle. Or else, here we see the obscure and the fascinating, out of the blue, but belonging in quite a different puzzle altogether.

'You weren't upset about that?'

'Look, we didn't even know that money existed. Neither did she. And as soon as she found out, she spent it. She and Thomas arranged the home, and she bought the painting. End of.'

End of.

One must fight one's prejudices, although usually I think anyone using the words *end of* as a complete sentence deserves to serve at least one month in a correctional facility.

'Why did she go into the home rather than just get the painting delivered to her house?'

A long, heavy sigh; impossible to tell whether it's aimed at the question, or her grandmother's circumstances.

'I've always thought it was her act of giving up,' she said. 'Throwing in the towel. You know the place? The Dunes? Not that you'll find much of a dune in its vicinity.'

'I've never been.'

'Look, it's lovely. I wouldn't mind staying up there just before I die. So, maybe she's happy, right? As far as anyone can tell, she's not aware of anything around her. She doesn't speak, she doesn't seem to take in information.'

'And the cost of the home is covered until she dies?'

'I think that's what Thomas sorted, yes, unless she cracks on for a lot longer than anticipated, I suppose. If that happens, well, Martin'll have to carry the burden. He can afford it.'

'Your husband?'

'Yes. I don't know what Thomas thought any more, we hadn't spoken about it in long enough. Money didn't seem to be a problem for him any longer, by all accounts. Not that that would necessarily have changed him, he could be quite dreadful.'

'He still visited his grandmother?'

'Huh,' she says, with the accompanying eye roll. 'Probably trying to get her to change her will. Spare me the eulogy for what a wonderful human being he was.'

I glance at the window, wonder about Sutherland. Can neither see nor hear him from here.

'I don't suppose you'll have too much to go on,' I say, 'but have you any idea why someone might have wanted to kill Thomas?'

'Really?' she says. 'I thought it was a random act of football hooliganism?'

'We don't think so.'

'Hmm,' she says, no particular surprise in her voice.

'That doesn't mean we have a definite point to aim at here. Like I said up front, we're just getting going. So, if there's any aspect of his life, or anyone in his life, that might give you some concern, then . . .'

'Well, Thomas really could be quite an awful man,' she says, 'so I imagine the list of potential assailants will be lengthy. However, I can think of nowhere better to start than with his wife.'

'She hasn't automatically confessed to his murder,' I say drily. 'What makes you suspicious?'

'The fact that anyone would marry Thomas in the first place would surely arouse suspicion.'

Beautiful. Family members give the best interviews.

'The marriage was about money,' she continues, '*so* obviously about money. Her husband had left her with nothing but that poor young boy. She was broke, and in need of someone who wasn't. That's all.' She pauses, shrugs, then says, 'I sound like one of those women on a Radio 4 drama, happily implicating someone else. I really don't know, Inspector, how could I? We don't like each other.'

'Will you go to Thomas's funeral?'

'Dear God, of course,' she says. 'I'm not a barbarian.'

'What about your grandmother?'

'Will she go to the funeral?'

'Yes.'

'Of course not.'

'Why?'

'She literally barely moves from the spot, Inspector. Well, she can walk around, she can go to the bathroom, but she gets led into the sitting room now and she spends her life in front of that damned picture. Her own, personal, self-imposed purgatory, for whatever crime it was she thinks she's guilty of.'

'Is it at all possible that Thomas confided anything in her?'

'Why would he? I can't believe it, but then, he did go and see her, so what did he talk to her about? I really don't know. Perhaps he told her secrets that he wouldn't tell anyone else, because he didn't believe the information was going anywhere.'

'Because your grandma doesn't talk?'

'No, Inspector, like I said, not at all. She rarely spoke when Grandpa was alive, and now she's just shut down completely. It's been three years since anyone heard her say anything. She's happy where she is, and that's it.'

The door opens, and Sutherland steps in. He nods a greeting-cum-apology at Euphrosyne James, then looks at me.

'How are we doing here?' he asks.

'I think we're more or less done,' I say, picking up on the urgency in Sutherland's tone. 'Everything all right?'

'We should get going,' he says.

A conversation to be had in the car. I get to my feet, Euphrosyne James following suit.

'Thank you,' I say. 'Excuse the abrupt exit.'

'That's all right,' she says. 'I'm glad I could be of help. Please do call again if you hear anything.'

She extends her hand, maintaining her guarded civility to the end. Nevertheless, when you interview people with money, quickly enough you pick up on the disdain, the fact that they think they're doing the police a favour. They're better than this, but for now, for these few short minutes, they will lower themselves to the appropriate level.

'We will.'

'Westbrook's been murdered, Singh's disappeared,' says Sutherland.

Sitting in the car, the short drive back down to Dingwall.

'Westbrook and Singh?'

'The two hedge fund guys on the board of George Bailey's.'

'I know.'

'Sorry, thought you were asking who they were.'

'You have the details?'

'Neither of them turned up for work this morning, neither was answering calls. Westbrook lived around the corner from the office, so one of his colleagues went to his apartment just before lunch. Door was unlocked . . .'

'Usually doesn't end well.'

'The guy enters, there's a shower room near the front door, there's blood on the floor. Looks like someone's used the shower to wash off, but not cleaned up. The friend walks around the rest of the apartment, into the bedroom, into the second bedroom, nothing, into the bathroom. Sees something lying on the floor, doesn't get what it is, a split second, then he realises . . . it's viscera.'

'Jesus.'

'Westbrook had been dumped in the bath, disembowelled, and his insides, well, just dropped on the bathroom floor in a heap.'

'Killed in the bath?'

'Looks like it. The police report Singh's fingerprints all over the bathroom, including on the murder weapon.'

'He left the murder weapon?'

'On the floor. A serrated kitchen knife, seven-inch blade.'

'He disembowelled someone he worked with, then fled the scene, leaving behind a tonne of fingerprints and the murder weapon?'

'I know. Either way you look at it, it's amateur hour. It's breaking every rule of concealing murder, *or* it's the crudest attempt at a set-up job since a nineteen-thirties Hardy Boys novel.'

I immediately think of *The Missing Chums* and *The Mystery of Cabin Island*, the books that first had my younger self interested in solving crime.

'Which Hardy Boys books did you read?'

'There was *Slaughter at Butcher Point*.'

'Funny,' I say. 'Which particular amateur act are the Met buying?'

'We'll need to speak to them.'

'Way too early to be making any kind of judgement,' I say. 'Any possibility there was something between them? They had a relationship that transcended work?'

A moment, and then Sutherland says, 'Sorry, right, you mean were they gay?'

'Yes, but not just that. Maybe Westbrook stole Singh's girl-friend, or maybe they were in the same chess league and their rivalry got out of hand.'

Low whistle and another dark smile from Sutherland, and he says, 'That's some chess league, by the way . . . Anyway, not that they said. The investigation hasn't progressed much beyond their working relationship at the moment, so it's way too early to be factoring in any of that other stuff.'

'We were talking earlier about what else we could add to the long list of things this case could be about,' I say. 'Chalk up another to the list.'

'We're going to need a bigger whiteboard,' says Sutherland, as we pull into the station car park.

Nice line, but Sutherland doesn't smile. That's him again, playing the part. Sutherland, the fool. The sad, tortured fool.

'How was Euphrosyne?' he asks, as we're getting out the car.

'Said her brother was not a nice man,' I say, car locked, walking back into the station. 'If we want a list of people who might've wanted to kill him, we should start with his money-grabbing wife. Plus, there's a grandmother who never speaks that we can go and talk to.'

'Does she write?'

'By the sound of it she doesn't communicate in any way.'

'This is the grandmother in the home by Dornoch?'

'Yep.'

'How much is she likely to know about Peterson's life?'

'He visited regularly. We've no way of knowing what he said to her, or in fact, if he spoke to her at all. Maybe the two of them just sat there, while he salved whatever guilt he had.'

'What guilt?'

'Aren't we all guilty about not visiting our grandparents enough?'

A moment of silence as we walk into the open-plan. Perhaps Sutherland is thinking of his lone surviving grand-parent, his grandfather who lives in sheltered housing in Stirling. I didn't mean it as a jibe, but I do know that he rarely sees him. For myself, the last of my grandparents died ten years ago, and I hadn't seen her in a year and a half before then.

'So, she's basically in a waking coma?' says Sutherland, snapping us both from the morass of self-reproach I'd plunged us into.

'Not sure. Apparently she spends all her days looking at a Brueghel painting. *Massacre of the Innocents.*'

'Hmm,' says Sutherland. 'There's a story. A print, presumably?'

'She bought it for two-point-four million.'

'Holy shit.'

'I like the sound of her,' I say, as we sit down. 'Sitting all day looking at a painting, even one as dark as that. Intriguing. There's a story there, no doubt, although of course, it's liable to have nothing whatsoever to do with us. Nevertheless, that's two-point-four million pounds just been thrown into the mix.'

'Holy shit,' he repeats.

'I'll give the home a call and see what they think.'

'I can do it,' says Sutherland.

'No, it's fine. I'll call.'

'Boss.'

Everything that needs to be said has been, and now we turn to our respective monitors and fire them up.

14

End of the day. Sutherland, Quinn and I are on a video call with the investigating officer from the Met. DI Strangways has already sent through images of the scene of the crime, several of which have been printed off and put on the noticeboard directly above the computer screen via which we're speaking.

Sutherland and I are sitting at the long table; Quinn joined us after we'd started, and is standing behind.

'They worked in a building that housed twelve hundred employees,' says Strangways. 'So, as you can imagine, that's a tonne of interviewing needs to be done. Just have to hope we get the time to do a thorough job.'

I take another look at the pictures that Sutherland tacked to the noticeboard. Westbrook's abdomen and stomach were slit, from the throat down to just above the pubic area. The skin and flesh were pulled back, although the ribcage was still intact. It was not necessarily obvious from the way the body was lying in the bath that the viscera had been extracted. The layman may not have been able to tell. The gaping hole reveals a bloody morass, with coils of tube and indistinguishable internal organs.

The photograph next to it shows the removed organs on the floor. They were scooped out by hand, attachments roughly hacked asunder. The third photograph is a close-up of the blade, which was dumped on the floor to the side of the bloodied bath mat, and there's a final photograph taken from the bathroom doorway, encompassing the entire scene.

'On top of that,' she continues, 'they had project partners all around the world. This could make for a very long investigation.'

'So, you're thinking it's work-related, rather than anything personal?'

'Open mind, Inspector,' she says. 'Just in those early stages, when anything can happen. Like going on a first date.'

She smiles, and takes Sutherland and me along with her.

'You've spoken to their managers?'

'Manager, singular. They had the same one. The two of them worked as a team, he said they were really close. Got along well, he never saw any problems. He's just done the annual report for them both, and said he could more or less have given them the same one. Both due a huge bonus at Christmas.'

'There's always money to follow,' mutters Quinn from behind.

'The more you find out, the more you see it's *Wolf of Wall Street* stuff in those kinds of places. We've been there before, and we'll be back.'

'I take it not for this kind of visceral brutality,' says Quinn.

'No, sir,' replies Strangways. 'But we do get all sorts. And here, as you'll have seen in the initial report, the victim had heavily consumed alcohol and cocaine in the hours before his death. That had no one reeling in shock. Once you add them to the mix, hold on to your pants . . . Anything goes.'

Hold on to your pants. I love this woman.

'Was there anything work-related the manager thought could've lit this particular torch?' I ask.

'Nada,' says Strangways. 'Just a couple of guys doing a regular job, were his exact words. But, look, I'm not even remotely convinced by that yet. We know how it is with these people. What these clowns call a regular job is the kind of thing that really gets some people's goat. There's all this industry, there are these men, and it's mostly men, feeling incredibly important, all this testosterone, but what are they actually generating? They're not feeding anyone, they're not entertaining anyone, they're not producing anything. They're moving electronic money around, they're generating more electronic money, the price of this goes up, the price of this goes down, x billion pounds gets wiped off of whatever. It's just a game, and the little guy, the working man at the bottom, that's the guy who gets fucked. These people, if they screw up, maybe they lose their job, maybe they just lose their Christmas bonus, but they still drive home in their BMW, more than likely with a white powder moustache, to their apartment overlooking the Thames.

'So, look, I should shut up, you can tell this kind of thing triggers me. But are there people out there who want to cause harm to the brokers and the finance manipulators? Damn right there are. And will there be people there who want to harm each other? Yep. When there's this much money in play, there's always the potential. And you add drugs and alcohol, it's toxic. At the moment, everything's on the table.'

'Did you get any specifics on their dealings with George Bailey's?' I ask.

'Didn't know to ask at the time,' says Strangways. 'We've still got people down there. I'll give them a call, and report back.'

'OK, thanks, appreciate it. Any gut instinct on where this is going?'

'You know the ropes, Inspector,' she says. 'Oftentimes it's the outlier, the thing from left field, right? So here, we have your guy. Seems like nothing much, and it's hardly the kind of thing we can suddenly devote ninety per cent of the investigation to. But you never know. But I tell you what; the weirdness of it, the grotesqueness . . . We had a case last year.

Guy fell out a twentieth-floor window, embedded on a spike. You remember that?'

'Sure. What happened with that?'

I can feel Quinn wincing behind me, Sutherland nodding.

'Everyone wanted it to be a suicide. It was easier that way.'

'It wasn't?'

She makes the appropriate, ambivalent gesture.

'Tough call. But the guy was up to his armpits in laundered Russian money, right?'

That sinking feeling.

'Now, sure, he may well have killed himself because he was in way over his head with people who were completely off the chain. But he had money, he wasn't bankrupt, so you'd think if he was scared he might at least try running.'

'Did you get anywhere with the investigation?'

'Like I said, everyone, and I mean everyone, wanted it to be suicide. There was no investigation to speak of. Carpet, brush, boom-shang-a-lang, man that's all she wrote. Holy Jesus.'

'How does that relate here?' asks Quinn.

There's no harshness or impatience in his voice. Obviously thinking the same thing as Sutherland and I.

'The crudeness of the set-up,' says Strangways. 'Feels like it's been done by someone wanting to create a story, yet not caring if the story holds up to close inspection. So we give the press what we can give them, they sniff around a little more behind the scenes, they get a grotesque murder story set in the heart of the financial district, which they absolutely love by the way, they get cocaine and booze, and that's all they care about. They don't want complexity or nuance, they want drugs and evisceration. And so . . . I don't know, it just strikes me it's the kind of thing the Russians would do. Balls out bullshit. They do what they like, and for all that there's a new Cold War, and for all the fearmongering, for all that government are trying to clamp down, there's still a shit-tonne of Russian money in the West, and by God, we don't want to lose *that*.

'So, my bet is that Davinder Singh died at the same time as Alan Westbrook, and his body will never be discovered. Or, if it is, it'll be ten years from now when the Russians have moved on and they don't care any more. Anyway, I don't know the specifics yet of what Westbrook and Singh were working on, but it's the City and they played with an awful lot of money, so there's a good chance that some of it was Russian. How about your end? Any Russian angle up there?'

I stare at the screen for a moment, and then turn to look at Quinn. Quinn glances at me, stops the curse crossing his lips, then turns away.

'Ah,' says Strangways. 'Welcome to my world.'

Driving home, traffic out of nowhere. News on the radio. Damp night, window open, the fresh smell of late autumn in the air. The occasional pedestrian scurries by beneath an umbrella, the evening passes in a damp blur.

The news rumbles on, I drift in and out. The same stories, fought over and over again, day in and out, decade after decade. People never change, the arguments never progress. It's just the voices, and the overall tone, which get worse and worse as the generations pass from one to the other, and our times are cursed by the rise of the dictators.

I've been thinking about Leia Marcus, although I have unusual clarity about the situation. I'm not tempted to call her, I'm not tempted to turn up on her doorstep, like some fool in a Richard Curtis movie. I have taken the idea of her – the idea of Leia Marcus and me going out for dinner, shar-ing a bottle of wine, going back to my house or the manse and going to bed, the normal interactions of a couple in their thirties and forties who are drawn to one another – I have taken all that and parked it, to be dusted off when this affair is done.

And in making the decision I'm fully aware that perhaps I'm just tossing it aside, never to be picked up again, Marcus never to be thought of again. Next week I won't go to church, nor the next; two weeks' absence will become four, five will bleed into months. Then one day next year I'll decide that maybe I could go to church again because I need the space, but I won't go to the local kirk. I'll avoid seeing the Reverend Marcus, and I'll take myself off to Muir of Ord or Conon Bridge.

Some day we'll see each other in the street in Dingwall, and she'll be passing by with a man at her side, and we'll say hello and there'll be a look there. The look that says what might have been, but we didn't even give it a go. And I won't know anything about the guy she's with, but deep down I'll feel he's not right for her, not in the way I would have been, and that I let her down.

The story runs through my head, with the flow of the Danube in springtime, each stage as clear and definite as the one before, and however it plays out, I know that the first part of it, where I don't call Leia Marcus while this investigation is ongoing, will at least come to pass.

And then, with a kick in the face, my thoughts are suddenly yanked back into focus. The story of the murder in London is on the radio. Car in first, slowing to a red light at roadworks at the bottom of the hill. The cause of the traffic. That moment between green lights, when traffic is going in neither direction.

That they're reporting the murder on the national news is not unexpected. A murder in the City of London is always going to get the attention of the media. The official police line is given, and then:

The police have refused to comment on reports that the victim had been disembowelled . . .

I'd rather that detail wasn't out there, and I'm sure the Met would too, but keeping the lid on in the twenty-first-century information shitstorm is impossible.

Cars start to approach from the opposite direction, headlights picking out the drizzle.

There are also unconfirmed reports that the murder might be linked to the death of businessman Thomas Peterson in Dingwall in the Highlands on Saturday.

The stock market began the week badly, with traders warning of the worsening economic situation as the British government limps—

I turn the radio off with a stab. Unconfirmed reports? Does that mean the Met leaked it off the record? Or has someone else managed to pick it up along the way?

Must be the Met.

I'm staring around, searching for someone else to drag into this, someone else with whom I can share my annoyance.

'What in the name of God did they do that for?' I say to the empty car. 'They couldn't have cleared that with us first?'

I lift my phone but who would I call?

The Met? What would I say to them? Am I going to tell them how to do their job? Or Quinn? What would that achieve?

I take a deep breath, try to let the frustration that has been winding up inside me dissipate. Phoning anyone when I feel like this would be of little use. Another deep breath, let it go for the day. All those lousy nights' sleep are catching up, but I can go home, have something to eat and look through the papers I've brought with me.

The cars from the other direction peter out, time passes, the red light changes to green.

15

Eleven minutes after midnight, sitting at the table, the window streaked with rain before me. Have been yawning, almost non-stop, for the past fifteen minutes. Two glasses of wine, a minute-steak, oven chips, green beans.

Sucked into the mundane drudgery of searching through financial paperwork and endless websites, trying to get my head around the complex finances of George Bailey's. Largely failing. Time passing quickly, so that I've barely noticed how long I've been sitting here. Made my supper of minimal effort, ate it in ten minutes. There have since followed a couple of hours of reading that already feel wasted.

The dog days of the investigation, the days that come too soon. There's the set-up; the crime and its immediate aftermath; the interviews with the family, the gathering of evidence; the discarding of unnecessary baggage, the narrowing down, the follow-up interviews. Often, of course, we quickly know the area of the investigation on which to concentrate. And sometimes, like now, we have no idea.

Either way, it comes to it, sooner or later. The drudgery of detail. The part they omit from fifty-eight-minute TV episodes, or cover in twenty-second montage scenes. The slog. Searching through paperwork and files, scanning the Internet, dissecting statements, fact-finding and cross-checking. In short, doing the job, in all its dog-days and dog-nights tedium.

We don't yet have the specific details of George Bailey's accounts. Neither the bank nor Natalia Kadyrova have been that forthcoming. The Clydesdale have at least given us details of the companies with which Bailey's did business. The full list of smaller funeral directors they bought over in the last five years, and some of the debtors and the lenders, the investors and the middlemen. Well aware, however, that they've only given us information we could have acquired ourselves from HMRC. Sutherland's contact at the bank saved us some time, that's all, but she hasn't given him anything she maybe shouldn't have.

Long stretch, look over my shoulder into the kitchen. Not too late for a coffee, not for me at any rate. I've never had the don't-drink-coffee-too-late thing. Never made any difference to me whether I have a cup at seven a.m. or one thirty in the morning, and as a result I have the sceptic's view of everyone who claims to be affected by it. People want things for themselves, even if it's just an inability to drink coffee after midday.

But what do I know of how others feel?

'Come on,' I say aloud to the empty room, mind rambling, 'just go to bed.'

Another yawn at the thought, accompanied by that uncomfortable feeling of what will come to me in my sleep. Troubled dreams, and the demons and monsters that lurk there. The guilt.

I take one last glance at a page of detail on Stravinsky Finance, one of the many companies investing in Bailey's, and then close it down and log off. All these businesses, every one that we're looking at, they're all the same. They each have expensive, polished websites, full of young, dynamic, diverse people with white teeth, looking incredibly earnest, or incredibly happy, while they make millions of dollars in the nebulous global solutions business, saving the planet along

the way. And you know that every single person in the photographs is a model with artificially whitened teeth, and that
not one of the companies has the slightest interest whatsoever in the planet, other than a wider investment in how they
can rape it.

Computer off. Close the lid, push it away across the table.
Stare out at the grim night. Intend to get up, but I sit here, as
though restrained at my wrists and ankles. Tiredness closes
in, like the relentless clouds of an oncoming storm.

I look along the beach, bleak and grey, as far as I can see.
There are no tables. I do not know what is waiting for me,
though the bleak setting is familiar.

I start walking, eyes straight ahead. The cloud is low, the
stretch of the beach does not seem long, the far distance lost
in the murk of smeary rain and mist and sand.

At last. A woman crying. That's what I've come to expect.
I don't know her, I don't know for whom she cries. It does
not matter. It is the sound of it, as it finds me, opens me up,
crawls inside, down my throat, into my belly, inhabiting me,
taking me over. The grief I caused. And then she's gone,
though the feeling remains. The horror of guilt.

I stop. Something else. I remember the old blind man. He's
not supposed to be here, there's no reason for him to be in
my head. So far he's the only imposter. This is not him,
however, not here to my left. By the back of the beach, in the
shadow of the dunes.

There is a bed. Very strange. A bed on the beach. And
there is a figure – hard to make out, dark, Gothic – leaning
over a sleeping man. The sheets are pulled down, the man on
the bed is naked.

The glint of a knife, though it is impossible to tell the
source of the light that causes the glint. A spurt of blood, the
body shudders, and then a slow squirming of red from a long

wound, as the knife is drawn down over the flat belly, from the bottom of the ribcage down to the groin.

The dark figure pauses, and then places the knife back at the top of the cut and this time plunges it in deeper, another stabbing movement to drive it in further, and then the knife is dragged, two-handed, back down the length of the bloody slit.

The figure pauses again at the bottom. The wind dies. In the claustrophobic silence of the beach, the man on the bed sighs gently. A final breath, a gurgle in his throat.

The knife is laid aside, and two hands in black latex gloves are placed together, back-to-back, inside the split, and the abdominal cavity is pulled apart. Then, with a great slurp, the hands are inserted in the cavity, and the viscera are lifted out, a tangle of organs, tubes and dark red.

The left hand holds the viscera against the pelvis, and then the figure lifts the knife and quickly hacks away at the connecting tissue and tubes, so that the mass is freed. Blood sprays messily into the air. One particular stream traces a beautiful parabolic trajectory, to the left, over the white sheets. This mélange of internal organs is then pushed to the side, onto the bed.

'Look. Look.'

I don't remember deciding to say anything, but there they are, the words out of my mouth.

The dark figure does not turn.

'Look,' I say, 'the phone's ringing. You ought to get it.'

Nothing.

'I said, the phone's ringing.'

Quiet. Insistent. Nothing.

I look round. Someone should get the phone, but there's no one else here. There isn't even anyone sitting at a desk, which is odd, because usually there are people at desks, and people at desks quite often have phones they need to answer.

I don't see why the call would be for me, and the mysterious surgeon's hands will be covered in blood, so he likely wouldn't want to lift the phone in any case.

Why do I think the dark, Gothic figure is a man?

'The phone!' I shout.

I bolt upright. The chair shifts beneath me with the sudden movement. I'm in the dim light of the sitting room, staring at the rain against the window, mouth dry, my brain encased in all-consuming disorder, a feeling like someone has just shouted in my ear, the words still echoing through the empty chamber of my head.

The phone is ringing, and the dog days of the first murder are about to be turned into the sirens and the frantic rush of the second.

16

Sutherland and I are standing at the back of a bedroom in a care home by the sea, near Dornoch. Very early morning, the wind blowing, the rain falling when we arrived, the sound of the sea loud on the shore as we walked towards the house. Inside it's completely silent. In this room the curtains are open, but the double or triple or quadruple glazing keeps the night at bay.

I knew what we'd be coming to as soon as I was juddered awake by the phone. Not the feel of the place, the door, the room, the curtains pulled back, the table by the window with the single chair, the two armchairs, the sadness of the solitary wooden ornament on the mantelshelf. But this, to the right of where we stand: the double bed, the old man lying, his hands by his sides, his pale face in repose, the dark red of the blood that is splayed around the bed in contrast to the sickly blue pallor of his skin. His entrails dumped on the duvet.

The mind constructs imperfect pictures, yet I look down on the aftermath of the evisceration and it's a scene that precisely followed the last. The one I witnessed. The murder, followed some time later by this, the victim lying in silence. Outside, the night has yet to give way to morning, the first light of dawn in the distant eastern sky yet to show, but the beam from the lighthouse at Tarbat Ness blinks resolutely into the dark, a few miles, due east, across the sea.

That can't be my lighthouse, I think. The beach here, the one down from the care home, stretching away to the left, isn't as long as the beach that I walk in my dreams. It can't be the same beach, so this can't be the same lighthouse. It must just be a coincidence. Like this disembowelment.

Precognition is in all of us, though only ever when not looked for. Think nothing of it, as we must think nothing of the boundaries of space and the beginning of time. There is no explanation that can make sense to us with our limited understanding.

I think of the Reverend Marcus, and don't doubt that she would have an explanation.

The SOCOs arrived not long after Sutherland and me, three of them, white-suited and gloved, Dr Hamilton among them. He's currently standing by the side of the bed, looking down on the corpse. There's a local constable at his side. I didn't ask him to stand there. I wonder if he's fearful that the corpse will spring back to life, and make a move on the doctor. The director of the home, Holly Littlejohn, is by the doorway, her face pale and hard set, her knuckles clenched white, her shoulder-length hair a striking, luminescent silver.

This home, The Dunes, is the one we'd been intending to visit anyway, the home where Thomas Peterson's grandmother, Louise Worrell, resides. At first I jumped to the obvious conclusion that she would be the victim, but I ought to have known better. I'd seen the victim, and knew it to be a man. And here lies Graham Strachan.

Now just after six in the morning. The residents are all still in their rooms, though the elderly have a habit of rising early, and already one can hear the distant suggestion of movement, as the collective entity of the home begins to stir. There has been, so far, neither sight nor talk of Louise Worrell. The fact that we've been drawn to a place that was already on our radar could be entirely coincidental, and yet there's the awful method of Graham Strachan's death, killed in the same manner as Alan Westbrook in London.

The results of the evisceration, the splay of Strachan's guts, have been dumped on the bed beside him. There's blood smeared over the sheets and the headboard, and around the carpet beside the bed, with a trail leading to the bathroom. Strachan's eyes are closed, his face relaxed.

We're standing together watching the scene unfold, as if this is the kind of thing we all see every day up here. Yet it is utterly horrific, and, we can at least hope, a once-in-a-life-time experience. Just the act of being in this room will mean that everyone here should be trauma risk assessed in the coming days. This is the stuff of nightmares and cold sweats, waking visions and personal horror.

Perhaps I wasn't the only one experiencing all that before I even got here. That I saw as bad, sometimes worse, as a result of IEDs in Afghanistan, makes little difference to me, and obviously none to anyone else.

'What d'you think?' says Sutherland, who has looked away from the bed and is staring at the wooden sculpture. 'Would you say that was porn? Like, wood porn?'

His voice does not display much interest. In most other crime scene situations I'd be giving Sutherland the *is this the time for that?* look. But not here. Because this is the time for mundane conversation. This is the time for clinging to anything that isn't what's directly in front of us.

Every swallow feels like holding back the malicious thrill of bile.

Funny how Sutherland should see it. The figure is made of pale wood, maybe twenty inches high, and is of a naked woman, standing alone, staring at the ground, her arms by her sides. She looks lost. Wretched. I look upon her and do not even see that she is undressed. I see desolation.

I don't answer. Sutherland waits for a moment, then does not seem bothered that I have no comment.

'We could be anywhere,' he says, finally looking away from the sculpture. 'We could be on the seventieth floor of an apartment block in Dubai. There's no way to tell what's outside that window. A hermetically sealed environment.'

The building is old, but has been expensively redesigned, repurposed and retro-fitted. Given our interest in Mrs Worrell, and this horrific crime that's currently in front of us, we'll need to get into the workings of the home, of who runs it, but it has the feel of expensive, purpose-built luxury. This is a home for people with serious money.

'How was the murder discovered?' I ask, checking my watch.

'Nurse doing the rounds noticed the door was slightly ajar,' says Sutherland.

'Careless or contrived?'

'The nurse says she walks the corridors once an hour. If the killer knew her routine, he could have timed it so it didn't matter whether the door was left open.'

'Hmm . . .'

'You ever seen anything like that before?' he says, making a small gesture towards the corpse, as though needing to establish that he's talking about the evisceration, rather than the view from the window.

I don't answer, and Sutherland nods after a while.

'Helmand, I suppose,' he says.

'Yes,' I say, though I'm not going to elaborate on the circumstances. 'Different, of course. It's . . . it's about expect-ation. What you're prepared for.'

I smile at that line, as if we're all just breezily waving away roadside carnage in Afghanistan because we saw it coming. Doesn't matter that fifteen people have had their body parts sprayed all around, because clearing it up is in the job description.

'It's not like you get used to it,' I add, then dismiss that part of the conversation.

About to suggest it's time to move on, and that we should take the director off for a chat, when I stop, turning my head to the side, listening. We look quizzically out into the corridor and then turn upwards, trying to work out where the sound is coming from.

A lament is being played on the fiddle, the sound filling the building. Slow, haunting, melancholic.

It doesn't appear to be on the same floor, yet it is so clear it feels like the entire building has stopped dead to listen to it. A perfect soundtrack to the early morning, as though John Williams has been brought in for dramatic licence.

'Jesus,' said Sutherland. 'Where's that coming from?'

The ethereal sound seems perfect for where we've come, for this bizarre series of events, a murder wrapped in unspeakable horror, a storm-battered old house on a bleak stretch of November coastline.

'One of the residents, presumably.'

The words are automatic. There's that strange, uneasy feeling again, and this time I know the root of it. The fiddle. The lament.

I knew it was coming. It's the fiddle that plays when I'm walking on the beach, even though I cannot think of the sound of the fiddle when I'm there. That tune, in all its melancholic horror, plays for those watching, as the lonely figure walks barefoot along the sand in an old, black and white, surrealist movie.

'I hope so,' says Sutherland, smiling uncomfortably.

I stare at the ceiling. Do I know what's coming next? So many portents, and yet I seem incapable of getting ahead of them. At the top of each hill, there is always another path leading upwards, rather than a view down below.

There's nothing there, not even on the edge of my thoughts. The longer I stand here, the more familiar everything seems, but that's all. There are no premonitions. Not yet, not here in a plain bedroom, conducting a murder investigation.

I snap my fingers, my hand down by my side, literally snapping myself out of it. Mind on the damned job. Do what needs to be done, do the thing directly in front of you.

'Come on,' I say, 'let's speak to the director.'

'I'd ask that you wait until later this morning,' says Littlejohn.

'We need to do it now,' I say, glancing impatiently at my watch. The time doesn't matter. 'We'll be as sympathetic as possible, and we understand how upsetting this is for the residents, but you saw the same thing in there as we did. If the murder was committed by an intruder, then we need to make sure no one's hiding in the home. If it was committed by one of the residents, or one of the staff, then we need to ensure that no one destroys evidence, and both processes start now.'

'No one could have done that!' says Littlejohn, horrified at the suggestion.

'Someone did it,' I say.

'Yes, yes, someone did it, but not my staff, not one of my residents. They're hardly capable. Most of them can't lace their shoes.'

'That's the kind of thing we need to talk about, Ms Littlejohn. But for now, right now, we need to lock down the building and check every room. This is not a do-you-mind conversation. It's happening. This is your chance to let us know if there are any residents with whom we should be particularly careful, that perhaps you'd like a member of staff to accompany us—'

'All of them!'

'So be it. We need—'

'This is the second morning in a row they'll be waking to awful news, and you clearly do not understand how upsetting that will be.'

She stares harshly across the desk, her silver hair perfectly framing her face in the harsh, bright overhead lights of the office.

'What?'

'Another resident died on Sunday night.' A pause. 'Mr Cummins.'

I glance at Sutherland, who shakes his head.

'Tell us about Mr Cummins.'

'I told the police already,' she says, voice crisp, her tone picking up a notch at the realisation she has the opportunity to go on the offensive.

'You reported it to Dornoch station?'

'Yes, of course.'

'Tell us about Mr Cummins.'

I know where this is going, and I'm not going to give her what she might well see as a minor victory of an admission of ignorance. If there was any reason we should have known about it, Dornoch would have told us.

'Mr Cummins appeared to have passed away in his sleep,' she says, coldly. 'He had advanced dementia, and barely communicated. Nevertheless, he'd had his monthly check-up last week, his heart was fine, and I decided to notify the police as the death was unexpected.'

'There's an autopsy?'

'There should be at some point. No one's holding their breath, I might add.'

'Someone dying in a care home can't be a particularly peculiar occurrence. You have a sense this transcends that?'

She doesn't answer, and I don't leave her much space in any case.

'We'll factor that in, but it makes it even more imperative that we get on with our investigation, and it really doesn't matter how early in the morning it is. We need to start right now. Floor by floor, room by room. We have nine available officers, and I'd like to begin in the next five minutes. You have sufficient staff?'

Littlejohn doesn't answer. She seems frozen, and it's impossible to tell whether she's thinking it through, or whether the awfulness of the moment has suddenly caused her brain to lock.

I stand quickly, surprising her, impatience finally taking hold, snap my fingers twice and say, 'Director Littlejohn, we need to get going. Do you have enough staff?'

'I think so. I'll need to . . . I'll need to join you.'

'Get hold of people, get us a plan of the house, and let's move.'

The sound of the fiddle weaves its way through the fabric of the building, a lamentation for the sad life and violent death of Graham Strachan.

There are forty-three rooms, not including the various ensuite bathrooms. Thirty inhabited by residents. The sitting room, the kitchen, the restaurant, the sun room, the games room, the laundry, the library, the prayer room, the office suite of five rooms, the staff room, four bathrooms, the maintenance room and two storerooms. There are corridors and stairwells, and the fiddle travels up and down and along every one of them.

It seems the disemboweller of Graham Strachan, the nameless horror, has left the building. The home and the grounds are in lockdown, but it's too late; the door has been closed long, long after the malevolent spirit has bolted. The wind still blows, and down at the quay at the foot of the slope, three small yachts still rock from side to side, the ropes still clang monotonously against the masts.

The rain falls, a fine, soaking drizzle. The four police officers now posted outside are prepared for the weather. Jackets retrieved from cars, boots squelching through grass. Our presence grows in number, officers called out in the early morning, as the grey light of dawn crawls over the land.

Room to room we go. Some residents cry, some panic, some stare, silent and fearful, from beneath the covers, sheets drawn up to their necks. Some do not yet wake.

The night passes, day breaks, and no more harm is done. Yet, there is nothing to be found. No clue, no murder weapon, no trace of blood outside Strachan's room. The killer swept in with furious force, and blood was spilled. And that, for now, is all we have.

17

Tuesday mid-morning. Dull day, the dark of night taking a long time to leave, and finally replaced by a grey light, washed with rain. The clouds are low, even and thick, with barely a contour. A solid ceiling of grey.

I'm in Quinn's office, joined by Chief Constable Darnley, who's travelled from Inverness.

'You found nothing there?'

'No trace of blood anywhere other than in the victim's room,' I say. 'Would seem the killer washed themself down in the shower in the victim's ensuite, and then walked back through the room without stepping on any blood.'

'No footprints?' asks Darnley.

'None.'

'There was nothing outside?'

'We set up lights, but we haven't found anything so far. We'll get on better in full daylight.'

All three of us look out the window, turning back to the room at the same time.

'I think you might need to keep the lights on,' says Darnley drily.

'First thing this morning wasn't the best circumstance. Hopefully the day, into the afternoon, will produce better results.'

'What about Mr Strachan's family? Are they local?'

'There's a niece in the south of England, that's all. She sends number puzzle books, Killer Sudoku, every month.

He'd do three books' worth of puzzles inside two days, and then, I don't know, vegetate until the next lot arrived. He liked walking down by the sea, watching the tides. At night he'd sit at his bedroom window, in the dark, and watch the light from the lighthouse. Always slept with the curtains open. He didn't speak to anyone generally, didn't have any friends, although he did say to one of the nurses that he could follow the blink of the lighthouse beam on the bedroom wall as he lay in bed. Given that it's over eight miles away, that seems unlikely.'

'People see all sorts of remarkable things,' says Darnley.

'Also, Director Littlejohn told me in a whisper that she thought he might be gay, as if that would somehow explain no friends and little family.'

'The victim had no especially close relationships with anyone else at the home? Residents or staff?'

'Not off the top of Littlejohn's head, but it's on the list of things to explore.'

'And how about a connection with this disembowelling in London on Sunday evening?'

'Way too early to say. We have to work on the assumption that this care home murder is a completely different case. We just don't know at the mo—'

'What d'you need?'

'A fully staffed ops room here in Dingwall for a kick off . . .'

'You need extra staff from Inverness?'

'Not yet. I'll need Sutherland up at the home with me, and out asking questions. I think Constable Cole can run the room for the moment, she's ready.'

'Yes,' says Darnley.

'I'll speak to Dr Hamilton, then get back up to Dornoch. We'll coordinate with London, but I don't think there's any need to go down there. We can keep things as they've been for the moment, but maybe we could make sure some of the Dornoch police stay on this for now so that—'

'Of course,' interjects Darnley. 'Anything else?'

Darnley's great, but I'm not used to this level of support from higher up the chain. I have a frivolous thought about asking if I can get a twenty per cent pay rise and six weeks more annual leave, though what on earth I would do with it I don't know. I can barely fill my weekends.

'I think that's all for now.'

'Good. I'll take updates through David, but don't feel you need to call in every twenty minutes. Do your job; if you need anything else, staff it up through the Chief.'

'Yes, ma'am.'

I look at Quinn, who's been silent throughout, then turn and leave the room, closing the door behind me.

Stop outside for a moment, look around the open-plan, and allow myself the regular thought that I wish Darnley was in on every meeting I had with Quinn, meaning I'd never have to listen to him, then back to my desk.

'I've spoken to London, I've seen the video and photographs. This is completely different.'

I look at the corpse of Graham Strachan, lying on its back on a table in the morgue. He stares at the ceiling, apparently in horror, although of course that is just us, the detached voyeurs on death, endowing the dead eyes with a fear we expect them to have. They're eyes, they're dead, there's nothing to see.

The rip in the stomach has been pulled apart. Dr Hamilton has further cut open the ribcage, separating the two halves. The viscera, so brutally removed, are in a low-sided tray on a smaller table behind Hamilton. The top of the table also contains a reference book, a lamp, a small tray of surgical tools and a glass of water.

'Explain it to me,' I say.

'Pathology in London confirmed their attack had been carried out using the knife that was then left on the bathroom floor. This one here was done more delicately, with a surgical instrument. A scalpel, more than likely.'

'It was done by a trained practitioner? A surgeon, a doctor?'

'Hmm . . .' says Hamilton, leaving it at that.

I give him a few moments, as we both look at the bloody mass of the eviscerated abdomen. Finally I look up and say drily, 'Or a magician perhaps, or a lumberjack?' when I realise Hamilton really isn't going to say anything further.

'It was someone,' says Hamilton, 'and I'd say they knew what they were doing, but it's not like the viscera have been cut out in such a precise way they could have been put back in and reconnected. This is a neater job than London, yes, but what this really implies is more about intent and the state of the assailant, rather than the eviscerator's ability with a scalpel. And Mr Strachan here was at least unaware of proceedings, having been knocked out by chloroform.'

'What d'you mean about the state of the assailant?'

'In London we had a brutal and savage attack, which might have been premeditated, but was still perpetrated at the height of passion. Think of the splay of blood, the tumult. Here we have cold, calculated brutality.'

'There was still quite a spread of blood, over the sheets, the carpet.'

'Somewhat unavoidable with a disembowelling,' says Hamilton, 'particularly one not done in a surgical theatre. What you had in London was . . . it was a splatterfest, in the modern vernacular. This . . . this isn't that. It's for you people to sort out. This'll keep me occupied for a while, and I'll let you know if I come across anything else.'

'Can you see any connection with the death at the football on Saturday?'

He stares down at the corpse for a while, then slowly lifts his eyes.

'What are you thinking?'

'I'm thinking we live in a relatively remote area of low population, and there have been two murders inside a few days, which seems kind of unusual.'

Eyes lowered, he gives this some thought, then reluctantly agrees with a low grunt from the back of his throat.

'No,' he says, nevertheless, 'but I'll have a look. They are so disparate, however, it's hard to see what that's going to be. I shan't stretch anything, but I'll see what I can come up with.'

'You know about the other death at the home?'

'Of course. We've had the body brought over. I believe the incriminating circumstances to be slight, but you're right, in light of this, and its connection to your ongoing investigation, it's definitely worth a look. I'm just going to give this one another hour, while I have the scent of blood in my nostrils, then I'll wheel out the other body.'

The scent of blood in my nostrils. Beautiful.

Hamilton looks over the huge, gaping wound that was the end of Graham Strachan and says, 'Leave me, Inspector, we've both got work to do,' and with a smile at the abrupt dismissal, I turn away.

18

Sutherland and I are standing down by the water's edge, looking out over the sea, the Dornoch Firth to our right. The small, L-shaped jetty, running out beyond a broad sandbank, is closed off. Presumably they don't want residents walking out there, but there are three small boats tied up in the lee of the L, so it appears to still be in use.

Early afternoon is so bleak the lighthouse at Tarbat Ness – the operation of the thousand-watt lamp controlled automatically by a light sensor – has not gone off all day. We're watching it, drawn to the magnetic beam, eight miles across the sea out to the end of the peninsular. I can see myself doing the same as old Strachan, sitting at a bedroom window, hypnotised by the light, and wonder how many of the other inmates do the same.

Shake my head. *Inmates?*

'What?' asks Sutherland, noticing the movement.

'Nothing,' I say, the moment broken. 'Just thinking about the residents, what kind of people we're going to find in there. What it means to give up your own home, and come somewhere for the last time. I guess they go out, and they can visit relatives, but still. This is it. The end. It might take a while, but you're giving up on everything else, or having the decision made for you, so here you go, to your home by the sea, to sit out the rest of your life on the sidelines. What does that do to your head?'

'Yeah,' says Sutherland. He sounds downbeat, his voice low. 'I've been wondering about that too. Some still have football on the TV, they all hopefully have family, but what's a two-hour visit once a week, in a week of a hundred and sixty-eight hours? They have all this time, and where do they go? They regress into the past. That's what they've got to hang on to. And if they're lucky, they remember the good times. Most people do. But what if . . . what about the ones who are haunted? What do they think about when they're sitting there, in morbid silence? All day, every day. Perhaps their family never visits, their contact confined to an awkward twenty-minute chat on a shakily held tablet they don't understand. What of them?'

'Sounds like this place is getting to you already. We've only been here a few hours.'

'More likely two years working with you, sir,' he says drily. Funny.

'Bitterness festers,' I say, 'and yes, there's a huge step from the bitterness of a potential dementia-inflicted pensioner, to the disembowelling of one of their fellows. But this is where we are. There's been a brutal murder in a care home, and we definitely need to start with the staff and the residents. An open mind, and who knows what we're going to learn from the lives of these people?'

We turn and look back at the house in the grim afternoon light. There are double doors, currently locked, leading out the back of the house from the large sitting room. Along the ground floor, windows on the dining room, and along to the offices and sleeping quarters of some of the staff. The residents' bedrooms are all on the first and second floors, with a view either over the Firth, or back over the small airstrip and the golf course.

We can see five people sitting at windows, one of whom, a woman on the second floor, has been watching us since we appeared in her line of vision. One of those looks that we could feel on our backs.

'This place,' says Sutherland, 'if you don't mind me saying . . .' and then he lets the sentence drift off.

'Go on, Sergeant,' I say, the accepting smile in my voice if not on my face.

'It's creepy as fuck,' he says.

'Yep,' I say, 'that it is. It shouldn't be, really. It's a nice old building, it's had the shit renovated out of it, and yet, as you say . . . creepy as fuck.'

The woman on the second floor lifts her hand, looking like she will touch her ear. The hand hesitates in the air, and then softly rests against the side of her head. Her head leans in to the touch, as though comforted.

Her eyes do not leave us.

Fifteen minutes later, and I haven't moved far. A few metres, inside the wall at the bottom of the garden, near the gate that leads onto the short promenade from which the jetty extends. Still standing with my back to the sea, looking up towards the home.

The clouds remain low and flat, the rain falling softly around us. No other residents are outside, but there are upwards of fifteen officers going over the grounds, looking for any sign of illicit approach or getaway.

I'm with the director, Holly Littlejohn. We're both wearing waterproof jackets, hoods pulled up. I bought my waterproof in a sports shop. Littlejohn got hers at the kind of designer store that supplies power clothes for the executive wanting to make an impression.

'That's a pretty low wall behind us,' I say, without turning to look at it.

'We're not a prison.'

'There are no residents who might wander off?'

'A few, but it doesn't matter. Whenever there's anyone out here – and I should say that it's not the weather that's keeping them inside today, but your team of investigators – we have two members of staff with them.'

I'll ignore the line about the investigators, as well as its pointed delivery, as if the real outrage here is the police sticking their noses into the business of Geras Holdings, corporate owners of The Dunes.

'I have a lot of questions,' I say, a level tone, trying to reset the conversation, 'and I know we covered some of it already, but you were clearly in a state of shock, as was everyone here. So, if it's all right, we're going to start from the beginning.'

'Yes, of course,' Littlejohn replies.

'As soon as you heard about it, as soon as you saw what had happened, what did your gut say?'

'What d'you mean?' she asks stiffly. 'My gut wanted to throw up, Inspector.'

'I want to know if, before you'd considered all the options, before your brain had had the chance to kick into life, did you immediately think, oh God, this is because of X, or this must be as a result of Y, or that'll be Z, he was bound to do something like this? Maybe, under careful consideration, you disregarded the thought as being too ridiculous, but just for that fleeting moment, did anything cross your mind?'

'No,' says Littlejohn, barely letting me finish.

'OK. Under careful consideration, does anything come to mind?'

'No.'

'Did Mr Strachan have any particular friends among the other residents?'

'Mr Strachan did number puzzles. That was all he ever did. I told you that this morning.'

'And I just told you we were going over it again. Did he speak to the others at all?'

'No. Kept himself to himself.'

'Did he have a relationship with any particular staff member?'

'He spoke to the staff, but he was gruff and blunt and not especially popular.'

'How unpopular?'

A moment while Littlejohn shows the question, and its implication, the disdain she feels it deserves, then she says, 'Not very popular, but on a scale of one to ten on whether or not someone would want to rip his insides out as a result, I'd say it was about a zero.'

'He never had visitors?'

'His niece, the one who sends the number puzzles, visited . . . I don't know, in June maybe. That was all. He did puzzles, he did them quickly, he didn't talk to people.'

'He was on the spectrum?'

'If you mean the maths genius, rude to people spectrum, oh yes. Although, to be honest, he wasn't that rude, and I don't think he was that much of a genius.'

'Any connection between him and Mr Cummins?'

Littlejohn snorts, and then clears her throat with a cough to cover the unattractiveness of the sound.

'Coppers gonna cop, I suppose,' she says.

'Heard it,' I say, although to be honest, I've never heard anyone say that before. 'Was there any connection be—'

'No, Inspector, I don't know of any connection, although the staff might be able to tell you otherwise. But really, I cannot believe that there would be anything to link these two deaths. I mean, look at them.'

'Mr Strachan's death was unexpected, right?'

'Of course!'

'And Mr Cummins, you thought he was about to die?'

'No, but . . .'

'So, his death was also unexpected.' I hold her gaze for a moment, before annoyingly stating the obvious. 'Look, we have a connection.'

'Well, regardless of whether or not there's a connection, I'm sure you'll find one,' she says with obvious irritation.

'As long as we find the truth.'

'How noble.'

The part where I reset the tone of the conversation didn't go so well.

'Has anything happened in the home in the last few weeks? Anything unexplained, anything untoward?'

'Nothing happens here, Inspector. That's how we sell the place, that's one of the reasons we can charge so much money. People send their parents or grandparents up to this quiet, beautiful spot, where no one ever comes. They live in relative luxury, and they know that literally nothing will ever happen.'

I turn and look out over the pale, sandy shore out to the grey sea, where the grey clouds merge with the water. Personally, if I were spending as much money as these people, I'd rather be looking at a Swiss lake and mountains.

'How about Mrs Worrell?' I ask, turning back to join Littlejohn in staring up at the house. There are lights on in about half the windows, as the residents and staff compensate for a day that's unlikely to see natural light of any consequence.

The woman in the window, who could not take her eyes away from Sutherland and me, is no longer in position. The shadow of her, the feel of her, remains.

'What about her?'

'Did she ever have anything to do with either Mr Strachan or Mr Cummins?'

Littlejohn looks curiously at me, brow furrowed. Finally, just as I'm about to nudge her for an answer, it seems to click.

'Ah, right. We heard about Mrs Worrell's grandson. Now two people who lived in the same home as Mrs Worrell have died . . .'

I'm getting the look of derision that the detective knows so well. Sometimes it's directed our way because we're throwing ideas around, searching for anything that works, and it might be deserved. And then there's this, this woman here, who's looking at me as if I'm a fool, putting two and two together to make seventeen.

'Yes, yes, I see it now, I'm sure that's the connection you're looking for, Hercule. Shall I assemble the guests in the library?'

She looks earnestly at me, awaiting the reaction.

'Can you think of any connection between Mrs Worrell and either of the deceased?' I ask.

Hercule . . . Usually it's Taggart or Morse.

'Have you spoken to Mrs Worrell yet?' asks Littlejohn.

'No.'

'Mrs Worrell has no connection with anyone. We don't know whether she chooses to not talk, or simply cannot talk. Her vocal cords are in perfect working order, according to Dr Raven. Maybe there's a psychological impediment. Or it could also just be that she doesn't *want* to talk to anyone. She never makes eye contact, never appears to hear anyone, never interacts with anyone on any level. Still walking, breathing, eating and using the bathroom, so she's not going anywhere any time soon, but there is no communication.'

'Dr Raven is the house doctor?'

'Yes, Anne. She's . . . yes, she's the doctor.'

'Mrs Worrell stares at a painting all day.'

'Yes.'

'There's no possibility that she's, I don't know, like Terry Gilliam's jailer character in *Life of Brian*? Puts on an act in public, quite a different person in private?'

'I don't really know what you're talking about, but if you're asking could she have been having a relationship of any sort with anyone that we don't know about, the answer is absolutely not. She is mute. She at least appears to be deaf. She is lost to the world, and all she's got left to cling to is that ghastly painting. A few weeks ago, I decided to move the painting from her room, out into the sitting room. I thought it might have some effect. At least she'd have people around her, rather than her sitting in solitude all day. The doctor didn't agree, but the doctor doesn't agree with much I say.'

'And it didn't work?'

'No. Look, she's been examined, and there is no recognisable neurological explanation for her condition, which is not the same for some of the others in a similar state. But she is lost to the world, Inspector, that is certain.'

I lower my hood and listen to the soft surround sound of the rain, the quiet hush of the waves on the shore. There's no sound from anywhere else.

If the wind is in the right direction, you can likely hear the traffic on the A9 from here. We can see an occasional car on the bridge across the firth, but what there is of the wind is taking the sound inland.

Now Littlejohn also removes her hood, and we stand in silence. Rain falls, officers in capes move in and out of the bushes that have been planted in the last couple of years down the walls that mark the sides of the garden.

'I'd like to speak to her now,' I say, after a while.

'Good luck,' says Littlejohn. 'Would you mind if we recorded your conversation for training purposes?'

19

A baby ripped from his mother's grasp, a soldier on the point of stabbing a child, another chasing a woman through the snow.

A soldier urinating against a wall, another dragging a child from a house.

A man trying to hide a child.

Soldiers stabbing viciously into a group of infants.

Soldiers armed with an axe, a log, a halberd, trying to break into an inn. We need not ask what's on the other side of the door.

A mother grieving for her dead son, the snow turned bloody red.

A crowd, standing over a murdered child, berating a soldier. Next to them a woman, her dead child in her lap.

A single soldier stabbing a child, next to him another stabbing a baby held by a woman.

A small crowd mourns.

The sitting room is large and elegant. A refinement to the décor, no television in here – there is another small sitting room with a television – the walls hung with eighteenth- and nine-teenth-century, pre-Impressionist artworks, a drinks cabinet (locked), several shelves of books and three large bay windows overlooking the Dornoch Firth as it stretches out to sea.

This is where the money is, the new frontier of corporate advancement, reaping reward from the rich.

There are six people sitting in chairs by the window, seven others around the room. No one is talking, bar one of the women by the window. Slightly detached from the others, she sits alone, her head in constant motion, moving slowly from side to side. Her voice is soft, her words imperceptible from my position at the door.

Behind the row of chairs by the window, there is a chessboard, a chair either side of the table. The pieces are set mid-game, but there is only one person playing, an old man who sits with a watchful eye on the board, seemingly oblivious to the room around him. He has one hand raised, about to make a move.

I'm drawn to the chess player at first, with a growing feeling of ill ease, even though he is not the reason I've come in here. Something familiar about him, though at the same time I know I've never seen him before. Something familiar about the game, the way the pieces are set up.

I wonder what's become of his opponent. Perhaps he or she has just gone off to the bathroom. Perhaps they died several months, or years, previously, and the chess player sits here, day in day out, waiting for his opponent to make a move that will never come.

I approach the board, standing side on, looking down at the pieces, and soon enough the reason for my recognition kicks in. The image of the chess player on the beach, the feel of it, the cold, silent desolation of the still, grey calm, sweeps over me, and I shudder. Then the clarity and vision is gone, and I'm back in this room, where no one makes a sound except a woman sitting in the far corner, muttering quietly to herself.

The old, frail hand is steady in the air, trapped in an eternal, indecisive struggle. And then, breaking the spell of it, the old man reaches out. Bishop to queen's rook seven. His fingers rest on the top of the piece for a moment as he considers the move, then he lifts them, and moves the board around.

It's on a swivel. I hadn't noticed that the board was a couple of millimetres off the table. And now he's black instead of white, and it's apparent there is no opponent. He is playing both sides.

He turns finally and looks up at me. Dead, blue eyes, disconcerting at first, a look that drills inside me, down into my guts, and then I remember he's blind. I knew that already. That's where the peculiar distance in his gaze comes from. The blind man playing chess, who somehow found his way into my world in the middle of the night.

'Inspector,' he says.

He looks straight at me, straight into my eyes. That's the unsettling thing about his look. The blind man who can see.

'Mr . . .?'

'Durin,' he says. 'They call me Blind Durin behind my back, but you don't need to do that. You can just call me Durin.'

'What do you see?' I ask, a peculiar question, yet one that seems entirely relevant.

He holds my gaze and then looks around the room. His eyes do not settle on anyone or anything, instead drifting slowly across the large windows looking out onto the firth, before coming back around to me.

I follow his gaze, a couple of seconds behind. A little closer to the front of the house, a little closer to the woman muttering to herself. Now, her words are clearer, and I hold my breath for a moment while I listen to her. The same phrase repeated over and over, and slowly it comes into focus, like the turn of an old-fashioned radio dial.

You know for whom she tends the weeping fig . . .
You know for whom she tends the weeping fig . . .
You know for whom she tends the weeping fig . . .

Blind Durin laughs without smiling, a peculiarly unsettling, low chortle.

'There's always something to see, Inspector,' he says, words emerging from his laughter. 'There's always something to feel in the air. Thought and deed do not just manifest themselves in the reflection of light.'

I turn back to Durin. Somehow I understand that he will know I'm now looking at him again.

'You know who killed Mr Strachan?' I find myself asking.

'I feel things, Inspector,' he says, bluntly. 'I am not psychic.'

'So, do you sense guilt in anyone?'

He holds my gaze in his particular way, and then seems to accept the validity of the question. His answer is, nevertheless, predictably opaque.

'There is guilt in everyone, Inspector.'

I don't say anything glib in response to that, although several things come to mind. There is guilt in most, sure enough, although the level of guilt is always linked to the temperament of the man or woman, rather than the act that induced the guilt in the first place.

'I'll leave you to your game, Mr Durin.'

'We'll speak again,' he says.

That peculiar feeling in the guts does not leave as I turn away, but I try to shake it off as I stand and look at the far wall.

To the right, as you enter the room, there is one painting that is not in keeping with the refined elegance of the port scenes and landscapes of the rest of the artwork. This is the late-sixteenth-century Brueghel, *The Massacre of the Innocents*.

Transferring the narrative of the tale of Herod's biblical slaughter of newborns to the sixteenth-century Netherlands, Brueghel depicted the panic of the townspeople, as Spanish soldiers and German mercenaries come to murder their male children.

There are dead babies, several more wrapped in funeral cloth, others being taken to or already being put to the slaughter. And it is this that Louise Worrell chooses to study every day.

Louise Worrell is sitting in what is her regular spot, staring straight ahead at the painting. I stand and watch her for a while, the peculiar life of the home continuing around me. Mrs Worrell rarely blinks, and she does not move. It is impossible to tell if there are any thought processes taking place. Her eyes do not seem to move from one section of the painting to another. Littlejohn related that Dr Raven thinks Mrs Worrell sets her eyes on a different spot every time she sits down, but does not change her area of study during any given sitting. If you can say she's studying, that is, as studying implies a good deal more thought than the doctor thinks her capable of.

After a while, I lift a chair from a small table, place it beside Mrs Worrell and sit down. She does not look at me. I do not look at her. Together we stare at the painting, and while it's a calculated position at first, placing myself as much as I can in Louise Worrell's shoes, I become lost in thought about the case rather than the Brueghel.

I'm curious, now, to hear from Dr Hamilton. Expecting little else from his examination of Strachan, it is Cummins's cause of death that interests me. That will be key. Not, of course, that it will necessarily help us pin down our killer, but it might inch us closer to an explanation.

I need to check my phone, but I've already put it on silent and turned off vibrate, not wanting to be disturbed. I don't expect Mrs Worrell to suddenly start speaking to me, having not spoken to anyone in years, but if I'm going to make any attempt to get through to her, this isolated woman lost in her pitiless, sixteenth-century universe, then I need to blend with the atmosphere.

I don't like the painting. I'm not sure that many would. I enjoy those old Dutch winter landscapes, the generic frozen-lake scenes, but not this. I'm quite sure that Mrs Worrell doesn't enjoy it either. That's not why she bought it. That's not why she's looking at this retelling of Biblical brutality.

'The director told you about Thomas,' I say, my voice low and soft in the grey light of the sitting room.

I didn't think about starting to speak, the words just appeared on my lips. I don't even know how long I've been sitting here. It's just time to talk, that's all.

'That's why we're here,' I continue. 'Maybe you'll have picked up what happened this morning, and maybe you know the other old man, Mr Cummins, died a couple of days ago. But I'd been intending to visit you anyway.

'I understand Thomas had been coming more often recently.'

A beat. Two beats. Time passes.

'That's how it is with grandchildren. They control the narrative of the relationship, doling out visits and conversations like they're doing you a favour.'

I stop for a while, mind wandering back to my own grandparents, random conversation coming in fits and starts.

'I had a gran who demanded visits, and so I went every week. If you missed a week, you'd be quizzed. Where have you been? Her other grandchildren didn't visit as often, but at some stage I'd set the precedent for myself, and I was held to it. Didn't make me the favourite, it was just expected. Then there was my other grandmother. Never seemed to bother either way. She must've enjoyed seeing me just as much, but she never complained. So I visited less.

'And that's how these things go. You're young, and you don't realise it. Time passes and people die. Life goes on . . .'

I let the thought and the words drift away. I glance at Mrs Worrell, almost apologetically, it feels, for saying too much. She has not moved. I look beyond her, out of the window.

From the murk, a small rowing boat has appeared on the sea, approaching from the northern shore of the firth, a lone figure, his back turned to the beach, laboriously pulling the oars.

It hadn't been my intention, nor a tactic, to start talking about my own grandparents, yet the words had come. And from somewhere I think of the fact that Peterson's mother is dead, and that Mrs Worrell lost her daughter, which is unquestionably the most awful thing that can happen to any parent.

I wonder what other heartache Mrs Worrell has suffered to bring her to this position, where all she has is this painting of bloody infanticide, where communication with the world is so beyond the pale, she has psychologically shut herself off from it.

I'd been sceptical about her lack of a neurological condition. There's so much about the brain that's unknown and can't be known until a patient is dead and their brain has been examined. And when someone like Louise Worrell dies, who will take the time, and meet the expense, to dissect and study her brain?

Now that I'm here, however, the thought has vanished. There may have been no way to truly know, but I can feel it from her the longer I sit here. The woman has retreated from life, for reasons unknown, but it is through choice. There is no great revelation in this, except that it comes to me as I sit in Mrs Worrell's company.

Her arms are resting on the wooden arms of the chair, and now I rest my arm beside hers and slip my fingers softly into her old, frail hand. There is nothing for a moment, and then I can feel a slight return of pressure in response.

The room is quiet – no sound from outside, no voices from other rooms, no footfalls along the corridor, no sound from the other residents, even the murmur from the far corner swallowed by the silence – and for a time that will be all too brief, I lose myself with Louise Worrell, and feel the escape.

I stand alone in the corridor, next to a large, modern, family portrait. Mother, father, three sons, two dogs. It looks American.

I missed five calls while sitting with Mrs Worrell. Three from Sutherland, one from Cole, one from Hamilton.

I call Hamilton first, as his call was half an hour ago. The fact that he hasn't tried again within that half hour doesn't mean there's no urgency or importance in what he has to report; rather, Hamilton is not the type to pursue anyone who's looking for help. He knows I'll get back to him when I have the time.

He answers with the words, 'You have another murder on your hands.'

'Mr Cummins, I presume,' I say, straight down to business, quite used to our pathologist's disdain for small talk.

'Of course. He was suffocated.'

'Crap,' I mutter.

'A compress to his face, held over his nose and mouth. I assume there were no signs of a struggle at the scene of his death?'

'They initially assumed natural causes, so I can, in turn, only assume that there didn't look to be anything suspicious about it.'

'The police didn't record anything?'

'They were called, obviously, but by the time they got here, Cummins's room had been straightened out, a sheet pulled over his head. The director, Littlejohn, said there wasn't much straightening out to do in the first place.'

'You can trust her?'

'Not sure yet, but Cummins was found by a nurse and examined by the doctor, so that's up to three people who would've had to have been in on any wrongdoing. Was there much force applied?'

'No. If there had been a struggle, I doubt it would have been much of one. There's little sign of agitation about the face and mouth. Indeed, if I was told that this had been carried out with the victim's agreement, I wouldn't be surprised.'

'The handkerchief wasn't laced with anything?'

'No, not like Strachan.'

'Possible he was just in a deep sleep?'

'I don't believe so. This man was naturally docile, or else compliant.'

'And do you have a time for me?'

'Too early to be any more specific than previously reported, between the hours of nine and eleven on Sunday.'

'OK, thanks, Roger. Anything else to report from Strachan's death?'

'He's still dead,' says Hamilton, a finality to his tone, then he adds, 'I'll call if I find anything,' and hangs up before I can say goodbye.

I stand for a moment, the happy American family of five and two dogs at my shoulder – I can feel their presence – sorting out what needs to happen next.

So now we have two murders here at the home, there was the murder at the football and there was a murder in London. The timing of the murder in London and the murder of Cummins more or less ensures they had different killers. Not unless someone made an implausibly fast trip south after killing Cummins. And anyway, why should they be connected? Why should any of the murders be connected, apart from these tenuous links, barely holding the whole thing together?

Quick check of the time. Unsurprisingly, I spent too long sitting with Mrs Worrell. If Quinn had seen me, he wouldn't have been happy. Quinn is not the type to believe that sitting in silence is any way to conduct an investigation. Just as well he's not a detective.

Time to speak to the house doctor, and members of the nursing staff, and time also to let Littlejohn know how Cummins died.

There's something tough to like about Littlejohn that I can't quite put my finger on. Perhaps it's just because she's the face of this establishment, corporate care with a smile, where money comes first and the care comes second. Where people are clients and commodities and numbers and statistics and bottom lines and problems to be managed. Caring about residents, the lives they have lived and left behind to come here, won't be in Littlejohn's job description.

As I walk along the corridor on my way to the next interview, I can feel old Durin, those blind eyes on the chess set, and somehow also on my back, watching me as I go, haunting my every step.

20

We sit, both of us momentarily with our heads tipped slightly to the side, listening to the fiddle. Took a few seconds, but I realise finally that Lisbet Bauer, the fiddle player, is playing 'In the Bleak Midwinter'. The tune, invariably maudlin, is beautiful in her hands.

'There's no sign of Christmas,' I say, suddenly having the thought.

'How d'you mean?' asks Nurse Marc Caddow.

We're in a small office. A desk, two chairs, a filing cabinet, a telephone on the desk, a small plant on the filing cabinet, a Scottish Coasts calendar, and in the corner a tailor's dummy on a wooden frame, the dummy painted after the style of Alphonse Mucha, the Czech, with a couple of jackets hung around its shoulders.

'Out there, in the real world,' I say, and he smiles, 'there are mince pies in the shops, and Christmas trees everywhere and adverts on the TV, and signs in windows and "Merry Christmas Everybody" playing everywhere you go. It starts slowly in September, then as soon as Hallowe'en's out the way, boom! But here . . . there's nothing.'

'Orders from head office,' he says. 'They're very traditional. You can't do Christmas until December 1st, and then you're all in until the 26th, then phht, back to black, if you know what I mean. Same in all their establishments worldwide. I kind of approve.'

'Yeah, I guess, though I'd go for not starting until the 24th of December myself.'

Caddow laughs, and then silence comes again, and for another moment we listen to the fiddle.

'Mrs Bauer never got the memo,' I say.

'Mind of her own,' says Caddow, 'even if none of us exactly knows what it is.'

'OK, I'm just catching up here,' I say. 'You were on duty last night?'

'Got off at eleven. I do the rounds last thing, then I head home. That's my usual shift. Got woken up at, like five after six this morning, they asked me to come in.'

'Five after six? December 1st?'

He smiles, makes a small eye roll.

'Watch too much Yank TV. Used to drive my girlfriend nuts.'

'Who called you this morning?'

'Holly. Ms Littlejohn, sorry.'

'How'd she sound?'

He laughs, blurted out. 'Yeah, you know Holly. Kind of an automaton. I mean, she's like that normally, but this morning, you could tell ... she was trying even harder to keep it straight, you know? Like, automaton-plus. Automaton times a thousand.'

'Did you know Mr Strachan well?'

'Sure,' he says. 'Well as anyone, but that's not saying much.'

'Why?'

'Kept himself to himself. Did his daft wee puzzles, didn't really speak to people. You've got to love his taste in sculpture though, eh?' A moment while he pictures the wooden figure in Strachan's room, then he smiles and says, 'We're all being kind, right?'

'How d'you mean?'

Another smile.

'*Old Strachan, liked his number puzzles* ... Give us a break, eh? He spent all his time in his room with his naked wooden bird, art as he called it, pulling his pudding,' he says, making the quotation marks sign around the word art as he speaks.

'You know any reason why anyone would want to kill him?'

'Nah.'

'D'you know if he had any disagreements with anyone? Any even minor arguments?'

'You know, there's nothing, man. It's kind of weird, right? I've worked in these places before, and they're usually hotbeds of infighting. All these old buggers, full of resentments. And the daughter they hate, or the old dead friend they've held a grudge against for fifty years, they're not around, so they take it out on the guy across the hall. *He took my walking stick; that's my seat by the window; he stole some of my booze; look, I marked the bottle and there's a bit missing . . .* But here? You see very little of it.'

A moment.

'Maybe all the bitterness has been replaced by weirdness,' he adds, then laughs. 'Like, this place is kind of weird, right?'

'What'd you do last night?'

A moment, then he smiles.

'Right. Classic Feds. Where were you between the hours of whatever and whatever? Was he really disembowelled? I mean, really? That's what they're saying. That is some fucked-up shit, man.'

'Yes,' I say. 'Where were you between the hours of eleven last night and six this morning?'

His expressive face now shows respect that I am actually asking after his movements, then he says, 'Went home, had some toasted cheese, surfed the old net for a while, went to bed about one.'

'Anyone to vouch for you?'

He watches the American TV shows, so he knows the score.

'Nah,' he says. 'Not in a long time. Look, man, I was sat in front of my MacBook. Presumably the government was recording me the whole time through the camera, am I right? You can check that.'

He smiles. Sitting close to him in this small office I get the vague scent of disinfectant.

Ten minutes later. Same position, different nurse. Keira Williams. The aroma of disinfectant is much stronger in this one. She was the nurse who discovered Strachan's body. I wouldn't be surprised if the disinfectant comes from her bathing in it to try to rid herself of the horror.

'There'll be no one left by the end of this,' she says. A vacant stare, can't look at me, eyes vaguely directed at an indistinct spot on the carpet. Shock. Or affected shock. 'There's three people already pulled their parent out. Another couple looking into it, though the director might have talked them out of it. But what could she tell them? We don't know anything. Not really.'

She finally manages to lift her eyes to mine, searching, and says, 'Do we?'

'Do you look in every room in the middle of the night as part of your rounds, or did you just look in Mr Strachan's room because the door was ajar?'

'Ajar,' she says. 'That time of night, we'd never just barge in on them.'

'You hadn't heard anything prior to that? Seen anyone?'

'I answered these questions already,' she says. She swallows.

'Sorry, but I do need to go over it again. It's always possible that something might come back to you.'

'Well, no. I've been trying to think, maybe there was a sound or a thump or a creak or a something that I dismissed at the time, but . . .'

She lets the sentence go; her eyes drift away again.

'How well did you know Mr Strachan? He seems to have been a detached character.'

She swallows again, deep breath. Holding back the tears this time, she steels herself. Another deep breath, straightens her back, various bodily tics as she attempts to keep it together.

'I know what they thought, what the others thought, but I was fond of him. I brought him puzzle books sometimes. He did them so quickly, I couldn't keep up.'

She laughs at that, a laugh that almost ends in tears.

'We had a laugh sometimes. When he was in the mood.'

The words run out, she swallows, looks off to the side. I feel there's more, so I give her a moment. Around us the home sounds busy, voices and footsteps, the distant call of the fiddle weaving in and out it all.

'And now they all come,' she says, her voice ever more distant. 'Concerned relatives. Will my dad, my grandmother, my whoever be next?' A beat, a slow blinking of the eyelids. 'How many are thinking, I hope so . . .?'

The lowered eyes drop even more, until she's looking at her own hands, the fingers clasped in her lap.

21

The Dunes' car park is almost full, thanks to the presence of the police teams and the influx of all those concerned family members.

I'm taking the metaphorical equivalent of a cigarette break, standing next to Constable Leuven from Tain station, getting a breath of air. She's young, but then they're all young.

The cordon has been set up about fifty yards down the driveway, the press and curious public not permitted any closer. They all looked coolly at me as I exited the front door, the latest addition to the entertainment, not convinced I will have anything to add to the *grand guignol*.

There are several officers on duty, although none of them are, at this moment, particularly active. The search of this side of the grounds is complete for the day. And the day itself will not last long, the afternoon drawing to a very early close thanks to the low, claustrophobic cloud.

It's quiet, bar a solitary figure wearing a yellow sou'wester, pacing up and down pushing an old-fashioned, manual lawnmower along a narrow patch of lawn, the blades trundling ineffectively over the wet grass. There's something hypnotic in the repetitiveness of his movements, and Leuven and I stand and watch him for a while.

'You know this fellow's story?' I ask.

'That's Mr Laine,' says Leuven. 'One of the patients. Residents, sorry. Apparently he needs to cut the grass every day.'

'Any particular reason?'

'I haven't asked.'

Silence, but for the rotors churning over wet grass. A pause as Mr Laine gets to the end of the short row, then he turns and the noise resumes.

'People have things they need to do,' says Leuven. 'We all do. He's achieving no less than someone who spends all day scrolling, or playing a game, on their phone.'

'And it gets him out in the fresh air,' I say, words automatic and banal.

The rotor blades are set much too high, so that the grass is not being cut at all, springing back up behind Laine every step of the way.

The blades trundle. The watchers are silent, the police disengaged. In the distance, beyond the building, there is the suggestion of the sea, but the wind is low, the water becalmed. Where we stand, one can smell the sea, rather than hear it.

Laine stops for a moment before making his turn. Perhaps this is him stopping. He must stop at some point, although it need not be light-related. I can imagine him still cutting the grass at this time a month from now when it will be pitch dark.

He lifts his head and looks at us. He's not interested in the crowd beyond, nor in the rest of the police officers. Just Leuven and me. His eyes are dark, his face pale, his look as haunted as that of the crowd at our backs, and then he lowers his head, he turns the lawnmower, and once again, after an interval that seems much longer than the few seconds it must have been, he's pushing the old green machine over the slender strip of lawn.

My phone rings, snapping the moment. Leuven and I acknowledge the call, then I walk a few paces away from her, taking the phone from my pocket, idly staring at the house. The trundle of Laine's lawnmower.

'Inspector Dundee,' I say. 'What have you got?'

There's a pause, which I suddenly realise is down to me formally calling her Inspector, and so find myself saying, 'Croc, sorry.'

Her laugh is light and genuine.

'I've been doing some digging for you. It can get confusing. Thank God I've seen *The Big Short* and *The Wolf of Wall Street* so I know what I'm talking about.'

She laughs again, and I can't help but laugh with her.

'Anyhoo, I came across something here I thought you might be interested in. And, just before I tell you, I'm going to say that you'll find it fascinating, but I can't let you do anything with it yet.'

'You're telling me off the record?'

I can see her smiling down the phone.

'Yes, I'm telling you off the record.'

'Scout's honour,' I say.

'I found a very interesting transaction between a couple of LLCs in London.'

'Limited Liability Companies?'

'Yep. It's a standard money transfer ploy. An individual sets up a company, in this case Goldhawk Road Holdings, and another individual sets up another company, in this case Goldhawk Road Financial. These two companies don't noticeably do anything. The first, however, sues the second company for undisclosed reasons. Civil proceedings, all under cover of the court. They both engage a lawyer for an hour or two, and then Goldhawk Financial pays Goldhawk Holdings three million pounds in compensation. We never know what they're being compensated for.'

'They're not actually compensating them for anything . . .'

'Sometimes it's a way of making an illegal payment, and sometimes, as in this case, both companies were established by the representatives of the same umbrella organisation with the intent of moving illegal money into the mainstream.'

'Laundering.'

'Laundering,' she repeats.

There's a pause and I get the vaguest hint of her taking a bite of something. I picture Croc Dundee at her desk, in her ripped jeans, snapping off a square of dark chocolate, popping it in her mouth.

'How does this apply here?' I ask.

She takes a drink. I see the mug of tea in her hand.

'The parent company in this case is the same financial services business, a branch of a Russian bank.'

'There's a thing.'

'Yes it is. BK. The Bank of Kolymagrad. Which is, you will not be shocked to hear, the bank at which Natalia Kadyrova worked before she came to Scotland.'

'And Goldhawk Holdings?'

'They put that three million into George Bailey's, which funded part of their expansion programme.'

There's a pause in the conversation while I think this through. That the principal Russian investor in the enterprise was laundering money through London won't shock anyone. It's a matter of what we can do with this information, and how it impacts on our investigation.

I look around the unchanging scene. Leuven has wandered off to talk to one of her fellows. Laine's head is down, the blades of the lawnmower turn in the night.

'So, tell me about this being off the record,' I say.

'Look, this is liable to just be the tip of this particular iceberg. We have to tread pretty carefully in these waters. You start arresting Russians for spreading dirty money in the City, and London would be bankrupt by close of play.'

Funny.

Doesn't mean they shouldn't do it.

'So, it's way too early, and I mean, way, way too early for us to be taking this anywhere near a procurator or the CPS in London. And it could well be, when we get into the weeds, that they haven't actually done anything technically wrong.'

'Just another smooth move from the Dick-Booths,' I say, distractedly.

'I don't know who Dick Booth is,' she says matter-of-factly, 'but yes, it could be a smooth move from someone. There's a lot more water to pass beneath this particular investigative bridge before we can press a charge.'

'So I'm banned from asking Kadyrova about it?'

'I can't ban you from anything,' she says, 'but I'd ask that you didn't. And I'm sorry, but the Chief Constable put round a request for updates from everyone involved in the investigation, so I'm going to feed it back to her, and I'll be asking the same thing of Darnley. Everyone just needs to keep schtum for now.'

I don't immediately respond, taking another look around the static scene, the Edward Hopper that is the car park at the front of The Dunes.

This is the quagmire we allowed ourselves to fall into after the collapse of the Soviet Union, and it's just going to keep getting worse and worse until someone at the top of government has the balls to do something about it. And not pretend balls, not give-a-tough-speech balls, but actual, legislative balls.

'I am going to see Kadyrova again,' I say, 'but I won't mention the thing.'

'Cool with me,' she says, 'but maybe you should staff it through your chief. Get yourself some cover, in case the boss comes looking.'

'If I staff it through my chief, he'll err on the side of caution. He'll eat, sleep and shit caution, then he'll take caution away for a romantic weekend in the Cotswolds. I need to speak to Kadyrova about Westbrook and Singh, our two guys in London, and I can do that without mentioning the money trail.'

'Oakie doakie. I'd be super-grateful if you didn't.'

'We're good. But thanks for the heads-up, I appreciate it.'

'No bother. I'll let you know if I come across anything else that seems particularly relevant.'

We hang up, and my phone starts ringing again almost immediately. It's time to head back inside and kick off the next round of interviewing, and so I walk towards the front door as I answer Sutherland's call.

'How's it looking, Sergeant?'

'Sir,' he begins. 'We have a bunch of hits on the e-fit of Peterson's killer, but there was one in particular, sorry, several in particular, naming the same guy. So, we've got the warrant out for him, but he hasn't been brought in.'

'That's not gone to the press, has it?'

'Not yet, we didn't want him to run.'

'Good. Where are we looking?'

'Inverness. Known to the local police, bit of a thug, but a clean record nevertheless, which would explain why we didn't previously pick up face recognition.'

'That'd be a breakthrough. You've got a name?'

'Steven Priestly. Unemployed, but hadn't claimed benefit in two years. Got kicked off because he was making no effort to get a job.'

'Anything else?'

'That's us for the moment,' he says.

'OK, thanks, Iain. Feels like we're managing to get into it a little bit.'

'What about up there, sir?' he asks. 'Anything?'

'Just had a good chat with Croc Dundee, but we won't go there yet. Otherwise, a lot of nil returns. These people up here, the residents, they don't argue with each other. They've all come here to decline into comfortable human obsolescence. There may be the odd resentment floating around, and a lot of them are damned weird, but there's nothing that really grabs me.'

Past the constable on the door – I've forgotten his name – and back into the bright warmth of the entrance hall.

'People to speak to,' I say, by way of bringing the conversation to an end.

'I'll leave you to it,' says Sutherland. 'I'm sure you're blending in well, sir.'

A beat.

Somehow that line is a kick in the teeth of the conversation. If we were together, if there was a comedic exchange of expression, it would be nothing. If we were existing in our usual semi-comic state of well-being, it would be nothing. But we're both out of sorts, Sutherland's mood has been grim for a while, and there was a strain in his voice, as though trying to force a joke out of something that he maybe thought not entirely untrue.

'Sir,' he says, with a certain contrition.

'Sergeant.'

Phone back in my pocket, and off to find Littlejohn and Raven.

22

Late afternoon, sitting in the director's office. Littlejohn, Dr Raven and I. Two teas, one coffee. The room is too warm. The fiddle is playing again. I've yet to see the fiddle player.

'Lisbet always plays in her room,' says Littlejohn, 'always with the window open, regardless of the weather, regardless of the temperature. The seasons blow in the window and blow through her life, and she plays with the weather.'

She takes a sip of tea.

'I don't mean she plays Vivaldi's "Spring" in May, Prokofiev's "Troika" in December. Her playing . . . she transcends, her playing transcends the tune. She can make *The Nutcracker* sound like summer, "A Song of Summer" like the falling snow. She expresses herself through the music, happy, sad, wistful, desolate. And now her lament fills the halls.'

She finishes the sentence with a softly thrown, theatrical hand.

'And she's completely deaf,' says Dr Raven, who has been sitting in silence. Her voice is so detached she could be speaking in another room, part of another conversation.

'Yes,' says Littlejohn. 'Deaf since birth. The woman has, quite literally, never heard music in her life. One would think it extraordinary, but one sees so many remarkable things among these residents.'

The story of the remarkable Mrs Bauer hangs in the air for a while, a companion to the equally peculiar Mr Durin, the blind man who can see so much, as the sound of the fiddle weaves in and out the fabric of the evening.

'Aren't there residents who get annoyed by it?' I ask.

'If you're wondering if they're all drugged,' says Littlejohn, 'well, no, they're not. They are made docile by this place. The wealth of it, the number of staff per resident. We run after them, attend their every whim. We are paid to pander to them like they are toddlers about to erupt into a supermarket tantrum, although in most cases, they are quite happy.

'And yes, there were complaints about Lisbet's playing, particularly when she played in the middle of the night, so I ordered a mute for the fiddle. She didn't seem to mind. One of the staff puts the mute on the instrument before bedtime, and removes it in the morning.'

She looks at her watch as she speaks.

'We could hear her playing at six o'clock this morning,' I say.

'Yes, odd. Lisbet must have removed it. She must have known what was going on. You know, some of them . . . can feel things. Lisbet can feel things. She plays the mood of the house. Maybe that's why so few complain. Her music is the soundtrack of the day. We'll miss her when she's gone.'

'She's going somewhere?'

'Everyone dies,' she says, although her tone is vague, whimsical almost.

'What does that mean?'

'Just what it means, Inspector. We are in charge of a facility where people come to die.'

'You're not a hospice.'

'No, we're not. But still, we take care of the old. They come here and find peace. And they die.'

'But don't they usually go off and die in hospital, or in a hospice somewhere, looked after by—'

'Yes, of course,' she says, her voice losing its whimsy

beneath the weight of pedantic questioning. 'I just mean, our residents are old. They die, it's what happens. Most will not die on the facility, but we witness the fading away.'

'I'm still not entirely sure why you called the police after Mr Cummins's death.'

'Mr Cummins's son is a practical man,' says Littlejohn. 'He lives in Hong Kong, hasn't seen his father since the spring. The death was unexpected, of course, but he knew his father was happy here.'

A politician's answer, giving background rather than addressing the question.

'We officially declared Mr Cummins dead at eight-o-five in the morning,' says Dr Raven. The doctor finally seems to engage, either having been listening throughout, though she didn't appear to be, or sensing that the time has come for her to properly pay attention to the conversation.

Littlejohn glances at her. In the look I see a dislike that I'd only vaguely picked up on before. A second becomes two, then three, and it's all there. The women tolerate each other, but something has happened between them in the past, and now they get through the days, working around each other. Maybe it started with a decision on a particular resident, maybe a love affair that soured, maybe it was nothing specific. People rub each other up the wrong way all the time.

'He hadn't been ill, though,' I say.

'No,' says Raven. Her head is absolutely still. Dark hair cut in a younger woman's bob. 'I only ever saw Malcolm on his monthly check-up, and that was as recently as last week. His heart was fine, blood pressure, all other vital signs . . . all fine.'

'You didn't recognise a cause of death when you examined him?'

'It seemed he had passed away in the night. He was ninety-one, after all. I thought his heart must not have been as strong as we thought.'

'So, why did you call the police?'

Raven glances at Littlejohn. The look says that it was Littlejohn's decision, not hers, and so Littlejohn can explain it.

'We have a routine when one of the residents dies,' says Littlejohn, 'but on this occasion, since Mr Cummins had seemed sound physically, and the news was obviously going to be something of a shock to his son, I decided we should cover our backs.'

'And the police were not at all suspicious,' says Raven, tossing in a comment from the cheap seats.

'It was an unexplained death,' says Littlejohn, 'and it was better that we cover ourselves. The police certainly were curious that we made the call, and it was hardly high priority. But Mr Cummins's son is a serious man, and I wanted everything to be above board. Anyway, we are now where we are, and we know we were right to have called them in.'

'Did Mr Cummins have any enemies?'

'People do not have enemies in this place, Inspector, they really don't. This is . . . it is what you see.'

'Nothing is ever what you see,' I say, and am immediately embarrassed at my own glibness. Must've read that line in a nineteen-thirties crime novel.

She doesn't answer. The eyes turn back, but the look remains vacant.

'Are we done here?' she asks instead.

The line *we've not even started* is about to cross my lips, but stalls on the back of my annoyance at my previous pulp-fiction cliché.

'Not yet,' I say mundanely. 'Who was the last person to visit Mr Cummins?'

She holds the empty look. After a while she says, 'It's been so long. It must have been his son.'

*   *   *

On my way out, I stop by the sitting room, which waits for me in half-light. Dinnertime. The residents have all relocated to the dining room, or back to their rooms. The chessboard has been vacated, but the game remains in play. The chairs around the fireplace are empty. The seats by the window lie empty. Mrs Worrell has gone for the day, and now the Brueghel looks bleakly down from the wall, no one to impress or depress.

The windows are streaked with rainwater, and in the far distance the light of Tarbat Ness blinks methodically, dim through the mist and rain.

I walk over to look at the painting, although the details are not clear in this low light. I stand with my back to the room, casting a shadow on the edge of the Brueghel, thrown by the small table lamp in the far corner.

Death and art.

I think of sitting in the church, looking up at the vision of Saint Sebastian, and the Reverend Marcus sitting next to me, talking about the art of dying.

My thoughts do not dwell on the saint. Leia Marcus does not leave me so easily, however. Perhaps I can find a place for her, somewhere in among the limping depression and the nightmares and the long-deserted beach where I am stalked by guilt. A corner, where she can wait for my attention. Standing here, I struggle to even remember why it was I went to speak to her the other evening.

Peterson, of course. Peterson. The first death, quickly being consumed by all the others.

I try to focus on the painting. The drama of sixteenth-century infanticide that plays out on the wall, as it does in here every day. Blood in the snow, the anguish of the parents, the horror of so many dead children.

'You know for whom she tends the weeping fig.'

Blood freeze. I can feel it. Warm liquid turned to ice.

I compose myself. The woman in the far corner was here this afternoon, the words spoken over and over, and she is still here now. I must have missed her when I came in.

I turn.

The room stares emptily back at me. The seats by the window are empty. The room in half-light, starved of life.

She's not there.

I search the room for the memory of the sound, but there's nothing. There are no words to be plucked from the past, and now I don't know if I really heard it at all.

I don't turn back to the picture. The infanticide behind me, I walk from the room, along the corridor and back out into the dark, dank night.

23

When you work overseas with the security services, invariably your cover is the Foreign & Commonwealth Office. Chances are your office is at the embassy in the first place, and to anyone on the outside you're a diplomat, and you work in the political section. Only in jokes would you be termed a cultural attaché.

The cover is bland and dull, which is what it's supposed to be. And as part of that cover, you find yourself at cocktails and events, mingling with other diplomats and civilians, pretending to be someone you're not, pretending to care about domestic politics and economics, or perhaps genuinely caring about it, if you're invested, and good at what you do. And having a good cover *is* being good at what you do.

I'm reminded of it as I walk into the small ballroom at the new Hilton DoubleTree in Inverness. The feel of a diplomatic event. The hum of conversation, people standing around with drinks in their hands, waiting staff circulating with trays of canapés.

I lift a glass of orange juice from a tray, stand not far inside the door and survey the scene. At the far end there is a cellist playing. Rachmaninoff, I'd say. To her right, and also by the door, there are security guards. Two men in dark grey suits. Perhaps they're not armed, yet security is clearly what they are.

The room is full, though people are not tightly packed. Dress code is smart casual. I'm not out of place in my jacket and tie. I scan the crowd looking for anyone I recognise, picking off a few faces along the way. A couple of Inverness city councillors, the manager of Caley Thistle – perhaps they have a Russian in their squad at the moment – a banking executive I interviewed a year or two ago about a fraud case involving a car tyre repair start-up.

Chief Constable Darnley is here with her husband. I'd rather she wasn't. I don't recognise the two men to whom she's talking. Duty calls presumably.

The Russian Consulate in Edinburgh operates pop-up days around the country, taking their show on the road. Promoting Russian culture and business. Spreading the word through soft power, which is not, it must be said, their usual method. They're obviously looking to cover as many bases as possible in their quest for world domination. They will get their backsides handed to them by the Chinese regardless.

Natalia Kadyrova seems a little over-dressed for the occasion. Perhaps she didn't read the invitation properly, perhaps she's off somewhere else afterwards – although I'm not sure where that would be in Inverness – or perhaps she just likes the attention wearing a black dress requiring several feet of body-tape will bring.

I start to make my way through the throng. Largely people are speaking English, although I pass two couples conversing in Russian. I always struggled to speak it – was never anywhere near the quality required to use it effectively in the field – but I always did, and still do, understand it well. The Russian conversations I walk past are as bland as the English ones, the politics neutral and relaxed, the words about the weather and its effect on the national psyche.

Kadyrova sees me coming, looking past a man in a light grey suit, top shirt button undone, no tie. I wonder if she'll make me try to extract her, or will hide behind him, but instead she touches him on the arm as I approach, excuses herself and walks towards me.

Her dress is ankle length, black, split to her waist from the ankle up and split narrowly to the waist from the neck down, though it reveals nothing of her small breasts. Her long hair is down over her shoulders.

'Inspector,' she says, and she lifts her drink an inch or two in acknowledgement, then takes a sip. Vodka-tonic, I'd wager. 'You are back for more.'

She glances around, her eyes coming to rest on the security guard by the cellist, then she turns back with a smile.

'Perhaps my complaint did not reach you.'

'We both know we didn't harass you, so perhaps I can just ask you some more questions without there being any drama.'

'And in what capacity will you ask questions, Detective Inspector?' she says. 'Investigating officer, or former officer of MI6?'

Poker face, inch-perfect delivery.

Of course she knows who I used to work for. Why wouldn't she?

'What can you tell me about Alan Westbrook and Davinder Singh?'

She smiles at that, at me not getting into a stupid game.

'You look unhappy, Ben,' she says. 'Perhaps you should drink something stronger than orange juice.'

Ben. Goddamn, I hate this. This sport, the constraints of it. In my old life there'd be a level playing field, but that doesn't exist here. She's the Russian businesswoman investing in, and toying with, the Scottish economy, and I'm the public servant, answerable to Police Scotland and the media.

'What can you tell me about Alan Westbrook and Davinder Singh?'

She lifts her eyes momentarily, as though she's dealing with an incorrigible child, then takes another drink, lets the moisture sit on her lips for a moment, before licking them and smiling.

'Of course I know names,' she says, 'but I do not know people.'

'You never met them?'

'Why would I meet them?'

'You, and they, were the money behind George Bailey's.'

'I do not know people,' she repeats.

She holds my gaze for a moment, and then glances over my shoulder. Another second, she smiles at someone – or no one, I'm not looking to see – and then she turns back, with a look about her that says she's completely lost the thread of our conversation. *What was it again?*

'Tell me what you do know about them.'

She takes another drink, each one a tiny sip, each one to allow moisture to rest on her lips, and now she lightly touches the emerald pendant around her neck. Perfectly manicured nails, clear gloss.

'I don't know what you're doing with the rest of your evening, Miss Kadyrova, but you look like you've somewhere else to be. So, why don't you stop sipping vodka and obfuscating, and just tell me about Westbrook and Singh?'

The look of superiority, the look that says she's in complete command of the conversation, refuses to leave her face.

'It is gin,' she says. 'We are not all cliché.'

I give her a blank look.

'And after this,' she continues, 'I go home. Perhaps you'd like to come. We could make love. That's what we do, isn't it, Ben?'

That's what we do ... Spies like us.

'Westbrook and Singh.'

Another lifting of the eyes, before finally we come to it. It'd be so much easier if people didn't feel the need to play around the edges of a police interview until they deemed the time right to engage.

'I do not know them, Inspector,' she says, the fun physically ejected from her tone. 'This is digital age. Everything is online. Business, politics, war, sex. Everything that happens, happens by computer. Look at foolish Americans, they elect buffoonish moron because of Facebook. Teenagers don't have sex, they send videos, pictures. Flux in stock market is no longer caused by frantic, shouting men on floor, it is computers responding to small change in currency and stock value. When democracy dies, it will not die from invasion and war, it will die from within, crushed by social media.

'George Bailey was no different to any of these things. I was more involved because I was here, in town. I met this man, Peterson. The other two were names on screen.'

'You never even had a video conference?'

'You're not listening.'

'This was getting to be big business, and you—'

'It was not big business, Inspector. It was small business. Tiny business. I come to country with half billion dollars. I invest six hundred thousand in George Bailey. Loose change, that is all. George Bailey is nothing.'

'Two men involved with it have now been murdered,' I say, ignoring the six hundred thousand lie, 'the other has disappeared, and here you are, sipping gin and tonic, mingling with what stands for power and influence in Inverness.'

'There is no power and influence in Inverness.'

'Two people have been murdered,' I repeat, trying to stay on track.

'When money is involved, even these small amounts, people are always murdered. Your trouble, you British, is that you do not yet face your new reality. You are nothing. It is over for you. The British have gone the same way as the empires of old, the Mongol, the Byzantine, the Roman. They come and they go, and now you have gone.

'We have saying in Moscow. The British love to play Monopoly, now they are Old Kent Road.'

She holds a serious gaze for a moment, and then she smiles. I wonder if that line was written by the Kremlin, then passed around all their agents in the UK to be used to bring a conversation with the British establishment to an end. Because where do you go from there? How can you argue a case so perfectly and accurately put?

'Ben,' says the voice coming up behind, and I turn to see the Chief Constable approaching. She nods at Kadyrova, says, 'Natalia, I'm just going to take the inspector off for a moment, I'll have him back with you in a jiffy,' and indicates for me to follow.

Kadyrova and I share a final glance, she says, 'Of course,' and then she turns away and is manoeuvering herself into the midst of a group of five in an instant.

How often, I think, do we encounter rudeness and entitled arrogance among the public, and how often do we have the gratification of eventually locking that person up?

Often enough.

Darnley and I take a few steps away. The Chief Constable doesn't have a drink in her hand. People without drinks in their hands at cocktail parties always seem innately suspicious. She looks moderately unimpressed, rather than censorious, which is good, because I really don't want to stand here getting a row from the headmistress.

'Really, Ben?' she says.

I take a drink. Not hiding behind the glass, but have no intention of defending myself.

'The consul complained to my office yesterday. Next time they'll complain to Holyrood, or they'll take it to Westminster, and I really, really don't want some moronic government minister breathing down my neck.'

I nod an acceptance. It's not like I'd want any of that lot interfering in my day-to-day.

'What were you speaking to her about?'

'Her relationship with the partners in London.'

'And?'

'She barely knew they existed.'

'Really? George Bailey's is but a speck on her portfolio?'

'That's about the size of it.'

She looks away, back round the room, making sure not to look in Kadyrova's direction. I can see her pause as her eyes scan past the Russian consul, before she turns back to me.

'I read the update from FCU. You didn't mention any of that?'

'No.'

'OK, good. We'll leave it that way for the time being, please.'

'Yes.'

'And maybe ... look, Ben, I don't want to be *that* asshole chief, but please, run it by me if you're going to talk to her again.'

'Boss.'

'Thank you. Now, I know it's not late in the evening, but I'm ordering you not to go back to work. Go home and get some sleep. You look terrible.'

I wake in the night. Eyes wide open, staring at the usual spot on the ceiling, shadows thrown by the soft light outside that penetrates the curtains. I listen to the sound of the house and can hear nothing but a crushing, absolute silence.

The beach. That's what woke me.

I'm alone, but it feels like I shouldn't be. And tonight I don't want to be.

I was walking along the beach, the light unusually fiery, the sea rumbling noisily up onto the shore. It was all so different, a red glow in the sky. I didn't know where I was.

And then there was a woman sitting at a desk, but this time it wasn't Elizabeth. Elizabeth of the perpetual knife in the guts. It was Holly Littlejohn, her silver hair tinged red by the sky.

Her eyes never left me. I did not stop. I held her gaze for a few moments, felt her judgement, and kept on walking, the whole time her voice in my head. *They come here and find peace. And they die.* Words softly spoken.

Even though I walked on, and she fell away out of view, the words did not end. Over and over, round and round, the click and hiss of the stuck needle.

Candy sitting at a desk. Candy, the next in line. Candy, with bloodshot eyes, wearing a man's shirt. I recognised the shirt.

'Where's your shoes?' said Candy. Candy was not smiling.

I didn't know what that meant. As I walked, I looked down at my feet. I wasn't wearing any shoes. My socks were damp, my feet were cold.

I walked past Candy, and she was out of sight. I felt she was no longer on the beach, yet the words continued, mingling with the soft, sinister voice of Littlejohn.

'We could make love. That's what we do, isn't it, Ben?'

Lifted my head, looked left, looked right. Looked at the dunes, looked out to sea. The mist and the red glow and the blip of the lighthouse. I did not see her anywhere, but I recognised that voice. Kadyrova. She was a ghost.

Then another desk, as though I'd moved on, through one reality into another. Someone else was waiting.

'Your own personal, self-imposed purgatory,' said Euphrosyne James.

She was leaning forward on the desk. There was a trickle of blood from her lips, her lips were bared, her teeth clenched. The beautiful goddess, vengeful and bitter.

Her words wrapped around me. Wormed their way inside. She was not wrong. I knew it as soon as I heard it. This was why I was here. My own personal purgatory.

'I woke to a peculiar dream this morning.'

'At some point in the past.'

By the dunes. Two more people sitting at a desk. The desk was no bigger than the others, so that Croc Dundee and Moira Reynolds were sitting side by side, their arms pressed together.

I woke to a peculiar dream this morning.

I kept walking. Their voices, all the voices, continued behind me, an unavoidable word jumble. Sentences overlapping, bumping into each other, altering the meaning. The sky above blood red, an intermittent glow away to my right, the usual beam, less distinctive and swallowed up in this strange light. And then, time folding back in on itself, time getting lost in a swirl of voices, and then there was someone else. In the distance, to the right, where the sea touched the shore.

She was not sitting at a desk, instead standing at the water's edge. She was naked. Standing still, arms hanging by her sides, staring at the sand. Before I realised who it was, I recognised she was in the same pose as the wooden sculpture in Graham Strachan's room.

That's what this is about, I thought, but even as the thought formed, I didn't know what it meant.

Eventually I could see her face. I don't know how long I was walking towards her. She wasn't staring at the sand after all. She was staring at nothing, her expression lost and forlorn. She did not look at me as I approached, as I passed, as I walked on.

I did not stop. It felt too painful. Reverend Leia Marcus was consumed by pain and regret. She did not have the hope of Saint Sebastian. She seemed bereft. She did not speak.

I walked until she was out of sight, and I did not turn back. The sea continued to barely touch the shore, the wind seemed non-existent, the voices howled in my brain.

And then nothing. The voices stopped. The feeling I had, that Leia was still behind me, disappeared. I was alone in silence. The grey of the beach, the monochrome scene with which I was so familiar, had returned. Silent waves upon dull sand, the beach stretching away into the far, hazy distance. Out to sea a thick haar, monotonously picked out by the blink of the lighthouse beam.

The awfulness, the horrible sadness of this place, consumed me.

A few yards ahead of me there was a large plant, in its grey pot, on the sand where the sea touched the shore. A *Ficus benjamina*.

I walked forward and stood by the plant. Looking towards the dunes, I could see a final desk. There was a man sitting at it, his head in his hands, sobbing.

I wondered if this was my man from the office window two days ago, but when he looked up, and we held each other's gaze, I saw that I was looking at myself.

And that's where I was when I woke up. And the memory of it, a confusion of voices giving way to grief, has stayed with me. Lying in bed in the middle of the night, staring at the ceiling. Three fifteen.

All those women. Some of it makes sense, I think. They've all been in my head in the last few days.

This evening, for a moment discarding the decision to not speak again to the Reverend Marcus until this was all over, I drove past her house on the way back into Dingwall. The Old Manse. I don't know if I'd've rung the doorbell at ten fifty-one in the evening if there'd been a downstairs light on, but the only light was in a bedroom window. I was close, never-theless. I got as far as turning off the engine in the car.

This is what we do, I thought as I sat there. The ex-spy, the hero of the story. Get out there, boldly, and romantically claim the woman.

And then, from nowhere, to the rescue, came the thought that this is what the heroes of old would do, when the stories were all about the men, the woman just there as fodder. *Don't be a dick, Inspector*, I said quietly to the car, and another wave of depressive self-loathing came in, and I drove away.

And so I came home, and sleep took me to the beach, and now here I am, wide awake in the middle of the night, and sleep will not be returning.

I swing my legs over the edge of the bed, stare out at the orange glow of the night, and then get up and walk through to the kitchen. Glass of water, then retreat to my familiar position, at the sitting-room window, in the dark, looking out over town down to the firth.

I wish there was somewhere, unrelated to work, where I could force my thoughts to go. But I have nothing. I work, I come home, I sleep, I go back to work. There's nothing else, and no one else, outside. And so, as I stand here, and I forcibly eject the melancholy, and the haunting, tormented eroticism of all those women in the same dream, the only thing I have on which to focus is the case.

Perhaps it's the macabre curiosity of it, but the first thing that comes to mind as I try to focus is the painting. The Brueghel. Louise Worrell's bane. Although the painting is, of course, a reflection of her curse, rather than the curse itself.

I sat with her all that time, and didn't really ask her anything in the end. Not because I thought it of little value, but because the time wasn't right. So I didn't ask if Peterson ever spoke to her, or whether he just sat in her company, working on his phone. I didn't ask if she had any notion of why someone would want to kill him.

Littlejohn and most others would say there's no point in asking those questions anyway. But I don't think so. Not with that old lady. There's still something there, however deeply it may be buried. Perhaps I need to find out what it was that caused her to withdraw in the first place. In the morning, I'll go back and speak to the granddaughter. The Greek goddess.

Close my eyes. Feel no tiredness.

Pick a victim, any victim. Graham Strachan, for example. The disembowelled man, the most grotesque horror that most of the force up here will ever come into contact with. Yet, there are so many strands bursting outwards, like the tangled piping of an old exploded steam engine, that Strachan's grotesque death has become just another pipe, another buckled cylinder in the mix.

From strand to strand my mind plays on, over and over. When will Strachan's niece arrive? How soon do you drop everything to clear away the remnants of a life in which you played little part?

A louder gust of wind, the rain noisily drills against the window.

24

Standing in a kitchen beside double doors opening out onto a patio. There is what will be an ornate floral garden in spring and summer, several high fir trees behind and the flat top of Ben Wyvis beyond.

Euphrosyne James is standing with her back to me, pouring warm milk into two cups. The radio is playing, the space it leaves behind filled with the sound of coffee, the machine spitting and gurgling.

My nights, such as they are at the moment, leave a black hole inside me, a nagging, melancholic shadow. The day at least allows me to escape the visions, if not the quality of regret they leave behind.

Milk in the cup, James reaches over and clicks off the news. We've been standing in silence, listening to three minutes of the daily run through the gamut of horror. Dictators everywhere, war and the threat of war spreading across the Earth, hospitals bombed in Yemen, slaughter in Asia, famine caused by civil war in South Sudan, the aftermath of last week's terror attack in London, infighting in the government, EU shambles, one awful story bleeding inexorably into the next.

The coffee expels its final spit, James pours the two cups, turns and places them on the table, and then we sit down in sudden quiet.

'Thank you,' I say, lifting the cup and taking my first sip.

Delicious and smooth, tasting of caffeine-infused decadence.

'It's so utterly depressing,' says James. 'I mean, here you are investigating the most awful murder, God, a man was eviscerated, and there's not even space for it on the news. Too many other horror stories. Good grief, what a world.'

'You were listening to the London news. GMS had us on at the top. Not that that's a cause for celebration.'

'You just want to scream at the radio. Why do we do it? Why do we listen? Every damn story, you just want to scream. Why can't people just live their lives, let other people live their lives, why can't we put as much effort into talking to each other and looking after those who need it as we do into war and hate?'

She lets out an exasperated sigh.

'Good God, that's how bad it is. I sound like a hippy.'

I smile, but she wasn't speaking with any humour.

'And did you hear that man,' she continues, 'the one with that old cliché, the *indomitable spirit of the British* nonsense?'

'You don't think the British are indomitable?'

'Yes! Yes, of course we are. But isn't everyone? Don't people just get up, dust themselves off and get on with their lives? Why are we any better? We have our terrorist attacks every so often, but what about the people in Syria and Yemen and wherever, the ones being bombed *every day*? And as soon as there's a ceasefire, they're out on the street with their orange stalls and their small pop-up cafés, and their whatever. Aren't they indomitable?

'They make it sound like when there's a bomb on the Underground, there are chaps in bowler hats sitting at the end of the carriage, who turn down the corner of their newspaper, look slightly perturbed, say, "Good grief, not again, this is intolerable. Do get me another cup of tea, Abigail," then go back to reading the cricket. But when a bomb goes off, there's screaming and there's panic, and then, at some point, those who weren't there can say it won't change their lives. Some people fight, some run, some freak, some go back to help, but goddamit, people are like that all over the world, aren't they? Aren't they? Most people are good people, and at the same time, there will be . . . fuckers . . . everywhere.'

She makes another loud noise of exasperation.

'I'm terribly sorry, Inspector. I shall get back in my box.'

'That's OK. And, for what it's worth, I agree.'

'Thank you. That's more affirmation than I usually get in this house. Now, what can I do for you? I take it you haven't discovered who killed Thomas?'

'I wanted to ask you about your grandmother. And no, sorry, we're some way away from identifying your brother's killer.'

'Grandma? What's there to ask? She didn't talk to you, did she?'

'No.'

'I need to go up there. You think she's all right? This was a one-off, right? There won't be, I don't know, like a string of murders?'

'The murder in the news turns out to have been the second. There was a suffocation the night before. Dr Raven, who I assume you know, initially assumed it was a heart attack, though they had at least reported it to the police.'

'Oh my God! Holly never told us that.'

'She should have done by now.'

'Oh, God. I need to get up there today. Are they safe? I mean, have you any idea . . .?' she begins, words and questions tripping over each other in a rush to cross her lips.

'I'm sorry, we really can't say for sure. But there are a lot of officers there now, and we're speaking with the management company about them getting in extra security staff until we have this cleared up. Three residents have been removed, and I imagine they can expect a few more once the news of the first death gets out. I suspect the reason Ms

Littlejohn has yet to inform the families is because she wants confirmation of the extra security measures before letting everyone know. I expect that'll happen sometime this morning.'

'Dear God. Who was it, the first murder?'

'Mr Cummins,' I say, and she holds my gaze while she thinks about the name. She takes a drink of coffee, Cummins clearly not known to her.

'It's not like that place needs any more reason to be . . . weird. I realise the level of care is exceptional, and the location has its stark beauty, but the people. The people.'

She says it in quite an affected way, not so far removed from Brando's *horror* at the end of *Apocalypse Now*, then waves away the thought. I'm not going to pass comment, but it's not like I don't completely agree. *The people . . .*

'Wait,' she says. 'Why do you want to ask about Grandma? I mean . . . she doesn't *do* anything. You don't think she's in particular peril?'

No one says *peril* any more.

'No, I don't. I can't say I'm entirely sure why I'm here, but it's definitely not because she's in any more danger than anyone else. But your brother was murdered, and two people have been murdered at The Dunes. There's also been a murder, and a disappearance, in London, of two people with whom your brother did business.'

'I heard about that. Dear God.'

'The starting point to it all is Thomas's death, and the thing that links him to the events in London is George Bailey's. One of those deaths was a similar death to the murder of Graham Strachan that you heard about yesterday . . .'

'Unbelievable . . .'

'And the thing that links The Dunes to Thomas's murder, and that had us aiming to go up there before we knew anyone had died, is your grandmother. Now, I have absolutely no idea what that connection is. None. And maybe it's just a coincidence, and not a very big one at that, but . . . I sat with her for a while yesterday, and there's something in there, I can feel it. In her head. You know there is.'

'Yes. I haven't heard her speak in so long, but yes, I know she's not like the others.'

'The others?'

'There are a few up there, the ones who never speak, where nothing ever seems to penetrate the sad outer shell. Nothing in, nothing out. You must have seen them in the sitting room. Vegetables.'

She looks disgusted at herself for the use of the word.

'Sorry. But Grandma, I've never quite given up hope, even though it's been so long.'

'Tell me about her.'

She takes a deep breath through closed lips, blinks a couple of times, looks away to the trees and the hills. Whatever's coming, it's not easy to talk about, and I give her the time.

I look around the kitchen, my eyes falling on the dark red KitchenAid. A large one, with the six-point-nine-litre bowl. I bought one of those for Olivia once. She rarely used it, but she did sometimes sit in the kitchen and look at it the way Mrs Worrell looks at the Brueghel.

'She always had a tough time,' says James, having managed to put herself in that place where she can talk about a painful past without reliving it. 'I mentioned it before but . . . well, I didn't tell you the half of it. Grandpa was a complete bastard. You don't see it as a child, do you? He kept the worst of himself for when there was no one else around. He drank, he philandered, his moods swung all over the place. I expect now his personality would have a label, but really he was just a bastard. He shouted at her, he abused her, he treated her like shit and he made her life miserable.

'And then, one day, he killed himself. Maybe she knew it was coming, but no one else did.'

'How old were you?'

'Oh, it was three years ago. Obviously, by then, we all knew what he was like. We understood. We tried to get her to leave him, but she was shutting down. Had been for a long time. And then he was dead. Just like that.'

She snaps her fingers.

'So both your mother and your grandfather committed suicide?'

A moment, her eyes drop, her gaze drifts off into the distance.

'He abused your mother?'

Another beat. Here the police officer sticks the knife into the still-festering family wound.

'Is it relevant?'

'Probably not,' I say, 'although it's always hard to tell.'

'Yes. And yes, sexually abused her. From the age of seven.'

Now she holds my gaze, the look demanding to know if I've learned enough of her family secrets.

'Your mum told you that?'

'Yes, at some point in between Daddy leaving and Mummy killing herself. I don't remember exactly when.'

That's a lie, but not a terribly important one.

'Was it possible your grandmother killed her husband?'

Deep breath, lips pursed as she comes to terms with the fact the conversation is not yet over.

'No one could have blamed her, but she was out when it happened. She was sitting in Corner on The Square in Beauly. She used to go there most days, just to get away from him. She was their most regular customer, and she never spoke to anyone. They brought her a coffee and an Empire biscuit, and she took a long time eating and drinking, and then she'd go home.'

'And she was seen in there at the time your grandpa killed himself?'

'I don't know, Inspector. You can check the files if you like, I'm sure you'll be able to locate them. She was at the café, Grandpa put a gun in his mouth and blew the top of his head off.'

'Where'd he get the gun?'

'It was a handgun he'd had since the war. He'd never fired it, and I mean, he never even fired it in the war. It was German. He picked it up in France in 'forty-four. Hung on to it. Had three bullets. He was quite proud of that gun. Wouldn't be surprised if he used it to threaten Grandma. Then he used it to kill himself.'

'Was there any suggestion it was an accident?'

'You can check the file,' says James drily, 'but it's pretty hard to put a gun unintentionally in your mouth. I doubt he was using it as a toothpick.'

'What then?'

'How d'you mean?'

'What did your grandma do after the suicide?'

'She was dumbstruck. I mean, literally. She said a few words that day, but by the next day . . . she just sat there. She'd been shutting down, like I said, talking less and less, but then almost overnight, she turned into the woman you see now. Then there was insurance,' she says, now snapping her fingers in rapid succession, 'and the money, and Thomas arranging for her to stay at The Dunes, and the painting.'

'How did she even buy the painting?'

'She instructed the solicitor who'd arranged Grandpa's will. When we asked him about it, he said she came to the office, she talked him through it, explained what she wanted.

The painting was about to come to auction in London, here's my starting price, here's my limit. He didn't need to go to her limit, by the way. She asked him to discuss it with neither Thomas nor me, she signed the papers to authorise him, and then she stood up in his office, and said, and here I quote, "I've said enough." Then she left his office. She hasn't spoken since.

'I sometimes wonder ... it was obviously an active decision to shut down in the first place, but after three years sitting in a care home I doubt she could speak even if she wanted to. I think she might be gone.'

'What is it with the Brueghel? A particular favourite?'

'Gosh, really, nobody knew where that came from. Yes, she always liked art, insomuch as Grandpa allowed her to enjoy anything, but that painting? We couldn't begin to imagine. Thomas tried to get the sale annulled, typical of him, but there was nothing he could do. She hadn't been declared incompetent or unable to look after herself, she'd signed it all off. And now we are where we are, and she spends her days looking at the horrible thing.'

She makes a gesture of hopelessness.

'What d'you suppose she thinks about while she's looking at it?'

'I can only imagine she constructs narratives around the people in the picture. Creating the story of it. I like to think she has this incredible eight-hundred-page novel written in her head.'

She smiles for the first time since we sat down, then the smile slowly dies away.

'Wishful thinking, I'm afraid,' she continues. 'She just stares at it, lost in it perhaps, but other than that ... Who knows?'

'And this painting is going to the Kelvingrove, and neither you, nor Sondra Peterson, will ever see the benefit of it?'

'There you go, Inspector. Like I said yesterday, it is what it is. Perhaps you can speak to the merry widow and see what she thinks? Perhaps she's already made plans . . .'

She lifts her eyebrows at me, as though there might be some great and amusing conspiracy to be uncovered, and then glances past me, taking a pointed look at the clock, staring at it, until I play the game and follow her gaze.

'*Fugit inreparabile tempus*,' she says, 'so, if you don't mind . . .'

She couldn't just have said *tempus fugit*. I won't be the only person she is determined to hit over the head with her education.

There's a thought there, the basis of an idea that's swirling around, waiting for me to be sitting alone in a car, accompanied by a suitable silence and thinking time.

My phone rings, the volume set loud as ever, the tone shattering the short silence that was only going to end with me getting up from the table and leaving. Lift the phone, make no apology to James.

'Sergeant?'

'Got another body,' says Sutherland, an urgency in his voice.

I get up quickly and walk from the kitchen, waiting until I'm in the hall before speaking.

'At the home?'

'In a skip in Merkinch.'

I process that for a second, running through the options. The drama may seem to have many parts, but the number of players is small. Could be the artist Grey Davies, but I settle on the man identified from the e-fit in the murder of Peterson.

'Steven Priestly?' I say.

'Yep. Decapitated.'

'You found his head in a skip?'

I've walked quickly to the door, looking out of the side window over the stretch of bleak morning.

'Head and body both there, just not attached to one another.'

'K,' I say. Jesus. How many more? 'Goddamit. Ping me the post code, I'll be there in twenty.'

25

I step out of the car and close the door. Stop for a moment to look around, gauge the set-up and the police presence, the spectators and the passers-by. Rain is falling, and I've no rain jacket, no hood. There's an umbrella in the car, but I don't bother with it. Funny how an umbrella can be seen as a sign of weakness sometimes. Real men just get wet. Real men don't get the flu and die of stupidity. I think of that as I get out the car, but still don't take the umbrella.

The yellow skip, paint faded and chipped and defaced, is sitting at the side of the road in the middle of a small housing estate in Inverness.

There are five police cars and an ambulance. The area around the skip has been cordoned off, with a small crowd dotted around the perimeter. Others stand at windows. Curtains pulled back, two or three at some, one guy with a bottle of wine at his lips, another couple with cups of coffee.

I approach the break in the cordon where there are two officers, and show my ID. The officer glances at it, nods respectfully and takes a step back. Sutherland is standing with his back to the skip, waiting for my arrival, wearing a dark blue rain jacket, the hood pulled up, hands in pockets, face as downcast as the weather.

I stop in front of him, and then together we take another look around the scene.

It's a bleak, wet, miserable day. The sad faces of the crowd, police officers huddled against the rain and the cold, a few parked cars, a house boarded up nearby, an open piece of ground in the middle of the opposite side of the road, with the old frame of a swing, a gnarled, dilapidated fence, weeds growing all over through the cracks in the concrete.

'Maybe it's nice when the sun shines,' says Sutherland. 'When you can hear the gulls and smell the sea.'

'Very probably,' I say. 'Because people love gulls.'

He smiles grimly. I look past him, and my eyes meet those of a teenage boy standing at a window beside one of his friends. I hold his gaze for a moment, and then he raises his middle finger and puts a can of Monster to his mouth.

I turn away, looking at the skip.

'We're sure it's our guy?'

'Sure as we can be for the moment,' says Sutherland. 'We'll need to get the face and head as presentable as possible, then get Roddy in to see if he recognises him. The face is, at least, pretty much unscathed.'

'It's just the neck, eh?' I say, and Sutherland shows that grim smile again. 'Whose patch are we on?' I add, looking around.

Sutherland indicates a woman in a dark blue rain jacket, hood down, head soaking, who's standing in a doorway, interviewing another woman, who is under cover, her arms folded over her chest.

'DI Grant,' says Sutherland. 'She's cool with us being here, knows the score.'

'I'll speak to her in a minute.'

We walk over to the skip, acknowledging the officer standing next to it wearing a huge, plastic raincoat, and look down inside. The skip itself is empty, except for the naked body, the head and the two white-suited scenes of crime officers, kneeling down beside it.

'Gentlemen,' I say.

One of them continues about his business, while the other – Inspector Tomes, chief of forensic branch in Inverness, Lyle as we call him – looks up and smiles.

'Ben,' he says. 'Glad you could make it. You've usually got a head for this kind of thing.'

He holds my gaze for a moment, and then laughs as I look at the detached head, beside which he's currently kneeling.

Lyle turns back to the head, at the same time indicating the other officer, currently kneeling over the rest of the body.

'Constable Turing, one of our newbies. We're calling him Newbie for the moment, waiting to see if it sticks.'

Turing gives Lyle the kind of glance you might give a difficult teenager – we've all given Lyle that look, but he's likeable and good at his job, so no one ever complains about his teenage surfer-dude schtick – then he looks round briefly and we exchange a nod.

The introduction concluded, they continue their work, waiting for me to ask the questions, something I don't do straight away.

The situation is clear. The man was decapitated, his body dumped in a skip, the skip dumped in a housing estate. If this is the man who killed Thomas Peterson, then there are a few options. This is a completely separate act of violence, enacted on a man who lived in a violent world; someone took their revenge; or someone is covering their tracks.

I turn away, looking over the small crowd. No press. There are two people holding their phones in our direction. They'll likely be broadcasting on Facebook Live, and there'll be someone in a newspaper office in Inverness or Glasgow watching the feed, writing up a report that'll be padded out with quotes garnered as much from social media as they will be from witnesses or from the police. Chief Constable Darnley's words will be juxtaposed, and indeed diminished, by being placed alongside the trivialities of Twitter.

'The skip just got dumped here overnight?' I say to Sutherland, dragging myself back.

'The guy in the house over there saw it being delivered at three in the morning. He was playing *Battlefield*, heard it getting unloaded, looked out the window.'

'He saw the people who left it?'

'Just the truck. Didn't notice who was driving, didn't notice what kind of truck it was, didn't get a number plate.'

'I'll have a word with him. So, we don't know if the body was dumped in the skip later, or whether, as would seem more likely, it was already in the skip when it was delivered?'

'Correct,' says Sutherland, 'but I think we should assume the latter.'

I look back down, Lyle and Turing with their heads bent to the task in hand; Lyle examining the severed neck, Turing running a gloved hand across the bare abdomen. Looking straight down inside, I notice the knife, placed up against the side of the skip, not far from Lyle's foot, streaked dark red and sitting in a small pool of rain-washed blood.

'You've confirmed that's the murder weapon?' I ask.

Lyle glances over his shoulder at the knife.

'We'll need to get it back to the lab,' he says, 'but it looks like it. I mean, a possible set-up aside, it's obviously the murder weapon. Just depends if there's any reason to plant a false lead. The guy's been dead a while. At least twelve hours. You'll need the doc to give you more precise timing. As you can see, the knife's a decent size. Brutal bit of kit, really. I'd say he was stabbed in the throat, that killed him, then they'd have had to saw through the neck.'

'Knife's sharp AF,' says Turing, without turning.

Lyle nods. A pause, as though he's going to add something of note, then he repeats, 'Sharp.'

'So, somewhere there's going to be a lot of this man's blood?'

'Aye,' says Lyle. 'Coupla litres at least.'

'But not in the skip?'

'No, and it hasn't dripped anywhere, so he'd been dead a while before his body was tipped in.' He looks at the knife, thinks about it, then adds, 'The knife dripped a little. Maybe they dropped that in first, then . . . I don't know yet.'

'Anything yet to help identify where he was killed?'

'Nope,' they answer in unison.

'Someone's been to his house?' I ask, turning to Sutherland.

'One of the locals had been around looking for him, based on the e-fit, but they hadn't effected entry.'

I look back down at the corpse. He'd been in his mid-twenties, regular build, good muscle tone, no extraneous fat on his body.

'About eleven stones, you reckon?'

Lyle looks over at the body, Turing looks over at the head, back to the body, then they say, 'Eleven and a half,' at the same time.

'It's likely to have taken a couple of people to lift him in here,' I say, more to myself than any of the others.

'Yep,' says Lyle.

'Possibly,' says Sutherland.

I study the corpse for a while longer, watching the men at work. The slow processes, the painstaking work, funded from the public purse that the public never sees. Work, nevertheless, that needs to be completed, and if the slightest mistake is made a defence lawyer will wring that mistake dry.

'You'll get the report to us soon as you can?' I say.

'Yeah, we'll give you a heads-up,' says Lyle. Turing snorts.

Rolling my eyes, I turn away, Sutherland falling in beside me.

'Could've been worse,' he says, without much trace of humour. 'Think of the gags he could've made if the victim had had a penile-ectomy.'

'Penectomy,' I say.

'Really?'

'Yes.'

'That's the word?'

'Yes.'

'Nice. I'll start using that in conversation.'

I give him a glance, and off we go, through the rain and misery, to speak to Detective Inspector Grant.

26

We've come to Priestly's apartment on the hill above Inverness. A new building; he was living on the top floor – the fourth – with floor-to-ceiling windows in the sitting room and bedroom, and a view looking out over the city and the Moray Firth, Ben Wyvis in the distance beyond.

We stand together, staring out at this bleak day, as the lights of the city get brighter by the minute, the afternoon turning to premature evening. There is, naturally, no sign of Ben Wyvis, we can just be fairly certain that it's still there.

The room behind us has been furnished with Scandinavian simplicity and style. Clean lines, pale fabrics, white walls hung with square images of modern art, pastel colours in regulated formation. There is also a sixty-inch television on the wall, opposite a white leather reclining armchair.

'You want to talk about it?' I say, the first words either of us has spoken in a couple of minutes.

Hesitation, then Sutherland inevitably says, 'Talk about what?'

'There's something up, Sergeant. I'm just asking.'

I can feel him standing next to me. His agitation.

'You think it's affecting my performance?'

'No.'

A beat. I don't want to say that I'm asking as a friend. He knows that already. His implication that I might be asking because of work is just an avoidance mechanism.

'Pots and kettles, sir,' he says, an edge having crept into his voice.

That's a tough one to argue, and that's the conversation brought to an end. I don't blame him. If Quinn were to sit me down and try to get me talking about my own dark internal monologue, I wouldn't give him an inch. So, I give Sutherland another few moments, but it's apparent that the silence will just linger uncomfortably until I choose to break it, and then I turn away from the window and look back over the apartment.

'We need to get hold of this guy's bank records,' I say.

Sutherland turns back round with me, his agitation not entirely leaving with the change of subject. We both look at the desk at the back of the room. There's a cord for a computer, and a mouse, but the desk is empty.

'You suppose someone got here before we did?' he says.

'Possibly,' I say. 'Or Priestly might just have taken it with him. Gloves on, let's have a look around.'

My attempt at getting inside Sutherland's head officially abandoned, he pulls a pair of thin latex gloves from his pocket, slips them on and goes to the desk, while I do the same and move into the bedroom.

The apartment is well appointed, expensively and neatly furnished, but it is small. A sitting room, an open-plan kitchen off, a bedroom, a bathroom. Perfect for the single, unemployed young man with a lot of money.

There's a giant bed. What is the name of the size above super king? This bed is enormous. I walk over to the cabinet on the side of the bed that Priestly obviously slept on. There's a near-empty glass of water, a stylish white lamp, a copy of *The Fellowship of the Ring*, which I lift and thumb through, noting that it's well read, possibly by several different people. The edition is from 1973. I'd guess the book has been in Priestly's family all this time, rather than that he needed to buy a second-hand copy for reasons of penury.

Top drawer of two in the bedside cabinet: a gold ring; a

leather bracelet that looks unworn; a newer print, not so well read, of *The Two Towers*; a half-used bottle of Durex lube; an unopened packet of Durex Thin Feel Condoms; a black Moleskine notebook; a generic football medal, dated 2014; his passport.

A quick look through the passport. No stamps, although that's not so unusual any more, and especially as the passport itself is dated six months ago. Open the notebook, hoping it might yield something extra, but am quickly disappointed. Completely blank.

The majority of these Moleskine notebooks, out there in the wild, will still be blank. Lovely gift, rarely used, like the latest kitchen gadget or a twelve-month gym membership.

On to the drawer beneath. It's stacked almost to the top with pornography. Stare down at it for a moment, contemplate lifting them out, choose instead to have a quick leaf through, and then close the drawer. The SOCOs will be round later, and they can have the pleasure of looking through the drawer, magazine by magazine.

Straighten up, walk to the window and take another look across the city. Here we are again, infringing on someone else's patch. Nevertheless, we have Darnley on our side, as always, which makes it easier. The thought of it, of working with another area, reminds me that I really need to get in touch with the Met. With them being the big city people, and us the detached northerners, it's hardly out of the question that they would make a discovery or breakthrough and neglect to pass it on.

There's a chest of drawers on the other side of the bed, doubling as a bedside table, a built-in wardrobe with mirrored doors, a doorway through to the bathroom and another large television on the wall opposite the bed. Propped against the wall, to the side of the television, is an acoustic guitar, the fretboard gathering dust.

Sutherland walks into the room as I'm opening the top drawer of the chest of drawers.

'They've been in, haven't they?' he says.

I turn away from the small right-hand drawer at the top, packed full of Calvin Klein and Hugo Boss skin-tight trunks.

'Pretty clean,' I say. 'They've left his passport, but only because it doesn't tell us anything.'

'There's nothing,' he says. 'Sure, we get little tidbits of the guy's life. He liked REM and Fall Out Boy, he played football, he . . .' he looks around the room, 'I don't know, played the guitar . . .'

'Not very often. He did like his porn, though.'

'He was twenty-five and single,' says Sutherland drily. 'But the nuts and bolts of his life. It's gone.'

'Likely there'll be no prints,' I say, 'but we still need to check. You see the CCTV on the way into the building?'

'Yep,' says Sutherland. 'It's one thing clearing out a guy's apartment, it's another altogether hacking a system and erasing memory.'

'Hmm. That might tell us something.'

'If he was being paid by the Russians, or some other big-time player, then they'd have the tech people to get to the CCTV.'

'Let's find out what we can about the guy's life,' I say, feeling the fire begin to burn in a way that's been lacking today. Maybe it's the mention of the damned Russians. 'Perhaps we can get somewhere in this investigation through the back door. Can you put the call through to make sure the SOCOs get up here, then check out the CCTV?'

'I'm on it,' says Sutherland. 'I'll finish up here first, just in case, then I'll get hold of building management. I'll look at what they've got, as far back as they go, see how often he went in and out, who he was with.'

'Thanks,' I say. 'I'll head down to speak to the locals, and give you a shout when I'm done.'

'K.'

And with that, back out the door and quickly down the stairs of the apartment block, large windows all the way down the stairwell, the last of the afternoon disappearing as I go.

Waiting in a small office for DI Grant, looking at my phone, staring at an image of Brueghel's *Massacre of the Innocents*. It's not precisely the same as the one with which Louise Worrell spends her days, but I wasn't able to find that exact one. Perhaps there isn't one on the Internet to be found.

Looking at the detail, the parents protecting children, the massed ranks of German mercenaries, the guards, the urinating soldier, it feels like one of those random, off-the-cuff things you find yourself doing as a police officer. Quite probably it has no relevance whatsoever. This case could have nothing to do with Louise Worrell, in which case it certainly has nothing to do with Brueghel. Or possibly, somewhere in this mass of detail, there is a clue.

The door opens behind me. I click off the phone and slip it into my pocket.

'Inspector,' says Grant, a woman not much younger than me, ginger hair clipped short, not so far from a buzzcut. 'Sorry to keep you.'

'Plenty to keep me busy. What can you tell me about Priestly?'

She hands over a thin file, a few pages in a folder.

'I printed it off. Thought you might be old school, like me.'

'Definitely old school,' I say, smiling.

'There's not much, but you're right, he is . . . he *was* a curious case. Everything here dates from a couple of years ago, and earlier. Petty little thug, never going to be anything, or go anywhere. Suspected in a couple of break-ins, nothing ever came to court. Five arrests for assault, never charged. Always on the cusp, never quite made the cut. Or maybe he threatened people into silence. Either way, slipped through the net, I'd say. And then he went quiet. Thought maybe he'd just upped and left, gone somewhere else. Didn't recognise him at first from the e-fit. I see that was a nice apartment he ended up in.'

'Yes,' I say. 'Classic tale of a small-time hood suddenly getting rich.'

'I'd say he got taken onto a payroll, and one with deep pockets.'

'There's nothing in there to indicate who that might've been?'

'Nothing jumps off the page. Although, to be fair, we are snowed, so . . .'

'All right, thanks, Inspector. Anything else?'

'It's all in there. We'll do what we can, usual procedures, and we'll keep in touch.'

'Yep, thanks. Same here.'

And with that I'm gone, already opening up the file and quickly looking through it as I walk along the corridor, down the stairs and out the building.

27

'Seriously?'

I can hear Hamilton's disdain down the line.

'I have a fourteen-year-old boy coming in to possibly identify the man who killed his stepfather,' I say, 'and I'd really rather not present him with a head on a plate. It's not an episode of *Game of Thrones*.'

'Seems not dissimilar from the way you're going this week,' comes the response, with an added tone of reproach, as though I might be personally responsible for the disembowelling and decapitation.

'Nevertheless,' I say, as ever taking a certain bleak enjoyment in Hamilton's disdain, 'the boy's mother is chippy enough as it is, and I don't want her suing the police for traumatising her son. So, like I was saying, here's what I want you to do. Place the head, supported, as if it were lying back. Put the body in position, as though the two were still attached, and then cover the brutal slit in the neck, so that the boy will just see the face.'

'Is that all?'

'Come on, Roger, really?'

'You sure you don't want me to sew the head back on? Then when you come over, we could blast the body with electricity and see if we could get him to come back to life. You could ask him questions.'

'Are you finished?'

'I think so.'

'Thank you,' I say. 'See you in twenty minutes.'

Roddy Peterson has an air of excited tension. He looks scared and nervous, yet in a way I know that if I said he didn't have to be here, he'd want to stay. He wants to see the body, just as much as he's scared to look at it.

His mother stands next to him, holding his hand. He absolutely doesn't need his hand held, I'm sure of that, but Sondra Peterson needs to play her part. The hand-holding is about her, not him.

Hamilton is standing by the body, entirely detached. He doesn't do the people part of the job, always leaving the conversation to the accompanying officer.

'You're ready?' I ask.

Sondra Peterson looks at her son as though he were five and about to go to the dentist.

'Sure,' he says.

He lifts his eyes to Hamilton, who does not engage him, then the doctor lowers the sheet from the face.

There is a second sheet, which is folded up just beneath the chin. There is no sign of the fatal laceration around the neck. The face is composed, the eyes and mouth closed, the hair combed. Steven Priestly could be sleeping.

I watch the boy, half an eye on the mum. Straight away I can see the disappointment in his face. He's built up an image of what he was going to see, the horror of the grotesque decapitated head, and it isn't there.

'Yeah, that's him,' he says softly.

'You're sure?' I say.

'Yes, sir,' he says, and his mother gives me a quick look. The one to say she herself is never afforded such respect.

'Had you ever seen this man before he attacked your stepdad?'

'No.'

'And not inside the ground?'

'No. Wasn't looking at anyone, though.'

'OK, thank you, Roddy. You've been very brave. What about you, Mrs Peterson? Had you ever seen this man before?'

The brow crinkles, furrows, the eyes narrow in curiosity.

'What d'you mean?'

'Just like I said. It's not an unreasonable question. Did you know your husband's killer?'

'No,' she says quickly. 'I mean, what are you implying?'

'I'm not implying anything.'

Peterson's tone and the automatic suspicion needn't necessarily mean anything. There isn't a single police officer not used to it.

'No, I've never seen that man before in my life.'

'Very well,' I say, then with a glance from me, Hamilton pulls the sheet back over the head of the corpse.

They watch with solemnity as the sheet is drawn up, and then Peterson turns harshly to me. Again, this whole thing is my fault.

'We can go now?'

I look at the boy, who's clearly embarrassed by his mother, then I nod and lead them to the door. There's an officer waiting outside to take them through the building, Peterson turning away without another glance. Roddy gives me a look that I can't quite fathom. Apologising for his mother, more than likely.

Door closed behind them, I go back into the mortuary. Hamilton is by the body, and already the head and torso have been re-separated, the sheets removed. The head is now resting, the right way up, on the neck, the body laid out before it.

'That was quick,' I say. 'How long was I standing out there for?'

'You want to talk about work now that your little charade is over?' he says, folding up the larger sheet and placing it on a table behind.

'Would you have preferred to put the head on a pedestal?'

Nothing for a moment, and then Hamilton says, 'She was lying.'

I stare at the decapitated head, sitting there like a prop from a movie, and as ever, as I have for twenty years, feel completely detached from the horror of it.

'Yes,' I say, 'that was how it sounded. Can't decide, though, if she just has this awful manner about her.'

'Or whether she's lying,' says Hamilton. 'Because she's lying. But look, that's your business, and it's not like I want you telling me how to dissect a corpse.'

He looks up, expression utterly humourless.

'D'you have anything else to tell me about Mr Priestly?' I ask.

'I can confirm that the knife recovered at the scene was the one used to decapitate him. Solid, sharp and serrated enough to saw through bone. He was stabbed in the back of the neck. Hard to say whether that killed him straight off the bat, or whether he was paralysed for a few seconds before his throat was slit—'

'Lyle thought stabbed in the throat first.'

'That's why he does what he does, and I do this,' he replies, matter-of-factly. 'It's a strong knife. Back of the neck,' and he makes a stabbing motion, 'then the knife was inserted in the throat, pulled round, and then using the serrated edge, the neck was sawn clean off the body.'

'There would have been a large loss of blood, presumably.'

'Yes, Inspector, there would.'

'We have no idea where that happened.'

'Not my concern. He'd been drinking, but possibly not to the point of inebriation, there was some cocaine in his blood stream, but from at least twelve hours before he died, and he had, as is always the case with these people, had sex in the few hours prior to his death. He'd also eaten lobster, caviar, monkfish, tuna and salmon. The fish, but obviously not the shellfish, had been consumed raw.'

'Sushi?'

'That would be my assumption.'

'So there was rice?'

'No rice.'

'Sashimi then.'

'Presumably.'

'You suppose he'd been at a restaurant?'

'Hard to say. You can get sushi in a plastic box from Tesco for four ninety-nine. Half price if it's ready to walk to the food recycling on its own.'

'Less likely to get sashimi like that, though. OK, that might be an in.'

'I don't think we need feel sorry for him,' says Hamilton. 'Drugs, alcohol, sushi and sex, the guy went out with a bang.'

I look up, amused, but he spoke humourlessly.

'Anything else?' I ask.

He pauses, then reluctantly says, 'Yes, yes. We got the details of the DNA from the pubic hair retrieved from the underwear of the first victim. Seems so long ago, in murder terms . . .'

'And?'

'It was human.'

'Really?'

'We have DNA, Inspector. As with all such data, we need something to check it against. You have anything for me?'

The investigation has become so wide-ranging, that the matter of Peterson's sexual partner has been overtaken, and so I answer with an almost dismissive hand.

'Don't suppose you could run it to see if it has Slavic roots?'

'Sure,' he says, 'I'll get the answer to you two months on Saturday.'

'I think we know which way that strand of the investigation is going anyway.'

'If I find anything else, now that I can get on with the job, I'll let you know.

'OK, thanks, Roger.'

Hamilton grudgingly nods, then makes a small gesture to indicate the door, and I turn away.

Door closed, and standing outside the mortuary, the corridor empty in each direction, I stop, looking at the time. Contemplating lifting my phone to call Sutherland, when it rings.

'Sergeant,' I say, as I start walking towards the exit.

'You're going to be shocked.'

'The CCTV at Priestly's apartment has been wiped?'

'Yep. They usually keep a month's worth, with the day from thirty days ago being wiped at midnight every night. Inexplicably, they said, everything had been wiped up until last night at midnight.'

'It's a digital system?'

'Yes.'

'Are they looking into what happened?'

'Said they were, but I'll get Tech onto it. We can get a warrant, get inside their system.'

'Yep, please. And I've got something else for you. For us. Maybe we can start on it tonight, but it might take a while. It involves raw fish.'

'Of course it does,' says Sutherland.

'Meet me back at the office.'

'Boss.'

We hang up, then I walk out the front door of the building, into the dark of early evening, cars passing by, headlights picking out the rain.

28

Standing with Sutherland in Room 2, staring at the morass on the whiteboards. A man beaten to death at the football. His business partner disembowelled. The business partner's co-worker in flight, possibly dead. A care home resident suffocated. Another resident disembowelled. The murderer of the first victim decapitated. Russian financing, and laundered money. A bizarre collective inhabiting a care home: an old woman staring at a sixteenth-century infanticide painting, a blind man playing chess, a deaf woman haunting the corridors through her fiddle. Barely a motive taken off the table, just one vampire short of the full house.

I leave the expletive in my head.

'Isn't it possible that he just bought some fish, cut it up and ate it raw at home?' says Sutherland.

'Sure,' I say, 'but the chances of most twenty-five-year-old men doing that are slim, then when we factor in who this guy was, and what we know about him, I'm prepared to make the guess that he let someone else prepare the raw fish. There are only a couple in Inverness?'

'Yes, two, and another couple of fusion places. Then there's one in Aviemore, and another in Golspie.'

'You can buy sushi in Golspie?'

He holds up his phone.

'Says here. Asian fusion.'

'Hmm. I'll be going back up to The Dunes in the morning, I'll dive up to Golspie when I'm there.'

'Right. I'll get round the Inverness ones in the morning. If I don't get anywhere, I'll get his picture down to Aviemore, and after that, we'll spread it far and wide.'

'Good.'

I find myself stretching, look at the clock above the door.

'Think it might be time to call it a day. Come on, we can reassemble in the morning.'

'Like the Avengers.'

It's a Sutherland type of thing to say, frivolous and off-point, an expression of the juxtaposition between him being a strong and intelligent officer, and the child that still lives inside. This evening, however, in keeping with how he's been the last couple of days, the line is delivered with none of his usual facetiousness, as though there's someone else inside him, playing the part of Sutherland, saying the right things, just unaware of how they're supposed to be delivered.

If I hadn't tried and failed to get him to talk earlier, then this would likely be the moment to do it. With due reference to that previous exchange, however, I say, 'Yes, Sergeant, exactly like the Avengers,' and move to the door.

Lights off, back into the open-plan, leaving the door open on the wall of tragedy, watched over by the lonely ficus. The office is almost emptied out for the evening, Constables Cole and Rae the only officers. I get the sense of hesitation from Sutherland beside me, and then he walks positively ahead to his desk, and sits down at his monitor.

Cole glances over at us, and then goes back about her business. The little drama between them, whatever it is, continues. This, presumably, is what eats at Sutherland, and I can understand why he doesn't want to talk about it. I, for my part, for my own reasons, don't really want to hear about him and Constable Cole.

I sit down at my computer, shift the mouse, the monitor springs to life and I log in. Looking at your e-mails, when you haven't done it in a few hours, isn't really the same as calling it a day.

'You should get home,' I say across the desk, aware that Sutherland will know I'm not about to leave, and that he likely doesn't have too much to go home to either.

'I'll just run through these,' he says.

And so we sit, on the verge of leaving, like so many others in the world, going nowhere.

Ten thirty-one. Sitting at the table, late-dinner plate pushed to the side. Oven-baked fish in batter, chips, sugar snap peas. Lousy thing to be eating at this time of night, but then, most things are. I'll elect to count the two glasses of wine as fruit.

Table lamps on, music playing low – Dylan this evening, because there's no one here to stop me – ongoing second glass of wine at my right hand, the slim folder on Steven Priestly on the table waiting to be reread.

There's little of the night to be seen outside. Dark and grim, rain on the window, the light of the table lamps reflected back.

My phone – ever present on the table, waiting to deliver news good and bad – starts ringing, and I recognise the number as being The Dunes. I know before answering that it'll be the director, Holly Littlejohn.

Fisher has been up there today, and had nothing to report. A day without advance in the case, although perhaps we can take something, some little thing, from the fact that there has been no third murder at the home yet reported.

'It's not too late?' says Littlejohn, when I answer.

The line is fine, but her voice sounds as though it's in another world. For a moment I wonder if she's been drinking, but that's not it.

'I'm still reading notes on the case,' I say. 'It's fine.'

'Your officers didn't find anything new today,' she says, more a statement of fact than a question.

The obvious thought is that she's looking to find out what progress we've made, ferreting for information, perhaps so she knows where she has to construct her walls of defence. Yet, that doesn't feel like it. There's a deeper, richer quality in her voice. She is alone. Perhaps getting little support from head office, a solitary figure with no one to talk to, no one at home.

I don't know there's no one at home, but I got the feeling, that's all.

'No rogue fingerprints,' I say, deciding that there's nothing, in any case, I could tell her that I shouldn't, 'no overheard conversations, no unexpected murder weapons, no revelations . . .'

'No book of matches with a nightclub logo?'

'No,' I say, kind of smiling down the phone. 'We have a nil return, so far, which can be useful sometimes, but needs to be cast against another positive, and that's something we don't yet have. How are things looking up there?'

'Your officers are almost all gone . . .'

'Yes, there should just be two left. You have your security staff in place now, though?'

I know they do. The way of the world; the negotiation between what the police should pay, and what private firms should pay. Given that, in this case, the private firm is a large, US-based healthcare conglomerate, we were pretty insistent on them bringing in the staff.

'Head office authorised a team of eight contract security staff, and they've set up a temporary surveillance system and an ops room.' She pauses, but I don't fill the gap, as I can tell she has something else to add. 'That job is itself contracted out to a firm called Warranted Safety. I presume you know them?'

'I know the name,' I say.

I know too much about private security firms, but I doubt any of that will come into play here. This isn't the kind of operation where we'd have to worry about Warranted Safety.

'These people brought the works,' she says. 'It really isn't in keeping with the aesthetic of the home, and I worry for our residents, I really do.'

'What kind of works was it they brought?'

'It's like *Minority Report* in that room. Dear God.'

'I'll check it out tomorrow,' I say, 'but for the moment, I think you should be grateful they're there. Whatever you lose in aesthetic, you gain in safety, which, after the last couple of days . . .'

She makes a grudging sound of agreement down the phone, and then silence settles on the conversation. Another pause, this one instantly extending into the uncomfortable. She made the call, however, and she won't let the silence last.

'I heard on the news about someone being decapitated in Inverness,' she says. 'They're saying it's related to this?'

'It's related to the murder of Mrs Worrell's grandson,' I say. 'We don't know if that murder, or this decapitation, are related to the deaths at the home.'

'Dear God,' she says again. I get the feeling, from the way the words uncomfortably cross her lips, that she's moderating her language because she's speaking to the police.

'We'll get there,' I say, because it's the sort of thing one says in this kind of situation. 'We always do,' I add, reading lines written on rolled-up pieces of paper picked from the jar of platitude.

There's another silence, and I wonder if she's going to end the conversation the way characters regularly do in films, by just hanging up, but then the words are up and out and across her lips. 'I don't suppose you'd care to come up to the home for a drink this evening?'

The question asked, when the answer is already known.

'It's late,' I say, my answer in the tone.

'I suppose not,' she says. 'And I suppose I'm still a suspect in some strange way because you don't rule anyone out.'

I'm not going to comment on that either. She's right, of course, and it's hardly strange. At this point, literally everyone is a suspect. We have very little to go on up at that home, so I'm certainly not removing anyone from the list, least of all someone who calls up quite possibly to check if they're on it.

'Good night, Director,' I say. 'I'll see you in the morning.'

A moment, and then the line goes dead.

I lay down the phone, lift the glass, take a long drink of wine, let the liquid rest in my mouth for a few seconds. Place the glass back on the table, stare at the blurry window. In the background "Cross the Green Mountain' plays on. Try to enjoy the sensation of the wine in my throat, the taste lingering on my tongue. Another deep breath, and then open the folder.

I'll take a look through what is known of the brief criminal career of Steven Priestly, and then I'm going to go online and further investigate the work of the artist we've been calling the Monkey Man. Mr Grey Davies, someone we have been quite neglecting for the past couple of days.

29

Did I feel guilty about turning down Littlejohn's peculiar late-night invitation? I hadn't thought so. There's no way I was going there, there was no reason for guilt.

Yet there she was, back on my beach of guilt and premonition, alongside the old familiar suspects. My new haunting, seemingly getting more and more real as the days and nights pass.

There was the man with the gun in his hand, there was the girl with her head in the sand. One by one as I walked in hazy grey, they appeared from the murk. Some usual suspects, some people I never realised I'd hurt. Emotional friendly fire, or loved ones left bereft. Every now and again, the slam-dunk certainty, beginning, of course, with Elizabeth thrusting the knife into her belly.

There was Leopold, a bullet hole in the middle of the forehead, after a chase down dark alleys in Warsaw, January 2008. Staring at me as I walked past, the bruise still showing on his cheek from where I kicked him, right before I put the .357 SIG in his skull. His eyes had barely left me when there was an older woman, alone at a table, completely lost in desolation.

I didn't know her. A bereavement I never knew I caused. One of those about whom I never thought. You can't, can you? Who would go into this line of work if they were to devote guilt and regret to all those left behind?

I stood and looked at her, as though grief were a spectator sport. As though understanding would come. As though there was a possibility she would lift her eyes, she would look at me, and I could explain everything with a look. I could salve my guilt and her bereavement. *It's all right,* my eyes would have said, *it had to be done. For Britain. There's no need to feel bad about it. This is just the way things are.*

She did not look up. I walked on.

I stopped again at Holly Littlejohn. I don't remember feeling surprised that she was there, although it was peculiar. She wasn't staring at me. She couldn't. There were cockroaches crawling out of her eye sockets. And her mouth. She was naked, her body slumped in a seat, head back. Her skin was pale blue; the insects crawled down over her neck and chest.

Behind her, away out over the flat calm of the sea, the beam of the lighthouse blinked monotonously.

Walk into the office at eight seventeen. Another busted night's sleep, another haunting of the spirit. Feeling edgy and uncomfortable, the disturbed nights bugging me as much as this ridiculous scattershot case. Not really wanting to think about any of it. Just thinking about coffee, the great panacea. Concentrate on it. The coffee. The easy win, the achievable goal.

I found something last night as I trawled the Internet, buried in an indiscreet Facebook post from five years previously. In among the dull and the repetitive, the anaemic and the outraged, and in an instant the course of the investigation seemed to be laid before us. Yet, this morning, without further study, I have tossed that hope away, replaced by a grudging acknowledgement that this stuff is never so easy. Success is rarely won on Google.

Sutherland is at his desk, Quinn not yet in his office, several of the troops already at post. Straight to the coffee machine, look round, catch Sutherland's eye in our regular morning silent interaction, he nods, and I set up two cups.

The Art of Dying

Watch the flow of the liquid, the hiss and spit and gurgle of the machine. Not long, and Sutherland is beside me.

'You're late,' he says.

Again, the intention is comic banter, but the usual flippancy is absent.

'I admire everyone's dedication,' I say. 'If only there was the budget to give you all a bonus.'

'Not just us,' he says. 'Got a call already from County.'

'Moira Reynolds?'

'Yep, just off the phone as you arrived. Asked if we wanted to go round.'

'Did she say what she's got?'

'There's a guy sitting in her office who said he saw something at the game.'

I look at him, then glance at the clock.

'Really? Does no one sleep any more?'

'Doesn't look like it. She thought we should speak to him before he changes his mind.'

'Not happy talking to the police?'

'Exactamundo.'

'God, I love the public. Right, I'll take it now, before I head up the road.'

Look over at my desk.

'The e-mails can wait. I'll just stick a lid on this and get going.'

'Sir,' says Sutherland, and then he takes his own coffee and turns away.

Moira Reynolds is sitting back with her arms folded, her way of ceding the floor to the police. I'm across the desk from her, a small man in his early twenties sitting a few feet away. We're re-watching footage of the moment that Peterson stood at the game, turned and shouted to the rows of seats behind, and then turned back and sat down.

231

I'm trying not to look at Reynolds. I don't know why. Maybe it's because, as Sutherland jokingly surmised, there's a thing between us. One of those connections that just happens out of nowhere. Me and Moira Reynolds, both ex-security services, transcended by some other peculiar bond.

I don't need it. Leia Marcus is bad enough. I don't need thoughts of any of those other women, sitting dolefully at desks, on my purgatorial beach.

I try not to look at Moira Reynolds.

The small man, who has given his name so far just as Wolf, is identifiable on the screen as sitting a couple of rows behind Grey Davies, some way over to the left. He has a remote control in his hand, and he stops the footage at a point when Peterson still has his back to the camera.

'You see there?' says Wolf. 'You see that? That slight hesitation?'

Reynolds nods. She'll have watched the footage far more than I have.

'It's like his hand paused,' I say, 'but it's not obviously hesitation.'

'It was hesitation,' says Wolf. ''Cause I was watching the bastard, right? I mean, I thought it was quite funny, you know, when the guy makes the monkey noise. That's funny, right? Doesn't mean anything, does it? I mean, like, everyone says everything's racist nowadays, but is it really?'

'Yes,' I say, 'that was racist.'

'Aye, right, sure. Whatever. The guy does the noise, this bastard gets up to complain, and he's looking around, 'cause he doesn't know who it is he should be, you know, actively pious at . . .' and he laughs, 'you know what I mean, he's just like pissing in the wind, man, fucking snowflake, hashtag-SJW right? Then you can see, his eyes fell on the monkey guy, and that . . . that's when you get that.'

He points at the screen

'Right there, man. He saw the monkey guy and he hesitated. He stopped.'

'Why?'

'I don't fucking know, do I?'

Oh, I've never heard that line from an interviewee before.

'Why d'you think? It wasn't that the Monkey Man gave Mr Peterson any kind of reaction. He wasn't looking angry. In fact, judging from that, there's no reason why Peterson would even have known who it was who made the noise. You're sure he was looking at the right guy?'

'He was looking right at him!' says Wolf, his voice higher pitched. 'And I suppose if you're wanting me to guess, I'd say he knew him. Looked like he knew him. So you get that hesitation, and then he looks away from that guy and just throws some more do-gooding crap at the rest of us like it was our fault, then thankfully he shut the fuck up. Don't suppose he'll be doing it again, will he?'

He laughs, looks at Reynolds to see if he can include her in the joke, and the laughter quickly dies.

I indicate for Wolf to give me the remote, then rewind it to the start of the incident and play it through again. With this possibility in mind – the notion that Peterson catches Davies's eye, and it momentarily stops him in his tracks – the video seems to play out exactly as it ought to.

I glance at Reynolds now.

'You didn't spot this before?' I ask.

I don't say *I thought you were better than this*, but that's the implication of the question.

'I did,' she says, nothing in her tone to imply offence has been taken, 'but without context it didn't mean anything. Now we have the context.'

Not unreasonable. Indeed, a nice diplomatic out, explaining herself in such a way that I don't have to feel guilty for having cast aspersions.

'Why did you wait until now?' I ask, turning back to Wolf. 'You couldn't have come forward on Sunday or Monday? It was all over the news.'

Wolf does what one must consider the very definition of looking shifty, and says, 'Didn't want to talk to you lot, did I? Thought I'd leave it a day or two, see if someone else said something, or maybe the thing would sort itself out, then when . . . I mean, I don't know, conscience got the better of us or something. Thought I'd do my bit.'

'You're going to have to give me a name other than Wolf,' I say, 'and you're going to have to let me know how I can get hold of you again.'

The guy stares at me, the eyes shift to Reynolds and back again, gives it a moment, then he says, with some reluctance, 'Simon. My name's Simon.'

'You've got a second name,' I ask, 'or are you like a Brazilian footballer?'

A beat, then he adds, 'Aye, sure. It's Andgarfunkel.'

Another second, then there's the inevitable burst of laughter, and this time when he looks at Reynolds he keeps on laughing.

'Can you wait outside in reception, please, Mr Andgarfunkel?' says Reynolds, drily, and her tone is so straight it wipes the smile from his face, and he grudgingly gets to his feet and leaves the room, casting a baleful glance back at us on his way out.

I hadn't expected that. The door closes; Reynolds and I are alone.

'Everything all right, Inspector?' she asks. 'You seem a little distracted.'

'I'm good,' I say quickly, then add, 'You don't think he'll just run off?' as a means to move the conversation along.

'He's not the sharpest pencil in the case,' she says. 'He gave us his ridiculous false name, but he has a season ticket, so we already know who he is and where he lives. Luke Jefferson.'

'That's good.'

'And I've got something else for you,' she says. 'Totally unrelated, but it came up, so I thought I should pass it on.'

'Go on,' I say, and I straighten my shoulders, sit forward, a positive act of tossing dark, useless thoughts into a sealed compartment, to be brought out and fretted over later, or hopefully sealed away forever.

'I was looking into this man Grey Davies.'

'Haven't you done everything you need to do?' I ask, although there's no censure in my tone.

'You know the score, Inspector. Sometimes there's just the tip of the iceberg, and sometimes that iceberg is the size of a house. I decided to do a quick background, that's all.'

'Of course. What did you find?'

'I don't want to tell you how to do your job, or give you more work to do ...'

'It's fine. What did you find?'

'This guy sells his art in studios, and he's got his website, and the art is all modern and erotic.'

'I've seen it.'

'It's good, if you like that kind of thing. The man has talent, you have to give him that, although I'm not sure I'd have one of those things on my wall.'

I smile at that, but I give her the space to continue.

'However,' she says, and she lifts a finger to hold my attention, then she opens a MacBook, brings up a page and swirls the computer round for me to see.

Rembrandt's *The Night Watch*. Two images of the same picture, side by side. She lets me look at it for a moment, and then she moves the page on. *A Young Tiger Playing With Its Mother*, by Delacroix. Again, images side by side.

'There are more,' she says, 'but it looks like you may have an art forger on your hands.'

I've been nodding slowly since she brought up the Rembrandt. I'd already found a hint of this online myself, but had discounted it this morning. Perhaps my ready acceptance of further information from Reynolds is me succumbing to confirmation bias, but this feels more significant than that.

'Stay with me,' she says. I hadn't thought I'd been going anywhere.

'Now we go back to the Rembrandt,' she says, and she clicks onto *The Night Watch* again. 'Take a look at the character on the right-hand side, the lower half of his face cut off by the outstretched arm in front of him.'

I study the two pictures, that up until this point had seemed identical. Once the anomaly has been pointed out, it becomes obvious. And there are coincidences everywhere in the world, in all walks of life, and in all police investigations, but this, this right here staring us in the face, is no coincidence.

30

Park my car on Golspie Main Street, the A9 as it is, given there's no Golspie bypass. Get out, stand and take in the air. There's no view of the seafront from here, although it's only fifty yards away, the other side of the row of houses and shops. The morning air is fresh, though there's cold moisture in it, the sky low and dull.

I stand in front of a restaurant named Pure Asia. The sign in the window states that it's only open in the evenings.

I look inside, but the windows are dark and all I can really see is my own tired face, and Golspie Main Street reflected back. The outside paintwork is dark blue, with a thin yellow line running around the window. Pure Asia is written above the window, with a simple floral design either side. Minimalistic and chic, very little ostentation intended to lure in the customer. They either don't need to worry about customers, or they're confident their reputation will suffice.

I try the handle, hoping the kitchen staff are in early, already preparing for the evening. The door opens, and I step into the restaurant.

There are around fifteen tables. The walls are dark, though hard to see in this dim light if they are painted black, or the dark blue of the exterior. On one wall, a line drawing of the Great Wall stretches the full length. The opposite wall has a variety of black and white prints, depicting various trad-itional – or clichéd – Asian scenes.

At the back there are two doors. One, in the far corner, leading to the bathrooms, the other presumably to the kitchen. Between them is a large Japanese peace lily on the floor, above which is an etching of a naked woman. To the left, at the rear, there is a flight of stairs leading straight up, with a chain across at ankle height.

I walk forward, between the tables, to take a closer look at the picture above the peace lily. The woman stands in the same position as the wooden statue in Graham Strachan's room. Is that so odd? A woman, alone, forlorn, staring bleakly at the ground. Nevertheless, the picture says the same things to me, and it once again puts Leia Marcus in my head. She is this woman, those are her eyes.

The room is silent, no sound from the kitchen, no sound from upstairs, nothing from the road. A silence so complete, it's as if all sound has been vacuumed out.

I close my eyes. Steady breaths. In the darkness my midnight beach opens up before me, stretching into the hazy distance. I see Leia Marcus standing alone, bereft. I see the others, these people who have haunted me, sitting at desks in morbid silence. The silence of this room, the silence of this investigation, where intricate paths lead nowhere.

You know for whom she tends the weeping fig . . .

Suddenly there's a loud clatter from the kitchen, a pan falling to the floor, bouncing once, more clatter, a barked, 'Aw, fuckit,' and then footsteps. In an instant the place is all noise, movement upstairs, conversation in the kitchen, a further clatter of pots, and then the door to the kitchen opens.

A young Asian man, Indonesian perhaps, stops when he sees me, but doesn't look particularly surprised. Nor is he looking stressed about whatever disaster just befell the kitchen.

'Sorry, we're shut, mate,' he says, then adds, 'kinda obvious really. You want to come back the night?'

Accent is pure Glasgow. Wearing a white chef's smock, wiping his hands on a cloth.

I hold out my ID, but he barely glances at it.

'Inspector Westphall,' I say. 'You got a minute?'

'Sure,' he says, glancing back at the kitchen door. 'Just a minute. What's up?'

'Are there any members of staff here who were working on Tuesday evening? Can't say the exact time.'

'Waiters aren't in yet, obvs,' says the chef, 'won't be until, like, five thirty. What's the problem?'

I pocket the ID and produce the photograph of Steven Priestly.

'We need to know if this man was in here.'

He studies the picture for a moment in the dim light, then I can see the change in his eyes and he says, 'Yeah, sure. Can't say he was definitely here on Tuesday, but I know him. Sushi eater.'

The affirmation is so sudden and direct that I find myself staring for a second.

'What?' he says.

'You're sure? I mean, he wasn't that memorable-looking a guy.'

'Comes in here all the time. Wait, what? *Wasn't* that memorable?'

'He was murdered late on Tuesday evening, found his body yesterday. You don't watch the news?'

'Nah,' says the chef, his brow furrowing, eyes dropping. 'I went cold turkey on it after Brexit and Trump. Couldn't face that crap any more. The dude was murdered? Seriously?'

The word dude is just never going to sound right in any of the panoply of Scottish accents, but there's little to be done. Like an invasive species of crayfish, it's well established and here for the duration.

'Did you know anything about him?' I ask.

'He was just a guy, you know? He probably had a bit of banter with some of the girls, but that was it.'

'Was he ever with anyone?'

'Sure, always. There was a woman.'

'And he was with her on Tuesday?'

He shrugs, then looks round as another young man appears at the kitchen door. The guy from the kitchen ignores me, looks at the chef and says, 'The fuck, Marty? This shit's no cleaning up itself.'

Another strong Glasgow accent, another shrug from the chef, then he says, 'Got to go, Inspector, if I think of anything—'

'This is a murder enquiry,' I say, sharply. 'The teriyaki haggis can wait. Describe the woman to me.'

He looks at the floor, rubs his chin, a perfect demonstration of someone trying to remember.

'Older,' he says. 'Could've been his mum, I don't know. Or maybe his girlfriend, though, hard to tell with people. You have to pay attention, and I don't.'

I look around, look up at the small, discreet camera above the door. The chef grudgingly follows my gaze.

'Look, go upstairs. Speak to Janey, she runs the office. She's in already. She'll bring up the footage for you.'

'How long does it go back?'

'It's digital, man, goes all the way back to when it was installed. I don't know, year and a half ago. Can I get back to work?'

'Sure,' I say. 'Thanks, you've been very helpful.'

The chef looks surprised, and a little disappointed, and then turns quickly away. I step over the chain on the stairs, and then go up, two steps at a time. Now I can really feel it, and I know, in a way I hadn't when searching Priestly's apartment, that this is what making a breakthrough feels like.

31

I park my car outside The Dunes, stepping out into the rain. The umbrella, which I never use, remains on the floor by the front passenger seat. The walk to the front door is short in any case.

The investigation has life today, and even if I don't yet know how all the pieces fit together, at least the pieces themselves are beginning to take shape.

I pass a security guard on the door, show him my ID, and he immediately steps back and allows me entry.

What if someone turns up to visit a relative without any ID? Are they really not going to let them in? At least he wasn't armed, but as the awful Americanisation of everything continues, perhaps that's not so far off.

I step into the hallway and look around. The staircase that leads to Littlejohn's office is directly in front, the doors leading off the hallway all closed. I look at the picture of a stag on open moorland that dominates the wall to the left, and listen to the silence of the building. 11.45 a.m. and nothing is stirring.

A door opens, and Holly Littlejohn appears. In my mind, cockroaches crawl across her cold, pale corpse.

'Inspector,' she says, 'I got the call you'd arrived.'

'Very efficient.'

'Come on through, you can see the new ops room, then we can talk about what you'd like to do today.'

I follow Littlejohn along the short corridor to the room in which we'd initially set up, before the decision had been taken much higher up the chain of command than me to turn it over to the care home company's private security. These people have resources that Police Scotland don't, and the main thing here is that there's no more murder.

'I want to focus on Mrs Worrell,' I say. 'Have a look in her room, certainly have another look at the painting, and talk to her again.'

Littlejohn glances round as we walk along the corridor.

'You don't honestly think you're going to get any more from Louise than you got two days ago?'

'There's always something,' I say blandly.

'That square peg can always be squeezed brutally into the round hole,' she says. 'I expect you do a course on the subject when you join up.'

The insecurity, and the warmth, that she showed in her call last night are missing this morning. Indeed, it's as if she never called. I begin to wonder, and start to think through the conversation. Could it just have been something else I imagined, a mundane accompaniment to the more dramatic and surreal episodes?

She stops outside the impromptu ops room, then turns to look at me. Waits to see if I have anything to say to the last jibe thrown in my direction, then says, 'Welcome to the twenty-fifth century.'

She opens the door, ushering me into the room.

There are four people, two women, two men, all in blue security uniforms, with seven flatscreen monitors mounted on the wall, and a computer graphic of the floor plan of the building seemingly suspended in mid-air, with heat signature representations of where everyone is in the home and on the grounds.

Oh, dear God. A sleepy home in the Highlands meets American big business. Word must have gone around the boardroom, the share price must be in danger. Dornoch calls for aid, and America has sent in the high-tech clowns.

★   ★   ★

I'm standing in Louise Worrell's room, Littlejohn beside me, staring at a painting I've not looked at before. Mrs Worrell is not present, being in her usual position in the lounge, bound to the Brueghel.

'I'd love to know what you're looking for, Inspector,' says Littlejohn, 'and why you think Louise's room could possibly be of any relevance. From where the rest of us are standing, none of this has anything to do with her.'

Littlejohn left me for a while with the security guys. The set-up and the money and the tech might all look American, but the men and women are from the Highlands, a decent crew, just doing their jobs. Of course, they'll be watching us, and will feed back to head office. Police resources, police impact, police methods. In the long game, where the private firms take control of more and more state business, part of the slow decline to a giant-corporation-dominated dystopian nightmare that may not even need to be post-apocalyptic, every piece of information will factor into the whole, and these days at The Dunes will be just another statistic.

I got a look at the tech, the layout of their operation, and a reasonable level of confidence that nothing else untoward is likely to happen on their watch. If something does happen while they're here, then I doubt the police would have been able to do much to prevent it.

And now Holly Littlejohn has rejoined me, and we stand together, looking at a piece of modern art that, to my old-fashioned mind, is straight out of the my-kid-could-have-painted-that catalogue. I can imagine someone giving me the talk on perspective and colour and the luring of the eye to a particular point.

'You sound tense,' I say.

She doesn't respond, and I turn away from the painting to look at her. 'I'm sorry if I've come across as too demanding. It's our way, of course. We step into situations, and

243

immediately insist on answers before the blood has dried, the scent of the crime has gone cold. But I do understand how hard this is for you.'

She holds my gaze, but has no words. Perhaps she will think this my belated response to her reaching out last night, when it could just be pity, wrought by a late-night vision of death and decay.

'Your head office is in the US?' I ask, to get past the fact she's staring at me, unsure whether she should open up.

'There's an office in Inverness, which they opened after . . . there's us, and we have sister establishments dotted around the Highlands, Fort William, Invershin, one not far from the Castle of Mey, but yes, head office itself is in California, so still early morning there.'

A Pavlovian glance at her wrist. Her lips purse, she makes her decision to talk a little more openly.

'The Inverness office is really just a bureaucratic layer. Santa Monica calls the shots. They'll let me go. Hardly my fault, they acknowledge that, but it's happened on my watch, so what can I expect?'

'How's Geras Holdings faring on the stock markets of the world?'

'You haven't looked?'

'You think it's pertinent?'

'It's faring badly,' she says. 'Which means people are losing money.'

'How about you?' I ask. 'Do you have shares in the company you were given one year as a Christmas bonus?'

'Really?'

'Because that never happens . . .'

She smiles.

'They never gave me shares.'

'You have options if they do let you go?' I ask, deciding for the moment just to go with the flow of the conversation.

Perhaps she will, after all, give something away if her guard is down.

'No children, no husband, no parents. A clean slate. I'd been thinking I might give this another couple of years, and then ...' and she makes a take-off motion. 'Don't know where, don't know when, but now it looks like it'll be a lot sooner than I'd been intending.'

There was a flicker in the voice on the word husband.

'Going off to find yourself?'

'To find *something*,' she says. 'I have no one, Inspector. Just this job, where client turnover is measured in filled graves. Kind of makes you wonder, right? Isn't it the kind of deep, trippy thoughts you have at university, or high school even? *What's it all about?* Really, what is the damned point of any of it? We live, we do things, we grow old, we die, and whatever we leave behind also one day dies. That's it ... You're not supposed to think like that at fifty-one, are you? Aren't you supposed to have some sort of idea? Aren't you supposed to have found the right space within your own skin?'

'Tell me about your husband.'

I'm not sure where the question comes from. Do I really want to know about her husband, after all? It's the old-fashioned equivalent of disappearing off down a rabbit burrow on the Internet. You think you'll just check the weather, and somehow half an hour later you're reading about Charlemagne's defeat at Roncevaux Pass.

Her eyes lower, but she doesn't question how I knew to ask. I read it in her tone, and she will accept that she gives herself away. Perhaps it's happened before.

'He killed himself,' she says, 'although he didn't die. Not physically.'

I make no conversational prompt. The story will come in time. My own urgency in driving here has been put on hold, taken by the strange sense of time that exists at The Dunes, to be seized again when this moment is over.

'He was depressed. Deep, clinical depression. He'd lost interest in everything, could barely get himself out of bed most days. Refused to get help. He was dragging me, and everyone else he knew, down with him. When he talked, which was rare, his words were strange and dark. And then . . . I don't know where the idea came from. Maybe there's a theory out there, maybe there's an old story. He told me at dinner one night that he was sorry, but this incarnation of himself had to die. The following morning he was going to become someone else. A new name, new interests, new tastes, new life. Everything that he had in his life – I don't know . . . supporting Manchester United and watching snooker, listening to the Stones and Cream, toast and jam, vodka-tonic, fear of water and snakes – everything that made him who he was, he was going to discard. In order not to be depressed, he literally had to become a different person.

'That sounds . . . I don't know how it sounds. Stupid. A cheap way of saying, that's it, babe, I'm out of here.'

'Mid-life crisis?'

'He was twenty-nine. It wasn't a mid-life anything. That night he slept in the spare room, came down the following morning. We stood in the kitchen. I'd made breakfast, his usual breakfast. I was clinging on. Two slices of toast, two boiled eggs, orange juice. Classic denial on my part. He was wearing clothes he'd dug up from the back of the wardrobe. I knew the clothes, but I didn't know him. His face was the same, of course . . . but it wasn't him. He was a complete stranger to me. "Thanks for the overnight," he said. 'I'll let you know if I'm ever back in town.'

'His voice was different. A soft, east-coast accent. The posh end of Edinburgh, maybe. And then he left. I stood there, silent, confused, as he walked out. I had no words. I could almost feel myself reaching into my brain for something to say, like putting your hand in an empty bag. Nothing.

'Maybe some people would've thought it was a joke, but I knew it wasn't. He didn't take anything with him. Some money, but that was all. No bank card, no passport, no clothes. Left everything that he'd once held dear behind.'

'Did you ever see him again?'

'No.'

'Did you ever hear of him again?'

'I knew when he walked out I wouldn't.'

'What did you do?'

'I waited, even though I knew he wasn't coming back. A month after he'd gone, I reported him missing. Didn't tell the police all the details. In fact, this is me now, telling the police all the details. Long story cut short, he was declared dead several years later.' She laughs bitterly, and adds, 'It's what he would've wanted.'

I can imagine another detective making something of that story. Perhaps not here, right now, as there are too many other things to do. But somewhere, at some point, there would be incredulity. There would be questions of what was in it for them both. Was there an insurance policy? How else had she benefitted from having a man declared dead, when he most likely wasn't? Had they really never seen each other since?

I don't sense artifice in her. I'm not about to chase another story, and I believe her entirely. He's out there in the world, this new person, born at the age of twenty-nine.

She turns away, looks across the room to the window, and the view out onto the grey water of the Dornoch Firth. There is literally nothing out there. Nothing to see. No boats on the water, no one walking by the water's edge, not a seagull in the sky, the far bank of the firth lost in mist. As if the world were nothing but grey, stretching into the far distance, with the lone exception of the lighthouse, the beacon barely visible through the murk.

She's thinking the same thing I am. She's looking at the grey, she's thinking that this is all there is. There are no great questions to be asked, and so there are no great answers. Just grey, all the way to the edge of the world.

She shivers, visibly and dramatically, and then turns back. She's been a thousand miles away, and while she was only standing like that for a short while, it will have felt much longer to her.

'Inspector,' she says, as if she's just walked into the room and the conversation is starting afresh. 'I'm sure we both have things to do. You have any other questions?'

'Yes,' I say, deciding to go along with the change in tack. The other conversation, like life itself, had not really had anywhere else to go. 'When was the last time Mrs Worrell's grandson visited?'

'I thought we discussed that,' says Littlejohn, looking at her watch again. 'About three weeks ago.'

'And when he came, that was when you decided to move the Brueghel out into the lounge?'

'No, it was nothing to do with him. I did it afterwards. I'm afraid . . . Well, yes, I should have discussed it with the family, but I knew they'd say no.'

'Why?'

'People are conservative, Inspector. If there's a routine that isn't a complete disaster, they'll stick with it, that's all. They don't want to risk the status quo. I thought, nevertheless, that it might work well for Louise to move the painting out into the sitting room, and so I went ahead without seeking consent.'

'Were they happy about it?'

'No, Inspector, they were not.'

I go back to staring at the modern canvas in front of us, which has been hung on the wall next to the door. Of similar size to the Brueghel, it is entirely painted orange, bar one thick, wavy, horizontal dark blue line an inch above the bottom of the painting.

The wall that had contained the Brueghel is now bare.

'How long has this painting been here, Director?'

A moment, and then she comes and stands beside me, shoulder to shoulder. I can smell her perfume, a subtle note of jasmine.

'At least six months, I believe. Maybe a little longer.'

The smell of her, her presence right beside me, makes me lose focus for a second, and I have to retrieve the words so that I can take them in. *Six months, maybe longer.*

'And Mr Peterson brought it here for her?'

'No,' says Littlejohn, 'he never brought her anything, he really didn't.'

'Who brought the painting? Did it arrive in the post?'

I know it didn't arrive in the post.

'Mrs . . .' and she hesitates, trying to remember the name, then says, 'Mrs James, Louise's granddaughter. Euphrosyne. So, I suppose you weren't a million miles away.'

I can feel her looking at me, trying to see what I'm thinking, why I'm going down this line of questioning. It's not there for her, though, even though it's not a particularly complex theory. Her mind is elsewhere, that's all.

'I do need to get on,' she says suddenly, and there's a change in tone, as the director returns. 'You can find your own way down to the lounge when you want to speak to Louise?'

It isn't entirely obvious whether that had been a question or a statement of fact.

'Yes,' I say anyway, glancing at her. She seems a little discombobulated for a moment, and then quickly leaves the room.

★   ★   ★

The silence of the lounge is not all-consuming. It is one o'clock, and the life of the home continues around us, however subdued. The slow movement of a resident across the room, the quicker, heavier footsteps of one of the security detail in the corridor, the smoother, lighter footfalls of the nursing staff, the rustle of a newspaper, old man Thorpe clearing his throat. Occasional conversations from further away, sometimes a barked voice. There is a window open, and the sound of two motorboats out on the firth can be heard. One with a large engine, loud and grating, fortunately far off, and another, smaller boat, puttering close to shore. There is life out there after all.

In the corner the old lady's murmur continues, as much a part of the room as the carpet and the windows and the paintings on the wall. *You know for whom she tends the weeping fig ...*

I'm finished closing my eyes. It's time to look past all this weird crap and get down to business. Someone killed two men in this home, someone killed the killer of Thomas Peterson.

My eyes have been running over all the characters in the painting, but I've been moving too quickly, keen to find what I'm looking for so that I can get on. The wheels of this investigation are turning, and having stood for such a long time with Director Littlejohn, now does not feel like the time to slow to a standstill, to the pace of a care home. However, as I've settled into the rhythm of this room, where nothing ever happens and few words are spoken, I've accepted that I have to slow down. This is not going to be telegraphed, the painting will not cry out. Like my time spent sitting with Mrs Worrell a couple of days ago, I can forget the noise around me, the sounds of the home, and the sounds of the investigation, and allow myself to sink into the moment.

Does it matter if I end up being here for ten minutes or two hours? Time, as it does, will bend and fold or stretch and expand, and there's neither rhyme nor reason for it. This is how it is.

My eyes settle on individual characters, and I study the expressions on their faces. The horror, the anger, the hate, the fear.

'What would you be?' I say softly to myself.

I study the man with a stick in the right foreground, foot raised to kick in a door. Are we supposed to wonder who's behind there? Do we wonder his motives?

The face is not a face I recognise. I move on, after some time, to the man behind.

I'm aware that I'm quietly muttering to myself, a running commentary on the painting. Not particularly caring that I'm not alone, that Mrs Worrell is beside me, the cipher in the room.

'You're in here somewhere,' I say, a little more loudly this time. 'Where are you hiding?'

Absorbed now. No longer hearing the sounds of the rest of the room, from the corridors and rooms beyond.

'Other than in plain sight,' I add quietly.

Time passes. My eyes are rooted to the middle of the painting, bodies bent double in grief, the corpse of a baby cocooned in linen, the very slaughter of the title taking place in the midst of the anguished women.

Together we sit, Mrs Worrell and I, studying the scene, like two people in a gallery entranced by the same painting, oblivious to those around them, to other visitors, and those who pass fleetingly between them and the art.

'This isn't it, is it?' I say after a while, this time my words aimed at my silent partner. I've been thinking of saying something, of trying to engage Mrs Worrell, but when it happens the words just appear from nowhere in the room, as though someone else decided it was time for them to cross my lips.

Mrs Worrell, who looks at this painting every day, will know far better than I the truth of what I'm saying.

'This isn't the painting you brought in here. It changed when that thing on the other wall came here. Euphrosyne would've brought the other painting in a box, and she would've been seen to take an empty box out. Except, there were two paintings in the box when it arrived, and the original Brueghel went out.'

The words mingle with the silence, and are eventually swallowed up by it. Sometime later, those words have completely disappeared, and it is no longer entirely clear whether or not I said them. Maybe I just thought to say them. There is no recording of the words, and thinking about it, I can't be sure myself.

'If only you could have said,' I say, my voice a little more certain. 'I expect you noticed on the first day, didn't you?'

Almost as though I can feel a change coming in the atmosphere of the room, I'm aware that Mrs Worrell is going to move before she does. I turn to look at her. She sits absolutely still, as she does almost all through her day. And then, slowly, as I'd known she would, she lifts her arm. And then her finger, the bony, crooked index finger on her right hand, extends, and she points at the painting.

We are a couple of yards away from it, but it's clear at which area she's pointing. Just above left of centre, a horse tied against a tree, and in front of it a group, huddled in a tight bunch, around a man in an orange coat.

The finger, the old wizened finger, gnarled of skin and bone, is steady, constant at a point. I rise and step up to the painting. And now that I've been pointed in the right direction, now that I'm this close, I immediately see what I'm looking for. The face at the back of the crowd, a black hat, a spear or a stick sticking up behind his head. That was the face I suspected would be there, and which I've now found.

I study it for a few moments, take out my phone, bring up the painting of one of the similar originals from Brueghel and close in on the face of the man in the same position.

The change is obvious, as is the reason for it. Swipe the picture off my phone and take a photograph of Mrs Worrell's Brueghel. Then I turn, and in that moment the sound and quiet fury of the home returns. The voices from around the building, the pad of the residents, the thump of security. The motorboats on the firth, the wind in the trees, the sound of rain against the windows.

Time to get on.

'Thank you, Mrs Worrell.'

She has lowered her hand.

'We'll try to get it back for you,' I add, although I know the original painting will be long gone, the chances of ever finding it very, very slight.

She does not move, her eyes do not stray to me. I wait, give her another few seconds, and then make my move. Time to go. I've found the piece I'm looking for; now we just have to work out where exactly it fits.

Across the lounge, out into the corridor, and on my way. Take my phone from my pocket as I go. Have missed nine calls, and as I'm contemplating which one, if any, to return first, another call lights up the screen.

'Sergeant,' I say, striding past the happy American family of five, and two dogs.

'We're wanted in Inverness,' he says. 'The Chief is getting angsty.'

'That's fine,' I say. 'It's coming together.'

'Is it?'

'Yep. We've got the Brueghel and we have CCTV of Steven Priestly's final meal. He wasn't alone . . .'

32

Sutherland and I are in the office of Chief Constable Darnley, back through in Inverness. There's a lot of driving when you're an officer in the Highlands. Comes with the territory. It's mid-afternoon, the day outside dark and grey and wet, rain falling steadily.

Darnley is on the phone, while we sit on the other side of the desk and wait. I'm thinking it all through, trying to put it in some sort of order before we speak to the boss. Again I lose track of time, and I'm abruptly brought out of my ruminations when Darnley says, 'Very well,' having been quiet throughout the call, and hangs up.

She seems to take a moment or two to compose herself, fighting some inner rage, then she looks across the desk, engaging us both.

'When is it, d'you suppose,' she begins, 'that politicians get the chip inserted? You know the chip, the politician's chip? They all talk in exactly the same disingenuous way. Truth is something to be navigated around, avoided at all costs. No wonder we've ended up where we are. People are so desperate for politicians not to be disingenuous, they'll vote for morons who distinguish themselves by just plain lying every time they open their damn mouths.'

Neither Sutherland nor I reply. I wonder if that was another call about me speaking to Kadyrova, but if it was, I don't think Darnley's going to mention it. She takes another moment, letting whatever silent fury is boiling inside her slowly and invisibly escape, then she says, 'Right, thank you for coming over. I spoke to David earlier, but I hope you don't mind me taking more of a hands-on approach. This thing has rather been getting away from us.'

'Of course,' I say.

'So, where are we, Inspector?'

'It may not look like it, but I think it's beginning to come together,' I say. 'We've identified Thomas Peterson's killer as Steven Priestly, now deceased. Beheaded. He was killed late Tuesday evening. Prior to that, he had dinner at an Asian fusion place in Golspie with Sondra Peterson. And, it appears, they were regulars.'

'Bingo,' says Darnley, although there is not much of an exclamation to it. 'So, we can link the widow to the killer.'

'Definitely. But we have several strands here, and we can't as yet say what form the link takes. The obvious one, they were having an affair and her lover killed her husband, doesn't fit any narrative that we have so far.'

'A proper mystery,' says Darnley, without much curiosity. Still edgy from speaking to the minister.

'We have a witness from the ground on Saturday,' I continue, 'who picked up on a look exchanged between Thomas Peterson and the man who seemed to have started all this, Grey Davies, the artist. Peterson seems to have recognised him when he turned round to berate him.

'So, let's just park that thought for a moment. The one thing that links Peterson to the home in Dornoch is that his grandmother is a resident there. His grandmother is, for reasons unknown, lost to the world. She's just shut herself off.'

'Dementia?'

'It doesn't appear so. I'd say PTSD. She had a long, abusive marriage, apparently, though we don't have too much detail on that. She gets up, she moves around, she eats, but she doesn't talk, she doesn't seem aware of what's around her, except for one thing. She spends her days, entire days, staring at an original artwork, *Massacre of the Innocents*, by Brueghel.'

'Which one?'

'Which . . .?'

'Brueghel?'

'The Younger.'

'Yes, of course, it had to be. He painted several of those, maybe into the double figures.'

'Yes. She bought this one with money she inherited from her husband, then she invested the rest of her small fortune in funding the remainder of her days at The Dunes.'

'Didn't leave anything for her children or grandchildren? Well, the painting, I presume.'

'Not even that. It's been bequeathed to the Kelvingrove.'

'Holy . . .' says Darnley, but then chooses not to complete the exclamation with *cow* or *moly* or *shit*.

'She had one daughter, now dead, and two grandchildren, Peterson and his sister, Euphrosyne James.'

'The Greek goddess is added to the mix,' says Darnley dully. 'What happened to the daughter?'

'Committed suicide several years ago. Her death isn't in play here.'

'Go on.'

'Now, we come to Grey Davies, the artist who made the monkey noise, as part of the investigation. He has an extensive studio, obviously paints quickly and often. His subject matter is predominantly his girlfriend, his art is modern, edgy, erotic. However, although he has no examples on display in his studio, it's apparent from searching around the Internet that the man is a brilliant, brilliant, copy artist. I found one last night that I was a little sceptical about – a Rubens, *The Three Graces*, that someone claimed was a copy by Davies. Seemed unlikely, but the thought was there. However, today the head of security at County had come across a similar thing. She'd spent a little longer going down the rabbit hole.' I pause, a peculiar moment of insecurity, the words sounding false. Had she spent longer, or had she just done it more efficiently?

'You don't need the qualifier, Inspector,' says Darnley, perceptive as ever. 'What have you got?'

A moment of weakness, it would seem.

'She had a couple, including Rembrandt's *The Night Watch*. Perfect copy, except he had changed the face of one of the subordinate characters to a self-portrait.'

'Artists,' says Darnley. What else could be expected of them?

'Now we come to the Brueghel that commands the attention of Peterson's grandmother, Mrs Worrell. About six months ago, Euphrosyne James brought another painting of a similar size to her grandmother's room. It's modern art, a colour motif.'

'You think she brought in a duplicate *Massacre of the Innocents* at that time, and removed the original?'

'Definitely. I've just been looking at it, and the face of Davies is there, part of the crowd. It was a harder spot, as the figures in the Brueghel are much smaller than the figures in the Rembrandt, but it's him.'

'So, presumably James took the original away and sold it. Do we think she split the money with her brother?'

'If we factor in the moment of recognition between Peterson and Davies at the football, that seems entirely likely.'

'And what then of the meeting at the football? That was coincidental?'

'We don't have that yet,' I say. 'We do know, however, that the undertaker business, which Peterson was expanding vigorously across Scotland, was propped up on the back of laundered money and serious debt, and that Peterson had very little control of what was happening.'

'In short, he would've needed the money from the Brueghel. How much was it likely to have gone for?'

'Mrs Worrell bought it three years ago for two-point-four million.'

'Hmm. Would Peterson's share have made much of a dent in the debt his company was accumulating?'

'I'm guessing his share of the proceeds went nowhere near the company. Putting the money into the business would've been the same as handing it over to the Russians. He'd have to have been incredibly foolish to do that. I imagine the money was sent offshore from the moment it was transferred to him.'

'Perhaps we'll learn more from the Greek goddess. Have you brought her in?'

'Next on the list.'

'So, we have a company in debt, we have money launder-ing, we have theft of the painting, we can connect both Peterson and his sister to the artist, we can connect Peterson's widow to his killer.'

'That's where we are.'

'Just leaves the matter of why he was killed, not to mention the somewhat important business of a double disembowel-ling. Where are we with those?'

'All we have at the moment is speculation.'

'Go ahead and speculate,' says Darnley.

We wouldn't be having this conversation with Quinn. He would likely have mumbled something about the wasteful-ness of idle speculation, and sent us away with a demand for facts. As if this approach from Darnley will have us doing anything else.

'I think the business in London is classic Russia. I don't mean to labour the point, but these people ... there have been so many deaths when Russian money and the Russian government is involved. Young, Berezovsky, on and on. There's no thread, there's never identifiable proof, it's hardly likely it's the same killer, but the consistent theme is people die. They die. And not just in London. There's all this money, and cities and governments around the globe are afraid to lose it, and there are places where the Russians and their operatives pretty much do what they like.'

'What about Skripal? There was some pushback on that at least.'

'Even a broken watch is right twice a day,' I say, immediately regretting the cliché. 'It can at least explain Westbrook and the disappearance of Singh. So, why then do we have the repeat murder at the home?'

I have no answer to my own question, and look at Sutherland, who has been largely silent up until now. Darnley follows my look, although she's been making sure to include Sutherland in the conversation.

Although my question was entirely speculative, not really expecting Sutherland to have anything to say, he is ready for the attention to be turned on him.

'I was listening to the news on the radio on Monday evening,' says Sutherland, 'and they mentioned the murder in London.' I nod, having heard the same thing. 'Somehow they'd got hold of the stuff about the evisceration. Presumably someone at the company talked. And then, on top of that they had unconfirmed reports stating it might be tied to Peterson. Sounds like the Met did a bit of talking.'

'It's one tactic,' says Darnley. 'Get as much information out there as possible, right from the off. Nevertheless, I didn't realise they'd done it to us. I'll make a call. Go on, Sergeant.'

'That's all I know. But I wondered, is it possible that someone at the home needed to get rid of a couple of people, namely Cummins and Strachan? They tried to make the death of Cummins look natural. They hoped the police wouldn't be called, but they were. So then they took a different tack. They heard the news, they knew Peterson was tied to the home through his grandmother, and they thought, let's make this look like some great financial conspiracy. Let's send the police off on a completely different tangent. Let's have them looking for connections that aren't necessarily there.'

He finishes, he raises his eyebrows at me, he self-consciously shrugs to fill the space in the silence that follows.

'What d'you think, Inspector?' asks Darnley.

'I like it,' I say. 'Particularly with the likely attempt at covering up Cummins's murder. Very good.'

'I like it too,' says Darnley, 'but we could use some evidence. What's next?'

'We arrest Euphrosyne James. We'll have her on art theft, if nothing else. We also need to bring Mrs Peterson in for questioning, obviously, and Grey Davies. Possibly there are no grounds to arrest him, it's not illegal to sell a copy of a painting if the buyer knows what he's getting, although that might depend on what Mrs James has to say.

'But it looks more and more like this revolves around that painting, and it suggests someone at the home is involved.'

'If this is about art theft, where do the Russians come in?'

'I don't have that yet, but it can't be a coincidence, that doesn't make sense. Everything's tied together, we just need to pin it down.'

'What d'you want to do?'

'Get Kadyrova in.'

'You're going to arrest her?' she asks. Sceptical, rather than disapproving, but she has a point. 'The woman is not going to go to a police station of her own volition.'

We can't possibly get Kadyrova in. Take a moment, kick myself for expressing my wish list rather than my actual intentions.

'You're right,' I say, 'and yes, we don't have enough to make an arrest. But I do want to go and speak to her again, and I'll need you to have my back when it starts raining angry phone calls.'

'Go all in, Inspector. Sounds like you have a lot to do. Just let me know when you intend to see her, so that I can—'

She stops at the look on my face, my glance at my watch.

'Her office is less than ten minutes from here,' I say.

'Of course. Go for it. I shall expect the first call in quarter of an hour or so.'

We share a grim smile, and then she takes us both in with an end-of-the-meeting expression.

'Do you need anything else from me at this stage?'

'Not yet,' I say. 'I'll let you know.'

'Very well. You can keep me up to date through the Chief.'

And with that, we're leaving the office, haste in our stride, and I'm already working my way through the division of duty.

33

'You sound busy, Inspector. I won't keep you.'

'I can sit here until you're prepared to talk,' I say.

It's a lie, and she knows I'm lying. I need to get on, and I need to do better than this. I'm here relying totally on intuition, hoping that something will emerge from the conversation. A slip of the tongue, a misplaced word, a vague, unintended hint. And I'm fooling myself. Natalia Kadyrova has been trained well, playing everything straight down the middle. The classic dead bat, not a hint of the kind of smug contempt that allowed two FSB agents to claim they'd been visiting Salisbury to look at its world-renowned cathedral.

'No you can't. Never mind. I leave soon.'

'Where are you going?'

'Maybe Novgorod, maybe Yekaterinburg, I do not know.'

Can't tell if she's joking.

Sutherland was with me when we sat down, but his phone rang, he gave me the look that said he needed to take the call, and he went back outside.

I wondered then whether just to explode at her. Lose my temper, lean across the table, grab her by the shirt collar. Anything to break the mould of our conversations, where I ask questions and she self-assuredly refuses to answer. She is, of course, never going to answer anything, regardless of her place in this investigation.

Now that we're here, sitting in a quiet coffee shop down by the River Ness, the low grey river silently passing us by outside, I don't think I'm going to have to fake the explosion of temper.

Aleksandra Wiśniewski appears from nowhere in my head. I hadn't thought of her in a while, except now that I see her, she's sitting at a desk on a beach, her face bruised and bloodied, and I realise she must have been in my dreams at some point. I hadn't realised I felt guilty about her. Why should I have done?

We were in the same situation that I'm now in. Sitting in a small café on the outskirts of Łódź. I'd been in Poland for three weeks and no one, not even Vauxhall, knew I was there. Wiśniewski was taking the same conversational route as Kadyrova is choosing here.

She'd killed Harkins. I knew it, and she knew I knew it. I didn't lose my temper that afternoon, but I did get up, lean across the table and plant a fist in the middle of her face. A messy business, but as intended, it ended with me disappearing into the ether, and her in a Polish hospital, from where the authorities got hold of her. She was reported to have died in a prison in Warsaw six months later. 'Suicide.'

Chief Constable Darnley may be on my side, but I think putting my fist through Kadyrova's face would cross the boundary. No one who heard the details of the way Wiśniewski killed Harkins and his young family would begrudge what happened to her. All I've got on Kadyrova is suspicion and a wariness born of her demeanour and crushing good looks.

Still, this time the loss of temper may not be faked.

'You can't leave the country at the moment. Not until the investigation is complete.'

She lifts the coffee to her lips, a full mug, one that is likely four-fifths froth, can't possibly tip it back enough to get any liquid, then licks the froth from her top lip as she places it back on the table.

'You are funny, Inspector,' she says. 'I joke, but maybe I

leave anyway. I would like to see what passes for British border control stop me. It would be funny also.'

She glances down at the whitening of my knuckles.

'Perhaps it would be better for all of us if you weren't in Britain any more,' I say, playing the game. 'Maybe something is more likely to happen to you once you've left the country.'

This is the real thing. The real threat. The edge in my voice is not faked. And as the words spit slowly across the table, I can imagine tracking her down to some out-of-the-way hotel in an out-of-the-way town in Russia, and putting a bullet in her head.

I don't know how yet, but I know this woman is involved in these murders, and she will be involved in many more before she's finished.

'Here we have the difference between us, Inspector. You come with threats, I invite you only to bed.' Her voice is like ice. 'The offer still stands. Why not? You would surely have more fun fucking me than killing me? You are not a barbarian.'

Barbarian. Euphrosyne James used that expression. Anything to be read into that? You're clutching, Inspector.

I move forward. An inch. Two inches. Leaning into the fight.

'Maybe that's what we'll do,' I say, voice low. My brain is spitting. I hate that I have to speak to her as a police officer, rather than as an MI6 officer. 'And maybe when I'm lying on top of you, and I'm inside you, and you're about to come, and I take the gun you keep under your pillow and put it at your head . . .'

Goddamit.

Her expression does not change. My words run dry.

I've lost it. The words are there, some of the determination, but the things I used to have, the spite and the fire and the conviction, they're not what they were. *The gun you keep under your pillow?* Really? That's all you've got? Where are the vengeful thumbs pressing against the oesophagus? Where is the breaking of the bones?

And she knows it.

'Oh dear,' she says. 'Maybe we could just have sex for the fun of it. I mean, you can still get erection even when you're not going to commit murder, yes?'

We hold the cold gaze across the table. Whoever she really is, she is at the height of this game, and I've long since moved on. That's what the nightmares have been telling me. Time to face up to the past, because those days are behind you.

'But then, maybe it would just be pity sex, and no one wants that.'

To my right the door to the café opens, and here comes Sutherland to save me from my impotent rage. He does not, however, come into the shop, instead making a *time to go* gesture.

I give the beautiful Russian spy a last hateful glance, but do not give her any further malicious lines from which to feed, and then I'm at the door and breathing in the fresh river air.

A car goes past, noisily crunching through the gears.

'You look happy,' says Sutherland, no light in his voice.

'We need to get something on her before she jumps ship. That was stupid.'

'What was?'

'Showing my hand like that.'

'Did you actually have anything to show her?'

'You know what I mean.'

An edgy conversation, Sutherland going with the mood and the tone.

'She already knows we're interested,' says Sutherland. 'One more visit won't have changed anything.'

The rapid-fire conversation comes to an end. The sound of the car disappears around a corner three blocks away.

'You called me out here because you looked inside and recognised I was about to lean across the table and strangle her?'

'That was Candy on the phone. The station put her through. I think she might be enjoying this. Davies is at home, down by the loch. Fishing.'

Turn away. Take a breath, try to draw some calm from it, find myself staring at a gull on the bank of the river.

'Right. We should get over there.'

'We bringing him in?'

Start walking in the direction of the car, Sutherland falling in beside me.

'I'll use the threat of it to get him to talk, then bring him in anyway.'

The river runs silently beside us. Behind, and to our left, I can feel Kadyrova watch us go.

Davies is down by the lochside, a rod in his hand, the line settled in the water. Rain falling, he's wearing a green Barbour fishing jacket. We were directed by Candy, who greeted Sutherland and me wearing nothing but her underwear, and underwear that is barely up to the job.

I walk down onto the small strip of sand that's not quite a beach.

'Mr Davies.'

He's seen me coming, and has already turned away, his attention directed to his fishing line, which he is reeling in, the baited hook travelling quickly through the water. I know as much about fishing as I do about sixteenth-century art.

'We need to talk, Mr Davies, and you might want to give me your attention,' I say. I don't want to have to stand here for twenty minutes, trying to squeeze the words from him. 'If you don't, I can take you into custody, and we can talk at my leisure, instead of yours.'

Much easier to threaten a British national than a Russian citizen with God knows how much diplomatic back-up.

He turns, the dismissive expression already set on his face, then he notices Sutherland standing a few yards behind, waiting in case his involvement is required. Sutherland may occasionally have the look of the office clown, particularly with his doughnut fixation, but he's a big lad with an effective air of thuggish brutality about him when required.

The expression on Davies's face changes, he turns back to the loch, quickly finishes reeling in the line and walks a pace or two towards me.

'What?'

'Can you confirm that Thomas Peterson, and or Euphrosyne James, paid you to paint a replica of Brueghel's *Massacre of the Innocents*?'

A second, his gaze does not waver, his expression does not change, then he says, 'Fuck's Euphrosyne James? Is that even a name?'

'You don't know the name?'

'No.'

'Then it doesn't matter who she is. The question still stands with regard to Thomas Peterson.'

'The only reason I know who that guy is, is because you came to tell me about him two days ago. I mean, seriously, it's barely one step from planting evidence.'

'You'd never heard of him prior to that?'

'No.'

'You never did any work for him?'

'No.'

'We have reason to believe otherwise.'

'Right, sure. Testimony from Peterson himself, is it? Oh wait, he's dead.'

I take a moment, look away from him, watch the wind ripple over the water. Can feel it through my thin coat.

'You can be honest, or we can arrest you for conspiracy in the murder of Thomas Peterson and we can talk about it a whole lot more down at the station,' I say, still looking past him, to the loch and the mountain behind.

'Bullshit.'

I look over at Sutherland, indicating for him to come over.

'That's . . . wait, what the fuck?'

'I don't have time for this, Mr Davies,' I say, harshly. 'I don't have time to stand here doing this garbage. Now tell me what I need to know, or you're coming to the station. And if you think it'll be good for your name recognition to get arrested, then we can make sure this really won't be the right kind of name recognition.'

Sutherland comes and stands beside me, his face set hard, waiting instruction.

'How did you both come to be at the football on Saturday?' I ask. 'You often go together?'

'How were we together?'

'You were sitting in the vicinity of each other. Maybe you couldn't get seats next to one another.'

'Seriously? Look, all right, Jesus. The guy asked us to do the painting. I'd never spoken to him before, haven't since. No idea how he got my name.'

'Sure you don't.'

Lips tighten, eyes narrow, a flare in the nostrils.

'I did the painting, he gave me money, I don't know what he did with it. I've never seen—'

'When?'

'Do I look like I keep track of dates?'

Without a word from me, Sutherland takes another step forward, at the same time producing a pair of handcuffs. Davies looks at us, and then his gaze is directed behind, where, about ten yards away, Candy is standing, now clad in a thin dressing gown, holding a glass of wine.

'Did he tell you why he wanted that particular replica?'

'Ha! Believe it or not, the man with criminal intent did not go posting his plans on the fucking Internet.'

'You met him, though?'

When he finally speaks it's in a tone that implies he's doing us an enormous favour.

'Aye. He came out here. Looked at my work. You could tell he knew fuck all about art. He had an iPad with him, checked my stuff against the originals. I had a couple of copies on the go at the time.'

'So, we have an entirely coincidental meeting at the football, and all you were to him was an unexpected reminder of a past he was already putting behind him?'

Davies now switches to disinterest, looking back over his shoulder at the loch. It's time for him to return to the fishing.

'I'm just not convinced about the coincidental part,' I say. 'The two of you were involved in criminal activity—'

'There's no crime in painting a repli—'

'There is if it's done with intent, and I'm not convinced it wasn't.'

'Jesus.'

'There was criminal activity, there was a *coincidence,* and then there was a murder.'

'I've got fish waiting for me,' he says, starting to turn.

'You're coming down to the station.'

'The fuck?'

He looks at me sharply, annoyed, then worried as he turns to Sutherland. The usual calculation runs across his face, the one that we see fifty per cent of the time – *how exactly am I going to get out of this?*

'Look, why don't we go inside and get a cup of tea, chat over a biscuit,' he says, and you can hear him forcibly ejecting the irritation from his tone.

I hold his gaze for a moment, then turn to Sutherland. Candy waits behind, enjoying the sport of the arrest.

'Sergeant,' I say, starting to walk away, 'take him to the car. I'm going to have a word with Candy. If he acts up, cuff him.'

'Look mate, just give us a break, we can talk,' pleads Davies.

'You almost had me at biscuit,' I say drily, over my shoulder.

34

Euphrosyne James is sitting at the table staring straight ahead at the mirror. PC Ross is at the door, watching her, eyes fixed.

She looks ready to explode. They regularly do, of course, sitting in this position. If not ready to explode, then scared, or determinedly disinterested. James cannot see us standing on the other side of the two-way mirror, but she assumes we're here, as people usually do.

There's an edginess between Sutherland and me. A conversation needing to be had, yet I don't know if either of us knows what it is we need to talk about. The air needs to be cleared, we just don't know where to start.

'You want me in with you, sir?' he asks.

'Sure. As usual, any questions or angles you think I might've missed, speak up.'

'Sir.'

And that's all. The conversation can wait, and we head on out into the corridor. In a similar room on the other side of the hallway, Sondra Peterson is waiting. Two doors down, Grey Davies is being held in a box room, four walls, two chairs, one desk, no windows, no mirror.

The short walk along the corridor, and then I open the door to the interrogation room, indicate to Ross that he can leave, then Sutherland closes the door behind us and we sit down across the desk from James.

She stares harshly over the table. We don't give her an in.

'I am flabbergasted,' she says eventually.

Sit in silence, let them speak first. Unless, of course, you recognise you have an Angus Sinclair on your hands, a man who could sit in silence for the rest of his life staring at a police officer. Then you go in, get on with it and try to provoke them.

'I have literally no idea why you brought me here. Martin's speaking to his lawyer right now, and if you think I'm saying anything before she arrives, then you have another think coming, Inspector.'

'You know exactly why you're here,' I say, 'and it makes no difference to us whether you speak before or after your lawyer shows up.'

'I know why I'm here?'

I stare blankly across the table. Sutherland, too, keeps his eyes on James, waiting for the explosion.

James swallows, lips tighten, jaw clenches, unclenches. The traditional tics of the guilty. It's just a matter of what it is she's guilty of. Pinning her down for switching out her grandmother's Brueghel isn't really why we're here.

'You're going to have to help me out, Inspector, because I really have no idea. The way things stand, Martin is going to have to collect the kids, and do you think for one moment that I can trust him to do that without fucking the whole thing up?'

She wasn't this aggressive yesterday morning. How quickly the gods turn . . .

'The way things stand,' I say, voice level, 'you're going to be in police custody for the next forty-eight hours, and if we're happy we've got a case to take to the procurator, much longer than that.'

James leans forward, rubs her hands across her face, then straightens. Expression set hard. Scratches her hair, obvious head twitch. Not doing a very good job of waiting for her lawyer to arrive before talking.

'You're going to . . .' she begins, and then pauses, as if she has to physically force out the words. 'You're going to have to help me out, Inspector. Let's say we start by you telling me what you think I've done, and then I can tell you what I've actually done, and then maybe I can go and collect *my fucking kids* from school.'

Time to talk.

'You and Thomas were angry at your gran for spending money on the painting. You arranged with Thomas to get a copy made, then you switched the painting. Mrs Worrell worked that out, by the way. With there being no honour among thieves, you and Thomas fell out over it, then you and Sondra conspired to murder Thomas, as well as the two men at the home who'd become aware of what you'd done.'

James stares expressionlessly over the table. A moment, while my accusation becomes part of the fabric of the conversation and of the room, and then James's face finally becomes quizzical.

'Hard to know where to start,' she says. 'How, in this plan, did Sondra or I manage to kill anyone at the home? We broke in, in the middle of the night?'

'You're working with someone.'

'Ah.'

Another silence. Five seconds becomes ten. James's gaze never deviates from mine.

'You're wrong,' she says eventually, voice cold.

'Tell me what's right, then.'

'None of what you said is right, and I need to go and pick up my children from school.'

'When was the last time you saw Thomas?'

'I don't know. Christmas 1985 maybe.'

'When was the last time you saw Thomas?'

'Jesus.'

273

'Let's say that you didn't have Thomas killed, but you were involved in swapping over the painting. We know you're not going to run off if you're released, so why don't you co-operate, and maybe we can have you charged for the painting exchange and released on remand by the end of the afternoon.' The plainly spoken, barefaced lie; working a dream for politicians everywhere for generations. 'Keep pulling this bullshit, get your lawyer in, and give us nothing, then you're here for the full two days, and after that, we'll see how it looks.'

I turn to Sutherland.

'How d'you think it'll look, Sergeant?'

'Bad,' says Sutherland. 'Prison-bad.'

'Oh, for goodness' sake,' says James, 'I cannot believe this. I cannot believe you'd pull this kind of cheap stunt.'

'We can make a case to get you on art fraud and theft, Mrs James, which will be more than enough to send you to prison. There's no stunt.'

'Jesus. Martin's lawyer is going to eat you for breakfast.'

'Lawyers have eaten me for breakfast so often I'm on more menus than eggs Benedict. When did you last see your brother?'

'They came for lunch a week past on Sunday. Happy?'

'Thank you,' I say. 'How were things between Thomas and Sondra?'

'What?'

'Simple question, Mrs James, you don't have to read anything into it. Did Thomas and Sondra seem happy?'

James takes a moment, calculating where this line of questioning is going. Is it straightforward, can it trip her up?

'They were awful,' she says eventually. 'But then, they were always awful.'

'Why?'

Harsh tone, demanding that James just gets on with it, expecting everything, giving nothing in return.

'It was a rebound marriage for her. She needed Thomas to save face, after the last guy left. I don't know anything about him, apart from the fact he knew what he was doing. But she got her new husband quickly enough, and he was way more successful, or at least appeared to be, so she had her trophy.'

'What was in it for Thomas?'

'You've seen her, right? I expect she put out for him on occasion. She got self-respect, he got sex and a family he could pretend to give a fuck about. Marriage made in heaven.'

'D'you think she might've wanted him dead?'

'Look, I don't know where you're getting this thing about the painting being switched, but it wouldn't surprise me if Thomas did it. I mean, stealing from his own grandmother? Sure, why not? He was an asshole. And now, I don't doubt, Sondra's one phone call away from cashing in on the insurance. Why wouldn't she want him dead?'

James's words are picking up pace. Time to sit back and let her get on with it.

'So, what?' she continues, bludgeoning the silence. 'Could she have had him killed, is that what you're asking? Sure. Absolutely. And she was pissed off about the Brueghel, and Grandma bequeathing it to the Kelvingrove.'

'Was there anything to indicate, the last time you saw them together, that the situation had deteriorated, was worse than normal?'

'They came over, they were late, they were snarking at each other from the off. I mean, couples, it happens sometimes, especially when they're with family and they might be more comfortable, but this was brutal. Dear God. I mean, to act like that, it was quite appalling. Martin made this, you know, he ordered lamb from the local butcher. It cost close on fifty pounds. Seriously. And he started cooking it on Saturday morning, for Sunday lunch. It was ... they talk about meat melting in the mouth, but this? I said to him, you're wasting it on those three. Not that I really blame the boy, what's he supposed to do, trapped between those two awful people?'

'Did Sondra make any explicit threat to your brother?'

A pause. As always, it's for us to work out if the witness is taking a moment to decide whether to divulge information, or to make something up.

'I overheard them talking after lunch. We went for a walk round past the golf course. You've seen where we live. Took the dogs.'

'I didn't see any dogs,' I say.

'They go to doggy day care,' says James, the word 'doggy' juxtaposing bizarrely with her tone. 'I don't have time. They're Martin's dogs. I said from the off, if he wants them, that's fine, but don't exp—'

'What did you overhear?'

Another breath is exhaled through the nose, lips clenched.

'She said there was no way – no *fucking* way – she was authorising him spending the money on the company. I didn't know what money they were talking about. I didn't want to know. It was quite unseemly, but I did think, well that's them, isn't it? They're bad all the time, but my God, bring money into it, then what are they going to be like? It's like those little bitches you get in primary school, and you think, what are you going to be like, how awful a person will you be, once you've discovered sex?'

'They were arguing about what to do with the money, or how it was split between them?'

'Sounded like Thomas didn't want to split it at all.'

'Really?'

'Oh, classic, isn't it? You ask for details, then when I tell you something that might be of interest to you, you don't believe it.'

'Why didn't you tell us any of this before? You were happy enough to implicate Sondra. Why not tell us about the lunch?'

'I didn't think ruining the lamb was that big of a deal, but if you insist on investigating that, then that'd be great. Maybe we can get our money back from Sondra.'

I abruptly get to my feet.

'We'll start processing the paperwork, but if I were you, I'd get used to the idea of being here until at least this time tomorrow. We'll show your lawyer through when she arrives.'

'Jesus,' she mutters, the contempt contorting her face, then Sutherland and I are at the door, and I usher Ross back inside to stand watch.

'Seriously, Inspector, will you get the fuck back in here?' James snaps from behind.

'If the lawyer hasn't shown in the next twenty minutes, just take her to the cells, please, Alex,' I say.

I close the door, then Sutherland and I walk quickly along the corridor, not stopping at the door to the room holding Sondra Peterson.

35

We're standing at the office window, looking out on a bleak afternoon and the dark grey clouds over Knockfarrel hill, the ill feeling of the investigation weighing heavily upon us both. Cup of coffee each. Sutherland is finishing off a doughnut, eating with the enthusiasm of a long-distance runner grudgingly taking on one of those awful energy sachets.

The open-plan is quiet, although most people are still here. The world continuing to turn, the bulk of the work being done unrelated to this case. Outside, the dark clouds gather as we watch. On the hill, a flock of crows rises from the trees, as one, in an angry squawk we cannot hear.

'She was nice,' I say. Just words.

A beat. Sutherland takes a drink, his eyes following the flight of the crows.

'Yep,' he says after a while. 'I particularly liked what was more or less *I was happy for him to die because he ruined the lamb*. Holy shit.'

'There's something almost biblical about the conflation of brothers, lambs and death.'

'Do we believe her?' asks Sutherland.

Take another long drink of coffee. School break almost over.

'Not yet. Not until I've got another story I can believe more. Thomas got the picture done, Euphrosyne provided the means to make the switch. It fits. Until something else drops into our laps, we'll run with this.'

'OK,' says Sutherland, 'but . . .'

He lets the sentence go with an uncomfortable wave, lifting his coffee.

'Out with it,' I say. 'You can't end on "but".'

'I believe her,' he says, words squeezed out. 'Look, I know she has that wealthy air of entitlement. The kind of person who uses money to solve problems. If anyone pulls her up on it, she's going to have this sense of moral outrage, *how dare you?*' He pauses, doesn't sound happy about what he's saying. 'But she sounds honest. That's it.'

'You think we should release her to collect her children?'

'God, no,' he says, indignantly.

The circle of crows, having felt the call to move off into the afternoon, now returns angrily to its previous position.

Do they all land on the exact same branches they vacated a minute ago?

'Right,' I say, 'I needed the decompression, but we should get back in there.'

'Sondra Peterson?'

'Yep. I expect we'll find her equally forthcoming and agreeable. You can take this one.'

'K.'

Sutherland drains his coffee, lowers the cup, hesitates, and then wipes his mouth with his sleeve.

As we're walking back to work, I notice he's giving me something of a look, then finally he says, 'I'm on more menus than eggs Benedict?' He laughs. 'Really?'

I smile with him. Can't help it.

'That's a decent line,' I say.

He laughs again, and I can't help laughing too, as we walk out of the open-plan.

'It's a terrible line,' he says, through the joke.

'My scriptwriters spent hours on that. Just wait until you hear what they've done with the word *infamy*.'

He rolls his eyes, and suddenly, from nowhere, we're just laughing stupidly, giggling like children. A celebration of the release. Along the corridor we go, and even though none of it's been that funny, for a moment, just a fleeting moment, with the lightening of the mood, the crows are banished and it feels like walking out into the sun.

Sutherland pushes across a photo of Sondra Peterson eating dinner with Steven Priestly at Pure Asia two nights ago. Peterson looks at it, Sutherland and I watch Peterson. The silence in the room is thick. When she swallows, the noise is cacophonous.

'I had dinner with another man after my husband died. It's allowed, isn't it?'

She looks up from the photograph. Not nearly as pugnacious as Euphrosyne James. Peterson is worried in a way that James wasn't. Or maybe she just lacks James's innate sense of self-worth.

'This man killed your husband,' says Sutherland.

Another loud swallow. The clenching of the jaw. Her right hand forms into a tight fist, knuckles turn white.

'You were paying him for his work?'

'What? No. No.'

'Your son identified this man as Thomas's killer. You saw his corpse at the same time. You didn't—'

'I didn't want to say anything. Doesn't mean I killed him.'

'We aren't talking about how Priestly died. This is about how your husband died. Why he died. This is about you paying Priestly to kill your husband.'

'That's not what happened.'

'What *did* happen?'

She swallows, another thunderous sound. Here we go. The painfully extracted truth, or the painfully constructed lie.

'Steven and I had been having an affair,' she says.

Sounds weak. The clock ticks.

Sutherland gives it a moment, then, 'How long had it been going on?'

'Six months. About six months.'

Sutherland doesn't ask the follow-up, just holds a sceptical eye and lets her continue beneath its weight.

'Roddy walked in on us a few weeks ago. I mean, it's not like he thought much of his stepdad. Hated him. But he hated that I was cheating on him. I don't know who killed Thomas, I really don't. And neither does Roddy. I knew what he was up to as soon as he started talking to the photofit computer lady. He described Thomas's assailant as being Steven.'

'So, Steven Priestly didn't murder your husband?'

'No.'

'Your son just implicated him out of spite?'

A pause, then, 'Yes.'

'There were other witnesses who worked on the e-fit,' says Sutherland. 'It wasn't just Roddy.'

Silence. She's not very good at this. Eventually, she says, 'That's how it is,' while barely opening her mouth.

'What does that mean?'

'Maybe the real killer looked like Steven. Maybe the other muppets didn't really see him, they just wanted to be part of the process. That's what people do. They want to be part of things. But they didn't know, not really, so they just agreed with the description Roddy gave.'

Sutherland doesn't immediately ask a follow-up. Peterson squirms in the silence, but somehow manages to stop herself digging the hole any deeper.

'So, you knew Roddy was lying, but you didn't stop him. You couldn't say anything to the police?'

'Not without . . . the whole thing's a mess. I kept my mouth shut and hoped no one would report Steven for his likeness to the photofit. Then I called him, and we went out to discuss it. He was lying low, walking around in dark glasses and a beanie. I said to him he should go somewhere, even if it was just to a camping site in Cape Wrath. Just somewhere he could be invisible.'

'You must've been upset when you found out he was dead.'

We watch the calculations play out, before finally she says, 'Yes.'

'Any ideas who might've killed him?'

'No.'

'What about Roddy?'

Her eyes widen, the protective mother in her bursts to the surface. Good question. Brutal.

'You leave him out of this.'

'According to you, it was him who brought Steven Priestly into it in the first place.'

'Roddy did not kill Steven,' she says, voice cold.

'We'll need to speak to him.'

'You will not!'

Sutherland lets the vehemence of her tone dissipate into the silent room. Allows her to come down off the instant high of anger, her breathing heavy, face flushed.

'You need to think this through,' says Sutherland, his voice level. 'If you're lying, then you just falsely implicated your son in a crime. If you're not lying, then your son *is* guilty of a crime. Either way, we need to talk to him, and no amount of you getting annoyed changes that. We don't know everything or everyone who's at play out there, but it could be that someone killed Steven Priestly because he thought he'd killed your husb—'

'Of course I lied,' she says, the words shooting out.

Sutherland again allows the silence in the room, and when he decides it's time for her to continue, he does so with a contemptuous nod.

'What?' she says, the word stabbing into the hush that Sutherland had let fall.

'You just said you lied.'

'Yes.'

'So, now you're going to tell the truth.'

'Jesus.'

I smack my hand down on the tabletop. Short, sharp, the sound cracking through the room.

'Drop the damn tone,' I snap. 'We're trying to solve your husband's murder. Tell us why you were meeting Priestly on Tuesday.'

She didn't see that coming.

She holds my gaze for a moment, then looks back at Sutherland. Slowly her eyes drop to the table.

Here we go. I may have cut off the flow of lies, but only by cutting off the flow of words.

'I want to see a lawyer,' she says.

'Oh, for God's sake,' I mutter.

There's a knock at the door, it opens and Cole puts her head into the room, leaning on the door handle.

'Can I have a word, sir?' she says.

I turn to Sutherland. It's a wrap for now. We get up, walk out into the corridor, indicate for Constable Wright to step back into the room, and then close the door behind us.

'Everything all right?' asks Cole.

Can see that I'm angry, which isn't normal around here. Sometimes, listening to serial liars, one after the other, one's patience goes.

Sutherland stares at the floor.

'It's fine,' I say. 'What's up?'

'Just had a call from DI Strangways in London,' says Cole

'Clean forgot about her,' I say. Can feel the anger slowly dissipating. 'What's she got?'

'Turns out Westbrook and Singh were lovers.'

She holds my gaze. A good officer, Alice Cole, even though I'm likely looking at her as though this news is her fault. This news that skewers everything I've been channelling about Russian involvement in this business.

'Really? No one knew they were gay before? That's not the kind of thing that just pops out of nowhere.'

'They knew they were gay, but there'd been no talk of a relationship. Just two gay guys who happened to work together. She was a little defensive, but it's a fair point. It's not like, oh there are two gays in an office, they must be sh—'

'Yes, all right,' I snap. Of course that wasn't what I was implying. 'Do they have anything else?'

'Turns out there was a sex ring of some sort. Parties, swapping, that kind of thing. She says there are like fifteen hundred people working in the building, there's a bar on the top floor, and every Thursday evening there's an LGBTQI night. That's how it starts. Our two lovers were part of this *thing*, this particular group. The others managed to keep a lid on it for twenty-four hours or so, but someone finally cracked, and now they're all talking. Westbrook and Singh had something of a relationship. Singh wanted them to be monogamous and bale out of the parties, Westbrook wasn't having it. They split up, Singh was upset.'

'Any intelligence that he was going to commit murder over it?'

'No one seemed surprised, sir.'

'Shit. They haven't found him yet?'

'Nope.'

'So, no connection to Thomas Peterson and George Bailey's?'

'Strangways said the word in the office is that they likely barely knew that business existed. These people deal in hundreds of millions of pounds every day, so to them George Bailey's is this minor thing.'

'They're ruling out a Russian connection, then?'

'They can't one hundred per cent, of course. And the company deals with Russian money, but they're in the City, so of course they do. They also deal with Saudi money, Qatari money, Chinese money, and on and on. Just not British money, because there isn't any.'

'Dammit,' I say, eyes dropping, hands on hips.

'The inspector was keen to emphasise that things were quite intense between them. That's what the rest of the men in this sex ring are saying. Singh was intense. And, as we always surmise with that kind of business, there were a lot of drugs going on. Seems like no one is surprised Singh did what he did, nor how he did it.'

'None of them have any idea where he is now?'

'No. Best guesses are dead from a suicidal drug overdose or living in Thailand having sex with teenage boys.'

'Jesus.'

Can see Natalia Kadyrova sitting in that café, coffee cup hovering just beneath her smiling lips.

'So there never was a connection,' says Sutherland, trying to move it along, 'and it's just as we were postulating before. The disembowelling at The Dunes was an attempt to fake a connection that wasn't there.'

I let out a long breath, quickly processing and reassessing.

'All right, I'm not ruling out the Russians just yet,' I say, looking up, 'but I can't say I won't be delighted if we can. We'll leave Sondra and Euphrosyne to stew, and get back up to Dornoch.'

If nothing else, I need the head space the drive will allow. Thinking time. Hard to do when you've got two junior officers staring at you, wondering what you're going to say next.

'Let's not get ahead of ourselves,' I say. 'First of all we need to know when Davies delivered the painting. He'll cave far more quickly than either of the women. I'll speak to him now. Iain, check in with Fish, see how things are looking up there, tell her we'll be there within the hour.'

'All right if I head, sir,' says Cole. 'I should get on.'

'Of course, Alice.'

'Sir.'

Cole walks quickly away. Sutherland, poised to say something, has the words stall on his lips when she doesn't look at him.

I give him a more dismissive look than intended, annoyed at my own lack of hold on the case, my inability to see where everything fits. How quickly that earlier moment of light evaporated.

'For God's sake, Iain,' I say, once Cole is through the double doors, 'can't you just sleep with her and get it over with?'

He's behind me as we walk along the corridor to the room where Davies is being held. Answers with silence.

Stop at the door, hand on the doorknob, look back.

'Out of order, sorry, Sergeant.'

He's got nothing to say.

'Let's just do our jobs and try to get this wrapped up.'

'Sir.'

He turns and walks quickly away.

Deep breath, wishing I could have the last few minutes back, then I open the door and step into the small room. It's a similar set-up to the other two, except there is no large two-way mirror. PC Campbell is on the door inside, but I don't dismiss her, or even close the door.

Any objections Davies might have been about to voice about his incarceration are silenced by the look on my face.

'I've only got a minute. You've got that long to tell me what I need to know.'

He sucks in his breath, audibly, visibly. I know I'm right. He doesn't have the gall of the women. I don't yet know how those two have been lying, but they're not intimidated by being brought into custody. They'll tough it out until they're presented with incontrovertible proof. Often enough, of course, incontrovertible proof itself isn't enough to get the determined liar to change her tune.

Davies is different, though. The very idea of police custody scares him.

'What?'

'Tell me the process you went through with Peterson, start to finish, dates, and so on. Do it quickly.'

'Do I get out when I've finished?'

'Yes.'

No, obviously.

'Fine. What d'you want to—'

'When did Peterson first contact you?'

'About eight months ago. I don't know the exact date, but it was still winter, last winter, so it was a while.'

'Did you go up to The Dunes to look at the painting?'

'I wanted to. I mean, there're fucking hundreds of those Brueghels. I said I should look at the original. He gave me a photograph. But his Brueghel is almost identical to one that hangs in Vienna, so I went to look at that one instead. Peterson paid my plane ticket. Ryanair,' he adds, spitting out the word.

'How long did the process take then?'

'About six months.'

What?

'What d'you mean? You work quickly.'

'I'm a machine, but there was a queue. I had other work.'

'So, when did you hand over the completed painting to Peterson?'

Davies stares at the desk for a few moments, then finally lifts his head and says, 'End of August maybe. He came to collect it. I remember, it was hot as fuck. Don't get many days like that.'

End of August. Even if his memory is a week or two out, it's still several months after Euphrosyne James delivered the other painting to her grandmother's room. The switch, whenever it was made, was not done then. Of course, it doesn't preclude James's involvement, but it does mean the reason we suspect her is gone.

'Dammit,' I say, straightening up, standing back from the desk. In doing so Davies instantly, and visibly, relaxes.

'End of August?'

'Definitely.'

'Right. I'll speak to you later.'

'Wait, what the fuck? I—'

I can hear the abrupt end of the sentence just before I close the door behind me on the way out. He'd have known I was lying anyway.

Back along the corridor, quickly open the door at the end. Euphrosyne James is still staring straight ahead, looking angrily at the mirror, assuming she's being watched.

She turns slowly, and contemptuously, to look at me, but I don't even cross the threshold. No time for games.

'She can go,' I say to Ross. 'Take her to the front desk, sign her out. I'll speak to Mary on my way so she knows you're coming.'

'Sir,' says Ross.

'For God's sake,' says James, scornfully. 'You changed your tune quickly enough.'

'I'll know where to find you,' I say. 'You'd better go and get your kids before Martin inadvertently takes them to Disneyland.'

James emits a bitter laugh, and I'm gone, closing another door sharply on the investigation.

36

Heading north on the A9 once again. Sutherland travelling with me, silence in the car since we left Dingwall. There's thinking to be done about the case, certainly, but there's an uncomfortable hangover from my blunt assessment of how Sutherland could end his peculiarly strained relationship with Constable Cole.

Had I given it any thought, I wouldn't have spoken, so here we are again, and having duly thought about it, I'm not saying anything. So we sit in silence, concentrating on the investigation, tying strands together, creating the lattice that will be its backbone.

We're through the Nigg roundabout and heading directly north when Sutherland breaks the silence. Turns out it was just me concentrating on the investigation.

'I've already slept with her,' he says.

I could probably have worked that out if I'd put my mind to it.

'Sorry,' I say. 'Shouldn't have stuck my nose in.'

'It's fine,' he says, his tone not entirely indicative of some-one thinking anything is fine.

Rain falls, wipers sweep across the screen, headlights blur past in the dark grey of afternoon.

'You hid that well,' I say, after a while. 'How long had it been going on?'

'Oh, I don't know,' he says, little amusement in his voice, 'must've lasted a good forty-five minutes I reckon.'

I don't smile. He's not joking.

'What happened after that?' I ask, releasing the question into the discomfort of the car.

He doesn't respond immediately, but then he didn't tell me that he'd slept with Cole so that he could become coy and distant.

'Maybe I had guilt,' he says finally.

We drive on, the conversation coming in spluttering, scratchy steps.

'You're single,' I say.

'Yes.'

'Alice is single.'

Nothing.

'There's no reason for anyone else to be affected by it. I know you're her senior officer, but you don't have line management responsibility, and there's no reason why it should adversely affect your work.'

When he doesn't reply to that, I glibly add, 'As long as the two of you don't keep nipping off to the photocopying room.'

'Funny,' he says.

We don't have a photocopying room.

Silence.

I think of Sutherland and DI Natterson's widow, Ellen. He told me once that they'd had a thing. A very brief thing, behind Natterson's back. It didn't seem to have involved any conversation, just a passion that I must confess I didn't really understand. I wondered if, after Natterson's death, something might happen between them, but nothing was ever mentioned, we never saw Ellen around, then I heard she and the kids had moved down to Glasgow to be near her mum.

And yet, now, sitting here in an uneasy silence, I realise that it is likely about Ellen. I've spent two years not thinking about Sutherland and Ellen, two years not asking him about her, two years living my own life in my own world at the station. Sutherland, everything else aside, has spent two years emotionally invested in someone who, for reasons I can't comprehend, he's never going to have.

'Ellen,' I say eventually, when it's clear he's not going to speak.

We're not far from the turn-off to Dornoch now, and the conversation doesn't have too much longer to run. He doesn't reply, although a slight dismissive noise escapes his lips.

Quick glance, not as sure of myself now.

'Did you see her again before she moved down south?' I ask.

'Just once. She came to see me. To say goodbye.' The words are blades with which the memory cuts into him. 'She didn't actually say goodbye.'

That's all. Sutherland and Natterson's widow, unable to speak, consumed by a hunger for each other that they cannot live with, a hunger that condemns them to eternal unhappiness. A love that allows no space to breathe.

'Maybe you just need to force yourselves to be together. Push through the discomfort, see what there is on the other side?'

'And what if there's nothing?' asks Sutherland. 'What is life then?'

'Surely it's worth finding out?'

Another beat.

'That's not how it works,' he says.

A couple of minutes later, as we're pulling into the car park at The Dunes, he adds, 'It was time to move on. I thought Alice . . .'

The sentence drifts away, the thought unfinished, or at least, left unsaid.

I bring the car to a halt, turn off the engine, slip the car into first.

We sit in silence. Past the side of the house, the sea off the east coast stretches away in a murky darkness spray-painted by the crests of white waves. Across the sea the ever-present light of Tarbat Ness throws its intermittent, weary beam, diluted by the rain.

'Maybe you could speak to Alice,' I say. 'I'm sure Ellen would understand.'

'It's not about Ellen,' he snaps.

We stare straight ahead in angry silence. We could be the ones having the lovers' argument. Words unsaid. Me wanting to squeeze Ellen into the narrative, because I'd rather it was about Ellen.

He stares at the dashboard. I stare at the rain on the window. We need to snap the moment. I can't think of how it should be done, and so go for the quick, clean break.

'We need to get on. We can park the demons for now.'

He doesn't move, eyes locked on the dashboard.

'And what demons are you parking?' he asks eventually.

I don't give that conversation an inch.

'That's it for introspection, Sergeant,' I say. 'Come on.'

Our shared laughter in the corridor seems a hundred years ago.

'Right,' says Sutherland under his breath, and flicks the switch.

Work to do.

We stand by the window in Graham Strachan's room, returned to the scene of the crime. Sutherland, Fisher and I, needing a space to talk, away from the residents and the staff, free from the watchful eye of Warranted Safety.

We walked in here and none of us turned on the light. Perhaps at first we all left it to each other, but the crime scene seems in its element in the cold, grey light of late afternoon. The bed frame still in place, but the bloodied sheets and pillows and mattress gone. The chairs that will not be sat in. The statue of the desolate naked woman, the lacquer dulled by the afternoon, stands alone, waiting to be collected. Sold on, or moved to the house of a family member, if anyone will have her. In the deathly quiet of this soulless room, you can hear her weep.

I try not to think of her. I do not want her made flesh again in my dreams. I do not want to think, just now, of the Reverend Marcus.

The lights in the garden have just come on, casting dim shadows into the room, and through the mist and the rain the Tarbat Ness lighthouse holds us all in its sporadic dominion.

We talked at first. I reported on the timing of Davies's delivery of the painting, something I hadn't done in the stultifying silence of the car. However, soon enough the conversation dried up, now the room holds us, bound to its tragedy. As though Graham Strachan were still present, listening and judging, daring us to say something perceptive.

The silence becomes an invisible person in the room, one who dominates the conversation, not allowing anyone else to speak. How often this seems to happen. Do I allow it, or does it follow me around? The ghost at my shoulder, shutting down time, creating these spaces where no sound seems to penetrate. Now, Fisher and Sutherland have been sucked into the void.

Words come eventually. They always do. There are always words.

Fisher, the rationalist, with the need to force the narrative forward. When she speaks, however, even she seems taken by the moment.

'The great metaphor,' she says, her voice more detached than usual, filtered through frosted glass.

She doesn't say it, but we both know she means the lighthouse.

'How much are they needed any more?' she says, although she's not asking anyone the question. 'Technology moves on, they seem so dated.' A moment, and then she adds, 'Yet, there it stands. A certainty in all weather, at the end of the land, holding the people along this coast in its thrall. Reaching out to those beyond.'

Finally, Fisher's words, sounding so alien from the pragmatist, manage to draw us from our contemplative stupor.

'Maybe it's just the light at the end of the tunnel they all see before they die,' says Sutherland gruffly.

'No,' says Fisher, not quite removed from it, and then it's time for me to retrieve the investigation.

'A month or two after the copy was delivered to Peterson,' I say, and I can feel Sutherland and Fisher switching on beside me, 'that is, two or three weeks ago, Director Littlejohn decided to move the Brueghel out into the main body of the home. Within a fortnight, Peterson and two people at the home are dead.'

'There's a correlation between the timing of the painting being moved, and the murders,' says Fisher.

'Yes. We could do with finding something that links Cummins and Strachan to the—'

Fisher stops me with a movement of her hand.

'I've got it,' she says. 'The director mentioned that Mr Cummins had been looking at the painting last week . . .'

'Seriously?'

'And I went through the home's files on Cummins, and, believe it or not . . . he was an art historian.'

'There we are,' I say. 'Goddamn, we should've had that before.'

'I don't know,' says Fisher. 'It wasn't like it was his full-time job. The man was eighty-eight, and he studied art in the nineteen fifties. We're there now, sir, that's what's important.'

'And Strachan?'

'No one saw him looking at the painting, and the man was a mechanic by trade. However, it transpires he has an Open University degree in art.'

And the obvious settles like the softly falling rain.

'How many people knew that?' I ask.

'That's the thing. No one. I mean, no one knew anything about Strachan, but it's in his file.'

'Which means that someone on the staff knew.'

'Exactly.'

'OK,' I say. 'So Peterson gets a copy of the painting, he enlists the help of a staff member to swap the picture over, it gets left in Worrell's room, no one knows any better. Everything's cool. Peterson takes the painting away, sells it, splits the cash with the staffer on the inside. The plan's about as perfect as they could wish for, until . . . a couple of weeks ago Director Littlejohn decides to move the painting out into the sitting room, thinking it will be to Worrell's benefit. The staff member worries that it'll get noticed. There's a lot of money to protect here.'

'And we don't know if Cummins or Strachan said anything – seems unlikely with Cummins – but it could be that the perpetrator took them out the game just in case.'

'That works.'

'And,' says Fisher, 'I've checked the files, it doesn't look like there are any more potential art experts in their ranks. Hopefully the killing's stopped.'

'That's something, at least. So, how about the person on the inside? Any ideas? I feel like we can probably rule out Littlejohn, given that, if we're right, she created the issue for them in the first place.'

'She said Dr Raven was dead against moving the picture,' says Sutherland.

'Yes, she did. Quite vociferously so. And no one is going to have known those files like the doctor. Quite possibly, in fact, no one is going to have known them in detail *apart* from the doctor.'

'We should talk to her now.'

Still looking at the lighthouse. I wait for the blink of the light. Unable to talk until it's come, one-two-three-four, and the moment is broken.

'Yes,' I say. 'Let's just check out the lay of the land, get a feel for how things are and we'll call in on her.'

The conversation is done, the next stage in what we can hope will be the denouement is set, yet no one immediately moves.

The light at the end of the tunnel returns. Finally, after another cycle, it sweeps us in the direction of the door.

37

Standing with Fisher in the lounge, looking around the small gathering of the usual suspects. Blind Durin and Worrell, old, cantankerous Thorpe, Robinson and Crane. Others, like those three, who have not crossed the path of the investigation, sitting anonymously around the room, their lives no less important.

Darkness has fallen outside. The room feels stupefied. The murmur from the far corner, the incantation, is still there, but I can feel it, I can see her lips move, rather than hear it.

What does that remind me of? Phil Spector telling George Harrison he wanted to feel the acoustic guitars rather than hear them on *All Things Must Pass*. Haven't listened to that in a long time. There's a song on that album, 'Art of Dying', which makes me think of Leia Marcus. What she said about the stained-glass window in the church. Here we are, the interconnectedness of all things.

The song starts playing in my head. Fisher catches me smiling darkly to myself, and asks the question with a raised eyebrow. I shake my head, dismiss the thought, and Fisher turns away again.

A moment, she looks around, seemingly taking the temperature of the room, then says, 'I'm fascinated by the blind man, sir. There's something odd about him, right?'

We're waiting for Dr Raven. She wasn't in her office; now Sutherland's gone looking for her. I've got an uneasy feeling, wondering if Raven has somehow got wind of what we've learned, and has fled the building.

Perhaps that's not the root of my uneasy feeling.

I think of the blind man playing chess on the beach. It seems so long ago. It seems to have been surpassed. Those beach scenes continue to evolve. But let us suppose these people are appearing to me in the middle of the night for a reason. Why was Blind Durin, who has seemingly played no part in this business, the first from here to appear in my haunting, night-time narrative?

'Yes,' I say. 'There's something transcending the blind man and his game of chess.'

'Like the chess is a metaphor,' she says. A beat, she remembers the lighthouse, perhaps feels self-conscious about the platitude, and says, 'Another one.'

'It's the kind of place where they abound. Maybe we just look for them in these surroundings, where the old gather at the end. Maybe it's pre-ordained.'

'Pre-ordained?'

She gives me the look.

'Like the entire home is a statement of loss, an entertainment for the gods. Watching over the decline and fall of their finest creation.'

Talking as distraction. The thought of Blind Durin has troubled me since the first time I walked in here. The idea that he was already in my head. That he knew I'd be coming. How could Blind Durin *know* that?

'You don't think he'd be able to carry out a disembowelling, though?'

I can imagine Blind Durin doing pretty much anything. I don't reply.

'I was thinking,' and she pauses while she constructs the thought into a workable sentence, 'it's more that perhaps he understands what's going on around him. He understands truth and lies. For example,' and she pauses, as the thought is unusually fantastical for her, 'he might know the painting has changed. I can't think how he would know, and maybe if he was sitting there doing jigsaws while being blind, or playing Angry Birds on his phone while being blind, we wouldn't invest him with such power. But playing chess gives him this air of sagacity. I don't know, maybe it's skewing our view, leading us to think there's something there that isn't.'

'Chess, Angry Birds or otherwise, it does feel like he knows things he's not telling. Have you spoken to him?'

'I tried,' says Fisher. 'He was obtuse.'

Look at my watch, wondering what's happened to Sutherland, wondering if Dr Raven really has gone on the run.

'I think we should give it another go,' says Fisher.

The Durin of my dreams sits intimidatingly on the edge of my thoughts, at odds with the old man bent over his chessboard.

'Yes,' I say simply.

I glance at Mrs Worrell. Same position as ever, the same rapt attention granted the painting. I take a moment to watch her, and to wonder again what it is that holds her there, and then I approach Blind Durin, Fisher alongside.

'D'you mind if we sit down, Mr Durin?' I ask, standing by the chessboard.

You know for whom she tends the weeping fig.

I pick up the words in the silence of the room.

Blind Durin is bowed to the game, he does not move for a few moments. Eventually he lifts his head, looks directly at me with his cold, blue eyes.

'Inspector,' he says.

Fisher brings over a seat from beneath the window, and sits down beside me, as I take the regular seat opposite Durin.

'You're happy to talk?' I ask.

'Of course,' says Durin, then he turns, nods at Fisher.

I glance at the door, expecting Sutherland to come through at any moment. Expecting, in fact, that he will arrive at a run, Raven having fled.

'I'm curious, Mr Durin,' I say. 'Did you know that the painting, the Brueghel that's been hanging there for the past couple of weeks, is a forgery?'

Durin looks like he's giving this some thought, then he turns to look at the painting, or at least, to point his face in its direction. A moment, he turns back. His eyes rest on Fisher, then move back to me. His face is unreadable. This man could be the best poker player in the world, if he chose to be.

It was a leading question, and one I would not normally have asked. But Durin sees things indeed, and there seems little point in asking questions in shades of meaning.

When he talks he does not answer. His voice is low, spell-binding. The storyteller, a tale out of nothing.

'You've seen Mr Laine mowing the grass.' He doesn't frame it as a question. 'We had a Mr Laine, lived in our street. A few years after the war. We called him Crazy Alfred. He tended his lawn all day, and when he wasn't tending it, he would sit and stare at it. He didn't seem to work, he just worried over his lawn. It wasn't large. A patch of grass, maybe six yards by four, at the front of his house, behind a low, stone garden wall. The narrow border wasn't planted, although he did keep it clear of weeds.

'It got so that Crazy Alfred didn't even want to walk on the lawn. He cobbled together a device that allowed him to mow the grass without ever stepping on it.

'Then one year, I don't remember, maybe 'forty-nine, maybe 'fifty-one, there was a long, hot, dry summer. The instructions went out to stop watering gardens. A hosepipe ban, even if we didn't call it that back then. The talk around the street was that the rain would start as soon as the ban was introduced. It didn't. The ban continued for several weeks. Gardens wilted. Lawns turned patchy yellow and brown. But not Alfred's lawn. Alfred's lawn remained immaculate, lush and green. His grass continued to grow, Alfred continued to cut the grass without ever stepping on it. People on our street muttered darkly. We children, playing football on the road, picked up on the disquiet and watched, waiting to see what would happen.'

He pauses for a moment as he moves a chess piece, and then swivels the table around.

'The previous year I'd landed a ball in the middle of the lawn. I'd stood and looked at it for half an hour, my friends beside me telling me to bite the bullet and go and get it, even though none of them were offering, before Alfred appeared with a broom to delicately knock the ball off the grass. For the only time in my life I caught his eye as he tossed the ball back to me. For a second I got a sense of his pain, then he turned away.

'The police arrived at Alfred's house one day. Two of them, men in uniform. They left ten minutes later. They did not remove Alfred in handcuffs. Nothing changed as a result of that visit. The lawn continued to be beautifully lush.

'Then one night, several weeks into the hosepipe ban, someone covered Alfred's lawn in acid. The lawn was ruined, the soil was ruined. Pretty much everyone in the street stopped and looked at the lawn the next day. There seemed to be general acceptance that a necessary evil had been performed. No one was above the law.

'No one saw Alfred that day. He didn't appear to study the devastation. Not in the garden, not at the window. Most of them, the gawkers, of whom I was one, wanted to see Alfred. How would he react? Would Crazy Alfred do something to live up to his name? There would've been some hoping to see him weep. But there was no Alfred.

'Days passed. Still no Alfred. One day, a day when it rained, someone must have called the police. They turned up at Alfred's door and had to break in. They found Alfred hanging from the topmost rung of the bannister. They also found, as they knew they would because they'd been there previously, a room full of five-gallon bottles of water, which Alfred had had delivered. There was no food in the house. Whatever his source of income, Alfred had spent that month's provision on water for his lawn. Someone had ruined the lawn, and Alfred had killed himself. It was all we talked about on our street that summer. Crazy Alfred, who tended his lawn, and then killed himself because someone had destroyed it.'

Another pause, although this time he doesn't make a move, he doesn't swivel the board. Time has ground to a stop, as it has so often in this strange place. Neither Fisher nor I are saying anything until Blind Durin has reached the end of his tale.

'Years later my father told me the story of Crazy Alfred,' he continues. 'How his platoon had landed at Normandy. Thirty-six men. One survivor. He'd watched them all die. He'd been the nominated medic, and he'd tried, but had been unable to save any of them. He hadn't even been wounded. He spent the next year pushing through France into Germany. He helped liberate Belsen. He'd seen the emaciated living, the mounds of the dead. He'd held men and women and children as they'd died.

'After the war ... You've seen things, Inspector. I don't know where you've been or what you've done, but you've not been a police officer all your adult life. You've seen war, you've seen death. It hangs from you, like the sad mist of morning clinging to the last copse in an old wood. No one comes back unscathed. No one picks up their life as though nothing's changed, because they themselves have changed.

'And that war, people saw so much. They'd done so much. So much destruction, so much death. Some coped in ways that wouldn't be countenanced now, some coped in ways that allowed them to hide it completely. And some couldn't cope at all.

'Alfred coped by picking something simple. Something to concentrate on. The war had left him broken, consumed by hopelessness and failure. And so he came home and focused on a small patch of the world where he could have control. A small patch of perfection, that was all. He had seen the world, large and terrifying and brutal and out of control, and so he reduced his personal space to this tiny little area of grass. Crazy Alfred wasn't crazy at all. Just lost, and lonely, and scared.'

Another pause, like the adverts before the final sequence of a movie on commercial television.

'As well as all the bottles of water, the police found three empty bottles of sulphuric acid. Alfred, in so much as he could, had retained control until the end. Perhaps he'd tired of the muttering, perhaps he'd just grown tired. Everyone has to give up at some point. Alfred ruined his own lawn, and then took his own life.'

He makes another move, surveys the position of the game for a moment, and then swivels the board back around.

'Everyone has a story,' I say.

'Yes,' says Durin, 'they do. And yes, I thought it quite obvious.'

Somehow I know that he is talking about the painting, and that he was answering the question I asked several minutes, or half an hour, ago. Time has been lost again. Lost to Crazy Alfred.

No one is as they seem. There's always something behind the curtain.

'Why?'

'It feels different,' says Durin. 'It feels new. I passed by Mrs Worrell's room once when the door was open. About a year ago. I went in. I could tell she was there, I could tell there was a painting . . . that there was something old. Something with history. Think of all these old paintings, Inspector. Think of what Europe has been through since they were first produced. The war and the terror, the governments that have been toppled, the greed and the outrages of humanity. And yet, here they are, some of them at least, still surviving. You can feel it. They radiate history, the way a fire radiates heat.

'But this? This has nothing, it radiates nothing. It's like looking at a vacuum. Is it a good copy to your mind?'

'Very.'

'Hmm,' says Durin.

'Would you have any idea who changed it over? How they changed it over?'

Durin smiles at this, and I wonder why I've taken so long to have the conversation with him.

'That would be an interesting call for you, Inspector, wouldn't it?' he says. 'If I said I knew. If I said I'd seen it. How could you take that to the procurator?'

The blind man sees everything.

'What do you know?' I ask. 'We need to find out what happened, Mr Durin. We can worry about the successful prosecution later.'

I turn at a movement to my right. The door to the lounge opens, and Sutherland appears. I'd been worried that he'd be at a run. Instead he calmly gives me the thumbs-up and mouths, 'Got her' across the room.

I look back at Durin. He hasn't taken his eyes off me. Up until now I'd been feeling uncomfortable with the idea that Durin has been looking inside my head, but slowly it's changed. I don't think the story of Crazy Alfred was supposed to be about Durin himself, but the telling of it reveals his humanity. I know he can read me with strange and peculiar accuracy, but I no longer feel concern that he'd do anything with the information.

I turn away, back to the painting. Beside me, I can feel Blind Durin following my gaze, and we stare together at the scene of brutal sixteenth-century infanticide. Fisher is still sitting here, and I guess she's looking at the painting too, but she's not part of this particular narrative. The reason she was included in the scene has been removed, but she remains, sitting wordlessly at the side. This thing, whatever is silently unfolding now, is between Durin and me.

There is a still over the room, and over the house. For a moment, not a sound. Not the creak of a floorboard, not the sigh of a central-heating pipe, not the growl of a motorboat engine out on the sea.

38

'So who else had access to the files?'

In Dr Raven's office, Sutherland, Fisher and I. The room is brown. Strange. Brown carpet, light brown walls, dark wooden furniture. She has a smiling, black and white photograph of herself on the wall. Much younger in the picture. It could be captioned, *Doctor Anne Raven in happier times.* There are three framed certificates, and no other decoration. There's a tall, leafy, green plant on the floor by the window. Maybe it flourishes in sunlight, though it won't see much around here.

The room is illuminated by a standard lamp in the corner and a desk lamp to Raven's left. Her desk is a clutter of stacked papers. The computer monitor is on another smaller side desk, also to her left.

Lisbet Bauer is playing the fiddle, the tune weaving its way through the building as we've heard so often in the past few days. Indeed, it might be even louder in here, as though there's a portal between this office and Bauer's bedroom. Imagine this mournful tune, the soundtrack to your every working day. What would that do to you? How deeply into the pit of introspection would you fall?

I know my own answer, though at the moment I do not need the fiddle.

'I'm not getting the connection here,' says Raven. 'Maybe if you told me what I'm missing.'

She sounds annoyed, but not in a way that's unfamiliar. So many people are annoyed when being interviewed by the police. Everyone expects us to do our jobs, to keep everyone safe, to catch perpetrators, to lock them up. Yet they resent the police at the same time, wanting us to exist and solve crime in a vacuum.

Dr Raven is showing this kind of regular resentment. Either she has nothing to hide, or she's very good at covering for herself.

'This is about the painting,' I say. 'The Brueghel.'

Raven shivers, the very thought of it putting an ill taste in her mouth.

'I don't know what Holly was thinking hanging it in public.'

'She said you argued.'

'I bet she did.'

'What were your objections?'

'Really? We have a home full of vulnerable, elderly people.'

'It's not especially graphic. You could easily look at it and not immediately pick up what's taking place.'

'That's fine if this was a gallery, but there are people who spend their lives in that room. And really, what does that have to do with . . . I mean, you're here because of the two deaths. Why are we even talking about the painting?'

'You don't know?'

'I really don't, Detective. Why don't you tell me, then you can do that thing of trying to work out if I'm pretending to not know what you're talking about?'

Funny.

Accurate nevertheless.

Interestingly, her annoyance seems to be slowly dissipating, giving way to bewilderment. A resigned bewilderment.

'A couple of months ago, Mrs Worrell's grandson made an exchange, swapping out the original artwork for a near-perfect copy, presuming that Mrs Worrell either wouldn't notice, or wouldn't be able to say if she did. There was no

310

particular danger of anyone else noticing, as the copy was so good, and so few people saw it.

'And then the director decided to move it out into the open, and suddenly there were a lot more people with access, people who might've been able to spot it was a forgery.'

I pause, but she really doesn't seem to know where this is going.

'We know from the files of both Mr Cummins and Mr Strachan that they had some sort of art history background . . .'

'Wait, they were killed because they knew about art?' she asks.

'That's what we have at the moment,' I say. 'You have a better suggestion?'

'No, but that's preposterous.'

'The painting was bought three years ago for two-point-four million pounds. It's possible that it sold on the black market for far more. That's a lot of money to protect.'

Raven is silent. There's little to be said, other than an acknowledgement that many people have been killed in the world to protect a lot less than two-point-four million.

'So, the question is, Dr Raven, who knew that Mr Cummins and Mr Strachan had an art background?'

She stares blankly for a moment, and then the realisation hits her, the various stages of it coming in quick waves.

'Wait,' she says, voice suddenly showing renewed signs of kicking into life, 'you're accusing *me* of knowing. You think I killed Mr Cummins? You think I . . . gutted Mr Strachan?'

'Who else could've known the men had that knowledge?'

'Well, Holly for a start. Are you accusing her?'

'It was Director Littlejohn who insisted on putting the painting out in public. Why would she have done that if she was worried someone would recognise it for what it was?'

'Well, I . . .'

Raven lets the sentence go, then looks at the others in the room, Sutherland standing by the door, Fisher standing, seemingly casually, by the window. Raven is feeling it now. Hemmed in. All exits blocked.

'You're serious?' she says.

'Doctor, we seriously want to know who else had access to the files. Who else knew enough about these men to view them as a threat?'

'Do you think I killed Thomas Peterson as well?'

'Where were you on Saturday afternoon?'

'What?'

'You weren't at work on Saturday afternoon.'

'. . . No.'

'So, where were you?'

'It's none of your business.'

She sounds exasperated rather than annoyed.

'We're investigating a murder. You're a suspect. It *is* our business.'

'I'm a suspect? I help people, I cure people, I don't . . . I don't cut them open. I'm a doctor, for goodness' sake.'

'So was Harold Shipman.'

That was cheap, but sometimes the harsh jibes are just crossing your lips before you can stop them, and sometimes you don't want to stop them anyway.

'Oh, please.'

'And Josef Mengele,' Fisher tosses in surprisingly from the side.

'Crippen,' says Sutherland.

'Lecter?' says Raven, with the air of an irritated schoolteacher.

'Were you having an affair with Thomas Peterson?'

'What?'

'Thomas Peterson had sex earlier in the afternoon of the day he died. He wasn't with his wife. Was he with you?'

'I barely knew the man. This is appalling. It is appalling, isn't it? Now, if you would please leave.'

'You're coming with us.'

'No, I don't think I am.'

I get the exasperated look from her, then she turns and gives Fisher and Sutherland the benefit of the same confused stare. Fisher is no longer looking so casual. Sutherland is standing, ready, by the door.

'Iain,' I say, eyes still on Raven, 'you know what to do.'

'Oh my goodness ...' begins Raven, then she lets the sentence go, as she watches Sutherland cross the room towards her.

39

Bauer is still playing the fiddle, the sound continuing to drift insidiously through the building. There are so many stories locked up in this golden cage, and while some of them might be happy, and some residents might find this a natural and comfortable final chapter to a long life, there is also, inevitably, a well of sadness. Through Bauer the well finds musical form.

Early evening, wet and bleak. Unrelenting. Perhaps this awful week is almost over, although while there is still a killer at large and the precise motives for everything that has been done remain unclear, it's too early to say that the residents can sleep easily once more in their beds.

Whoever's guilty, I'm almost certain it isn't Dr Raven.

'D'you want me to get everyone together?' asks Holly Littlejohn.

Her voice is flat. Dead. Different from a couple of hours earlier. Something has happened in between, although not something she feels the need to tell the police about. The moment we shared earlier, when she felt able to talk about her former husband, who is neither an ex-husband nor a deceased husband, but in some strange limbo in between, has passed out of memory. We have slotted back into our prescribed roles. Director and inspector.

We're standing together by the window in the lounge, looking out on what's left of the view of the sea. No sign of life out there, the tide retreating in white waves.

'Who?'

'The staff,' she says. 'Get the staff together. Let them know that you've arrested Anne. It would help put their minds at ease. Once the staff know, we can, well, fan out among the residents, make sure everyone knows this dreadful business is over.'

I give Littlejohn a glance, one which she doesn't seem to understand, before turning away and looking around the room. She's preoccupied, which might explain why she just completely misrepresented what I said to her.

As usual, there are seven or eight residents in place, the line-up only slightly different from earlier in the afternoon. Everyone in their usual positions, with the peculiar exception of Blind Durin, who is sitting with Worrell, staring at the painting. There is, naturally, no acknowledgement from either of them that they are not sitting alone. Mr Thorpe is scowling at his crossword, and Nurse Caddow and Nurse Williams have just entered the room, standing by the door, Williams with a phone in her hand, Caddow a clipboard, watching over the residents with a distracted air. Robinson and Crane are by the window, having a sullen conversation about the continuing sullen weather. The old woman sits in her spot, her lips moving, but for now there is no sound.

'I told you I didn't want you to let anyone know,' I say.

'I haven't,' says Littlejohn defensively. 'I just thought, now that Anne's gone, maybe you wanted to get people together. It's been so oppressive around here. I may be finished, but I'd like at least to leave everyone feeling a little happier than they have been the last few days.'

'I don't want anyone to know,' I say, coldly, 'so please don't mention it in public. We'll tell them when the time is right.'

'Oh,' she says.

In Littlejohn we've seen several versions of the same person, the rollercoaster, as the consequences of what's happening here have unfolded. One death, two deaths, the police, the forensics, the clamour of calls from concerned family members, the calls from head office in the US. Big business doesn't mess around, and is not in the least forgiving. It doesn't matter who's to blame for the murders, or that the director in charge could barely be held responsible. Someone has to take the fall, someone high up.

Money. The root of every problem. Climate change and the banking crisis, the NHS and increasing knife and gun crime, and every damn issue you can think of in society. The solution is usually straightforward, but someone will lose money if that solution is implemented, so the government will be lobbied and badgered and threatened until big money has its way.

And here is no different. This isn't about the effect of these events on a community of the elderly, staying in the last place they'll ever live. This is about share price.

'What happens now?' asks Littlejohn.

'Almost dinnertime, folks,' says Caddow behind us. 'Five minutes.'

'Things are in progress, Director,' I say, Caddow's voice no more than a small part of the soundscape. 'This isn't about whether you get to leave everyone feeling fluffy once you're gone, if you do go.'

'Have you seen the Geras price on the S&P 500? There's no *if* about it.'

Her tone is bitter suddenly, but I don't think the bitterness is aimed at me. It's the first thing she's said since we started talking that showed any real investment in the conversation, presumably because it's what's currently on her mind.

'You've already had the call, then?'

Her lips are thin, her face tense. As before, I can see the internal debate, deciding whether it's worth her while to talk. Where did it get her when she talked to me before? If getting the story of her husband off her chest provided her with any kind of relief, that feeling has long since evaporated. Yet I know, as I watch her, that she's going to talk, if for no other reason than she has no one else.

'Seven years,' she says after a moment, eyes dropping. 'Phht! And thanks to events completely outside my control. What exactly was it I was supposed to have done to stop this? To stop two murders? They said I should have thrown money at security after the first death, because it was slightly suspicious. I mean, seriously? Can you imagine the godawful stink, the *stink*, if I'd asked for those funds, or if I'd gone ahead and authorised the spend? Maybe Mr Cummins didn't have a heart attack, so we'll just spend half a million on security, scare the shit out of all the other residents and have a queue of panicking relatives. Jesus. But here we are, a disembowelling is always going to free up funds, right?'

'I've had the call, and now await the official e-mail with the terms of my dismissal.'

'Every tragedy needs a scapegoat,' I say.

I may be enabling her victimhood, but she's right. No one likes the scaremonger. Everyone likes the person who says *don't worry, it'll be fine*, until it's that person who gets the blame when it's not.

'Yes,' she says. 'And I'm standing here wondering how it is I can refuse to be the scapegoat, and wondering what it is that I really should have done, and I don't know. And ultimately, it isn't about me, I have to remember that. I may have lost my job, but two people lost their lives, two families lost their father and grandfather, and I really ought not to be making this personal. My part in this sorry little drama is over, and off I go, out into the great blue yonder, worlds to conquer.'

'Play your cards right with head office, and they'll find something else for you. A recommendation, a nod and a wink.'

She nods, but doesn't wink.

'Yes. I let them rodger me from behind without complaint, they'll enable me to go and play somewhere else. The bigger the stink I make, the harder it becomes for everyone.'

She puffs out her cheeks. The bitterness hasn't completely gone, but the conversation has at least helped her a little.

'Am I clear to go home now and get pleasantly hammered, or d'you think I should stick around?'

I turn away to look around the room. There they sit, the care home residents. They have grown old. Age has wearied them, the years have condemned.

'I think if you go home, you're likely to get called back in again,' I say.

I turn back to look at her, her face expressionless. Here I am, taking away even her most basic relief.

'And I mean it,' I say. 'Tell no one about Dr Raven.'

40

We're all Crazy Alfred. Concentrating on what we can. Trying to exert an element of control over *something*. Hoping we can impose rules, that we can be something other than a pawn. Or Old Kent Road.

Most of us don't have Crazy Alfred's guts, though.

There is a flat calm out on the water. Clouds are low, visibility minimal, a still over the shore. Beyond the low cloud and the haar upon the water, the lighthouse beam barely dents the curtain.

Here sits Blind Durin, in his familiar late-night spot. Lights off, in the chair at the small table by the window in his room, looking out on the sea through smirry glass. The smirr upon the glass, the haar upon the sea, mean nothing to Blind Durin.

He has not heard about us holding Dr Raven. He does not know what we know, he is not aware of any developments. He knows, however, that the ugly drama that has overwhelmed the care home in the previous few days is coming to an end. The final chapter is on its way.

He seems neither scared nor tense. Whatever is going to happen will play out, either in some other room in the home, or right here, where he sits.

Somewhere in the building, Bauer still plays the fiddle, although the instrument is muted, the sound swallowed by the walls. The feeling of it is in the air, however, the terrible lingering of Bauer's sadness.

The door opens. No one knocked. There is the soft pad of footsteps, then the door closing quietly behind.

'You all right, Mr Durin? I didn't mean to frighten you.'

If the light is turned on right now, then the game is up. But if the light is turned on, then the late-evening visitor will not be here for the purpose that we suppose.

'Just come to tuck you in, old man,' says Nurse Caddow, when Durin doesn't respond. 'Sorry I didn't knock. Old Thorpe's a bit restless down the hall, complaining about every sound. God, that man is something else. He reminds me of some grouchy old guy in a Woody Allen movie, right? He should be Jewish and living in an apartment on the Lower East Side or something. Instead, he's Scottish and he's just miserable as fuck.'

A beat.

'Sorry, language. I know . . .'

Nurse Caddow is doing the rounds in the dark as he does at this time every night. Nurse Caddow would not necessarily turn on the light, particularly since it makes no difference to Blind Durin. Nurse Caddow might well be here for no other reason than the usual.

A long pause. Caddow is standing by the table, looking out the window, down over the beach. The window is slightly open, so that you can feel the low cloud and the damp, sense the strength of the darkness.

'I used to live by that light when I was a kid,' says Caddow, looking into the murk, watching the steady blink from Tarbat Ness. His voice is soft, holding a peculiar, elegiac quality that I don't recognise in him. The coarseness of his comments on Thorpe was more typical. 'I used to create stories, of ships seeing the light through the gloom too late, smashing on the rocks. And smugglers. I used to imagine smugglers.'

He pauses, but he's not finished his reminiscence. He's saying something other than what he's saying.

'I wasn't the smuggler, though. I was on the shore, I was the one who found them. Who stopped them.'

This is it. His act of repentance. Barely worthy of the expression.

'I was the good guy. I don't think I ever knew what they were smuggling. What do people smuggle any more? Other people? Drugs? Those things weren't in my stories. I didn't know about any of that, I just imagined right and wrong.' A pause for the sad laugh. 'Right and wrong . . .'

'Your voice betrays you,' says Durin. He doesn't look round at Caddow as he speaks.

Caddow doesn't respond at first. I wonder if this could be the moment. That it will come without fanfare, without explanation. But I don't think so. It is not yet time.

'What d'you see, old man?' asks Caddow. 'There are so many here who don't think you're even blind, you know that? You've got this . . . I mean, you're extraordinary. I don't know whether to call it a sixth sense, or whether you have some other strange thing going on that allows you to *see*. I mean, you're blind, and yet you can *see*.'

Caddow isn't looking out the window any more. He's standing in the dark, hands by his sides, looking down at Durin. Caddow's moment of regret has passed. He has faced it, he has briefly wallowed in it, now it's gone. Slowly, Durin turns his face up to him. In the dark grey light of the night, their eyes meet, and Durin holds Caddow there, locked in place. Stuck in silence. Waiting for Caddow to say something, or for Caddow to leave, or for Caddow to do something else. Something that he wouldn't normally do.

Eventually Caddow's voice appears once more. Softer still, the return of the regret. Caddow does not want to be here. Caddow has misgivings about what is going to happen. It will happen anyway.

'So, that's the thing,' he says. 'We don't know what you see, old man, and so we can't take any chances.'

He pauses again, possibly waiting for Durin to speak, to defend himself, to put forward a case. Durin has said one thing this whole time, however long that time has been, and he will not say anything else.

'You know the painting's not right, don't you?' says Caddow. 'You know that's what this whole thing's about. I mean, I wondered when the copper, the detective, sat with Louise the other day, I thought, does he *know*? But, I don't think so. He was just sitting there, playing at his job, thinking he could get inside Louise's head. The method acting school of detective work. *I'll know what she's thinking, and I'll be able to solve her grandson's murder.* Give me a break.'

The elegiac tone turns to acerbity in three or four sentences, but then he pauses, and when he starts talking again, the tone of regret is back.

'But you. I wondered about you all along, whether you'd pick it up. And today ... well, here we are, old man. Sad to say, though, I've been speaking to the boss, and I'm afraid it's your time. You're a canny old bastard. You'll choose your moment, and we can't let that moment arrive. Thought I might be able to keep my hands clean, but now there's no one else.' A moment, then he adds, 'It's on me. Thought my days of doing this kind of crap were long gone.'

There is light, bitter mirth in Caddow's voice. In the light of the dark night by the window, Durin closes his eyes. Accepting what is to come.

Caddow moves around behind him, soft footfalls on carpet. His dark shadow stands over Durin, he pauses. It is the moment only the most hard-hearted do not take before delivering the fatal blow. The last second before the murder.

In the night we sense the raising of the arm.

The lights come on, bright, harsh, cold.

Out of the darkness, Caddow is revealed, standing over Durin, knife raised. He turns, eyes wide, and Sutherland is upon him, swatting the knife free from his hand, wrestling him to the ground. The cry from Caddow, the exclamation of 'Fuck!', is barely aggrieved or shocked.

The tone is so understanding of what's just happened that if he'd said, 'Typical' it wouldn't have sounded out of place.

There is no fight in him. And why would there be? Revealed to be the perpetrator in that moment, where is he going to go, what could he possibly say?

Sutherland is ready to pin him down, to throw punches if necessary. Caddow is thrown to the ground, and lies there, unmoving. No protestation, no more cursing, a casual mercenary's lack of commitment to the fight at the death.

The door opens, Fisher enters, two other officers alongside her. With that, Sutherland gets up, straightens his shirt and tie, then walks over to the bed and lifts the knife.

Blind Durin is looking over the room, face expressionless, completely unmoved. He has not shifted an inch in his seat at the disruption.

'Everything OK?' asks Fisher.

'Yep,' says Sutherland, then he takes a small transparent bag from his jacket pocket, places the knife inside and lays it down on a chair on the opposite side of the room, away from Caddow.

'Looks like we have our man,' I say.

I walk across the room, from my position over by the bathroom door, and stand over Caddow. He's no longer pinned down, but he's still lying on the carpet, making no attempt to move. The two constables are also over him, awaiting orders.

'You're going to tell us who the boss is,' I say.

Caddow looks up, then laughs.

'Director Littlejohn?'

Act stupid. Give him the easy one. The easy denial. Test the waters. I know it's not Littlejohn.

Nothing. A smile perhaps.

'Dr Raven?'

Nothing.

'You just said you were going to do what you had to do, because the boss had told you. Who's the boss?'

Too many people in the room. It's not like I'm going to start breaking the guy's fingers, but with this many witnesses you have to be by the book. I don't want to put the others in a position where they have to feign ignorance on my behalf. There will be no foot placed with increasing pressure against his testicles. Or his neck.

'Who's the boss?'

'If you think I'm implicating the people who'll be paying for my lawyers,' says Caddow, then he lets the sentence go with a laugh.

I look to the two constables, making a quick decision – mostly so I don't stand here filling myself with more useless rage – and say, 'Cuff him, put him in the car, leave him there for the moment.'

'Someone stay on him,' I add, as an unnecessary afterthought.

'I'll take care of it,' says Fisher.

'Thanks, Fish,' I say, then look at Sutherland. 'Right, Sergeant, let's go and talk to the boss.'

Behind me, still on the floor, Caddow laughs.

41

Littlejohn is sitting behind her desk, back straight, arms folded. Her silver hair is starkly and attractively etched against the dark of the window behind her. The ornate clock on the wall to her left shows the time as almost midnight. The only light in the office is the lamp on her desk. The Dunes, for the most part, sleeps. The corridors are not illuminated, there is no panic among the residents.

Tonight, murder has been averted, and although word has not officially gone around, understanding has seeped through the walls. Stand down from your fear. Relax. Sleep. Evil has been vanquished, and tomorrow normal service – normal, quiet, undisturbed, melancholic service – will be resumed.

'You've had the official e-mail then?' I ask.

'Yes,' says Littlejohn. 'My position as director has been re-imagined, and I am released to pursue my career elsewhere.'

'Re-imagined?'

'Yes. There will not be another director. Instead, the home will have a ... I don't know ... an administrator or, God knows ... a guru, maybe. Principal Guru In Charge Of Ensuring No Murders Occur Among The Indigenous Octogenarian Population.'

I don't immediately ask a follow-up question, allowing that slice of acerbity to hang in the air. Sutherland stands to my side. No one else in the room.

Fisher is taking charge of the crime scene – such as it is, given that so little was allowed to unfold – and is working

327

with Nurse Williams, who reads Braille, so that we can take a statement from Blind Durin for him to read and approve.

Durin, himself, does not seem at all bothered or upset that someone was about to try to kill him. Perhaps the presence of two officers in the room the entire time relaxed him, or perhaps Blind Durin's vision allowed him to know no harm would come.

'*I've been speaking to the boss, and I'm afraid it's your time*,' I say. 'Nurse Caddow's exact words.'

No change of expression from Littlejohn. Instead a low, dismissive grunt from the back of her throat. Her attitude has changed once again. Earlier she wore a despondency that was forgiving of a more intimate conversation with the investigating police officer. Now, as a result of the e-mail from headquarters, that despondency has been replaced by the abrasiveness that we've met previously. Up and down, round and round she goes, taken by the storm.

'Who d'you suppose he was referring to?' I ask.

'Couldn't begin to think,' says Littlejohn, 'but I suppose since I was his actual boss, and we're all sitting here like this, and you're asking me questions with that tone in your voice, you're looking to imply that he was referring to me.'

'I really don't know, Director.'

'We've discussed that . . .'

'It would seem obvious,' I say. 'Yet, it was you who put the painting out in the main sitting room, which would seem to preclude you being worried about someone finding out it was a forgery.'

'It was a forgery? That's what this is about?'

She smiles in a *who would have imagined such a thing* kind of a way. The reaction seems so obviously fake that I immediately dismiss giving it any significance. And I don't answer. Not about to lay it all out for her. She can work it out for herself.

'So the original was replaced at some point, by Mr Peterson presumably,' she says, 'and this was fine while it remained in the relative isolation of Louise's room. Then it got put outside and . . . people started dying. Cummins and Graham knew it was a forgery?'

Cummins and Graham, like a pair of opening batsmen, or a sixties folk duo, their names forever linked.

'Their files suggest they had knowledge of art.'

'Their files? That's all you've got?'

I hold her gaze across her desk. I can feel Sutherland bristling behind me. He just wants to cuff her, take her in, force answers from her, and if, in the end, we release her, then so be it.

'*I* would have access to the files, that's what you're thinking?'

I still don't answer.

'I mean, we all do, all the staff. Anne, Nurse Caddow, all the nurses.'

I'll let her talk for the moment. Let her work it out. Or, possibly, let her reveal what she already knows in such a way that she's pretending it's only just coming to her.

'Anne didn't want me to put the painting out, you know that?'

'Yes.'

'So, if this boils down to the painting being a forgery, something you still haven't explained, why would I make it more public?'

'I don't know,' I say.

She gives me an insistent look, the expression that demands some kind of answer. *Well then?*

'Just because there's nothing obvious,' I say, 'doesn't mean there's not something there.'

'Well, when you find it, I'll be delighted to discuss it with you.'

Another beat. Sutherland rocks forward on his feet, rocks back again. She glances at him, looks back to me.

'I'm not sure why we're even having this discussion,' she says. 'You caught Nurse Caddow, and you already have Anne in custody. And . . . yes, and when I reported Mr Cummins's death to the police, she wasn't happy about that either. You know that too.'

I do, and it's another tick in the box of her lack of involvement. The point of this discussion was to see where she was as the story unfolded, but I'm getting nothing from her. No admission of guilt, and no feeling that there's guilt being hidden.

'What about Mr Durin?' she asks, her brow creasing. 'How could he have seen the painting was a forgery?'

'He may be blind, but I think we've all got a feel for his particular abilities.'

She lowers her eyes, stares at the desk.

'You know we'll get access to all your bank records?' I say.

Nothing, although she does raise her eyes.

'So, if you've been receiving payments, or if you're involved in fencing the original Brueghel, we're going to find out.'

Nothing.

'And we will get access to your phone records. In some cases, it's not out of the question that calls will have been recorded. Storage is so easy nowadays, all sorts of companies store phone calls.'

A beat. Still Littlejohn's face is expressionless, her arms folded.

'There are CCTV cameras everywhere, we have facial-recognition technology that makes those new *Mission Impossible* movies look like they were made in the fifties.'

Still nothing. Perhaps Sutherland and I can have another laugh later about the absurdity of that last bold claim. In reality, we're still trying to catch up with *Mission Impossible* technology from 1966.

'We have not started, but we will be able to piece together your life from the last two months, Ms Littlejohn. So, if you have anything to hide, you'd be as well getting it out right now.'

'If what you're asking for is a *de facto* plea bargain,' says Littlejohn, her voice flat and humourless, 'wouldn't I be as well waiting until I'd spoken to a lawyer?'

Of course she would.

'And anyway,' she continues, 'I don't know why you aren't putting these questions to the doctor.'

I don't answer, and after a few seconds Littlejohn nods in response to herself.

'Of course. You already have, or you will, or whatever. Playing all sides.'

She finally unfolds her arms and lays the palms of her hands on the desk.

'It's late, and I'm tired, and I'm out of a job. To be honest, you can do every damn check into my life you want, working back from now to the day Mum was wheeled into an operating theatre for an emergency Caesarean. I don't care. You won't find much of it very interesting, bar the strange instance of my marriage that I told you about earlier. But go ahead, fill your boots.'

She stares at me for a while, and when I don't immediately reply, she switches her gaze to the restless Sutherland.

'I'm about to walk out of here for the last time, gentlemen,' she says, getting to her feet. 'Stop me, arrest me, or . . . whatever, but we're done talking.'

'Who's in charge once you're gone?' I ask.

Nurse Williams is still on duty, but it hardly seems right that she should be left in control. And there has to be some duty of care from the police, since we're holding various members of staff. I'll need to speak to someone from Geras Holdings in the morning.

Littlejohn laughs.

'Ha! Well, the kitchen staff know what they're doing, maybe they can run things for a while. Can't be much worse than it's been the last few days.'

'Who's your contact at Geras in Inverness?'

Littlejohn rolls her eyes.

'Yeah, good luck getting hold of that Russian bitch. I'm sure she'll speak to you when she feels the time is right.'

I stare at Littlejohn for a few moments, then turn and look at Sutherland. His face is set in its familiar, understated expression.

You've got to be kidding. There may be a lot of Russians working in Scotland, but Sutherland already knows the answer to the question that crosses his lips.

'What's her name?'

We don't have a home address for Natalia Kadyrova, an oversight for which I'm now kicking myself. Not as much as I am for not already knowing her involvement with Geras. So many loose ends to chase, something was bound to get lost. An oversight bordering on incompetence. When the reports are written and the judgements are laid down, I'm just going to have to own up to it.

Calls are made, however, as Sutherland and I drive hurriedly through the night, back down the A9 towards Inverness. By the time we arrive at the BBC building on Culduthel Road, we have a warrant to search Kadyrova's office, and Constable Cole, who never left work, has her home address.

With her house being a detached lodge in the forest beyond Kiltarlity, I asked Cole to head there, accompanied by at least two other officers, prepared to make an arrest. Meanwhile, Sutherland and I approach security at the front of the BBC building, ID and warrants in hand.

The door is buzzed open for us, as we show our ID to the camera, and we enter reception. The guard, waiting on the other side of the glass, and wary at the arrival of the police so late at night, looks particularly startled when I hold up my phone, and show the copy of the warrant that has been issued, permitting us to enter and search the premises. Only when she realises that it's one of the rented-out offices and unrelated to the BBC does she relax.

'All right, Inspector,' she says, 'that looks in order.' You think? 'Second floor, I'll take you up. No one else about at the moment.'

'We've been, we can find it, thanks.'

'I presume the office'll be locked, and if you don't mind, warrant or no, I'm neither giving you a key, nor allowing you to put the door in.'

I look at the name badge, sewn onto the black security shirt. Notice the wedding ring.

'Mrs Hatton,' I say, 'of course. If you could lead the way.'

'Inspector.'

Through the next set of security doors, and then along a short corridor, past three office doors that lie open, to an elevator. I'd take the stairs, but think it best to defer to Mrs Hatton for the moment. Mrs Hatton does not look like she often takes the stairs.

'Do you know the people who rent this office?' I ask.

'No,' says Hatton. 'There're a couple of suites rented, but everything's contracted out these days, of course. Literally no one at the BBC has any idea who we're sharing an office with. Piece of nonsense, but no one ever listens to the likes of me. It's all about money, isn't it? Everything's always about money. They'd rent an office to ISIS so long as they paid the bill on time.'

She snorts derisively, a curt dismissal of capitalism that it rightly deserves.

'We don't deal with the initial security clearance,' she continues when we're in the lift, 'and once it's done, anyone who works here is just another person turning up with a pass.'

I'm about to ask a further question, but realise that it borders on small talk. If Hatton isn't aware of the company, then she won't be aware of Kadyrova, and there's nothing else to reasonably ask her.

Second floor, turn to the right and along the corridor, the way we came four days previously. We stop at the door, Hatton brandishes her security card and the door opens. Then she steps back, allowing us to enter ahead of her.

As we step inside, the lights automatically come on.

I walk into the middle of the room, where we've been so recently, Sutherland walking up beside me. Close my eyes for a moment, rub my hand across my face.

'Crap,' I say.

'There were a lot more pictures on the walls the last time we came,' says Sutherland, glibly.

42

2.31 a.m. Back in the interview room, Sondra Peterson having been brought over from the cells. I told Sutherland to go home for the night, and then made the decision that Peterson wasn't going to be left until the morning. She's been awake for half an hour, she's had a cup of coffee thrust at her. She's tired, irritated and scared. She sits across the table, while Ross stands at the door.

Maybe we've sorted the worst of this out, but to what end? We caught Nurse Caddow in the act, but then we set up the act. We currently have no proof that he murdered Cummins and Strachan, and we can draw all the conclusions we want from the fact that we caught him in Durin's room, but I can already see the look on the face of the procurator.

Three murders, and as evidence, one set-up job.

'We've spoken to Roddy's dad,' I say. 'He's getting an evening flight from Boston, later today, and he'll be in Glasgow tomorrow morning. It'll be up to him, and Roddy, to talk it through, see what they want to do for now.'

'Roddy's still at Mum's?'

'Yes.'

'She won't let Brandon take him.'

I make a be-that-as-it-may gesture.

'Roddy's future is uncertain, that's for sure,' I say. 'If you want to play a bigger part in it, or at least, be separated from him for a shorter period of time, you can start right now by telling us everything. Otherwise ... well, who knows how long it'll be before you and Roddy see each other outside of a prison.'

'I'll get bail,' she says, with no conviction.

'Tell me about you and Natalia Kadyrova.'

Sondra Peterson is not a natural at this. Few are. That's why so many in this situation hide behind contempt. It's the easiest way to fake it. Usually, however, with such people there's a blip in the contempt – however brief – when presented with a piece of information they weren't expecting.

Not entirely sure, though, why Peterson wasn't expecting this. She obviously hasn't thought through how it's going to go, deciding instead to fall back on self-denial and disdain.

The blip passes, the look of angry defiance resumes.

'She's gone already,' I say, abruptly. 'Got on a flight to Paris earlier this evening. We're making calls, but the chances are zero that she's not already on her way to Moscow, or who knows, Iran or Syria or Ecuador or some other country that's just going to tell the British that they can ...' Pause, lean forward on my elbows, forearms flat on the desk, 'fuck off ...'

I allow that to sink in. The satisfying moment when you tell the crook that their co-conspirator has fled the coop without a second glance.

'So, that's where we are, Sondra. Your partner in crime has gone, and she won't have gone off to live in poverty. You're here, and this time tomorrow she'll be in the Hilton Triple Gold, Fifteen-Star resort hotel in Bandar Sera Begawan. She'll be drinking cocktails, and you're ...'

I gesture dismissively towards the cup of coffee, gone cold, at Peterson's left hand.

'What makes you think she was my partner?' asks Peterson.

The classic tentative dip of the toe. *How much do you know? How much can I get away without telling?* Well, Mrs Peterson, we know a lot, and you're not getting away with anything.

'You didn't kill anyone, Sondra,' I say. 'You may, or may not, have been the mastermind behind all of this, we—'

'Oh, that was her, all right,' she says, voice bitter.

Here we go.

'Don't go . . .' she begins, then pauses, head shaking. 'Look, don't go thinking this was some kind of partnership. She was . . . I mean, she had money, she reeled Tom in like a fish on a hook. Did the same to me too . . .'

She lowers her eyes, stares at the table.

Here comes the regret, here comes the story. *My infinitesimal part in the narrative.*

'Tom had this great plan. Recession-proof business, he said. People are always going to die. Create a brand, become the Cadbury's or the Apple or the HSBC of the mortuary business. Jesus. And don't think . . . I mean, he wasn't like . . . he didn't *care*. He didn't care about people. He just thought it was a good business model. Probably right, right?

'That was before I met him. So it started well, and he was expanding just as he planned, but he needed money. And the bank . . . well, you know what the banks have been like since the crash. They didn't have the balls. So he found Natalia. Or, rather, she found him. Had all this money. Endless tonnes of it. He thought, it's Russian, maybe it's a little dodgy, but what the fuck, right?'

She looks at me for affirmation. She doesn't get any.

'Whatever. Then Tom's granddad dies, and Louise has all that damned money, and she doesn't talk and she doesn't, you know . . . That stupid woman, Euphrosyne, she thought Tom sorted it all by himself. But Natalia had this retirement home business, and he got Granny signed up for that, and handed over her money. He intended to use it all, and then she bought the picture. Just . . .'

Peterson laughs.

'I mean, she's switched on, right? I heard she just spent the last three years sitting up there like a vegetable, looking at the damn thing, but she upped and bought it in the first place.'

'You never went to see her?'

'Why would I?'

Of course.

'So then we had to come up with a plan to, you know, get the painting back, swap it out, whatever.'

'You hatched that when? You must've known from the start that she'd bequeathed it to the Kelvingrove?'

'I didn't hatch anything.'

I don't bother responding. I can throw in the odd question now, but there's no need to push her, no need to wind her up. The clockwork villain is running.

'Tom found this guy who could do the copy. The whole thing took forever. Finding the guy, then he says he can do it really quickly, but he took months.'

Peterson pauses, a recalibration. Common practice among the guilty. Stop every so often in the narrative, decide whether they're going to continue. This one has started though, and she's going to go on until it's all out there. Doesn't mean it'll all be true, of course.

'It was fine. Natalia had a guy up there. One of the staff. He helped Tom make the switch.'

'And Euphrosyne never knew anything about it?'

Peterson answers with an eye-roll.

'She can get to fu—'

'You don't have a name for us? The contact at the home,' I ask. We already have him, of course, the name and the man himself, but one can never have too much corroborating evidence.

'A bloke on the staff, that's all I know. Sounds like it was mostly women up there, that should narrow it down for you.'

For a moment she looks like she's going to add to the acerbic comment, a riff on causticity, but she doesn't have the conviction. She clearly doesn't like Euphrosyne James, but she wants to be her. She wants to have her money, and she wants to have her chutzpah when under interrogation. Instead, her bitterness and occasional barbed comments merely mask her weakness.

'The original of the painting's been sold already?' I ask.

'Thomas gave it to Natalia, and she was using some of her Russian contacts or whatever.'

'And had she sold it?'

Peterson is quiet. I can read her defensiveness, which is all the answer we need.

'We'd have got the money.'

'When?'

'She was driving the price up.'

'Or the painting was hanging on her wall, or she'd sold it and kept the money, or she'd given it to some contact in payment for something else.'

Nothing. I need to rein it in. She already knows they were duped.

'What did Thomas think?'

'He said they'd spoken, but he was giving her time. Expect she was keeping him happy with all the fucking.'

Another line delivered empty of the conviction she wants it to have.

'What happened when the director moved the painting into the sitting room?'

'Tom started panicking.' Heavy, dismissive sigh. The look that says, *if only they'd listened to me.* 'I mean, I said to him, you're being a pussy. Those old guys, what were they going to do? Who were they going to tell? Who was going to listen to them, even if they could speak?'

'Your contact at the home was telling Thomas he should be worried?'

'The contact was telling Natalia she should be worried. Natalia starts badgering Tom. Tom starts bricking it. Tom starts talking about throwing in the towel. Jesus.'

'What would it have been to you if he had?'

She scratches her ear.

'Well, you're right, I mean, it was him who was going to get it, right? Him. Not Natalia. Just him, and whoever was helping him out. But Natalia, of course, wanted her money, so she, I don't know, just kept on fucking poor old Tom to shut him up, right up to the day he died. Right up until the point she had him killed.'

I hold her gaze. The next question asks itself, and I'm just going to sit here in silence until Peterson answers it. It won't take long.

She takes a deep, loud, unattractive breath through her nose, her lips tightening into sphincter-like invisibility.

'Steven worked for Natalia. Then he started doing some stuff for Tom . . .'

'What kind of stuff?'

'Stuff. He came to the house one night, that was when I first met him. Happened a couple of times, then one night he turns up when Tom's away. Says he'd forgotten Tom wouldn't be there. You know how it is, right?'

'How what is?'

'We fucked.'

The apparent, crushing inevitability of sex.

'Don't judge me. Don't look at me like that. Look at what Tom was doing. If he was going to fuck around, then so was I. After what Brandon did to me, I deserved it.'

'Were you in love with Steven?' I ask. Of course she wasn't.

'What?' says Peterson, through an ugly laugh. 'Really? I mean . . . you saw Steven in the mortuary. You probably saw him naked when Roddy and I weren't there. He was fit . . . as . . . fuck. That was all. Tom got his Russian tart, and God knows who else, and I got Steven.'

'So, what happened to him?'

'Nothing to do with me.'

'So, what happened to him?'

'Ha!'

'Really? Come on.'

You have to enjoy the scorn of someone implicated in a triple murder.

'Natalia got Steven to kill Tom. I didn't realise until Roddy started describing him.'

'Roddy had met Steven?'

'No, thank God. So Tom was out the way, and Natalia decides she should take care of things at the home. She gets the guy up there, her contact, to let Steven in. He goes up, sneaks around, whatever, and he kills the two old guys. Steven was the hit man.' She laughs. 'Like something out of a movie. I mean, fucking Brandon was out of a sad, middle-aged, mid-life-crisis twat of a movie, and then Tom, the stupid arsehole, gets involved in all sorts of crap like that. The pair of them.'

'Why'd they kill Steven? Who killed Steven?'

'They killed Steven because he was also an arsehole.'

'That's not usually reason in itself.' Wouldn't be many of us left.

'With the first guy he murdered at the home, he says he tried to make it look like, I don't know, like he died naturally. He was supposed to kill them both on the same evening, but something happened. So, he had to go back the next night. Said to me he heard about the disembowelling in London, thought it might make sense to disembowel the guy up at the home. Thought it was funny. Of course, it made no sense at all, did it?'

'It tied the murder of Thomas to the home, which we wouldn't necessarily have done without it.'

'Exactly. I said that to Steven, but it was too late by then.'

'And?'

Peterson thinks about it.

'He got decapitated.'

'By whom?'

'Don't know. I expect Natalia was pissed off at him, and got one of her heavies to take him out. I mean, Russians, right?'

'Is it possible the contact up at the home killed Steven?'

'Sure. But then, it's just as possible she got some other guy to do it. The only certainty is, she won't have done it herself.'

And there's the story. As usual, gaps will need to be filled in, names will need to be slotted into place, different tales told from different angles to be squeezed into the same narrative, and ultimately there's a good chance we'll never have the full story. And since Natalia Kadyrova has fled the country, there's the added issue that any remaining suspects can point innocently in her direction and say, *she did it*.

If Peterson is telling the truth, the killer of Cummins and Strachan – also her husband's killer – is dead. One of the architects of the whole thing is dead, and the other is already beyond our reach.

I push my chair back and get to my feet.

'Fuck are you going?' she asks, surprised.

I stand across the desk for a few moments, then I turn away without speaking, look at PC Ross, say, 'Take her back to the cells, please, Alex,' and leave the room. As I close the door, I cut off Peterson's, 'What the f—?'

Put my head on the pillow at three minutes past four. Down off the high of results and a surprising level of completion, I come to bed flat and tired, wishing I didn't have to set my alarm for six. The wrap-up on a case this size will be, as ever, painstakingly long. The Russian involvement means there will be politics, and there will be questions asked about the investigation. We can only hope there will be no more blood.

43

The beach is empty.

Nothing changes. Everything about the expanse that stretches into the far distance is familiar. The whole scene washed of colour, until the sand is monochrome. Low, grey cloud, disappearing into an obscured, misty distance. The flat calm, the sea soundless as it washes imperceptibly upon the sand. Out there, somewhere, in the midst of the haar, the beacon blinks.

I see that beam in my dreams.

What then is this, if not my dreams?

I don't know how long I stand there. Time is an underground river, passing unseen.

Eventually I take a step, and then another. I am propelled slowly across the sand. There is a desk, and I recognise that this is what's supposed to happen. A desk, with someone sitting at it.

Elizabeth Rhodes. She does not change. Elizabeth will not leave me. Her face expressionless, her eyes on mine, she drives the knife into her stomach. Blood gurgles from her lips.

I do not stop to watch her. I do not stop for Elizabeth.

Dead now.

There is another desk. I recognise the man who sits there. Kovács, the Hungarian, defenestrated in Paris. He sits at the desk in a peculiar position. His back is distorted. One side of his face is normal, the other crushed. His one good eye watches me.

I'd never thought I felt guilt about Kovács. If he wasn't dead, I would be. Maybe, if it had played out differently, he'd be walking on the beach, and I'd be sitting there, spine bent and broken.

I walk on. Kovács does not disappear. I can feel his presence.

Another desk. This time it is Olivia, leaning forward on her elbows and forearms. Her eyes are poison. There is bile pouring in a constant, grey-green stream from her mouth, splashing on the table, running over the other side onto the sand. I do not stop.

Three more desks, recurring features. Khalil, a young Afghani boy without a father, and Alina from Kiev, and Daniel from the DRC, one after the other, the same every night. Are they always there? I feel that they might be.

There is something else. I stop, I look away from the blood in Daniel's eyes. I stare along the beach but this thing, whatever it is, has not yet found form. Nevertheless, the feeling begins at once to infect me.

Out of the grey gloom they come, these desultory figures. A man and a woman and a girl and a baby, the four of them dancing around a single scene, all with their parts to play. The monster, his wife, his prey and the infant, soon to be lost.

I come to a stop alongside them. This is why I am here. I'm supposed to watch. They do not watch me.

This man, who I know to be Louise Worrell's husband, is kneeling over his daughter's bed. The daughter is lying with her eyes closed, a tear on the side of her face. His hand is beneath the sheets. He unbuckles his belt, he pulls down his trousers. Louise Worrell stands by an invisible door, shouting at him. He stands, naked from the waist down, and shouts back. She approaches to protect her daughter, he slaps her viciously, and throws her from the room.

This scene has played out many times. I have not been here before, but Louise Worrell has. Times beyond counting.

In this scene, an amalgam of years, the horrors of abuse are concentrated, the pain caused by this awful man distilled into a dark, terrifying, brutal essence.

Louise Worrell retreats. She is lost. She is bereft. She does not care for herself, she weeps for her eldest child. And she weeps for her baby who will grow into this family, this life.

She leans over the baby's crib. Behind her the horror unfolds. There are so many times in this job when I think, *this is bad, but I've seen worse*. But I have not seen worse than this man. Euphrosyne James was kind to her grandfather.

Louise Worrell takes the small pillow from behind her baby's head. Her movements are slow, reluctant, forced from a well of desperation and self-loathing. She weeps through horrible sobs. She places the pillow over the baby's face.

I don't know how long I stand there. The scene does not change. On one side, the monster enacts his horror. On the other, a mother frees her child from what was to come. It is all she can do. And she will have to live with it.

The sand stretches far into the distance. The walls of claustrophobic grey cloud close in. The beacon beyond the haar is lost. There is no light. There is no hope.

I will wake later with the sadness of it coursing through me.

44

There is a quality of sedate calm at the home. Everything as it should be. The feeling in the air, of the return of the familiar, is tangible.

Outside, the clouds are unusually high, scattered, broken. The grey damp of morning has given way to blue sky over the Dornoch Firth and out to sea. At last, the lighthouse at Tarbet Ness has turned itself off, and now stands lone and distant on the promontory, picked out by the morning sun.

The usual residents are in their usual positions. Robinson and Crane looking out the window, Blind Durin at his chess set, old Thorpe, the curmudgeon, his face screwed up as he studies a crossword puzzle, Mrs Worrell staring blankly at the massacre.

Here, too, unusually, is Bauer, sitting at the window, looking out on the sea. Perhaps she does not lament for this day. Perhaps she is taking a break. Perhaps this is her lament, a baleful look upon a sea she will never touch, beneath a blue sky that is lost to her.

I notice the absence of the incantation from the old woman at the far end of the seating by the window, the silence, before I realise that she's not there. Seeing her seat unoccupied did not elicit the thought, but the lack of the sound eventually wormed its way into my head. That there is something missing.

I'm about to comment to Sutherland about her, when I realise that I don't know her name. All this time, all these days, I never asked. Why was that? I know all these people, even the ones who did not become part of the story. Thorpe and Robinson and Crane, several more throughout the home. But this woman, who was always here, I never talked to anyone about.

'Can you feel it?' asks Sutherland, standing beside me, and the thought of the old woman breaks like a wave on the rocks.

'It's like everyone's relaxed,' I say. 'The relief is tangible. The brutal murder has ended, to be replaced by the slow creep of inevitable death.'

Sutherland laughs. 'That you quoting from the brochure?' he says. 'The Dunes, for that natural air of melancholy.'

'That about sums it up. But . . .'

I take a look around them, this subdued crew of pensioners, then turn away and follow the gaze of those at the window out to sea.

'We can't all go out in a blaze of bullets,' I say. Voice forlorn, trying to latch on to the familiarity of regular conversation. Sutherland and I, worn down, clutching at past lives. 'They are content in the means of their slow passing. The real-life equivalent of Frodo and Gandalf going off to the Grey Havens.'

'A blaze of bullets?' says Sutherland. 'I must've missed something in Dingwall.'

'There was a woman there,' I say, indicating the empty seat at the far end, conceding to the need to talk about her. 'She was here every day, muttering to herself.'

Sutherland stares at the empty seat. Thinks on it for a moment.

'I didn't notice,' he says.

'She was always here.'

'I got a feeling about that,' he says, but the thought drifts off and he doesn't immediately elaborate.

Moments pass, and I say, 'You got a feeling?' to prompt him.

'Yeah.'

He hesitates, although I get the sense he's just struggling to put the thought into words, rather than not wanting to talk about it.

'Like there was something there. I don't know, like someone used to sit there but doesn't any more. Like none of the others wanted to sit in that spot. Like it still belonged to someone else. But if you saw someone sitting there, maybe it wasn't that.'

We hold the gaze for a moment, neither of us completely understanding the other, then I turn away and look back at the seat. The empty seat. I could ask someone at the home, but I don't want to. I don't want to know.

'You've spoken to Dr Raven?' I ask, some part of me deciding that it's time to move the conversation along. Get back to business.

Very early this morning we released her. Not being convinced of her innocence was not enough reason to keep her in custody, as we had no evidence on which to hold her. Suspicion may linger upon her, yet there is no one implicating her, neither strand nor story directly pointing to her guilt.

'Sure. I said you'd have a word too, not that she's very forthcoming.'

'Pissed off at us, I expect.'

'Aye. But she's been put in charge temporarily, so she's got other things on her mind.'

'She's been put in charge? Who . . .?'

'Geras. Not, of course, our Russian friend. Head office in California.'

'God,' I say. Try not to think of the quagmire of business dealings.

'Aye,' says Sutherland, then he looks at his watch. 'I should get on, sir, still have a few members of staff to interview. When will I tell Raven you'll be in?'

'Give me ten minutes,' I say. 'I want to have a word with Mrs Worrell first.'

'Sir,' says Sutherland.

He doesn't immediately move away, and we hold the slightly awkward, resentful gaze. This investigation has not gone well, but it's had little to do with the crimes that have been committed. Sutherland has been preoccupied, and I feel I've missed much, dragging around this crushing weight of guilt. We are both haunted, kicking out at that which is closest to us. At some stage it feels like it's moved beyond going for a pint and sorting everything out.

He doesn't move. He has something to say, but the words won't come just yet. Sutherland and I in silence, the room lost to us for a few moments, then he finally says, 'I know why Alice tends the weeping fig.'

That's all.

My mind is a blank. I do not know what to think of it, so my head, something in my head, blocks out the words, cannot even begin to formulate a response. Sutherland waits for a moment, but the words have been spoken, and now he turns away.

I watch him to the door, he does not look round, then I look back out of the window. Over the heads of Bauer and Robinson and Crane, past the empty seat at the end, to the beautiful blue-grey sea.

I know why Alice tends the weeping fig.

I look at the empty seat. I cannot think. Perhaps I just do not want to think.

I snap myself from it, physically forcing the thoughts from my head, by walking quickly across the room and standing beside Blind Durin. The chess game looks to be the same one he was playing the previous afternoon, the game further advanced, a few more pieces removed.

'Inspector,' he says. 'I liked that. Funny.'

He's looking at the board, nothing on his face to suggest he found anything funny.

'What?'

'The slow creep of inevitable death,' he says. 'Apt, although now I wonder. Will the melancholy be assuaged, will the residents be happier with their place in the slow decline, now they have witnessed the alternative? Death, sudden and brutal.'

I look around at them, and he finally lifts his head and follows my gaze.

'I don't know how this place felt before it started,' I say prosaically.

'Much like it feels now,' says Durin, 'but sadder. We'll see if the light relief of the morning lasts, although you will soon be long gone, Inspector.'

Those cold blue eyes hold mine for a short while, and then he turns back to his game.

'Thank you for last night,' I say, something he acknowledges with a small nod. 'No ill effects?'

'Of course not,' he says, but there is no tone in his voice.

He makes a move on the board, goes into his usual routine, studying the position of the pieces, committing them to memory from this side, then he swivels the board.

'Normal service has been resumed for the foreseeable future,' he says. 'The three wise monkeys are in position, defining this mournful establishment, even if Lisbet has downed her fiddle for the moment.'

He looks up, smiles that crooked smile again, almost chuckles at the three wise monkeys line, I presume, and then returns to his game.

Three wise monkeys. I hadn't thought of it before, yet I know exactly what he means. Durin, Bauer and Worrell.

'Caddow first used it,' he says, then he looks scornful at the thought of what Caddow had been going to do and adds, 'Stupid boy.'

I can't help smiling bleakly at the term, the dismissal of Caddow's attempted murder as though it had been some puerile prank.

'How did you know I'd be here?' I ask suddenly. One of those questions, formed from nothing.

'What d'you mean?'

'You were in my head, several days ago, like you knew I was coming. Lisbet's music, I could hear it. You were there, playing this game. This exact game.'

A pause. There's something coming in reply, but he keeps me waiting. Another one of those moments in this house; the clock ticking, yet time standing still. Finally the dead eyes look up at me, into me, through me, as they have done every time he's looked in my direction.

'I did not know you were coming. It was you who knew that I would be here. These are the stories we tell, Inspector. People with the same stories are drawn together. Whatever makes you, and that I do not know, you share with someone else. And if you knew you were coming, it's because that someone else brought you here.'

The eyes linger for a moment, and then he turns and looks over at Louise Worrell, her back to us, her gaze steady on the Brueghel. He leaves us there, hanging in this position, then he breaks the moment, turns back to the board and indicates, with the wave of a casual hand, that it's time for me to move on.

'Let us hope we never see each other again, Inspector,' he says, 'a pleasure though it's been.'

I place my hand momentarily on his shoulder.

'Thank you, Mr Durin.'

He grudgingly accepts my thanks with a growl and then I turn away, walk over to Mrs Worrell, lift a seat and sit down beside her.

My conversation with Durin at an end, the room is now

quiet. Outside, the wind blows lightly, the firth and the sea are silent. The only boat is a small, wooden rowing boat, the oars soundlessly splashing into the water.

I stare at the painting, the forgery, the face of Grey Davies now unmistakable. I wonder if Mrs Worrell has seen it all along, just as clearly as I do now.

This time I don't wait to make the only contact I can. I place my hand in Mrs Worrell's, and entwine my fingers. There is an immediate response, her fingers squeezing weakly in return.

I have seen her past. The process by which I saw her past I cannot understand, but I have seen it. Louise Worrell murdered her second child so that she did not grow up into a life of abuse. The guilt defines her and controls her. She is lost to this representation of infant murder, wallowing every day in its horror. Facing, and beholden to, her past.

I can but wonder why she did not take her children and run, or even why she did not kill her husband instead. I cannot hope to understand what she was thinking, all those decades ago.

The police officer in me will not be opening up an investigation. Some cold cases are best left alone.

Mrs Worrell is staring straight ahead, her eyes on the painting. I watch her for a few moments, smile sadly at the wonder of it, then turn back to the Brueghel.

How long was it I said I would be before talking to Raven? It doesn't matter. I'll come to the doctor eventually. For now, I'll allow myself to be taken by the same timelessness that haunted me when I last sat here.

'We'll try to get it back for you,' I say, the words forming in my mouth unexpectedly, the same words I said yesterday, 'although I'm not sure we'll be able to. But we'll look. And we'll keep looking.'

Not for the first time, my words seem to disappear in the past, so that I might never have spoken. This place consumes everything. Talking to Blind Durin feels like the sole anchor to real life. Everything else is in the grip of peculiarity.

I'm aware of the movement of Mrs Worrell's fingers, thin and bony, still entwined with my own. A slight squeeze, which I recognise as being in response to what I said. I must have spoken after all. Or, at least, she picked up on the thought by one means or another.

I don't look at her, just respond with a movement of my own hand. That's all there is between us.

'I'll come and see you again,' I say, aware that in the gentle touch of her fingers, I've made more contact with Louise Worrell than anyone else has in years.

'We can talk,' I add.

That's all.

EPILOGUE

Eleven thirty-one. Sitting in my familiar spot. Dining-room table, the last of a bottle of wine, rain against the window, the lights of the town stretching down to the firth.

Wondering if it's too soon to call Leia Marcus. Not that it might be too soon after the conclusion of the case, but that it is too soon for me, and this haunted world I inhabit.

Who knows what horrors tonight will bring? Who knows what I will find along that beach, or who'll be waiting for me? Leia Marcus may have offered, and I may be tempted, but it would be wrong to bring someone else into this world.

My phone pings, a text from an unknown number, the sound loud and clear in the silence that has consumed the room since Sinatra's *It Might As Well Be Swing* stopped playing.

I left work four hours ago. Since then I've been sitting here in a fug, mind wandering lazily and unhappily all over the place. I've barely thought about the case, barely been able to focus on anything. And so I don't automatically think the text message will be case-related. The case seems to be behind me, even though there remains the inevitable paperwork mountain.

Pull the phone over, open the text, sit and stare dumbly at the photograph.

The silence is overwhelming. I feel the clutch of useless-ness at my stomach, accompanied by the bile of rancour.

Natalia Kadyrova. On a beach. Little detail other than the sea and the sand and the blue sky. Impossible to tell

355

where she is, other than that her bikini points to the heat of the day.

She is not alone. Beside her, his arm wrapped around her waist, and smiling just as broadly, is Davinder Singh.

The message accompanying the picture reads: Just hanging with a friend! See you soon! xx

I turn the phone off and push it away from me.

Rain spatters silently against the window. The night has no stars.

Discover more books in the DI Westphall series

A dead man walks into a police station. He tells a tale –
bizarre as it is grotesque – of kidnap and organ harvesting.
John Baden's story of being held prisoner for twelve years
sounds far-fetched – but it's all about to get much,
much stranger.

Available now in paperback and ebook.

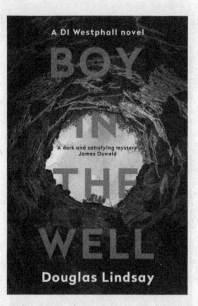

The body of a young boy is discovered at the bottom of a well that has been sealed for two hundred years. Yet the corpse is only days old . . .

Available now in paperback and ebook.

You've turned the last page.

But it doesn't have to end there . . .